THE

Somewhere beyond the fishing boat, across oceans, continents, was the man for whom she had done all this. Perhaps he worked on a newspaper or TV station in New York; perhaps he was rich and owned a long Spanish house in Arizona or Texas. Perhaps, even, he owned a yacht and gave parties where people played in the water, diving from the deck like members of the fishing boat crew. All she really knew was that if her father was alive in America she would find him.

Find him and kill him.

Donald James grew up in London during the Second World War. After graduating from Cambridge University he worked in Fleet Street and for the BBC, subsequently enjoying a highly successful career as a scriptwriter.

In the 1980s he turned to writing novels and has been translated into twelve languages. His last book, *The House of Janus*, has been published in several European countries, the United States and Japan.

He now lives near Cahors, in south-west France.

The House of Eros

DONALD JAMES

Mandarin

A Mandarin Paperback
THE HOUSE OF EROS

First published in Great Britain 1991
by William Heinemann Ltd
This edition published 1992
Reprinted 1992
by Mandarin Paperbacks
Michelin House, 81 Fulham Road, London SW3 6RB

Mandarin is an imprint of Reed Consumer Books Ltd

Copyright © Donald James 1991

A CIP catalogue record for this title
is available from the British Library
ISBN 0 7493 1125 8

Printed and bound in Great Britain
by Cox & Wyman Ltd, Reading, Berks

Contents

Revenge is a kind of wild justice.
Francis Bacon (1561–1626)

PROLOGUE

Saigon/New York City

The girl stood motionless in the band of deep moonshadow between the edge of the forest and the silvered sand. Waiting, she faced towards the open sea, taller than most Vietnamese women, her gleaming features an elusive mixture of East and West.

As she watched the changing shadows on the surface of the water she hummed softly to herself, olive arms clasped before her, her weight on one hip, a knee braced forward between the curtain folds of her long cotton skirt.

What tune was it? A favourite of the American days. Somebody had told her that. She tried for a few moments to stretch her memory. But she was too young. It was over fifteen years since the Americans had left. For her there were few memories there to stretch.

In response to something seen or heard she stopped humming. Standing quietly, she picked up her sandals and walked barefoot to the edge of the shadow. She could see now, where the moonlight shimmered on the sea, a dark shape moving east to west across her front, perhaps five hundred yards from the beach. As the boat came closer she frowned as she made her decision. The sail was the right shape, the black untidy rhomboid of the Cahn Roc fishing villages. The stern was low in the water, the prow high and curving. She looked at her watch, a heavy military watch. The time was right too. More or less.

Her jaws clamped together, her lips drew back over slowly revealed white teeth. It was her boat. Their boat.

Her gaze swept the horizon. To her left the faint glow of the city the world still called Saigon; then a dark, warm stretch of ocean until on the furthest horizon, the searchlights of the state police launches wavered and flashed like a storm at sea. She stood for a moment staring at the horizon, assessing the risk. Then she turned and walked back into the shadow.

A small pile of leaves and twigs lay in the hole scooped in the sand. 'Light the fire,' the girl said in the cultured Vietnamese accents of the city, 'they're here.'

A shadow moved. A young boy came forward, fifteen or sixteen, a wraith with a Zippo lighter. He dropped to one knee, clicked the lighter and applied the flame to the leaves and twigs. The tall girl stood over him, watching the fire play at the rim of the shallow pit. She looked once more at her watch, clumsy on her slender wrist, then she turned towards the sea as the flames leapt, umbering the sculpted lines of her face.

Almost immediately a light winked from the fishing boat and the black sail moved to turn the high prow towards the beach.

'They've seen us,' the tall girl said. 'Put out the fire.'

Handfuls of sand rattled on the unburnt leaves. The girl walked forward into the moonlight, barefoot, erect, suppressing her fear. On the horizon the searchlights still swept the rim of sea and sky.

Very slowly the fishing boat moved towards the beach, trailing a brightly incandescent wake. Spider fish leapt from the water; behind her night jars shrieked in the forest. She stood on the edge of the water now, her bare feet lapped by the tide.

A man's voice called across the water. She thought in her half-Western way that passwords should have been devised and answering patterns of flashlamps. But nothing like that had been agreed upon. The man called. She answered.

The boat pulled and drifted on its anchor rope. A dark figure leaned across the prow. 'Ola,' the figure said. 'Where are the others?'

The girl turned her head, a thumb and finger to her teeth and whistled a strangely melodious triple note. Creatures from the forest took up the call. On high rocks which rose from the sand six or seven figures appeared and stood like sentinels.

'Come aboard,' the man in the prow called to the girl. 'You don't expect me to do our talking on the beach.'

Again the girl hesitated. She had no way of knowing if things had gone wrong. Only instinct and small inconclusive indications. The fishing boat was right. The time was right. The man's voice carried the accent of the south-west Mekong. Of course he could have been put aboard by the government. Of course the fishing boat might be full of government coastguards. And if none of these things had happened the man might still plan to collect the money, murder them all and sail away, still in possession of his boat.

'Come aboard,' the man stood in the prow. He wore shorts and a T-shirt. At thirty yards she could not be sure of his age. She lifted the folds of her skirt and tied them round her hips. Then she walked forward across the ribbed sand and plunged into the warm sea. She swam with a facile overarm stroke, not directly towards the boat, a little to one side, then stopped, treading water.

Her imagination had been so much nourished by stories of a distant American lifestyle that she saw herself for a second, even now, at this moment of acute danger, as just a girl swimming off the coast of California, treading water beside a boatful of partying friends. In her mind's eye she saw a man standing on the deck, in the centre of a group of friends, a man dressed in white shorts and a white shirt, faceless, because she could not remember her American father's face. She shook her head, bringing herself back into the ugly, dangerous present.

The captain threw down a rope. He wasn't old, not much more than forty but his face was ravaged and his front teeth were missing. The girl caught the rope and pulled herself closer to the splintered gunwhale of the boat. He stood above her, his shorts a pair of cutdown jeans, his T-shirt torn at the armpits and frayed around the neckline.

She made no attempt to climb aboard. 'My name is Nan Luc,' she said. He nodded and made that throwaway gesture of the hand by which Vietnamese indicate they know, they are aware, they are unsurprised. 'How many crew?' she said, turning her face towards the raised deck and the reek of fish.

'How many men?' the captain countered, pointing towards the men standing sentinel on the rocks. 'They carry weapons,' he said. 'Our agreement was no weapons.'

The girl let her long legs float up to the surface. Lying on her back, one hand holding the rope, she pointed with her free hand towards the long knife in a leather sheath on the captain's belt. 'A knife is also a weapon.'

'A gutting knife,' he said. 'For fish.'

'Bring your crew out.' She kicked her legs so that she was upright in the water and hauled herself up on to the deck. The man's eyes were on her white briefs as she untied the skirt and let it fall around her legs.

When she stood before him the captain turned and hammered on the thin timbers of the deck house. 'Out here,' he said. 'All of you. Bring everything you want to take ashore.'

The men shuffled out on to the deck, a dozen or more of them, mostly in shorts, their eyes cast down as if in guilt at the array of weapons they carried, knives, an ancient seaman's cutlass, an old rifle or two.

Nan Luc walked towards the prow of the boat and signalled to the men standing on the rocks. Low voices carried across the water, hoarse whispered shouts, the higher tones of women. She turned back to the captain. 'Get your men on to the beach,' she said. 'I'll look at the boat.'

He smiled, his tongue jutting through the great gap in his front teeth. 'We'll smoke,' he said. 'To seal the agreement.'

She shook her head. Her heart was jumping. She shivered and rubbed at her wet bare arms. 'Put your men on the shoreline under the big rock,' she said. 'When I know the boat's empty I'll get the money.'

The captain's tongue leapt out like a lizard's. She was sure now that he had had no intention of keeping to the deal. Only what he saw as the armed men on the line of rocks had persuaded him. But she knew the rifles were roughly carved lengths of wood; the machine pistols tucked under their arms, no more than branches, snapped from the forest.

The captain looked again towards the men on the shore. He had stopped smiling. 'OK,' he said. 'OK.' He spoke to the men in words she barely understood. In ones and twos they jumped into the sea. Again the image passed through her mind of a Californian party night with friends splashing in the sea.

She turned towards the deck house and pushed aside the bead screen. Behind her the captain said, 'I was expecting a man.'

In the light of the kerosene lantern she saw a long, narrow room lined with bunks. The stench of fish rose from the gaps in the planking. 'All right,' she said. 'We'll go back to the beach.'

They came out on to the deck and she dived straight from the gunwhale into the sea. As her head broke the water she heard the captain dive in behind her.

From the shoreline two groups watched the moonlit swimmers, the seamen under the big, jutting rock, the refugees a hundred yards distant, their wooden guns held across their chests. As Nan Luc splashed through the shallows among a shoal of spider fish skittering across the surface of the water, a young man detached himself from the refugees and jog-trotted the distance between them. Handing a leather drawstring bag to her, he turned without a word and walked quickly back.

The captain of the fishing boat emerged from the sea behind her. 'A boat like this, a fine boat, is worth a lot more than you're paying.' It was as if he hadn't spoken. She opened the neck of the bag and tipped the contents into the sand. American dollars fluttered down among gold Napoleon pieces from the distant French past. She took up the hundred dollar bills and counted them. On the dark wet sand the Napoleons gleamed. As he watched she counted them back into the leather bag.

'Ten thousand dollars,' she said. He grimaced.

'That's what was agreed.'

'The man in Cahn Roc says five thousand is for him.'

'Even so, five thousand is a good price.'

'The man in Cahn Roc said you would pay the five thousand extra.'

'You're lying,' she said fiercely. 'You want your throat cut? You want the bodies of your men left on the sand?'

He recoiled. 'That's what he said. That's what the man in Cahn Roc said,' he muttered.

'Take the money,' her lips curved in a high, ritual contempt. 'Take the money and lead your men off along the beach.'

'If the government patrol . . .' he began.

'If the government patrol catches us, you are safe. They will learn nothing from us.'

He took the leather bag. 'The boat,' he said, nodding over his shoulder, 'was the living for ten families.'

She said nothing, staring at him, until he turned away and walked slowly towards the group of seamen. For some minutes they stood in conclave, their high voices rising higher. Then they straggled off along the beach behind the captain.

The refugees, men, women and six or seven teenage girls, twenty-five people in all, watched them go. The older women smiled, the uncertain smile of fear; the men threw down their stick weapons.

The first hurdle, Nan Luc said to herself. Just the first. She was trembling. She turned towards the boat.

Offshore the oddly shaped black sail from the fishing port of Cahn Roc rode on the glittering water.

Somewhere beyond the fishing boat, across oceans, even continents, was the man for whom she had done all this. Perhaps he worked on a newspaper or TV station in New York; perhaps he was rich and owned a long Spanish house in Arizona or Texas. Perhaps, even, he owned a yacht and gave parties where people played in the water, diving from the deck like members of the fishing boat crew. All she really knew was that if her father was alive in America she would find him.

Find him and kill him.

Inside the dark blue Mercedes the voice of Billie Holiday washed plaintively sweet around the shoulders of the driver. The air was cool, filtered, scented lightly with leather soap. Outside on the South Bronx Grand Concourse it was ninety degrees, humid. An early evening, late in the summer.

In this section of the city seventy-five per cent of the street population seemed to be under sixteen, black or Hispanic, uniformed in thick-soled trainers, T-shirts, jeans, and rasta knits or baseball caps, the peaks pulled asymmetrically to the side of the head.

No less than the car itself the driver of the Mercedes exuded affluence. Blond-haired, clean shaven, perhaps a little over forty, he allowed his eyes to travel along the broad red stripes of the arm of his shirt, to the banded cuff and come to rest on the gold links, hallmarked Dublin 1836.

Lifting his eyes from his hand resting on the leather wheel he pushed out his lower lip in minor irritation. The traffic had been running nose to tail, slowly but smoothly enough so far. Now on the slight slope he could see red tail lights ahead, rippling back towards him. He changed his foot to the brake, picked up the phone and punched buttons with his index finger. As he waited he looked up at the crumbling Art Deco tenement above him. The jacket of his business suit lay on the tan leather seat beside him. He flexed his shoulder muscles. After a game of squash he liked the low ache and even the faint buzz of fatigue. But he was eager to break out of the sweltering city into the countryside.

The Art Deco tenement stirred something in the depths of his memory. Billie Holiday was singing 'On the Sunny Side of the Street'. He let memory and the music wash over him. He saw the butt-end of Detroit; he saw himself as a twelve-year-old, blond-haired, bright as a button, already spending his nights running errands for the South Side street girls. Coffee, cigarettes, a few grams of this or a line or two of that. It kept him eating when no one else was going to. For what he did, he maintained, he had no choice.

In forty-two years there had been other times in his life when, as he saw it, Cy Stevenson had had no choice but to walk on the dark side. Mostly he was happy not to look back too much. Not to reflect. If he did, his answer was that today it was Cy Stevenson wearing a Jermyn Street shirt, the Egon Rossington suit; it was Cy Stevenson sitting in a new Mercedes 300 while others pimp-rolled along Soden Avenue, Detroit, or Grand Concourse, South Bronx, still looking to score in life.

He had scored. By his own efforts he had brought himself from Detroit to a family and home in Meyerick, upstate New York. Over here on the sunny side the only real danger was that there were time when the brightness could be too revealing. Sometimes it had been necessary to duck back into the shadow. Just now and again.

His wife, Sunny, was on the line.

'How's home life?' he said.

'Quiet.'

'What are you doing?' He settled comfortably. The traffic ahead was stuck solid.

'Nothing special. Lying back on the *chaise longue*, a kir royale in hand, wearing my usual black stockings, black skirt, black devoré blouse, a slash of red lipstick on my mouth and a certain familiar glint in the eye. As I said, nothing special. Why d'you ask?'

'I get it,' Cy said. 'The new gardener showed up.'

'Matter of fact he did,' Sunny said. 'He's doing a lengthy reconnaissance before coming back for the kir royale on the sofa.'

'How's he look?'

'OK. Name's Fitzgerald, call me Fitz. Tall, dreamy, good-looking boy.'

'Thus the black devoré. But can he garden?'

'Yet to see,' Sunny said crisply. 'Somehow I think he'd prefer to philosophise. How's the traffic?'

'So, so. Be about an hour, I guess.'

'What do you want to do tonight?'

He mused. 'Well . . .'

'Well,' she echoed. 'Mary's asked us over for drinks after dinner.'

'Definitely no to your sister.'

'Let's see now. How about stay at home, have a few drinks and fool around a little?'

'You're getting warmer.'

'I am,' Sunny conceded. 'It must be the thought of Gardener Fitzgerald, call me Fitz. See you in an hour. Home safe.'

Cy put down the phone. In his mind's eye he saw his wife do the same. For a moment he held the image before him of a tall patrician young woman, thirty-three just, her hair russet blonde, her mouth wide, ever smiling. Sexually it wasn't an image that moved him much.

Raising his eyes from street level above the aluminium grille of a liquor store, he caught sight of a pair of stone heads, part of the decoration of the old building. Even scarred and burnt by the city's acid air they were still recognisable as George Washington and Abe Lincoln.

Ahead the traffic was shaking out. His eyes brushed over the cabal of black teenagers on the street corner, their furtive dealings overlooked by two American presidents. He touched the gas pedal, sending the Mercedes silently forward.

In the cool air he shivered as he left behind the kids on the street corner. Perhaps it was the reminder of his own childhood in Detroit, a reminder of the sullen, loveless faces of those he had once lived with.

The car glided forward, past a clutch of Vietnamese food stores, past Vietnamese faces in the doorways, gestures, a restaurant painted in dirty red and gold. Cy Stevenson gazed at the scene, experiencing a micromoment of transference as if he were back in Vietnam. As he turned his eyes away he shivered again, more violently this time.

His Polish grandmother, back in those far-off days when he admitted to having a Polish grandmother, would have said that someone had just walked over his grave.

PART ONE

From Saigon

1

In a haunting memory, before other more true or false memories had displaced it, the child lay quiet, burrowed into a mountain of bedsheets, listening, above the warm reassuring voice of the American radio station, for the next hissing salvo of rocket shells. They had told her that her mother would never come back. Her Aunt Louise had gone away to America. Only the radio, the music and the warm voices brought her comfort.

The rockets hissed. Outside, the explosions seemed to roll along the old Rue Catinat and on, grumbling like oxen carts, across all Saigon. After a while there was a lull. Six-year-old Nan Luc knew that when the hissing demons stopped, they stopped for long enough for her to crawl from under the pile of bedclothes she trusted to protect her.

She switched off the radio.

The Eros Bar was silent. The Rue Catinat was silent. All Saigon seemed suddenly to be bathed in silence. Nan Luc walked out on to the landing. From there, looking down through a skylight, she could see into the bar where the music had played and the girls had danced with the GIs. Now broken glass littered the floor, sparkling like silent fire in an orange shaft of evening sunlight.

Nan Luc stood listening. She was a tall child for her age. Very erect. Self-contained. At first, when her aunt had left to go to America and her mother had not come back from the forest, she had cried herself to sleep. But she drew strength from the daylight hours. And from the radio. And the hope that somebody would come for her.

There was food in the big refrigerator, stored beside the hundreds of cans of beer. She took a bowl of rice and slowly climbed the stairs, picking at the white grains with a small dusty hand.

A mirror halted her. She always stopped for a mirror. She

always stopped and puzzled that she looked so different from most of the other girls in the Ecole Normale in the narrow alley known as the street of the deaf woman, the Rue de la Sourde.

At school they spoke French, the old colonial language. At home her mother spoke to her only in English. In the streets Nan Luc spoke Vietnamese with the accent of Saigon.

Downstairs there was a noise. The crunch of wheels over rubble. And women's voices. She ran to the window and looked out. A black car was parked in the street below, a Red Cross flag attached to the side of the windshield.

Two Vietnamese women in khakis, one with a Red Cross band on her arm, looked up at her. 'Come with us, Nan Luc,' the woman with the Red Cross band said. 'We'll find somewhere where you'll be looked after.'

Nan Luc looked down at the black car. On the side words were stencilled that, at the age of six, she could just read but not fully understand: The St Christophe Orphanage, Cholon, Saigon.

'Did my mother send you?' Nan Luc asked.

The women hesitated, glancing at each other and then up at Nan Luc. 'Your mother wanted you to come,' one of the women said.

Late in that first autumn of Communist victory, on the newly named Avenue Giap in the administrative district of what was now called Ho Chi Minh City, the well-dressed middle-aged Vietnamese woman left the entrance of the elegant French-built apartment block and stood in the sunlight as her car drew level at the kerb. By all but a few of the most privileged ladies of the revolution European clothes were no longer worn. In what the world still thought of as Saigon the right to wear bourgeois clothes or to be conducted across town in a chauffeured motor car was given to very few.

Sitting in the back of the Citroën, Bernadette Hyn looked what she was, a figure from the recent pre-revolutionary past. Admitting to no more than forty of her nearly fifty years, she was still, in a slender Vietnamese way, a strikingly beautiful woman.

As her car crossed stop lights or was waved on by policemen in khakis and sun-helmets, Bernadette allowed a certain curiosity to build inside her. For nearly a year now since the Americans had evacuated Saigon she had assumed her family irretrievably lost: her younger daughter, Louise, long departed, married to an American; Pham her elder daughter, a nurse in the defeated South Vietnamese Army, dead; and Nan Luc, her granddaughter, lost among the tidal wave of orphaned and dispossessed which inundated the south.

Lost and perhaps now found. Bernadette had put out enquiries as soon as she and her lover, the senior administrator Quatch, had been recalled from their duties in Paris. Of the dozens of orphanages in Saigon at the end of the war. Catholic or Bhuddist, English, German or Swedish run, most had by now been amalgamated into the new state system. A child named Nan Luc, without a known family name, of approximately the right age and with an American heredity had been taken into St Christophe's Children's Home, State Orphanage Cholon 7, as it was now known. The child's original notes recorded that she had been found living alone at the waterfront Eros bar-hotel. Nan Luc had apparently been admitted to St Christophe's shortly before the Spring Victory. Approaching a year ago now. A year in which the glitzy wealth of the American period had drained out of Saigon. A year in which the new Ho Chi Minh City had been changed to a grim, silent fortress. For everybody but those as well placed and determined as Bernadette Hyn.

The young matron who met her at the main gate of the orphanage was carefully courteous, uncertain how to address this perfumed lady from the already inconceivable past. 'I had the child brought into the courtyard, comrade madame,' she said as she conducted her visitor up to her office.

Bernadette crossed the room. From the window she looked down into a courtyard slashed by sunlight. At first she saw nothing but the lower barred windows and the round, plank-topped well in the centre of the cobbled courtyard. Then, in the shadow, she saw a movement. And a child rose from a stone bench and wandered into the sunlit half of the enclosed square. As Bernadette watched, the child, six or seven years of age, raised her head towards the dozens of small, barred dormitory windows. It was a small movement, puzzled and imperious, of a girl child unquelled by her surroundings. As the sunlight touched her face her eyes flashed a startling clear green. Her hair, chestnut in colour, fell in waves rather than straight down the sides of her face as might the hair of a purely Vietnamese child. Bernadette smiled grimly.

'When was your granddaughter last heard of?' the matron asked.

'The dates seem to fit well enough,' Bernadette said. She was in no doubt that this was her grandchild. She came into the middle of the room. 'And what did the child have to tell you about her family?'

The matron carefully studied the record. 'She made no mention of a grandmother. If she had of course . . .'

Bernadette waved the matter aside. 'I was on a revolutionary assignment in Paris at the time. But the child must have spoken of her mother?'

'Yes.' The young matron knew this was a point to be handled with care. The Hyns were clearly an old bourgeois family. A note on the record showed the child had even spoken of an aunt, Louise, who had left with an American soldier.

Bernadette tapped the desk impatiently. 'What did she say?'

'She told us her mother was a nurse in the jungle. From Nan Luc's description we concluded her mother might have worked for an American medical unit.'

'Erase that from the record,' Bernadette said brusquely. 'My daughter, Pham, served gallantly in a frontline Vietcong medical company operating clandestinely on the outskirts of Saigon. Enter the correction.' The matron bent over the record and wrote carefully. 'And her father?' Bernadette asked. 'Is anything known?'

'He was American, obviously.' The girl flinched as Bernadette stared at her coldly. 'Nothing further is known, madame,' she said hurriedly. 'When she first came here the child asked if this was America. She said she had been promised her father would take her with him. Most mixed blood children were told the same story, of course.'

'Were you at St Christophe's before the victory?'

'I was with a frontline company on the Danang sector,' the girl said proudly.

Bernadette nodded and turned back to the window and watched while the child, bored with her unexplained confinement in the courtyard, began to skip back and forth.

'How old is she now?' she asked the young matron.

'She said she was nearly seven. Tall for her age obviously. But as her grandmother . . .'

Bernadette lifted her hand imperiously. 'I was not present when she was born,' she said. 'I told you I was away in Paris, working for the Revolution.'

'Would you like me to send for her things, madame?'

Bernadette frowned. 'Her things? What for?'

'I thought when you took her with you . . .'

Bernadette glared at her irritably. 'Not at all. Nan Luc will stay here.'

The matron looked down. 'Is there anything you wish us to do for her.'

Bernadette shook her head. 'No. Treat her like any of the others.' She pressed a slim fold of US one dollar bills into the matron's hand. 'I'll be back to keep an eye on her.' She paused, turning from the window. 'In a year or two.'

The second visit to the orphanage provided Bernadette with a modest shock. Almost three years after her first visit she had driven across to Cholon and been taken into the young matron's office. Through a low glass transom she could look down on to a broad staircase up which groups of disciplined children climbed on their way to class.

'A good proportion of your children had American fathers, I see,' Bernadette mused almost to herself.

'This is the main orphanage in the city for Amerasian children. They are treated of course just like our own children. Or as much as is possible for a half foreigner.'

'You find them different?'

The matron shivered just short of revulsion. 'They're so big. Clumsy. Some of them look so American that you wonder what they're doing here.' Bernadette was silent. 'Worse than that,' the girl said, 'they take pleasure in speaking American among themselves. It's forbidden of course, but we have found it difficult to eradicate.'

'A foreign language can be an asset,' Bernadette said. 'A revolutionary asset.'

'In some circumstances,' the girl agreed cautiously. 'But for some of these children American is not a foreign language. We, the authorities, are convinced they consider it their *first* language.'

'My granddaughter too?'

'She speaks with great fluency, I am told. She has been reprimanded several times.' Bernadette stood, watching the flow of children across the hall towards the stairway. The young matron leaned forward. 'Just at the foot of the stairs now.'

The girl reaching for the baluster was still a child. Still unmistakably ten or eleven years of age but the young woman she would become was clearly prefigured. Bernadette gasped. She had never doubted her grandchild would be beautiful. All the Hyn women were beautiful. But she knew the addition of Caucasian genes invited the equal possibility of reducing, or compounding, that beauty. In Nan Luc's case there was no doubt, even as Bernadette looked at her as a child, that she would be an astonishingly beautiful young woman. And soon.

Bernadette turned to the matron. 'And what sort of child is she?' she asked. 'Disciplined? Will she take correction?'

The young matron nodded. 'Disciplined, yes. And ready to take correction . . .'

Bernadette heard something additional in the matron's voice. 'But what?' she said.

'Nan Luc,' the matron said slowly, 'will accept any correction without complaint.'

'Excellent.'

The matron fiddled with pencils on her desk. 'Nan Luc,' she said in a rush of words, 'lives in her own world. You can never be sure that the correction has changed her, changed her way of thinking. You can never be sure if, in the end, she has been *persuaded.*'

Bernadette nodded her head slowly. 'I recognise what you're saying, comrade.'

'Is there anything we should do?' the matron asked. 'She responds well in political classes. I have her reports here. She has quickness, intelligence.'

'And yet . . .?'

'Some of the reports consider her interest in anything American is unhealthy. Among the children she is considered a leader.'

Bernadette nodded. 'So. She has a will of her own. Later it will have to be broken. Goodbye, matron.'

On her last visit to the orphanage Bernadette braced herself for what she was likely to see. It was almost four years later and her granddaughter was now just fourteen years of age. When she watched the coltish young woman digging in the vegetable garden, she had turned away quickly and left without her usual small gift of dollars to the matron.

Nan Luc was on the edge of womanhood, the breasts swelling, the hips rounding, flashing bright smiles at the Amerasian boy working the next row. Exhilarated by her own youth.

At home on the Avenue Giap Bernadette stood in front of her long dressing-room mirror. Today she was wearing Western clothes. They suited her, she was sure of that. But her makeup now required renewal every hour or so. She turned from the mirror, sickly jealous of that young creature so carelessly laughing and moving her body in the orphanage garden.

But then again she was consoled by the fact that Nan Luc was after all her granddaughter. And in the old Vietnamese world to which Bernadette Hyn still secretly adhered, her granddaughter and her *possession*.

Memories of those far-off days in Saigon tortured Nan Luc still. As part of their education in the story of the War of Independence the children of Orphanage Cholon 7 were taken to see the former US embassy and dramatic accounts were given of the last days of the American invader on Vietnamese soil, the days when General Giap's revolutionary army was massing out beyond the airport ready for the last drive into the city. Each incident described by her instructors seemed to have the sharp edge of clarity; every rocket burst, every running man, the clack of helicopter blades, the piles of abandoned uniforms of the deserting soldiers and policemen of Saigon. And into these images Nan Luc wove her own. Of her American father frantically searching through the crumbling streets, of his arriving at the orphanage in creased khakis, a tall light-haired man with a yellow bandanna tied round his forehead. When she closed her eyes tight, she could hear his voice even, raised in anger as he demanded she be brought to him. 'I've a right to my own daughter, for God's sake,' he had sworn at the trembling women of St Christophe's.

As the first years passed at Cholon 7 Nan Luc came to believe absolutely in her images of that last day of old Saigon. And by extension she came to believe in a father desperate to take her with him to America. In her childhood years she saw him in increasing detail, as the tall man with the yellow bandanna, at the last moment finding her at the orphanage. But then what horror had occurred, what happening had separated them, caused him to lose her again among the rubble and piles of abandoned clothing along the road to the embassy.

The tissue of a child's memory is cobbled together. For the first years after the catastrophic days when the United States was leaving Vietnam, Nan Luc, in State Orphanage Cholon 7, cease-lessly recounted to the other orphans how nearly she had escaped to America.

In Ho Chi Minh City a French word had been adopted for children such as herself. They were called 'Ricains', the con-temptuous Paris slang word for Americans. With few exceptions they were tall, well-built adolescents, some of the girls with remarkable hybrid good looks, but all, nevertheless, carrying the scars of their dual ancestry. After the day's work they would meet together in the orphanage corridors, telling their stories, playing their parts, boasting of their American fathers.

'He's arranging to get me to Florida,' one boy claimed every night in a low, conspiratorial voice.

'My father just got a message to me that I would be living with my family in New York by summer,' another insisted to wry, disbelieving faces.

It was these hope-filled fantasies that affected Nan Luc as she got older, that brought her slowly to the conclusion that much or all of what she thought of as a memory was imagination. Why, after all, if her father had rescued her from the orphanage had he not been able to take her back to America with him? It was only one of many unanswered questions which began to raise doubts in her mind until brutally, almost deliberately, she pared her story down to the essentials of what she knew for certain. It was not much. She knew that the Eros Bar was not a figment. It was still there, its red door scratched and chipped, its tattered front boarded and thickly layered with revolutionary posters. She knew from the orphanage that her mother had died some time before the evacuation. Perhaps she remembered her mother, perhaps not. Perhaps the tall American she conjured up in her imagination resembled her father. Perhaps not. She knew only that among her uncertain memories she retained some certainty that there had once been love and trust in her life. But she had never succumbed to the wild hopes of the other Ricains of returning fathers who would carry them away across the sea. It was not that dream of escape that supported her, but another, more crucial to an orphan's world, the dream that she had once been loved.

On the day she graduated from the children's pioneer brigade Nan Luc was given a birth date. And a reminder of her strangely ambivalent status in the bright new world which victory had placed within everybody's grasp. She had stood before the matron of her new section and signed her agreement to a date and place of birth in the former city of Saigon.

'Today,' the matron had smiled sparsely, 'you become fifteen years of age. You know, you can see, that like some of the other children here, you are not of full Vietnamese parentage. It is your misfortune to have American blood.'

This open, unsubtle discrimination affected all the Amerasian children differently. Some became rebelliously attached to an America conjured up in their dreams. Others became fearful and guilt-ridden. Only the stronger spirits were able to retain some hidden attachment to the idea of an American father and freely embrace their childhood world at the same time.

Nan Luc was one of these. By the age of fifteen she had perfected the ability to keep hidden her secret American world so completely that she was appointed as junior instructor to the younger children in the exploits of the folk hero, Uncle Qui. This was an honour for a Ricain, a mark of trust.

The stories of Uncle Qui's fabled exploits came from the Ministry of Education theoretical section in five yellow instruction books. Uncle Qui was a ghost. To the Vietnamese mind a ghost is a powerful symbol of vengeance, so powerful in the Chinese-Vietnamese tradition that Mao Tse Tung once banned all ghost stories in China because they had come to represent vengeance for his own crimes. In Vietnam the vengeance Uncle Qui had the duty to exact was against the landlords and generals of the old Vietnam and against the false pretender Uncle Sam, the American warlord who lived in a Disneyland castle defended by napalm and agent orange.

To make the exploits of Uncle Qui real to the children, even the orphaned children of Cholon No 7, the Vietnamese family was always evoked. In each story the avenging ghost of the young jungle fighter Qui exacted vengeance on behalf of good fathers killed or sisters forced into evil ways. When Nan Luc raised pictures of the false Uncle Sam, the fifty tiny children hissed and spat while a picture of the ghostly Qui would bring them to their feet cheering. All the age-old traditions of the Vietnamese people were concealed in these stories: the family; respect for their fathers; and an utterly implacable belief in the right and duty to revenge.

From these children's stories, Nan herself absorbed what she might have absorbed from a family of her own. Brushing aside the evil American Disneyland of the yellow books, she still drank in the family aspects of the tales, the life of the village and the endlessly repeated gentle mothers and loving fathers, the rights of the Vietnamese family and the duty to defend it – and to avenge any wrong visited upon its members.

On the morning of her nineteenth official birthday Nan Luc walked the corridor towards the senior matron's office. Most of her friends had left at the age of fifteen. She had no sense of being singled out. Only her teaching post, she imagined, had kept her from an assignment to a reconstruction area in the north. The tiled floor of the corridor clacked emptily under her sandalled feet. It was the appointed hour. From this last interview she would discover where the next part of her life, perhaps the rest of her life, would be spent.

At the door to the matron's office she knocked and waited. Inside she heard voices, the matron's and a man's deeper tones. She knocked again. Straining, she heard footsteps approach. The door was opened by the matron who gestured to Nan Luc to enter. Inside, seated behind the matron's desk, was the rarely seen Director of Orphanage 7. The matron stood beside him.

'You know that today is the day you receive your assignment,' the matron said. Nan Luc nodded with the polite smile directed as required, first to the comrade director and then to the matron.

The matron indicated a folded pile of clothes on the corner of the desk. 'These are your possessions at the time of your entry to Orphanage 7. Ministry regulations lay down that all possessions must be returned on assignment day.' Nan Luc looked at the folded green gingham school dress of the past and the six-year-old's brown buckle shoes. A lump invaded her throat. 'There's one other thing.' The matron was frowning with distaste. 'You were wearing this at the time.'

She lifted a gold bracelet from behind the pile of clothes. Nan Luc took it from her and stared down at the thin gold band. It was inscribed: *To my daughter, Nan Luc – with all my love.* Inscribed in English.

'Ministry regulations insist these items should be returned,' the matron said.

The director nodded. He sat with a displeased, disapproving look on his face. 'I can see no reason whatsoever,' he said, 'why you should not be assigned to a reconstruction unit.'

Nan Luc waited, conscious of the bracelet in her hand, a gift which meant everything. A gift which meant that her father could not possibly have been an American soldier passing through on an R and R weekend in Saigon.

'In our country today every available hand is needed in the superhuman task of reconstruction,' the director intoned. Nan Luc dropped her eyes. The streets of Ho Chi Minh City were flooded with unemployed ex-soldiers from the Cambodian War. And yet something, politeness or policy, demanded they should pretend there was work for all, building the new Vietnam. 'I had given you an assignment to a military road-building brigade in the north,' the director said curtly. 'However . . .' he paused, the colour in his face deepening with anger, 'that order has been rescinded.'

Nan looked at him in astonishment. Who would, who could rescind an order from the director? 'I am no longer assigned to the brigade?' she said tentatively.

'Evidently not,' the director snapped. He was rising to his feet.

'Pick up your things,' the matron said.

Nan hurriedly scooped up the schoolgirl clothes.

'You have been assigned to special duties,' the director said. 'Your orders will be given to you as soon as they are available.' Nan Luc stood silent. For an Amerasian to avoid assignment to a work brigade was unknown. 'One more thing,' the director said, his mouth twisting. 'Your grandmother requires you to visit her this afternoon at her apartment on the Avenue Giap. You are dismissed.'

Nan Luc felt the shock pass through her, threatening to spill the child's clothes from her arms. Her grandmother? Living in a government apartment on Avenue Giap?

2

It was hot and Nan Luc had walked from the suburb of Cholon with her shoulder sack of possessions. She had never been in Avenue Giap before. Looking at number twenty-six now, she saw an old French apartment building with windows and *porte cochere* on a grand scale. And outside the house its own policeman in khakis and sun helmet patrolling the sidewalk.

As Nan Luc showed her pass and explained to the policeman the purpose of her visit, her real intention ran clearly through her mind. From this woman, Bernadette Hyn, who claimed to be her grandmother, Nan Luc would learn about her family. About her father.

She was announced by a houseboy formally in the old manner as Mademoiselle Nan Luc Hyn, and was perfunctorily kissed on each cheek by the woman who must be her grandmother. She found she was looking at a woman much younger than she expected, a woman dressed in European fashion, middle-aged certainly, but with that hard resistant handsomeness of the wives and mistresses of many South-East Asian leaders.

The apartment, Nan found immediately, played tricks with her sense of scale. She had been in no more than two or three private apartments in her life, single rooms mostly. Compared with this they were rabbit hutches. Here in her grandmother's apartment the walls, hung with rich curtaining or decorated with European paintings, seemed almost to fall away as the huge room expanded before her eyes. Ivory figures covered the surfaces of old lacquered furniture. Delicate scroll caskets sat in window alcoves.

There were no grandmotherly reactions from Madame Hyn. She surveyed Nan Luc impatiently. 'How dreadful those black pyjama outfits look on a girl. Oh, I know they're considered ideologically sound but God be thanked I'm free to wear my own clothes.' She walked away from Nan Luc as she talked. Then stopping in the middle of the room, she beckoned her closer. 'I'm taking you in to meet Quatch,' she said in a lowered voice.

Non-comprehension registered on the girl's face.

'Monsieur Quatch is my *bel ami*. He is also a provincial administrator. How else did you think you got a special assignment?'

'It was suggested you had intervened on my behalf,' Nan said. 'That's all I know.'

Bernadette smiled. 'Your grandmother might not have a conscience but she has influence. Now come and meet Quatch before the girl prepares his opium pipe and he snores the afternoon away.'

Her arm was taken firmly and she was led into an even larger room, the open windows shuttered against the afternoon sun. She made out bamboo screens, a desk and a portly figure in a white suit seated behind it.

'Monsieur Quatch,' the older woman said in French, 'allow me to present my granddaughter, Nan Luc.'

The man looked at her for a disconcertingly long time. In the silent room she could even hear his breathing. 'As beautiful as her grandmother,' his voice drawled in French.

'Nan Luc wishes to thank you for your help.'

As she became accustomed to the darkness Nan Luc saw a round white-haired head lolling to one side, a small open mouth, and reddened lecherous eyes.

'She has no reason to thank me,' the mouth said.

'I would wish to thank you all the same.'

A grunt came from the direction of the desk. Nan Luc searched for something to add but could find nothing. Her grandmother looked on with a faint smile.

The thin chimes of a clock broke a long silence. 'Three o'clock.' Quatch rose from behind the desk. 'I have business to attend to.'

As he hurried out her grandmother's smile broadened. 'His opium pipe is the only business he has to attend to, chérie,' she said in almost normal tones. 'Now let us go to my study and talk.'

They mounted a polished wooden staircase to a small attic room looking down on the Avenue Giap. Below, Nan Luc could watch the traffic, heavily laden trucks canted at strange angles, carts drawn by men and a swarm of bicycles enclosing them.

'Sit down, chérie,' the grandmother said. 'I have already ordered tea for us.'

'Thank you, madame.' Nan Luc sat in a high-backed chair beside a small brass-handled desk.

'You must call me Bernadette,' the other woman said. 'I'm nothing more to you now. Formerly we Vietnamese treasured equally our past and our future. Our ancestors and our children. But no longer. To each other we are no longer part of a living family. We are acquaintances. We owe nothing, we ask nothing of each other.'

Nan Luc understood she was receiving the terms of the relationship. 'Nevertheless,' she said, 'I am grateful for what you have done.'

Bernadette nodded her head dismissively. 'After the Americans left,' she said, 'I came to the orphanage, did you know that?'

'No.'

'You were happy enough, it seemed to me,' her grandmother said casually. 'You were being fed, looked after. I saw no reason to take you away.' She smiled. 'And if I am to be more honest I had no wish to advertise my real age by acknowledging a six-year-old granddaughter. In Paris I had become the mistress of Monsieur Quatch, you see. Most of the war he spent as a sort of unofficial ambassador in Europe. His work collecting aid from our many European friends was invaluable to the cause.'

Tea was brought on a tray by a shy-eyed girl no older than Nan Luc herself. She disposed cups and a teapot on the table and withdrew, half bowing as if leaving the presence of royalty.

'I must warn you that Quatch is not popular in some sections of the party,' Bernadette went on. 'Too French, too ambivalent politically. As a beneficiary of his influence you must take care. I think you understand.'

'I understand,' Nan Luc said. She had seen members of the orphanage staff fall from power.

Bernadette poured tea and handed Nan Luc a cup. 'And stay clear of politics. Everybody's days are numbered. My life could change overnight.'

'What would you do then?' Nan Luc asked.

Bernadette put a long slender finger to the side of her nose. 'I have made adequate arrangements, chérie. For the future.'

They drank tea from small, palely decorated cups.

After a long silence Nan Luc placed her cup carefully on the table in front of her. 'I have some questions to ask you,' she said. 'About my family. About my mother.' Bernadette raised her eyebrows, signalling reluctant permission for the girl to continue. 'I know nothing about her,' Nan Luc said. 'Apart from cloudy memories, I hardly know what she looked like. I know nothing about why she received a medal from the government. I know nothing of my father,' she added, 'except,' her hand brushed her face, 'that he was American.'

'These things you wish to know.'

'Yes.'

'Even though they are no longer relevant to your life today.'

'Even so.'

For a few moments the grandmother was silent. Then she put aside her teacup with the air of someone who has made up her mind. 'Some things I can tell you,' she said. 'Not all. This is my decision. It is not negotiable.'

'Very well. I accept that.'

The eyebrows fluttered. 'You say that now. When you have heard the little I am about to tell you, you will want more.' Nan Luc was silent. 'There will be no more, Nan Luc. Accept that now.'

'I will try.'

'Good.' Bernadette stood up and walked towards the window. For some moments she stood there looking down at the dusty bicycle traffic on the Avenue Giap. She reached across to a silver box on the table and took out an American cigarette.

'When I grew up, Hanoi was a city of dancing, of sidewalk cafés, of dinners *à deux*. For us, the bourgeois Vietnamese, a French existence. At home we spoke French of course, we gave our children French names, we dressed in French clothes. But the core of our lives was still the family. Our family. However many French universities we attended we could not be fully colonialised while the family remained a family. I was married just after the Communist war against the French began. I was not much more than your age and my husband, your grandfather, was given to wishful thinking. He believed the French Army would defeat Ho Chi Minh. Your mother Pham was born and a few years later, Louise, her sister. But still Ho Chi Minh was undefeated. Then at Dien Bien Phu General Giap turned the tables on the French. You know of Dien Bien Phu?'

Nan nodded. Revolutionary history was part of all orphanage studies. The victory at Dien Bien Phu had led to the agreement to divide Vietnam in two, a Communist north and pro-Western south.

'Of course, the war against the south continued. Ho Chi Minh's guerrillas naturally continued the war they were winning. For families like us, trapped in Hanoi, it was a time of grave decision.'

Nan Luc, watching her grandmother, could see her agitation in the sharply inhaled breaths, the incessant movement of her hands. Her cigarette burned unsmoked in a silver ashtray on the desk.

'We decided to come south. The family. There were perhaps twenty, twenty-five who set out. We drove as far as we could and then, like a pack of animals, took to the forests.'

'Did you survive, all of you?'

Bernadette snatched up her cigarette, ignoring the ash that fell on her Paris skirt. 'We were hunted by the guerrillas. We were attacked and some of the women raped by the montagnards, you know, those primitives who live on the high plateaux. My husband died of fever. We were scattered, tried to regroup and were scattered again. When I limped into Saigon I was alone. I had lost my husband. I had lost my two daughters, your mother Pham and my younger daughter Louise. I had lost my family.'

'What did you do? How did you live?'

'A clandestine member of the government in Hanoi offered me money to start a bar here in Saigon.'

'The Eros?'

She nodded. 'It was to be a place where Westerners came to relax. A place where people would drink too much and talk too freely.'

'You were working for Hanoi, even though you had just fled Hanoi.'

'To live in Saigon and to be subsidised by Hanoi, can you think of a better way of insuring against the future?'

'I see,' Nan Luc said slowly, 'and did Monsieur Quatch come to the bar?'

She chuckled. 'The Eros was his idea.'

'And how long did it take for you to find my mother?'

'Many, many years.' She shrugged. 'I found your Aunt Louise first. I was no longer looking, you understand. The Americans were arriving. One night at a party I told my story. A man there thought it was familiar. Of course, it was. It was the story of half a nation. But the names and ages fitted. Louise worked in a bar not half a mile from the Eros.'

'You all came together again?'

Her grandmother puffed her lips. 'We were not a family any more. A family is a unit which reveres the same ancestors, indulges the same children, nurtures the land of its ownership.' Nan Luc sat silently. She thought of Uncle Qui and the shattered, broken families he had reunited or revenged.

Her grandmother extinguished her cigarette and took another from the silver box. 'I brought Louise to the Eros. I moved in with Monsieur Quatch. She became manageress. A great success. The American boys loved her.'

'And Maman?' Nan Luc's head came up. 'Was she a bar-girl too?'

Her grandmother smiled. 'No, your mother was not like her sister. She did not take clients.'

The anger surged again in Nan Luc. The hypocrisy of this woman who could make a difference between a madame and a whore! She lifted her teacup and sipped at the thin cooling liquid. When she set the cup down again she had recovered her composure.

'What else would you like to know?' Bernadette enquired with an amused display of solicitude.

'I would like to know what happened to my mother in the War of Independence. Did she fight against the Americans?'

'Why do you ask?' her grandmother said warily.

'After the war she was presented with a medal. A posthumous Ho Chi Minh Star for fighting as a secret officer of the Liberation Army.'

'Are you proud of your mother's medal?'

'It has been useful to me,' Nan Luc said candidly.

Bernadette laughed. 'Quatch said it would be. It does me no harm, also,' she said.

'You mean Monsieur Quatch arranged the medal?'

'Yes. It involved a little minor doctoring of the record. Half of Saigon was trying to do that at the time.'

'So Maman did not fight in the forest.'

'She served in a medical unit. Unfortunately she chose the losing side.'

'She was killed in the fighting?'

'In the last days there were many deaths.'

Nan Luc took a deep breath. 'What was my father's name?'

Her grandmother shook her head impatiently. 'I don't know.'

'Was he here long, in Saigon?'

She shrugged. 'I was in Paris at the time.'

'Tell me anything you can about him,' Nan Luc said. 'Anything my mother said about him.'

'There's nothing to tell,' Bernadette said sharply. 'Your mother had an American lover. So did thousands of others.'

'You must know *something* about him,' Nan Luc said desperately.

Her grandmother looked at her coldly. 'Forget your father. You are Vietnamese. Your father is none of your concern. Any interest in someone you will never see is childish and absurd. I will not discuss the question.'

Nan inclined her head obediently as she had learned to do in the orphanage. But the gesture only disguised feelings of boiling anger and disbelief.

Bernadette took a photograph which lay face down on the secretaire. Glancing briefly at it, she pushed it into Nan Luc's hand. 'Have this,' she said. 'Pham, your mother.'

Nan looked down eagerly at the small black and white portrait booth photograph. She was a woman with thick black hair, olive skin and deep set eyes. Less than a woman perhaps. A twenty-year-old girl. Attractive without being markedly beautiful, a girl in a plain white blouse.

The roots of memory stirred in Nan Luc. She had remembered her mother as different. More filmically beautiful perhaps. But the stirring of the roots of memory brought with it a breathtaking sense of love for the woman represented by this stark black and white picture.

'And my aunt, Louise, what happened to her?' she asked after a moment.

'One of the lucky ones. Her *bel ami* was a US military policeman. I heard stories that he got her through the gates of the embassy by marrying her an hour before his helicopter took off. May they live in peace and harmony.'

'May they live in peace and harmony,' Nan Luc repeated.

'So,' her grandmother said rising. 'That is your once distinguished family history. The last years have not been uplifting. We can talk of honour no longer.'

'I have more questions to ask,' Nan Luc said tenaciously.

'Yes,' the other woman said coolly.

'My father, the American. Is there nothing you can tell me about him?'

'I see,' Bernadette said. 'You may be hard-headed and practical, but you still nurse the dream of going to America.'

'I am content here. But I need to know who my father is. His name. Where he lives. A photograph of him. Every Vietnamese child has that right.'

'You would leave for America tomorrow if you could,' Bernadette said. 'And so would I. But not as one of these wretched boat people. When I go to the West it will be in suitable style. By airplane to Paris.'

Nan Luc found herself overwhelmed by a sense of loneliness, of isolation, as she looked at the cool, over-made-up woman before her. She had lived as an orphan, her life organised in a cold efficient way, without love. More even than the half memories of her mother, dreams of her father seemed to offer that love, the warmth of a parent, a guide.

'I want to understand him,' Nan insisted. 'I want to understand what happened between him and my mother.'

'Dreams,' Bernadette said harshly.

'But at the end, when the Americans left, did he want to take my mother with him?'

'It wasn't possible. She was already dead.'

'And me?'

'I forbid you to ask me more questions,' the older woman

hissed. 'Your father is none of your business. You are a member of the Hyn family. That is enough.'

Nan Luc took a deep breath. 'I want to know his name. My name. I believe you know it.'

'Ah,' her grandmother held up her hand, the red-tipped finger-nails caught in a shaft of afternoon sunlight, 'they told me this about you in the orphanage. No more, d'you hear?'

'You refuse to tell me.'

'It is unimportant,' her grandmother flared.

'Not to me.'

Bernadette stood up. 'In the orphanage,' she said after a few moments, 'you had a reputation for having a will of your own. The world we live in is not an orphanage. Do you understand that, Nan Luc?'

'I understand the words,' Nan Luc said carefully, 'but not the meaning.'

'You have not wondered why I asked you here today?'

'Of course.'

'You have not asked why.'

'I was sure you would tell me if you required some service of me.'

'Not a service, ma'moiselle.'

'What then?'

Bernadette smoothed her cheek with the tips of her fingers and walked across the room to stand in front of a mirror. 'I am,' she said, looking at Nan Luc's face reflected in the glass, 'no longer a young woman.' She turned, baring her teeth in a smile. 'Of course I'm not an old woman either. I was hardly more than a child when your mother was born. She in turn was no more than nineteen, twenty . . .' She walked, almost skipped, in front of Nan Luc. 'I still, fortunately, have the body of a young woman . . .'

Nan Luc shifted in her seat as her grandmother stopped on the far side of the room.

'I live a life of great comfort, Nan Luc.'

'I can see.' Nan Luc gestured round the room.

'This life is entirely due to the good will of Monsieur Quatch.'

'Monsieur is an important man,' Nan Luc said.

'And important men,' Bernadette said smiling, 'require their needs to be *serviced*.' A silence fell on the room. 'I've known for a long time it cannot last for ever,' Bernadette said. 'To be the mistress of such a man is a great honour, Nan Luc.' Nan Luc's eyes opened wide. 'I do not intend to be discarded, you understand,' Bernadette said fiercely. 'For that reason I am resolved to choose my own successor. Someone of course who will make sure I am maintained as I should be maintained. Monsieur Quatch has always spoken favourably of such a progression.'

The idea struck Nan Luc like a thunderbolt. 'No,' she said, sitting upright. 'I will not do it.'

'I can teach you what pleases him. Already he has reason to favour you. Many, many years ago he remarked how pretty a child you were.'

Nan got quickly to her feet. 'I will not do it. He's old, ugly. I need to love a man.'

'You young fool,' Bernadette hissed at her. 'This is the greatest opportunity you will ever get. Look in a mirror. You're beautiful, yes. But you are a *hybrid*. The War of Indepedence wasn't fought for you, for hybrids!'

Nan moved towards the door. 'I would like to go.'

'Nan Luc!' Bernadette's voice was like a whip. 'You're still a virgin, I suppose.' Nan Luc blushed. 'Virginity is like excess weight,' Bernadette said. 'It does not become a woman. Listen, girl, what you've got men are fool enough to want. They'll pay clothes and comfort and food and drink for it. Unless you still believe, against the mountains of evidence, that´a woman can make her own way in a Communist society, you'll learn to use your one asset.'

Nan Luc looked at her in shock.

'You're fortunate that your grandmother is still a relatively young woman,' Bernadette said harshly. She walked across the room. 'I will dream up an assignment for you,' she said, suddenly smiling. 'Fool about a little. Experiment. Learn what pleases men. In a year or two you will think differently.' She cupped her hands under her small breasts and threw back her shoulders. 'Meanwhile I still have a little time yet,' she said, swaying to her own reflection in the mirror.

A few minutes later Nan Luc walked through the heat and dust and jangling bicycle bells of the Avenue Giap with her head slowly spinning. A thought or image would enter her mind only to remain incomplete, undwelt upon before being jostled out by another. First the toad-like Quatch. She was already indebted to him for releasing her from back-breaking labour for the next two years. Was it dangerous to accept? Was this what the bright new world would be for her, sexual bargaining and discrimination by race? She shivered as she thought of the man's small red mouth and strange thyroid eyes.

Reaching the corner of the Avenue Giap she flung off the images of Quatch and the slimy hypocrisy of her grandmother. Other thoughts jostled for attention as she pushed her way through the crowded streets. Most of all thoughts of her father. An American whose name, she was convinced, was known to Bernadette. But for some reason a name not to be discussed even now. All these years since her birth, more than fifteen years since the Americans had carried their flag from Vietnam.

Why?

3

Halfway round the world a taxi drew up before a small Paris hotel on the Ile St Louis. It was a little after dawn and the young American who stepped into the first rays of morning sunlight blinked and rubbed at his unshaven cheek as he paid off the driver.

'It's going to be a good day,' the driver said, nodding towards the pale sky.

The American's eyes roamed the balconied windows of the hotel. 'I wonder,' he said. In truth he was wondering behind which of these balconied windows his father had been murdered fifteen years ago.

Max Benning picked up his duffel bag and stood for a moment as the cab pulled away. Blond-brown hair, a little over six feet tall, lean but heavily boned, it was not difficult to see a north European ancestry. He was casually dressed: jeans, Chelsea boots, a pale tan patch-pocket shirt, a tan leather jacket hooked over his shoulder by an index finger through the tab. His face, now drawn from the half-sleep of an overnight flight, seemed to hold a permanent weariness. A foreign correspondent's face, those who knew him said; a classical mercenary's face, others thought, the face of someone used to sleepless nights and long marches. Meeting him for the first time, people overreacted to his physical presence. Most men saw him as competition; most women as sensual excitement.

The black duffel bag in his right hand was pulling at his shoulder socket. He glanced up at the brass-lettering that read Hotel Kandler and walked through the open door into the dark lobby.

The woman who emerged from the breakfast room and shuffled behind the desk was small with gypsy dark eyes, her black hair greying. While she went through the formalities of checking him in, Max took in the cracked pattern-tiled floor, the dark green panelling, the curving iron banister of the staircase his father must have climbed.

The old woman did not react to the name Benning on Max's passport. She pushed it across the counter and turned to reach down the key to his room. 'Number five,' she said. 'It overlooks the Seine.'

'*Merci*, madame.'

'Mademoiselle.'

'Mademoiselle,' Max corrected himself. He took the key. 'Have you been here long, mademoiselle?' he asked her.

'All my life,' she said. 'I worked here as a chambermaid, starting at the age of twelve. When my patronne died in 1960 she left the hotel to me.' She shrugged away the idea of gratitude. 'There was no one else,' she said.

'Do you remember, fifteen or more years ago, when a man was murdered here?'

'The German, yes.' Her black gypsy eyes held his.

'Do you remember his name?'

'Yes.' A caesura rather than a hesitation. 'The same as yours.'

'He was my father.'

She pursed her lips. 'He was a German.' She glanced down at his American passport.

'My mother's American. I was born there.'

'You speak French well. Like your father.'

'You remember that.' She shrugged. 'Will you tell me about that night?'

She lifted a flexible brass-ringed pipe from beneath the counter and blew a whistling note into the ivory coloured mouthpiece. 'Madeleine,' she said. 'Two coffees, please. And croissants.' She turned back to Max. 'Do you want to see your room first?' She smiled spectrally. 'It's not the same one.'

He shook his head, bent to pick up his duffel bag and followed her shuffling walk into the musty breakfast room.

They sat down at a table near a window. Something linked him to this woman with her odd bitter smile. He was not certain why he decided to tell this stranger the truth. 'My mother has always told me that my father was killed in a car crash a few years after I was born. It seemed a more respectable story.'

'Ah.' The exclamation was without expression: without surprise, disbelief, understanding or even encouragement to continue. 'And now at last she's told you the truth.'

'She's in a clinic in London,' Max said. 'She has a cancer. Her doctors say she's not expected to live long.'

The maid came in with coffee and a plate of croissants. The patronne pushed the plate towards Max. 'In those days,' she said, 'a small hotel like this might let a room or two on a permanent basis. A year say. Sometimes more. A lot of artists like to live like that. The top floor in some of these old places is arranged as a studio and sleeping salon. My old patronne used to claim Picasso lived here in 1905. Lying, I expect.' She poured hot milk in his coffee and broke a croissant so that the shards of its carapace scattered across the bare table.

'Early in 1974 a Vietnamese woman came here and paid me a year's rent on the top studio. She was the sort of woman some men like,' the patronne said.

'Beautiful?'

'Perhaps. A putain. A prostitute.'

'Local businessmen used to visit her?'

'Foreigners, mostly. A few French.' She sat back, thinking. 'I remember telling the investigating inspector at the time of your father's death. They never stayed long. Not really, on average, long enough,' she said without a smile.

'What was her name?'

'Mademoiselle Bernadette Hyn. Yes,' she said with some satisfaction. 'Bernadette Hyn.'

'Did she pay in cash?'

'Cash. Always. There was no shortage of money. When the North Vietnamese marched into Saigon, her *bel ami*, her pimp, became the new Communist *chargé d'affaires* here in Paris.'

'Do you remember his name?'

She puffed her lined cheeks. 'Do reptiles have names? Quatch, his whore called him.'

Max finished his coffee. 'Can I look at the attic?'

'Of course.'

'Will you come with me?'

'If you wish.'

They left the breakfast room and climbed the iron banistered staircase. Halfway along the corridor on the top floor, the patronne stopped and opened a brown-painted door. 'There's not a lot to see,' she said.

It was a bare, uncarpeted room with a good north skylight. A second room leading off it had a large double brass bed and a few pieces of furniture.

'Monsieur Benning was found on the floor,' the woman gestured carelessly.

Max walked to the skylight and looked out across the grey slate roofs gleaming in the spring sunlight. He tried to imagine his father standing here. What was he doing in this room fifteen years ago? What had he come for?

'The police recovered a knife,' the patronne said. 'They talked of suicide.'

'But you don't think so?'

'Who knows what really happened?'

'How long did the woman live here?'

'A year. But she had been in Paris longer than that. Long enough to adopt our ways. A foreign whore who thought herself better than a French patronne.'

'Did my father come here just that one time?'

The woman gave her strange savage smile. 'One time was enough, monsieur.'

He caught a few hours' sleep. At just before midday he made his way down to the Rue Boileau where the Vietnamese embassy stands. Max Benning had been a journalist long enough to be without real hope. If Bernadette's lover had become *chargé d'affaires* he wasn't going to get much from the embassy. But it was still worth a try.

In the high ceilinged interview room the furniture was a mix of Louis Philippe and splay-leg 1950s Formica. Faded posters of young Vietnamese soldiers waving forward their advancing columns covered the walls; posters of a revolutionary struggle long ago won and lost, the corners curling down where the blue tack had hardened and lost adhesion. Sitting alone in the room, watching the slant of sun through the unwashed windows, unable to hear the slightest movement beyond the double door, Max waited half an hour for the first clerk to return with further questions and a second half hour for him to come back again.

But he didn't come back. Instead the door opened and Max was confronted by a girl, simply dressed in a black skirt, black pumps and a sleeveless white blouse. He stood up. He registered olive green eyes and hair that was dark chestnut and slightly waved. An Amerasian girl. It seemed to him that she could not fail to see the effect she had on him but she moved unselfconsciously behind the desk in the centre of the room and invited him to sit down.

She began speaking in fluent English, the accent American, the usage at times just slightly unpractised. 'Mr Benning,' she said, her eyes on the file she had laid open in front of her, 'I understand you are anxious for information about a Madame Bernadette Hyn who once resided at the Hotel Kandler here in Paris.'

'I gave the clerk all the details,' Max said. 'My father was found dead in Bernadette Hyn's studio apartment in early 1975.'

'May I ask why you are seeking this information all these years later, Mr Benning?'

'Until twelve years ago I believed my father had died in a car crash just after I was born. My mother chose that as a suitable version of events for a growing boy.'

'I'm sorry,' she said, carefully. 'I was asking from a personal interest. It was not an official question.'

He realised that, behind her spectacular green eyes, she was deeply troubled. 'My name is Nan Luc Hyn,' the Vietnamese girl said suddenly. 'The Bernadette Hyn you are enquiring about is almost certainly my grandmother.'

'Jesus Christ,' Max said.

She put her head down and read rapidly through the notes, turning the pages quickly. He waited until she looked up. The features were put together with that unique felicity that a Vietnamese mother and an American father sometimes brought about.

'I don't think I'm going to be any help to you,' she said. 'My grandmother, Bernadette Hyn, was an official of what was known as North Vietnam. She was working for one of our senior representatives in Paris, Vo Tran Quatch. In my notes it is written that the accusation of murder was an American attempt to discredit the work of Franco-Vietnamese friendship which Monsieur Quatch was engaged in.'

'Sounds as if the CIA have a lot to answer for.' She looked down at her notes, momentarily confused. 'OK.' Max sat forward. 'You mean somebody picked a passing German tourist off the street, murdered him and dropped the body in your grandmother's apartment?'

'According to my notes.'

'That's all you have to say?' Something in her expression cancelled out the inadequacy of her words. Something that appealed to him to understand she had no alternative. He stood up. 'Will you have lunch with me?'

'That would be impossible,' she said, flushing.

'Why impossible?'

'I seldom leave the compound.'

'You must sometimes. How about tomorrow?'

'Tomorrow I have some errands to do at lunchtime. I'm sorry, Mr Benning.'

Max got to his feet. 'Your grandmother, is she still alive?'

'Of course.'

'In Saigon?'

'In Ho Chi Minh City, yes.'

'Did she never tell you about the day the Americans planted the body of a German tourist on her living-room carpet?'

Nan Luc looked at him evenly. 'There are many things she has not told me, Mr Benning. My grandmother has lived a very full life.'

'I bet,' he said. At the door he paused. 'If I were to just catch you between errands, say at twelve-thirty in the Brasserie one block down, would you have time to talk a bit more about this very strange story?'

'Official business is always discussed here at the embassy, Mr Benning.' She stepped forward and opened the door for him.

'Then we'll just talk about how much we both like Paris.' Her eyes opened wide, incredibly green, set in a flawless blue-white. He thought of the brightness of emeralds. 'Try to make it happen,' he said quietly.

'Please, Mr Benning . . .' she whispered.

'Will you try?'

He could see her teeter on the edge of a momentous decision. 'Don't wait past one o'clock,' she said through the crack in the closing door.

She knew it was an utterly reckless thing to do. She had delivered a file of documents to the Elysée palace and had spent some of the few francs she possessed on a taxi back to Rue Boileau, gaining nearly half an hour on the Metro ride. With a little leeway claimed for waiting time at the Elysée she calculated that she had the best part of an hour. An hour to meet an American.

She had no real doubt about what would happen if she were found out. Free time did not exist for the junior members of the embassy. It was not so much forbidden as unthought of. And to spend an hour as she planned, an hour carved out of her official duties . . . her heart raced at the thought of what she was doing. Even more at the thought of why she was doing it. It was the first time in her life that she had had lunch with a man alone. It would be almost the first time in her life that she had done anything that was not part of an organised event, approved or endorsed by the state she lived in or the politics she was expected to live by.

She left the taxi in the shadows of a narrow road no more than a few yards from the Brasserie. She could see it up ahead in the sunlight. She could turn now and walk away. Or she could continue the few yards along the ruelle, step out into the sunlight and enter the Brasserie. Where the American waited.

'No wonder you can't take your eyes off her, chérie. She's adorable,' the French woman said to her husband. Max, at the next table, glanced up to see Nan Luc hesitating at the door of the Brasserie.

As she walked in he got quickly to his feet and touched her hand in greeting. She gave him a quick smile, then her eyes flicked rapidly round the room, before coming to rest on the large, lettered window that gave on to the sidewalk.

'There's a garden out back with one or two tables,' Max said. 'Would that be better?' She nodded quickly and he led her through the bar.

In the garden, around the white painted walls, four or five tables were arranged, each set with cutlery and glasses on a pink paper cloth. When the waiter had taken their order they were alone in the paved, glassed-in garden room.

'Are you different because you have an American father?' he said.

She smiled. 'That's why I look different.'

'It's more than looks,' he said. 'I don't believe there's another girl at the embassy who would have dared come here today.'

She laughed. 'I'm sure you're right, Monsieur Benning,' she said.

He thought of how the embassy might react if they discovered she was having lunch alone with a Westerner and felt a twinge of guilt at the risk she was taking. 'I don't have to say I'm glad you came,' he said.

'I can't stay long.'

'I know that. I guess you don't get a lot of time to see Paris?' She was silent. 'Dumb question,' he said. 'I'll try again. Tell me about back home. Were you born in Saigon?'

'Yes.'

'And your mother?'

'She served in a South Vietnamese medical unit during the war. She was killed just before the end.'

'What happened to you?'

'My mother's sister had gone to America, my grandmother was here in Paris. I was put in an orphanage. I stayed there as a pupil and later a teacher until my grandmother found me.' She said all this in a rush of words as if trying to put it behind her.

'And your grandmother arranged the job in Paris?'

'Yes,' she said neutrally. 'Monsieur Quatch is a very influential man in our government. He was once the *chargé d'affaires* here in Paris.'

'Can I ask you – do you believe this story about the CIA picking a tourist off the sidewalk . . .?' She hesitated, then shook her head. 'Do you know what really happened?'

'No. If I did I think I would tell you.'

'I think you would. Do you know you're totally unlike anyone I expected to find working at the embassy?'

She smiled enigmatically at him. 'Perhaps I've reason to be.'

The waiter rattled plates down on to the table with that efficient indifference of the Paris professional. With a rapid twist of his wrist he poured wine into first Nan Luc's glass then Max's.

'How long have you been in Paris?' Max asked her.

'A few months. After I left the orphanage I did a semester at Hue University before being posted to Paris.'

'You were one of the lucky ones.'

'Perhaps,' she said with the first touch of coldness he had felt coming from her.

'Have you been to the Louvre or the Beaubourg?' She shook her head. 'Have you had an apéritif at the Deux Magots or dinner at a restaurant in the Bois de Boulogne?' She was silent, looking down at the table. 'I'm sorry,' he said. 'I didn't mean to hassle you. It's just bad luck you're not able to do things like that.'

He knew that he meant his bad luck. 'Would you like to hear what I got from the French police?'

'Yes,' she said cautiously. 'I would.'

'I talked on the phone to the Commissaire of Police in charge of the case. Retired now. A man named Borel. First he agrees your grandmother has a complete alibi. She was somewhere else at the time of my father's death. From there on he seems to have a completely different version of events.'

'How different?'

'Borel doesn't see my father as a casual victim of the CIA. Or just a tourist looking for a good time. He says his enquiries revealed my father and Quatch had been seen together twice in the previous week at a café near Quatch's office.'

'Did he say why they were meeting, your father and Quatch?'

'No. I don't think he knows for sure. But he has ideas. He's agreed to meet me tomorrow morning. Talk a little more about it.'

Nan Luc was silent. After a moment she said, 'Will you believe me if I say I have no interest in covering up any responsibility Monsieur Quatch might have for your father's death?'

'And does that hold for your grandmother, too?'

'My grandmother had an alibi, you said.'

'She could still know much more than she told the French police.'

'Yes.'

They sat in silence while the waiter served them choucroute and Toulouse sausages.

'Normally someone else would have dealt with your enquiry,' Nan Luc said. 'When my colleague saw my grandmother was involved, he brought it to me.' She paused. 'I'll help all I can.'

'Why?'

'I believe you have a right to know the circumstances of your father's death.'

'You're not just here to protect your grandmother's part in this affair, then?'

'Here?'

'Here in the restaurant, having lunch with me.'

She thought for a moment. 'I'm here because I want to be,' she said. 'Is that good enough for just now?'

'That's good enough.' They drank, first touching glasses. He felt a powerful need to know as much about her as he could in the short time they had. A need to ply her with questions. 'Tell me what life's like in Vietnam today?' he said.

'Hard.'

'But hopeful?'

'I'm not sure.'

'Do you have a man back home? Boyfriend, husband?'

She held him with an amused glance. 'No . . .' Then the half smile faded. 'You've never been there?'

He shook his head. 'I was too young for the draft.'

'We Vietnamese . . .' She paused. 'The Vietnamese people,' she seemed to be correcting herself, 'believe in race. Ambitious young men in the administration prefer not to be seen with girls who too obviously have American fathers.'

'Tell me about your father.'

'I wish I could,' she said. 'Beyond the fact that he was an American, I know nothing. Not even his name.'

'Was he a soldier?'

'If he was, it was not an R and R romance.'

'That's not what I was trying to say.'

She shrugged. 'There were thousands, tens of thousands. But this was different. When I was born he gave me a bracelet.' She touched her wrist. He looked down and saw a gold band length-ened with a thin strip of base metal. 'If ever . . . whenever, I get to America, I'll look for him.' Those clear green eyes held his. 'It's important to know our fathers. That's what you're doing too, isn't it? Looking for your father?'

'Yes.'

'Why did your mother tell you he died just after you were born?'

Max shrugged. 'My mother's lifeblood is a sort of chilly pride. She couldn't bear the idea my father wouldn't live with her any more. She found it easier to pretend he was dead.'

'Did he never try to see you?'

'He never knew I was born. Never knew I existed. She was too proud to tell him she was pregnant.'

For a few minutes they ate in silence.

'When she told me all this,' he said slowly, 'I was surprised how much I felt involved with the life of someone I'd never even seen. How much I wanted to know what happened to him between the time he and my mother split up and whatever happened here, in Paris.'

Her eyes met his. 'I always believed we felt differently, East and West, about such things.'

'I don't know,' he said. 'Perhaps someday you'll tell me how it is with you.'

'It's simple. To find my father, to get to know him, is the most important thing in my life.' Embarrassed, she glanced down quickly at her watch. 'I must go now,' she said.

'Are we going to get a chance to meet again?'

She drank some wine. 'It's not easy.'

'I know that.'

She thought for some moments. 'Tomorrow night I have to attend a lecture on European Community Aid Policy,' she said. 'Their press office issues a résumé.'

'You mean maybe you could play hookey.'

She laughed, suddenly delighted. 'I've never been in school in America but I know that phrase, Mr Benning. Yes, maybe for an hour or two I could play hookey.'

Marc Borel was nearing seventy, short, powerfully built, a monk's fringe of black hair semi-circling a tanned, bald dome. 'My doctor has told me my liver must not be seen within ten metres of a bar,' he said. 'Since, so far at least, my liver and I are inseparable, I don't sit in cafés any longer. I hope you don't mind a walk in the Parc Monceau, Monsieur Benning.'

'Not at all,' Max said, falling in beside him. 'I'm sorry about the liver.'

Borel shrugged. 'I suppose you've already made up your mind that your father was murdered. You're a journalist. You have a feel for these things.'

'This is not my kind of journalism. I write about eco-disasters rather than individual tragedies, but I know enough to guess this isn't the story of a john knifed by a pimp when he wouldn't pay for favours received.'

'No.' Borel felt about in the misshapen pockets of his old houndstooth jacket and found a pipe and an oiled tobacco pouch. Early April sun lightened the bare gravel alleys. 'Do you know what your father did for a living, monsieur?'

'No. I know he left Germany as a very young man shortly after the war. I know that he was in the French Foreign Legion when he married my mother.'

'Then you also know he served the French in what was then known as Indo-China.'

Max nodded. 'Captured. Released a few years later. After that it's a blank. What did he do?'

'Most importantly, your father was a scholar, my friend,' Borel said.

'A scholar? I saw him as a businessman, maybe. But not as an ex-paratrooper turned scholar.'

'There have been many great soldier-scholars, monsieur. Your father was a leading authority in many areas of Imperial Vietnamese art and culture. When I was investigating his death I came to admire him considerably.' They stopped while Borel completed the filling of his pipe. 'Almost alone,' Borel continued, 'he was responsible for saving many valuable items of Indo-Chinese antiquity from the ravages of the war. While the fighting was raging round Hue, Peter Benning rescued centuries old manuscripts from the old Imperial library. Much survives today in the museums of Vietnam entirely thanks to him. Today's Vietnam has reason to be grateful. *You* have reason to be proud.'

Max shook his head, wondering if his mother had known any

of this. 'You're not suggesting this had anything to do with his death?'

'In my investigations,' Borel tamped down his pipe, 'I discovered, as I told you on the phone, evidence of two meetings at least between your father and Quatch.'

'What did Quatch have to say about that?'

Borel laughed. 'Quatch is not an easy man to deal with. Even less so when it was obvious that he was about to become a senior figure in a united, triumphant Vietnam.'

'What did he tell you?'

'He told me Peter Benning had fallen in love with Bernadette Hyn. That he had gone to her apartment and thrust a dagger into his breast. I don't think he cared much whether I believed it or not.'

'Could it have been suicide?'

'Possible, but unlikely. I'll spare you the gruesome details.'

'So what did happen?'

'Quatch killed him. Or had him killed.'

'Why?'

'Ah, that I don't know.'

'Do you have any guesses?'

Borel stopped to light his pipe. Expelling puffs like gunsmoke he glanced up at a bruised purple cloud moving from the direction of the Boulevard Malesherbes. 'I think Quatch was more than just a representative of Hanoi,' he said. 'I think he had a business sideline.'

'Antiquities?'

Borel nodded. 'Smuggled ivory statuary, manuscripts, *objets d'art*. Your father caught up with him in Paris and Quatch put someone on to kill him. I don't think it's a very complicated story. The complications began when, about a week after your father was killed, the Communists were victorious in Vietnam. Quatch became *chargé d'affaires* here in Paris and the Quai d'Orsay told me not to upset a representative of the new Vietnamese government.'

'You gave up the case?'

'With Monsieur Quatch about to be the next ambassador to tread the purple carpet, I had no choice ... I was in any case offered an excellent promotion.'

'Which you accepted.'

'Without a trace of shame, Monsieur Benning.' Heavy drops of rain began to speckle the dry gravel in front of them. Borel dragged from his inside pocket a tam-o'-shanter in a Royal Stewart plaid. He put it on, carefully adjusting it round the line of his tonsure. 'What do you think?' He touched the peak and cocked his head in a Maurice Chevalier gesture.

'Ridiculous,' Max said.

'You're an honest man, monsieur,' Borel laughed. 'That's enough walking for one morning. It's almost lunchtime. My liver craves the bonhomie of a little bar I know just through the gates. There.' He pointed.

A clock somewhere across the river rang midnight. Across the Seine from the Ile St Louis, Paris pulsated with the sounds of traffic and music and people. In front of him the Hotel Kandler was dark but for a small lamp burning somewhere deep in the lobby. Max stopped outside, searching his pockets for the front door keys the patronne had given him.

He was surprised at the acuteness of his own disappointment. Nan Luc had not turned up at the café where they had arranged to meet. He had waited for almost two hours, drinking his way through half a dozen pastis and a day-by-day account by the barman of this year's Tour de France.

'Do the Vietnamese embassy staff ever come in here?' Max had asked him cautiously.

'Seldom,' the barman said. 'And then I think only senior members perhaps.' His lower lip turned down in a grimace.

'You're happy enough they stay away?'

'I was a conscript in Indo-China in the fifties. Myself and half a million other Frenchmen. They're a hard people. More than dedicated. Suicidal. I could have told the Americans who came after us.'

From the café Max had gone to the Château de la Muette. He was pretty certain she had not attended the Aid Policy lecture. Waiting outside the iron gates as the lecture ended he watched the Third World delegates leave the building. She was not among them.

He had gone back to the Avenue Boilleau, to the Vietnamese

embassy. Through the padlocked gate he had stared at the infinitely depressing combination of a pagoda roof style and a white tiled fifties façade. There were no lights visible behind the shuttered windows, no light in the oriental portico.

He had returned to the café, ordered another pastis and sat for another hopeless half-hour. The barman told him stories of what life had been like in Saigon while Max drank and wondered how real it was, his certainty that he would never see her again. Not real at all, of course. Just an acute reflection of the ache he felt to see her enter the bar and cross towards him.

'I'm sorry your girl never turned up,' the barman said. Max lifted an eyebrow in surprise. 'The Vietnamese girl you were here with in the garden yesterday.'

'You remember.'

'Not easy to forget. I had a Vietnamese girl when I was there. She came from a village in the Mekong Delta. Nice people. Peasants and a bit more. Not just a service romance.' He poured himself a pastis. 'She was pregnant when I last saw her.'

'What happened?' Max asked him.

'What always happens. The winds of war.'

'Just like that. You never saw her again?'

'I was posted north. Took some shrapnel in the leg. The Army shipped me back to France.'

'What happened to the girl?'

The barman shrugged. 'I still sometimes think about her. They never give up, the Vietnamese. Whatever it is, waiting, fighting, hating. Maybe even loving too.' He finished his pastis and drew a sharp breath through his nose. 'If ever ... whenever ...'

'What's that?' Max said. It seemed to echo a phrase Nan Luc had used.

'They say it a lot out there. The women especially. If ever it happens ... whenever it happens ...'

'What is it?' Max said. 'Resignation?'

'Not the Vietnamese.' The Frenchman shook his head. 'They *make* things happen. I could have told the Americans that, too.'

Max bought the barman another pastis and bade him goodnight. The Frenchman lifted his glass as Max put a handful of francs on the bar. 'Sorry about the girl,' he said. 'One thing you can be sure of. She didn't just forget.'

Back in the lobby of the Hotel Kandler a shadow moved through the darkness of the breakfast room. From the shuffle of her espadrilles he recognised the patronne.

'I hope I haven't kept you up, mademoiselle,' Max said.

She shook her head. 'I have a message for you, Monsieur Benning. A young woman named Nan Luc telephoned. She says she regrets she will not be able to continue work on your case. She is no longer at the embassy. She was called home to Vietnam this afternoon.'

4

Bernadette Hyn seethed with anger. 'Make sure you understand, Nan Luc. Nobody has given you nine lives. The moment Benning's son came to the embassy you should have cabled me cipher here in Saigon.' Bernadette swerved the Citroën round a clutch of cyclists, blasted her horn and accelerated down the road from the airport to Ho Chi Minh City. 'I warn you,' Bernadette hissed. 'Monsieur Quatch is not in a forgiving mood.'

Nan Luc kept her eyes on the road ahead. 'When the reception clerks read the list of enquiries Max Benning presented,' she said evenly, 'they brought them straight to me. I had no reason to know you didn't want me to deal with the matter.'

'He should have been turned away. Commonsense should have told you that you were not in Paris to supply information to an American journalist.'

'Who was Peter Benning?' Nan Luc said. 'Why was he killed? I think his son has the right to know these things.'

'The matter's closed.' Bernadette threw her a look of savage fury. 'Open it again at your peril.' She brought the car to a squealing halt as the head of a long column of students began to pass across their front.

The two women sat in silence, Bernadette rapping with her scarlet fingernails on the plastic steering column, Nan Luc remembering all the other youth demonstrations she had taken part in: the long columns winding their way through the dusty tracks of the countryside behind Saigon, the times when, as the banners were shaken and the chanting against China or America taken up even more strongly, the peasant women in conical hats would look up from the paddy fields. Sometimes a child or two would wave, but through most of the long, trudging marches only the water buffaloes, the movement of their great heads slowly following the progress of the column along the banked road, registered the passing of the dispirited demonstrators.

With a sharp and sudden touch of anguish she thought of student demonstrations she had seen in Paris where young people marched because they felt strongly about something. Now she watched the demonstrators crossing in front of the car, their weary chants paying slogan lip service to unfelt international hatreds, and tears rose in her eyes.

Bernadette thrust the car into gear as the last of the column passed. 'You're a fool, Nan Luc.' Her anger bubbled over again. 'After Paris you could have gone on anywhere. London, even Washington.'

'And what will happen now?' Nan Luc asked.

'You will go to one of the provinces. And you will never, on any account, talk to anyone about anything Benning's son told you in Paris.'

The main square of the city of Cahn Roc, capital city of Cahn Roc province, was hot and dusty as the old Dodge truck coughed and wheezed to a stop after the journey up from Ho Chi Minh City. The balconied buildings set back behind the line of palm trees were French colonial in style, run-down now with paint blistering and peeling from the doors, and broken windows stuffed with rags. But the people had a lighter air than those in Saigon. The same swarms of cyclists emerged from side roads in a cascade of tinkling bells, the same dusty evidence in the form of broken café tables existed from a life more generous than the present. But the girls' high-buttoned blouses were in fresh contrast to their billowing black trousers and officials in straw helmets chatted and exchanged civic information on street corners.

It was almost, Nan Luc thought as she swung her linen bag on her shoulder and headed towards the flag-draped headquarters building, as if a café might materialise in a dusty shop front or the faint sound of American music might rise above the cyclists' bells, above the revolutionary pop song, endlessly and triumphantly repeated from the square's loudspeakers, 'Hue, Saigon, Hanoi'.

She stepped through the open doors of the administrative building into the deep shade of a tiled hall. A cast-iron staircase rose in an elegant sweep to the next floor. High panelled doors stood in pairs on either side of her. Nothing indicated who might be working behind the doors; nothing guided the visitor to where enquiries could be made. Then a woman's voice rose from behind one of the doors and Nan Luc took a breath, knocked on the door and entered.

She was in a large room with a surprising barrel-vaulted ceiling, some parts of which had lost its plaster and exposed the dusty laths beneath. A large, cracked inscription still reading *Liberté, Egalité, Fraternité* curved along the line of the barrelling. Three or four desks were placed at random angles in the room, each occupied by a woman in a high white jacket. The faces of the four women were turned towards the door as if they had been sitting in this posture all afternoon.

Nan Luc entered and closed the door behind her. 'Good afternoon, sisters,' she said politely. 'I am Nan Luc the new recording clerk.'

The women reacted immediately, all four rising from their seats and executing something resembling a clumsy bow. 'It is a privilege to meet you, comrade recording clerk,' one of the women said in a husky, nervous voice. 'But this is only the charges and sentences office. The offices of Provincial Administrator Quatch are upstairs.'

A few minutes later she stood before the toad-eyed Monsieur Quatch as he smiled a gold flecked smile and congratulated her on her appointment to the Cahn Roc Provincial People's Court.

'I have to thank you, monsieur,' she said warily.

'There is no need to thank me, mademoiselle,' he said with his frightening smile. 'You can be sure I have kept an eye on you. Even though it has been at a distance.'

'You are very kind,' she said, her thoughts racing ahead.

He looked down at papers in front of his desk. 'I can rely on you to understand, however, that even I cannot extract you from any further indiscretions. The death of Peter Benning lies within realms of state policy. It is therefore beyond discussion. In any event the matter is closed.' As he echoed her grandmother's words Nan Luc was still at a loss to know what they meant.

She watched him pull down the lapels of his white jacket. His strange eyes moved round the room from an unmoving toad's head. 'I understand, monsieur,' she said.

He rounded his desk and guided her to the door. 'Do your work here as you're capable of doing it and you will hear no more about it. The episode in Paris has already been expunged from your record.' His hand on her bare upper arm, he led her to the door. 'Simple accommodation has been allocated to you in the town,' he said. 'For your use during the week. We will get to know each other at my river pavilion at the weekend.'

Nan Luc stiffened. He held her arm, his round head angled enquiringly. 'With respect, monsieur,' Nan Luc said. 'No.'

He looked up at her. His hand dropped from her arm. The round, wet mouth quivered slightly. She was rigid with fear. The refusal had leapt out before she had considered a way of rephrasing it, softening it.

He opened the door slowly but she knew that she was not yet dismissed. 'Remember my words, Nan Luc,' he said. 'I have chosen you for a very special part in the theatre of my life.' He looked at her coldly. 'I will not be refused.'

He swung open the door the rest of the way and inclined his head for her to leave. Her last sight of him was as he smiled, owlishly, like a benign professor. But his tongue was darting, moistening the bright round of his mouth.

On the day of her arrival at Cahn Roc, Nan Luc was introduced to the new provincial prosecutor, Kiet Van Khoa, a forty-year-old veteran of great battles at Hue and Da Nang. A dedicated servant of the state, Van Khoa saw his role as maintaining the legal purity of the revolution. He was not in any sense a democrat. Though fully aware that the original Vietnamese Declaration of Independence had, ironically, been modelled on another, more famous declaration, Van Khoa never allowed that to lead him to the belief that the people should choose. The law chose. The law was the creation of ancestors, the government and above all the wisdom of the late Ho Chi Minh. There was no room left for doubt.

Yet despite a relentlessly undeviating line on the law, Van Khoa, his dark hair flopping forward over his dark-olive forehead, pointing to the map with the only finger left on his injured hand, was still able to give real sympathy and consideration to village boundary disputes or fishing rights on the river banks.

From the first anxious day Nan Luc was plunged into work. There was little civil crime except occasional incidents in the capital Cahn Roc itself. Most of her duties were echoes of the reverberating problems caused by the American war. A village which had been flattened in the US Army urbanisation programme might have had land annexed by a half dozen neighbouring villages. But if the scattered families of the village returned, even to huts blackened by the fires of a decade or more ago, the land itself was an inalienable part of their family heritage.

Each week Nan Luc, under Van Khoa's supervision, struggled with two or three blue folders of such cases. Sometimes the same cases were presented again by other villages who believed their sacred claims were being flaunted and the high-pitched disputatious voices of the villagers filled the old colonial courtroom with claims and counterclaims. It was all a long way from the glib solutions of Qui, the gentle ghost of the Ministry of Education's yellow-jacketed volumes of propaganda stories.

To Nan Luc's intense relief Quatch was absent from Cahn Roc. Some of the junior clerks spoke of an administrators' conference in Hanoi and Van Khoa briefly confirmed that Quatch would be absent into the rainy season. Her problems with Quatch deferred, every day Nan Luc went out in the departmental jeep, her straw sun hat held firmly on her head and discussed and sometimes arbitrated claims with the leaders of the village families. For herself, a product of the city, it was an often moving introduction to an age-old Vietnam.

She was close to being happy. A cloud descended on her every time Quatch's name was mentioned, but for the moment a confrontation with the administrator was a problem deferred. She thought of Paris often, of that day in the Brasserie and of the American she had risked so much to spend an hour with. But these thoughts of Paris were to her so incredibly distant they resembled more those of an older woman reflecting on the irrecoverable past.

It was not long before Nan realised that the ever smiling Van Khoa possessed influence. Where or how this influence was exercised Nan had no idea. But the typists in the downstairs office and even Nan's subordinates, the three women counter clerks, all contrived to give Nan Luc the idea that Van Khoa was different. If she needed something he lifted the telephone and spoke to some department of government in Ho Chi Minh City. Usually he would get what she wanted: the loan of a winch-truck – US Army, reconditioned – to clear shattered tree trunks from an old road between two villages; a spare part for her jeep; emergency medical supplies when a fire leaping through a village bamboo thicket hedge, trapped and burnt the villagers. And there was something else that impressed everybody about Van Khoa. The way he spoke of Quatch, without that intimation of deep respect for the administrator's power which was the accepted style among all the other officials.

There was another area of her duties which soon brought daylight fantasies and recurring dreams. It was the role of the coastguard to supervise the fishing boats of Cahn Roc province, those strange, black-sailed wooden ships she could see at sunset from her window, motionless on a blood-red sea. The relative proximity of Thailand to the north was the problem. Should a fishing boat disappear it might have gone down in a storm. It might equally have been sold to a group of refugees. Sometimes it fell to Nan Luc to investigate.

These duties kept Nan Luc busy deep into the summer. She remained, though always anxious about the return of Quatch, moderately content, if not happy. She was lonely, with only Van Khoa to provide the sort of company she wanted. But above all she was becoming obsessed with the thought of what might have been, with the thought of America. Every night she watched the black rhomboid sails of the fishing boats go out into the Gulf of Thailand and wondered why they would choose to return in the dawn.

More and more as the year lengthened memories of Paris occupied her waking dreams, memories that came in clean-cut snippets. Two young people walking together by the Seine, a family Sunday lunch at a café off the Boulevard St Michel, a group of Americans at a foreign aid reception at the Swedish embassy. And an unobtrusive but ever present regret that she had not been able to meet Max Benning that last night before she left the West for ever.

For ever? At night she looked out across the ocean at the black sails of Cahn Roc and let all her memories or part memories of her childhood filter through her mind. Somewhere a garden hung with bright coloured flowers. Grass of a vivid, dark green. In a child's memory she saw a tall, fair-haired man in a light suit. He held a large coloured ring, like a deck quoit, in his hand. Smiling, he was about to throw it to her . . .

In these days of loneliness at Cahn Roc Nan Luc suffered more than anything a recurring desire to know her father. The ache was more than a thinly disguised desire to leave the land in which she felt cut off by her mounting scepticism and her hybrid appearance. The desire to know the man who had fathered her was, ironically, purely Vietnamese.

But it pointed her always towards America.

Her fear of Quatch's return was constant. She recognised now the quizzical movement of Van Khoa's eyebrow whenever she referred to the subject. Since the administrator's absence Van Khoa had spent more and more time in the past weeks working in Quatch's office. Many of the officials believed that he was about to be appointed Quatch's deputy. Even to Nan Luc it seemed that Van Khoa was dealing with fewer and fewer legal issues. She discovered her mistake one afternoon when she had been forced to ask his advice on a particularly complex problem in one of the outlying villages.

When he had given his opinion she thanked him and turned to leave the room. 'Just a moment,' he said. She stopped, her hand on the door. 'After all these months working together it would be wrong for me to go without saying goodbye.'

Nan Luc stiffened. The fear of loneliness enclosed her. She had not fallen in love with Van Khoa, she knew that. She saw little or nothing of him in the evenings. But she had become very dependent on his company at work.

'You're leaving,' she said in a voice as flat as she could make it.

'For the moment. Perhaps for a long while. Perhaps for ever.'

'I shall miss working with you,' she said guardedly.

He bowed his head. 'Nan Luc . . .' He paused. 'I had thought to ask you to marry me. There, I have blundered it out . . .' He left the words hanging hopefully in the air. With a sharp movement of his head he threw his hair back from his thin face. His injured hand was held behind his back.

She kept a tight hold on the door handle and began counting in her head. She knew that she was in danger of saying yes. She knew that she was in danger of committing herself to a whole life in which she had no belief. She kept her hand on the door handle and her eyes down.

'Very good,' he said quietly. 'Perhaps I understand.'

'It is not . . .' she began.

He held up his good hand. 'You have no need to explain. I have watched you carefully these months, Nan Luc, and I have one warning to offer you.'

'A warning?'

'Yes. I know you dream of America,' he said slowly. She could feel herself blushing. 'I see the movement of your head, the tiredness disappear, whenever America is mentioned.' He paused. 'It's an empty dream for you, Nan Luc. Abandon it.'

Before she could answer he changed the subject with a gesture of his injured hand. With the other he took a thick file from his desk. His tone changed, became more formal. 'When we were discussing your village problem a few moments ago,' he said, 'you were resting your hands on this file.'

'Yes,' she said, puzzled at his rapid change of subject.

'Let us imagine that you had altered your position. Perhaps your arm ached. You exchanged hands. Clumsily . . .' he smiled, 'if for you it's possible to be clumsy. Clumsily. So that you pulled this file to the floor.' She looked at him without understanding. 'The file would fly open,' Van Khoa said. 'You would catch a glimpse, no more than a glimpse, of its contents. It would however be too late for you to do anything about it.'

She shook her head, not understanding. 'Too late for what?'

'Too late for you to warn anybody.' He moved and stood beside her. He made no attempt to conceal the mutilated hand now. 'Perhaps you would see something like this.' He flicked the file open so that one or two pages fell back on one another. She looked down. The face of Quatch stared up at her. In another photograph her grandmother and Quatch together . . . He closed the file. For the first time she registered that it was a red prosecution file.

Her grandmother and Monsieur Quatch were about to be arrested.

5

Nan Luc awoke early. From her sleeping mat she watched, through the room's high single window, a long slow dawn climbing from the east. It touched a thin strip of cloud with copper fingers. It outlined in black the giant palms which marked the end of the streets and squares of the capital, beyond which lay dense forest. If she raised herself on one elbow, turning her head, she could see further, beyond low roofs to where the fishing boats streamed back towards a stone quayside that poked like Van Khoa's single finger out into the shimmering black sea.

She rested for a moment on her elbow thinking how much she loved this land, thinking nevertheless how much she wanted to leave it. Only slowly did she become aware, as it seemed to her, of her own rhythmic, steady breathing.

And then of another rhythm, different, faster. Her throat tightened. Her head spun towards the corner of the room. She saw a dark, crouching shape. She came to her feet and in desperation snatched a candle-holder from beside the bed. Perhaps she forced out words. More likely, she thought afterwards, the words were trapped in the fear that seemed to have swollen her throat.

The crouching figure moved. Shuffled like a vulture about to tear at flesh. Then relief flooded her, anger, a desire to laugh at wild images of carrion birds as a familiar voice said in precise French, 'It's me, chérie. Your grandmother.'

Nan Luc could make out now the crouching figure, her chin still resting on arms crossed above her knees. 'What in the name of heaven are you doing?' she said. 'Why didn't you wake me?'

Her grandmother got to her feet. 'I arrived in the middle of the night. I saw the house list downstairs and the number of your room. I thought I would sleep a few hours after my journey.'

'You've come from the city?'

'By lorry-bus, my dear. Can you imagine? Twenty peasants and me.'

'I'll light the candle.'

Bernadette put her hand on Nan Luc's arm. 'Wait for the dawn,' she said. 'A few moments.'

'At least I can make you tea.'

Her grandmother nodded and went to sit by the window while Nan fuelled and lit her US Army field stove. 'What are these lights bobbing out there?' she asked as Nan Luc made the tea.

Nan glanced out of the window as she crossed the room. 'Fishing boats coming back,' she said.

Bernadette nodded. 'Ah, yes. It's well known in government circles that Cahn Roc port is one of the least secure places along this coastline.'

Nan Luc didn't answer. She knew that her grandmother was talking about the boat people. But officially the boat people didn't exist. Safer, even with Bernadette, to say nothing.

She took down the tea caddy and spooned out tea into the pot. Her grandmother's eyes closed and opened. For a few moments Nan thought she was about to doze off but with an effort she rubbed at her eyelids and turned from the window to watch Nan Luc's movements across the room.

Nan knelt by the stove in her white linen pyjamas, her rich hair falling across her face. Bernadette came forward. Her hand reached out to stroke her granddaughter's hair, her lips curling downwards as she felt the girl stiffen.

'I intended to come into Saigon tonight,' Nan said. 'As soon as my work allowed. I wanted to warn you.'

Bernadette smiled. 'Too late, chérie,' she said.

'Quatch is already under arrest?'

'Not yet. But we both know it's a matter of days, hours even. He is watched day and night. This is why I'm here like this.' Nan Luc waited. 'You remember, chérie,' Bernadette said, 'that I once told you we were both free of any responsibility for each other, that the old family ties of Vietnam had burst long ago.' Nan Luc stood, the teapot in her hand. 'You can see that I was wrong,' Bernadette said.

A chill crept through Nan. 'In what way were you wrong?' she asked.

'I come here in a lorry-bus full of peasants. I come in the night. I sleep crouched in a corner.' Bernadette turned in her chair to look at Nan. 'I daren't wear my Paris clothes, my makeup, perfume. Not in a lorry-bus with twenty peasants.'

Silently Nan Luc handed her grandmother her tea.

Bernadette took the thick white cup and raised it to her lips. For a moment or two she drank, silently. Then she put it aside. 'I am in great trouble, chérie,' she said. Nan Luc took her tea and sat cross-legged on her sleeping mat. 'I am in great trouble,' Bernadette repeated, 'because Monsieur Quatch is in great trouble.'

'He is a provincial administrator,' Nan Luc said carefully. 'The most senior figure in Cahn Roc. What is his crime?'

Bernadette shrugged. 'He has made too many enemies with his French ways. A year ago he was reprimanded by a member of the government, a minister. He took no notice. He continued to live as a colonial governor.'

'There must be other things.'

'That was an outward sign. There are other things.'

'More serious?'

'In power he has lost his awareness of danger. He forgets Ho Chi Minh with his simple khaki shorts and sandals. It's a long road to travel from Uncle Ho to Monsieur Quatch.'

'There's more,' Nan Luc said.

Bernadette nodded. 'Perhaps more than I know. He dines on *foie gras* and *magret de canard*. He drinks the best châteaux from the appropriated cellars of the old French colonists. All this costs money. Where, it is being asked, does that money come from?'

'The trouble you talk about, Bernadette. Has it anything to do with the death of Peter Benning?'

Her grandmother pursed her lips. 'Better you know nothing if you're to help me.'

'I can do nothing to help.' Nan stood up. 'You came here, I've no doubt, to ask me to speak to Van Khoa. But you must understand I am not on a level to talk to Van Khoa about a provincial administrator's case.'

Bernadette was watching her carefully in the lightening dawn. 'I know that, chérie,' she said. 'I've lived through it all.'

'So why did you come?'

'I came to ask you to do something for *me*.'

The emphasis on the last word made Nan Luc stiffen. She got up and poured her grandmother more tea. Then went back to the sleeping mat and resumed her cross-legged position. The sky was light now, pouring brightness into the narrow room, revealing the old French bentwood clothes rack on which Nan Luc hung her two black pyjama working suits.

Bernadette let her eyes drift down to the sandals neatly arranged beside it. Blue files were piled up on a scarred but once fine directoire desk. A partly open drawer showed the edge of neat, folded underwear.

Bernadette smiled. 'Perhaps because you have never owned more than very little, you cannot appreciate what it means to own much.'

'Perhaps. How could I know?'

Bernadette nodded. 'I had prepared myself for disaster,' she said. 'I thought I had.'

She paused, cupping the heavy tea-bowl in her hands. 'In a Swiss numbered account I have 100,000 francs. Swiss francs. For the last five years I have possessed a valid Red Cross passport and suitable papers.'

Nan Luc's eyes widened. 'You're free to leave Vietnam whenever you wish?' Bernadette smiled. 'Why not use your passport before you're arrested too?'

'Simple, chérie. Because Quatch acquired the passport for me. It still rests in its original wrapping on the top shelf of his safe.'

'He refuses to give it to you?'

'Of course. There is nothing altruistic about Quatch. He has *never* performed a service without the thought of reward, however distant.'

'Then why is his position so desperate?' Even as she spoke Nan Luc knew she was only putting off some evil moment. 'He must have many friends in the government.'

'Rats are said to leave sinking ships. He is now alone. Since he came back from Hanoi he sits in the apartment on Avenue Giap listening to Berlioz in a haze of opium smoke . . .'

'Why have you come here?' Nan Luc said suddenly, in desperation.

Bernadette looked haggard, old, in a shaft of sunlight. 'I must have my passport. I cannot sink with him.'

'But he won't give it to you . . .'

'He likes to tease me. He goes to the safe and dials the first three numbers. He tells me what they are. But there are three more.'

'And in return for those three numbers?'

'He wants *you*.'

Quatch saw himself as a victim of the War of Independence, as no more or less a victim than a woman with a womb shrivelled by agent orange; or a man missing a leg or a hand. He considered his war, his part in the struggle, had been equally dangerous.

As a young man he had, like many sons of the Vietnamese middle-class, studied in Paris. Small, plump and studious he had gravitated naturally towards the seriousness of the Sorbonne's Marxist clubs. He had met a girl, a French girl, short, plump and studious like himself. With her encouragement he began to attend meetings claiming independence from colonial rule. One night, after police broke up a meeting in the Billiard Hall at Montmartre, he found himself sharing an overnight cell with the guest speaker, a thin, balding drystick of a man in an ill-fitting suit.

Among the revolutionary leadership the story of that night in a cell spent talking with Ho Chi Minh would be recounted and exaggerated over the years. It was soon believed that Quatch had been acting as Ho Chi Minh's private secretary at the time of their arrest, that on matters of youth policy and political education for the youth of Vietnam Ho Chi Minh relied extensively on the advice of his young assistant.

Not surprisingly Quatch had made no great effort to deny these stories. He was arrested and questioned several times. In the revolutionary underground his reputation grew. When the time came to return home the movement found the money to bribe someone to remove his dossier from the files of the French police.

Back in Vietnam, as the war between the Viet Minh and the French Colonial Army intensified, Quatch had lived as a prosperous businessman in Saigon. In fact, on his return from France, he had been appointed political officer of the city's clandestine Viet Minh battalion.

He had lived on his nerves. But although he thought he knew all the weapons ranged against the Vietcong, he did not. He never understood that the weapon that was turned against all of them, French soldiers, American advisers, clandestine political officers, members of the government of South Vietnam alike, was the same secret, unheeded weapon: Saigon's unique ability to draw a man into a net of decadence; to destroy the morals and then the morale of soldiers on both sides; to confuse aim and ambition, mission and motive. In Saigon you could *die* of pleasure. No corner of the imagination, however frightful, went unsatisfied in the bars and clubs of the narrow alleys off the Rue Catinat. But only the strongest could survive, only the strongest could keep separate purpose from possibility. There were strong spirits on all sides, of course. But Quatch was not among them.

In Saigon he had begun trading: antiquities to the Americans who were arriving in increasing numbers. In Paris, when he was assigned as a propaganda official, he had greatly expanded his business. Using his old connections in Saigon he had sent out men to loot the unguarded temples in the forest. Diplomatic privileges had made transport easy; and the dealers of Europe had grasped the opportunity with both hands.

Peter Benning had been his only problem. The almost monkish, scholarly figure of Benning had pursued him from the beginning, breaking up his forest looting parties, threatening his organisation in Saigon. And when, in the days of approaching victory, Quatch had been posted back to Paris, openly now, as North Vietnamese representative, Benning had followed him there. Followed him, hounded him and threatened to expose him.

It had been no great problem to have him killed. It had cost Quatch no more than a $1,000 mixed bag of drugs to a Vietnamese student. Even the fact that the fool had killed Benning in Bernadette's apartment had been no more than a short-term problem. The French government had seen to that. The French government and the North Vietnamese Army which had just marched into Saigon. As the now official Vietnamese *chargé d'affaires* in Paris, Quatch was left strictly alone.

When he heard that he was to be promoted to a post back home in Vietnam Quatch collapsed with frustration. He saw himself as a Westerner, a Parisian, a victim of the degeneracy he had been called upon to live and work in.

Once back in Vietnam he had felt the world close round him in the grim, pitiless city that victory had made of Saigon. Too dangerous now to experiment with his pleasures he had begun to search the dream world of opium. Sometimes he would emerge from it, purged and lusty as a youth. But less often now. Except when he thought of Nan Luc.

Quatch had often found it curious, the effect the girl had upon him. It was, he had no doubt, the mix of East and West, the luminous olive skin, the chestnut hair and the clear green eyes of another continent. Genes, he reflected, married in curious ways. This girl had been immensely lucky. Her mother's beauty might easily have been lost. And yet this girl had all this. And the fullness of figure of a young American girl allied to the lithe slenderness of Vietnam.

But most of all was the challenge. She was polite, she smiled, she inclined her head gently, but beneath it all you were aware of a powerful sense of self, the self-protective aura of her will.

Which he would break.

He realised of course that, for himself, escape was now impossible. Since Van Khoa's investigation had begun opium had been his escape. More opium and more, only emerging, like now, from that soft brown world at the thought of Nan Luc and the drama he had planned for her to take the leading role in tonight.

He had bathed and dressed in a new pressed white suit. He had walked into the salon and, without calling a servant, had mixed a little mineral water with grenadine. He had sat, for an hour, his almost unblinking eyes watching through the glass doors into the hall and to the main door itself.

And now there was a sound on the stairs.

Nan Luc knocked on the apartment door and trembled at what she was about to do. She had found herself unable to refuse.

'For just an hour in a man's bed,' her grandmother had pleaded. 'My liberty, my life even, for just one hour in his bed. You can't refuse me, Nan Luc. In a re-education camp I would be dead within a year. Carrying stones, clearing roads . . . please, chérie, for one hour in his bed!'

She had thought of appealing to Van Khoa, then realising the absurdity of asking him to help her grandmother escape. She had thought of begging Quatch for the passport, then realised this was equally absurd. She was trapped. One hour in a man's bed for her grandmother's liberty, her life even!

She waited for almost a minute and knocked again. The hope rose in her that he was not there. Then, from beside her, Bernadette's thin arm came past her and seized the ring handle of the ornate door. 'He's there,' she said. 'He's waiting.' Bernadette turned the handle. As the door swung open she was muttering, part to herself, part to Nan Luc. 'The passport. The Red Cross passport . . .'

Nan Luc stepped into the hall. Behind her Bernadette closed the front door. Across the wide hall she could see through the glass doors into the salon. Monsieur Quatch sat at his desk, a glass of red liquid raised to his lips.

'We are a family.' Bernadette fussed around her granddaughter, brushing the hair from her face. 'A family has duties to each other . . .'

Nan Luc pushed her hand away. 'I have decided,' she said, 'I'll get you the passport when you give me the name of my father.'

Bernadette's face stiffened. 'You must understand,' she hissed. 'There is to be a trial. Almost any information might be used against Quatch.'

'Is the identity of my father important in this trial?' Bernadette hesitated. 'Is it?'

The older woman nodded vigorously 'It could be. If Quatch found I had given you your father's name I would never get my passport.'

'Look at it another way,' Nan Luc said coldly, 'you will never get your passport *until* you give me the name.'

'You're here now. You can't turn back.'

Nan looked across to where Quatch sat, still forward in his seat, the glass of grenadine to his lips. 'You can tell Quatch I have no intention of doing what he wants me to do.' She made to turn away.

'Stop!' Bernadette swung her round with surprising strength as Nan Luc reached towards the handle of the glazed door.

'I will tell you his name,' she whispered. 'You must never say

I told you. To anyone. Not to Quatch. Not to the People's Court you work for. Do you agree?'

Nan Luc nodded briefly. 'His real name. Not a name you make up on the spot.'

Her grandmother looked at her for a moment. 'Very well. Wait here,' she said.

She ran from the hallway to the staircase which Nan Luc knew would take her up to her room. Again Nan glanced at Quatch. There was no doubt that he was aware of her standing on the other side of the glass door, but he still gave no sign. Instead, he stared fixedly at the wall beyond his desk.

Bernadette returned scuffling along the corridor. In her hand she carried a folded paper. 'It's all I know about him,' she said. She pulled Nan Luc back, out of the line of sight so that the two women would have been invisible from the salon, and thrust the paper at her.

'What is it?' Nan Luc said.

'Your birth certificate.' Bernadette's face was tense with fear. 'I'm risking my life,' she hissed.

Nan took the folded yellow paper. Opening it she saw a document of the old Republic of South Vietnam, written in Vietnamese and French. Next to her own name, her mother's name. Next to her mother's name, in the column headed *Père* was written: C. Stevenson, New York City.

Bernadette snatched back the certificate. 'Now you know,' she said. 'His name. There is nothing more to know.'

She pushed Nan forward towards the glass door. 'The passport,' she said. 'Your part of the bargain.'

His head had not turned towards her, so that he sat, shoulders hunched slightly forward in his white suit, as if listening to somebody, invisible to Nan Luc, on the other side of the room.

Nan Luc crossed the hall slowly and paused in the doorway to the salon. There was no one on the other side of the room. No one on the hard yellow striped Empire sofa, no one standing with a hand resting on the base of the great bronze of Diana, the huntress. No one to help her. No one to see what she was about to do.

The heavy curtains had been drawn against the darkness outside and silk shaded lamps lit the room. She remembered when she

had first been here how impressed, awed, she had been at the size
of the room and the magnificence of its furnishings.

Monsieur Quatch came slowly to his feet. 'You do me a great
honour, ma'moiselle.' She said nothing. 'Something to relax you.
Cognac?' She nodded, too abruptly. 'You must not be alarmed,'
he smiled. His toad eyes raked the room. 'At least,' he said. 'Not
very alarmed.'

'My grandmother, Bernadette, must have her passport,' Nan
Luc said, dry mouthed.

'Her Red Cross passport.' He nodded as if considering the
matter for the first time.

'Unless you give it to her . . .'

He was pouring brandy with one hand. The other he lifted to
silence her. 'No, ma'moiselle, you will not speak to me like that.
Your role is to be soft, pliant, submissive. You do not threaten
your provincial administrator. You do not threaten Monsieur
Quatch.'

'I was not threatening Monsieur Quatch,' Nan Luc said. 'I was
simply reminding him of the terms on which I'm here.'

'There are no terms,' he said airily as he carried the brandy
across to her. 'There, my dear, sit down. Let me talk to you. Look
at you.'

She remained standing. 'There *are* terms,' she said firmly.

He poured brandy for himself. 'You're not a virgin, are you?
You *have* known a man?'

'The passport, monsieur.'

His mouth twisted. 'Known in the biblical sense. Carnal knowledge.' He licked his round lips.

She stood up. 'You think me a fool,' she said.

He smiled, with something approaching charm. 'No, Nan Luc,'
he said. 'You think *me* a fool. If I were to give you the passport
now, you would leave.' She remained silent. He shrugged. 'Understand, Nan Luc,' he said, 'the passport means nothing to me. It
is a device to obtain your favours. Now you force me to speak
openly. You rob the moment of any romance it might have. A
man and woman, drinking cognac together, a young inexperienced woman and a mature world-travelled man, there should be
some warmth between us, some electricity in the air.' He watched
her shiver of revulsion and walked across to refill his glass.

'Now, since you insist, I will tell you about the passport. It is not in the safe. It is in the keeping of a friend, a mutual friend. Bernadette knows him well, Monsieur Ba Hoa. I will telephone him now, in your presence, to tell him to give it to Bernadette tomorrow in the forenoon. That is the best arrangement I can think of which will also ensure you play your part to the full.'

'You could also telephone later and tell him not to hand over the passport.'

'Don't waste my time, Nan Luc. I have little left. I care nothing for your grandmother's passport, whether she has it and uses it or not.' He paused. Then added abruptly, 'There, as I said, it's the best I can do.'

With a sick, sinking feeling, Nan Luc said. 'I've no choice but to trust you.'

'None,' he smiled.

'Then I will keep my side of the bargain.' She saw in front of her the overfed body and the soft, prominent eyes. She forced her thoughts away from him. To an office perhaps among the skyscrapers of New York or to an apartment as large as this. To a man now known to her as Stevenson. 'It is enough,' Nan Luc repeated. 'I will keep my side of the bargain.'

And she touched the child's bracelet she wore on her wrist. *To my daughter, Nan Luc.*

6

Cy Stevenson turned his blue Mercedes into the drive of the Meyerick County Country Club and enjoyed the slow crackle of the gravel under the heavy car. He could see the parking lot to the right of the club building, already occupied by forty or more of the world's most expensive production automobiles. He could see the striped awning which gave covered access to the side door of the club and he could see the Meyerick County building itself, long, low, white clapboard with a stone tourette rising from the far end, a solid building twice as high as the club house, its limestone tailored, its windows Victorian Gothic.

Cy Stevenson, in his early-forties now, was still slender enough to boast the easy movements of a young man. He wore pale chalk corduroy slacks and a well-cut, dark green, almost black, blazer with black English regimental buttons. Buttons of the English regiment, he related, which had been first raised in America as the 62nd Royal Americans, and was now, in the modern British Army, called the Greenjackets. His English grandfather, Cy now regularly told enquirers, had served with the Greenjackets in the First World War.

His brushed pale blond hair gave him the look associated with an older man, the impression of solid decisions judiciously taken. But his easy, even toothed smile was contrastingly boyish. When he had married into Meyerick County, club members had found in him just the balance of qualities that appealed to them. Within five or six years he had been elected president of the club committee.

As Cy climbed from his car, Anita Simpson, emerging from the back of her Rolls Bentley, waved to him across two or three glistening car tops. 'Cy,' she said, 'Cy darling. We don't usually meet you here on Fridays. Are you changing old habits?' She was walking between the cars towards him. 'Or starting on some new ones? I'd say that it was high time you did . . .'

She leaned forward to kiss him on the cheek. Anita Simpson, a widow of one year's standing, was not the only club woman of mature years who found Cy Stevenson's apparent faithfulness to his wife, Sunny, an exciting challenge. Two years into his presidency and he could have slept with a dozen or more women at the club, but he politely diverted every approach. Those women who discussed the problem openly decided he had a dragon mistress in New York. It was the only answer.

There was another. And that was that Cy's loins were not much stirred by big Caucasian women. His wife, Sunny, tall, shapely, by any normal standards a very attractive woman, in fact left him cold. His preference was, and always had been since his days in the orient, for the slender olive-skinned girls of Saigon.

He had not found it difficult to arrive at a solution to his problem. With Sunny he played games. Maybe she saw through them, maybe not. But he made an effort to seem a considerate, passionate husband.

His real passions were satisfied elsewhere. Sunny's family wealth made it unnecessary for him to earn. Instead, with her initial support, he had devoted his time to the Meyerick Fund, a local Vietnamese charity, headless since the death of its founder, a local philanthropist named Philip Rose. The work of fund-raising was varied and challenging; more important, the opportunities to meet young Vietnamese women in New York were frequent and satisfying.

'No change of habits,' Cy said to Anita as they crossed the parking lot. 'We have a fund meeting tonight. Third Friday in the month.'

She slipped an arm into his. 'Do you have time to have a drink with me before your meeting?'

'Of course.'

Over Spritzers on the terrace, Anita acknowledged friends and rivals and listened impatiently as Cy talked about the Meyerick Fund. 'No,' Cy said ruminatively, 'when I took on the Fund after Philip Rose died there were just 300 contributors. Most of them members of this club. No criticism of Philip Rose, he was a great guy, a visionary I guess is the way you'd describe him. He knew the fund could be big. But didn't really understand modern communications.'

God, Anita Simpson was thinking to herself, if only I could turn this man's attention away from his boat people. She knew instinctively that he wasn't a saint. She recognised too many of the signs. But he had never, never once offered her the slightest encouragement.

She allowed herself a few minutes of erotic fantasy as he talked about the Fund's attempt to help boat people settle in the States. Then seeing her friend and rival Marsha Knox stop in the doorway to the clubroom she pulled herself up short. Marsha knew all too well the way Anita's thoughts ran when Cy was around. The two women had talked about it often enough and in erotic details over late afternoon gin and tonics. Now when Marsha waved, in an attempt to get called over to the table Anita turned away.

'Hell, I've had enough of being health-conscious.' Cy Stevenson looked down at his half-finished Spritzer. 'Just time for something more substantial. Join me?'

She smiled a refusal. With a brief kiss on his cheek, Anita wandered away between tables. Cy checked his watch. He could use a drink. A real one. He had been a fool wasting time on a glass of watered wine, trying pointlessly to impress with his moderation.

He walked across to the bar and greeted the bar manager in a loud voice. 'No problems, Vic? All running smoothly?'

'A drink, Mr Stevenson?'

'Just while we're talking. That new wine merchant is working out OK, then?'

They had said all this before. The manager handed almost two inches of Glenmorangie to Stevenson. 'Yes,' he said, 'I think we made a good move there, Mr Stevenson. I'm very pleased with their range of Burgundies.'

'Good, good.' Cy gulped the whisky in two swallows and was already turning away. 'Great.'

As if by sleight of hand the glass had already disappeared from the bar top. Vic Impari knew his job.

Cy Stevenson climbed the stone spiral staircase of the tourette, the only remaining section of the original Victorian building. After the disastrous fire of 1947 the new clubhouse had been built to adjoin it. He stopped at the first row of Gothic windows, taking in the view across the tennis courts.

Someone was coming up the spiral staircase behind him. He turned. The Reverend Hector Hand smiled much of the time. But his tensions were apparent to anybody who had known him for five minutes. He hated youth and he hated Communists. He affected to find both groups behind any disturbance of the American way of life. But he had served three spells as a professional soldier in Vietnam.

'Hello there, Cy,' he said to the waiting Stevenson. 'I've said it before and I'll say it again. You have a great club here. Quiet, orderly, everybody taking their modest pleasures in a good old-fashioned American way.' Did he know? Did he really know what some of the membership got up to, Cy wondered briefly before he dismissed the idea. No, the Reverend Hector Hand of the 22nd Church of Christ the Lord was not sending anyone up. The 22nd? Stevenson had asked once and found that apparently you could count established Christian churches this way from St Peter on. If you chose.

They walked together up the last twenty steps and reached a landing with a large dark arched oak door before them. Stevenson opened it, standing aside for the Reverend Hand, and then followed in himself.

There were five men and two women round an oval conference table in the middle of a light, sunny stone-built room. Portraits of distinguished club members hung on the walls. A gigantic view of the old clubhouse, before the fire of 1947, had been temporarily removed from the wide chimney breast above the stone fire surround. In its place, for the duration of the committee meeting as tradition demanded, a large portrait of the founder of the Meyerick Vietnam Fund, Philip John Rose, had been hung. It showed a formidably stern, confident face which might have been painted closer to the beginning of the twentieth century rather than towards the end.

'Good morning, good morning,' Cy Stevenson said and the Reverend Hand echoed. He shook hands with the first two men, Oliver Digweed and Colonel George Savary, and rounded the table to kiss the two women. The first, thin angular Helen Rose, the founder's widow; then adding a quick hug for Mary Page

Butler, his wife's sister, before passing on to shake the hands of the two brothers, Gus and Arne Anderson, blond Scandinavian types, owners of a series of swimming pool installation companies throughout Meyerick County and beyond. Both had served with the Marines in Vietnam.

He came towards the last man, Jason Rose, the Vietnam veteran son of the founder, and Mrs Rose. 'Don't move, Jason,' he said, squeezing his shoulder. 'How did the tests go?

Jason turned his sightless eyes on Cy. 'You know what doctors are, Cy. Maybe we can operate, maybe we can't. New developments, new techniques, more tests, more maybes.'

Cy clapped him on the shoulder and turned back to his seat. 'Finlay not here?' he asked Mary.

'Correction, Finlay here,' a voice said in a mock oriental lilt behind him.

Cy smiled indulgently as he turned his head. Mrs Rose looked impatient; Mary Butler watched expressionless as her husband shook hands with Cy. Fin Butler was a handsome man, in his early sixties, a wealthy polo player who travelled regularly in pursuit of his game, who had photographs of himself at home with Prince Charles in polo dress and one, much admired by his friends, of bending to kiss the hand of Princess Diana with a pleased, feisty smile on his face. His qualification for service on the committee was a brief stint as voluntary observer with the International Red Cross in Saigon.

Mary Butler glanced across the room as her husband Fin circled the table apologising and shaking hands. She caught Cy's eye and gave a guilty start. She sometimes, not often, wondered what might have happened if she had been a dozen years younger when Cy had first come to Meyerick. A dozen years younger and unmarried, of course. She found him an uncommonly attractive man. That was not to say she had been happy about Sunny's wedding. Eight years ago she and Sunny had nearly fallen out on the subject. She had warned her younger sister there were male gold diggers aplenty. And for a long time she had continued to think Cy was one. But things had settled down. Cy had worked hard on the Meyerick Fund and although she still didn't entirely warm to him as a brother-in-law, a truce had been declared between them. Perhaps, Mary thought, it would never be a hundred per cent on her part – but what little acting was necessary was no longer difficult for her.

Cy Stevenson called the meeting to order. 'Before we start today,' he said, 'I'd like to welcome George Savary to our merry band of brothers and sisters. I'm sure we're going to benefit greatly from his experience and common sense. Good to have you aboard, George,' he parodied himself.

In the murmur of agreement from the others he turned to Oliver Digweed and asked him to distribute copies of the half-yearly accounts. 'Strictly speaking,' he said, 'this meeting is reserved for financial matters. But let me just check everybody's OK for the Fund luncheon next week.' A murmur of assent passed round the table. 'Fine.' Cy sat back in his chair. 'Now, ladies and gentlemen, your chairman invites you to examine the half-yearly accounts.'

While the trustees read the columns of figures in front of them Cy picked up the phone in front of him and dialled the bar in the clubroom below. 'Vic,' he said, 'send us a selection of drinks. Some champagne and something for me,' he grinned.

The trustees were making exclamations of surprise at the figures in front of them. Mary Page Butler was reading off the figures to Jason Rose in a low murmur.

'This is astonishing, Cy. Really great.'

'I said I thought we were heading for a good half-year,' Cy smiled, 'but even I didn't think we were on course for a bull's-eye.'

'Wonderful, Cy,' Colonel Savary said. 'Quite *wonderful*.'

The Anderson twins smiled and shrugged. 'We can do no more than repeat what George has just said.' Arne spoke without the need to consult his brother. 'We think it's wonderful.'

'Miraculous,' Hector Hand intoned.

'Good on you, Cy.' Finlay Butler grinned at him across the table. 'A million dollars, wow!'

'And commitments I see,' Mrs Rose said, 'for nearly three-quarters of a million dollars for the next half-year. I must say we look as though we might run right off the chart.'

She was forcing a smile which did not come naturally to her face. She was in fact deeply resentful of the success Cy Stevenson had made of the fund she and her husband had started.

When Vic Impari and two bar waiters had brought the drinks,

Finlay Butler raised his glass to Stevenson. 'Well done, Cy. We all respect what you've done very much indeed.'

'Thank you, Fin. Thank you all.'

A cough from the Reverend Hector Hand swung attention to him. 'Ladies and gentlemen, I do apologise, but I'm rather short on time. I've no wish at all to diminish Cy's achievement in scoring the bull's-eye but if we could get on to other business . . .' He waved his glass of Perrier at them as if they were wild New Year's revellers draped with streamers.

'This *is* our business, Hector,' Cy said firmly. 'If the dollars don't come in there are no dollars to go out.'

'Quite,' Hand said. 'No wish to diminish . . .'

'Turning to the monies out column,' Cy went on, 'you will see that we have increased our support to New York Vietnamese societies to seventy-five thousand dollars. Frankly it's still not enough. I think we should look at a substantial increase next time round.' There were murmurs of agreement round the table. 'One hundred thousand dollars for language teaching. We'll vote on each item, of course. But how does everybody feel about that?'

'Same as they do about all the other items, I guess,' Fin Butler said. 'What we can do is never enough.'

'Big item,' Cy Stevenson moved on down the list, 'is repairs to settlement houses.'

'I'm a new boy here,' the colonel said. 'Does the trust *own* these buildings?'

'Mary runs the housing committee,' Cy nodded towards his sister-in-law.

'We bought them two years ago,' Mary told him. 'Mostly in the Bronx. Repairs are running at two-fifty thousand dollars a half-year.'

'That's a lot of money,' the colonel said.

'There's damage, racial problems,' Mary said. 'I was there last month with the surveyor. We had one apartment burnt out. Racial attack. I think at our next meeting we may have to face the possibility of letting these buildings go. The money can maybe be used more effectively elsewhere. Sorry, Cy,' she said, looking towards the trust chairman. 'Thought I should just plant the idea.'

'Sure.' Stevenson poured himself another whisky. 'Mary and I have discussed the problem, as you gather. But let's leave it over. Next item, fifty thousand dollars administration.'

'I don't know how you do it,' Arne Anderson said. 'Most people couldn't administer a hamburger stand on that sort of money.'

Cy Stevenson grinned. 'I pull in a lot of favours. Next. Clothing fund stays at fifty thousand. That's levelling out now. And last item: clandestine.'

'Over five hundred thousand dollars this half-year,' Colonel Savary read in astonishment.

'We get the results,' Hector Hand said. 'Every dollar we pump in contributes to the downfall of the system there.'

'If I may say so, Hector,' Cy said carefully, 'that is not what this part of the fund aims at.'

'Eventually, surely,' Hector Hand said angrily. 'Eventually we're looking for a change of system in Vietnam. Am I wrong, Mrs Rose?'

Mrs Rose hesitated. She knew this to be deep water. 'Cy,' she said, 'I think you should restate the guidelines for Colonel Savary's benefit.'

'OK.' Cy took a long drink from his whisky. 'Sure. With pleasure. Our clandestine fund is aimed solely, I repeat solely, at making it easier and less dangerous for the boat people, as the world now calls them, to leave Vietnam. We deal, as you know, with the one province of Cahn Roc only. So our route is Cahn Roc–Thailand. We use money to bribe officials and the Cahn Roc coastguard.' He looked towards the Reverend Hand. 'It is not part of our remit, nor of our intention, to subvert the Vietnamese government itself.' Fin Butler, Digweed and the Anderson brothers nodded.

'But anything we can do to that end . . .' Hand persisted, 'propaganda . . . whatever . . .'

'We don't do,' Cy Stevenson said firmly. 'You have to trust us on this one, Hector. Many of the people we bribe wouldn't touch the money if they thought our real object was subversion. They are intensely proud and patriotic people. Proud of the government they've got. As it happens it's a Communist government. We can't change that, Hector. We're not trying to.'

'Let's move on, please,' Colonel Savary said. 'I repeat, I'm a new boy.' His face creased in concern. 'But I must say that I had no idea, when Helen first approached me, of the proportion of the fund allocated to clandestine purposes. Almost a million dollars a year. How is this money distributed?'

'The bulk of the money is transferred from our own bank here in Meyerick to a Swiss numbered account,' Cy said.

The colonel looked alarmed. 'Just that? Is that all the trustees have the right to know?'

'Now, George,' Arne Anderson said, 'we have the absolute right on this committee to know as much or as little as we choose.'

'You mean not all committee members know all the details?'

'Need to know, is our guiding principle,' Gus Anderson said. 'We haven't thought it necessary.'

Colonel Savary flushed. 'How many members of this committee do know who is the account holder in Switzerland?'

'I do,' Oliver Digweed said. 'Myself, Mary, Mrs Rose and Cy of course.'

'But not the other members.'

'Frankly I don't see the need to know,' Fin Butler said. 'Unless of course we are questioning the integrity of Cy or Ollie here or indeed,' he raised his eyebrows, 'of Mrs Rose.'

'This is not a light matter,' Mary interjected. 'Colonel Savary, George, has a genuine concern. He was clearly not aware that he was being asked to join the Fund Committee under these conditions. And of course in fairness to Cy and Ollie, he couldn't really be told in advance.'

Mary Butler had always taken her duties as a trustee very seriously. It was in the public service tradition she had been brought up in. When Philip Rose had first returned from a fact-finding visit to Vietnam and proposed the fund, Mary had been in enthusiastic agreement. Philip, herself and Mrs Rose had comprised the first committee of what was then a tiny fund collecting money mostly from members of the Meyerick Club.

Of course Philip Rose would hardly recognise the Fund now. It was astonishing, Mary thought, watching Cy across the table, how quickly he had established himself. For a while he was seen by others in the county too as something of an adventurer. He was known to be without money of his own and there were the inevitable mutterings that he had simply married Sunny for her inheritance.

But the rumours had died quickly. Cy was popular, especially with the women of Meyerick, and had soon shown himself willing and able to take on the sort of organisational work the community always needed. The Fund, headless after the death of Philip Rose, needed someone like Cy. Fin Butler had argued strongly that he should be appointed chairman. Mary had finally agreed. For some months Mrs Rose held out but in the end she too had reluctantly agreed. Because of her part in promoting Cy, Mary felt a special responsibility to the fund. Sometimes she worried about the gigantic growth in income Cy had generated in less than a decade. Sometimes, too, she worried about the annual clandestine payments they made, although everybody who had ever been to Vietnam said Cy was right that bribery made the world go round there. Nevertheless she understood George Savary's concern on hearing about the secret account.

'If I might usurp Cy's role for a moment,' Mary said, 'I think the whole committee would fully understand and sympathise with George if he felt he could not continue.' There were supporting murmurs from round the table.

'No,' Colonel Savary said with a touch of stubbornness, 'I don't wish to resign. I'm not calling anybody's integrity into question. But I do feel I should know who is the recipient of this large sum and how exactly it works for us. I was in Vietnam myself, not as long as Cy was, of course, but over a year. My estimate of the people is that they are polite and tough and above all corrupt. I'm just asking who are we paying and how do we know we are getting value for money.'

Fin Butler looked at Stevenson. 'Perhaps it's time, Cy, that we all knew more.'

'Sure . . .' Cy Stevenson nodded. 'I agree with Fin. Perhaps it's time the committee as a whole knew. On reflection I can't see how we can take corporate responsibility otherwise.' He poured himself a drink and smiled across the table at Mary. 'My third or fourth time in Vietnam,' Cy began, 'I met a merchant in Saigon. Forget now exactly where but I had seen him in a number of bars up and down the Rue Catinat before we actually spoke. Strange man, very frenchified. Well I was a young man at the time but I wasn't that new to Vietnam. When we got talking he gave me a tip or two. You know, where the action might be taking place.'

'How did he know?' the colonel said suspiciously.

Stevenson laughed. 'He knew because he was a member of the Vietcong political committee for what *they* called occupied Saigon. For all I know he might have been the head of the committee.'

'You mean he was spying.' Jason Rose said.

'Yep. He was spying.'

'What did you do, Cy?' Fin Butler said.

'As soon as I realised, which was pretty soon, I went to Saigon Intelligence Center and told them what I knew.'

'What did they say?' Hector Hand leaned forward, unable to guess how Cy might be vindicated.

'They said, go mind your own business. They said they knew all about this guy. They even implied he worked for them.'

'Did he?'

'Like most people there he probably did deals.'

Colonel Savary shook his head in disapproval, but of what – the US Army Intelligence, the Rue Catinat or himself, Cy Stevenson – was not clear.

'That was the way things were there, colonel, my man is now provincial administrator of Cahn Roc.'

'The seaboard province?' Savary said.

Cy nodded. 'The province through which, since we began our operation, more refugees have passed than through most of the rest of Vietnam put *together*.'

'When did you propose the deal to him?' Fin Butler said, frowning.

'I met him in Geneva,' Stevenson said. 'Just after I became Chairman of the Fund I attended an aid conference. I remember I looked up and saw my former friend. He waddled across and was his own affable self.'

'Is that when you made the arrangement?' Hector Hand asked.

'No. But that's when the idea was broached. By him of course. The deal was made when Ollie Digweed and I went back to Geneva at his invitation.'

'What was the deal?' Fin said. 'I mean exactly.'

Stevenson waved his arm. 'Of course there was no way of keeping him to the details, there was no fine print you understand. But essentially for the money he guaranteed the coastguard be kept sweet. He guaranteed the police would look in the other direction. Substantially of course. There had to be some token arrests. But we have reason to believe that even those are small in number.'

'OK,' Fin said.

The colonel's face was shadowed with doubt. 'I know the world over there is not as we see it from here.'

The men and women round the oval table were silent. Cy raised his glass. 'From this seat, the way I see it is that we raise our glasses to Monsieur Quatch.'

'And,' Mary Butler said, 'to Cy Stevenson.' There was a discreet round of applause and glasses were raised.

Looking back on the meeting, Cy Stevenson thought of it as the high point of his career.

7

She awoke at dawn, her mind a blank, the surface of an unruffled pool. Her eyes remained closed. Slowly sensations edged their way into her consciousness. A draught of cool morning air brushed her legs and her face. She breathed to capture its full flavour and heard a gurgle in her nose and throat. Like having a bad head cold. One hand was heavy on the bed she lay on. Some unidentified weight pressed on her stomach. Her skin seemed caked with thin mud, a sensation she identified immediately from the orphanage visits to the river bath. To be among the last into the hole dug into the mud beside the river was to emerge caked with a thin slurry of mud which dried in the sun . . . to feel like this.

A strange ache pervaded her body. An ache made bearable by the soft filtering of her mind from the orphanage bathing hole to lunch with the American in Paris.

Perhaps it was an hour before she woke again. The thin shaft of sun, falling through the gap in the curtains, was hotter, uncomfortable on her face. This time she was aware of the reek of brandy and another odour, sweeter, somehow sinister. Something warm and liquid slid down her thigh.

She was conscious now. With clarity suddenly. And crazy with fear as she opened her eyes and sat up. In a mirror opposite she saw a face. Screaming with terror she stared at the bloodied shape that faced her. Blood-caked like the mud of the river. Blood in her nose, her hair, blood on the back of her hands and streaked up her arms, blood on her shoulders and rounding her breasts. Blood on her belly and in dried smears across her legs.

She tried to rise from the bloodstained bed but something restrained her wrist. Looking down, she gasped with fear.

Shivering, she remembered.

They had stood in the vast salon. He had poured her more

cognac and walked back to lean against his desk, silent, appraising, watching her drink.

'Why do you think you will be arrested?' Nan had asked.

After a long pause he had nodded. 'Let us say simply that I know that I have come to the end of this one particular road.'

'You seem not too distressed.'

He had smiled. For the first time she noticed the jaggedness of his lower teeth. 'Not too distressed, you say? Well, perhaps not. I am, you see, inside my white suit, spats and walking cane, truly a Vietnamese. An oriental. Bernadette has often said the same.'

'A fatalist?'

'Perhaps. I have been sometimes touched by the beliefs of some of the sects. Belief runs deep.' She felt a momentary leap of hope. 'It runs deep,' he said with his jagged-toothed smile. 'But the surface waters are turbulent.'

She shivered.

Taking her arm he raised her from her chair. 'When I first saw you,' he said, 'I recognised immediately a quality in you. Something which one day would be worth a sacrifice.'

He gestured to her to walk before him into the adjoining room. No more brightly lit than the salon, it was dominated by a huge bed spread with a red silk cover. The bedhead was of dark teak, intricately carved and set with decorative brasswork, brass lions and elephant heads and pictorial incised panels.

'Is it not magnificent?' Quatch said behind her.

He came to stand beside her and together they stared silently at the bed. Her eye was caught by a sequence of line drawings on the brass panels. A young peasant girl holding a bunch of lilies was bending towards the headstone of a grave. Three exquisitely drawn panels described the girl . . . the shock which made her drop the lilies . . . and the hand rising to welcome her from the grave.

'I see you know the story of the hand from the grave,' Quatch said. 'It is, of course, our own Vietnamese version of the myth of Greek antiquity, of the beautiful Persephone snatched into the Underworld. But the Vietnamese story is more subtle, more ambiguous. The question it poses is this: is the corpse that pulls her down attempting to defile her beauty? Or somehow trying to capture it for himself for ever?'

'I don't understand,' Nan Luc said cautiously.

'I'm sure you've heard it said that beauty like yours, Nan Luc,' he said softly, 'drives men wild. A hackneyed old cliché. But it contains a truth. Such beauty drives men mad because love is an inadequate way of possessing that beauty. Mad with the frustration of beauty such as yours some men see destruction of it as the only satisfying solution.'

She stood beside him in the bedroom every nerve end alive with a sick fear.

'Undress,' he commanded.

'The passport,' she said. 'You have a telephone call to make.'

'Payment first,' he said bitterly. 'I see you have the mentality of a whore.'

He motioned her to sit and she sat on the edge of the red silk coverlet. Taking her hand, he lifted it as if to kiss her bent wrist.

'The passport,' she said.

'There is no need for a telephone call,' he said. 'It is here. In my desk drawer.'

She took a deep breath. 'I wish to see it.'

'Of course.'

He was still holding her wrist with one hand. He seemed to her to be bent awkwardly to the right. For a moment he fumbled. Then his other hand came up and a cold bracelet circled her wrist. As the metal cuff clicked he stood away from her in triumph. She stood bolt upright, her arm pulled rigid by the movement. A thin chain attached her to the bed.

'Undress,' he said again.

She shook her head, too shocked to speak.

Quatch roamed in front of her, mewling with delight. He had thrown off his jacket and waistcoat, and now continued in a wide half-circle round her, sometimes moving forward quickly to brush her hair with his palm or squeeze her breast. As she turned away from him he ran his hand from her shoulder down the curve of her back. 'Perfect,' he said.

His hand left her. She was half aware of another, different movement. Then the stick fell across her back breathtakingly sharp, sending a shooting pain through her body. As she turned to defend herself he hit her again, blows, she now saw, from a pliant bamboo cane. She was screaming in pain as the first blow struck her across the face and she fell forward on to the bed. Too weak to speak she lay there across the crumpled red silk coverlet as Quatch poured cognac. Breathing heavily he put the bottle down on the floor and straightened up, watching her with his head cocked to one side.

Her mind was still working, however uncertainly. She was chained but she had seen that the blows, the very pain she suffered, was for him an absorbing sexual experience. And a man sexually absorbed was off his guard.

'I could teach you many things,' he said. 'But it would take time I no longer have.' She watched him while he lifted his glass and drank the cognac. 'You must beg,' he said. 'Plead with me.' He paused, his lips formed thoughtfully in a round. 'Perhaps you are more wilful than Bernadette,' he mused. 'I would like to think so.'

She moved, taking the weight off her left arm, her free arm.

'Bernadette,' he said, like a schoolmaster reviewing a former student, 'was not *naturally* submissive. But she grew, before long, to be appreciative of the things I taught her.'

A moment's inattention on his part would enable her to reach the only weapon available to her, the heavy, almost full bottle of cognac. She moved, her knee protruding through the torn pyjamas. Her free hand stole towards the bottle. He watched, savouring the movement of her legs. She swung the bottle. It bounced off his shoulder and rolled back towards her.

With a grunt of surprise, he had fallen to his knee, his head hanging forward within range of another blow. She swung again, crashing the bottle against the side of his head. He screamed, half rose and fell forward, face down upon the coverlet beside her.

Nan Luc twisted her body to look down at him. He was groaning, barely conscious. The back of his head, where the black hair thinned across the skull, was at her mercy. Panic thoughts surged through her mind. One more blow, she knew, could kill him, could deliver her from this horror. Trembling madly she lifted the bottle, hesitated, lifted it again. One more blow to kill a man. To kill a man like Quatch.

Exhaustion sapped her resolve, her hatred. Her arm fell. She watched Quatch roll clumsily away from her as her aching hand released the bottle.

At the end of the bed he crouched, his hand to the side of his head. Breath soughed from his rounded mouth, sour enough to reach her across the foot or two that separated their faces. Pushing himself to his feet he stumbled to a chair and lowered himself into it to sit, his small, glittering eyes never leaving her.

He beat her. Rested, and beat her again. Tore off the last shreds of her clothes and beat her again.

Half blind with pain she lay crouched on the bed in a foetal position until the blows finally stopped. She had begged him and pleaded with him and screamed in pain. Now she lay back looking up at him and their eyes locked together. The thought that he might kill her hung between them.

He spoke and the words meant nothing to her as she faded in and out of the most compelling need to escape into sleep. Hours or minutes fused. Minutes or hours. Sometime, as her eyes opened, she was aware that he was crouched over her, pushing her legs apart, grunting like an animal.

His face was just inches away, sweat pouring from his forehead, the breath hissing through his broken teeth, the eyes red with madness. Somewhere in the room she could hear her own voice, pleading . . .

He was reaching for something now, something behind her head, fumbling past her shoulder as he thrashed from side to side on her body. When his hand rose it rose with the glint of steel. In the soft lighting from the lamps, the blade glowed yellow.

Paralysed, as he pushed inside her, she watched the angled wrist and the yellow glowing blade. Then his exultant scream filled her consciousness, and she saw, without understanding, the spurt of blood and the bloody hand stabbing and stabbing the blade into his *own* neck.

Through the night, from every moment's sleep she woke in terror as blood dripped and burbled from his body across her shoulders and face. Through the night she pushed and struggled to roll him off her, his inert weight a deathlock, an embrace she fought to break; until at last his body rolled from her, thudding to the floor on the far side of the bed.

Standing now, straining on the chain attached to her wrist she could see no more than his crooked arm and bloodied hand. Her legs ached and trembled. She looked at the mound of sheeting and twisted blankets on the bed, soaked and stained black-red to almost pink. She wondered how two bodies could have so much blood.

On the floor beside the bed, the bamboo cane lay. With it she reached out to where Quatch's jacket was draped across a chair. Hooking the coat through the air until it fell on the bed, she searched the pockets until she found a slim folded wallet of keys. Awkwardly she began to try them on the lock of the metal cuff that clasped her wrist. At the third or fourth key the lever turned and the cuff fell away.

Without thinking, almost as if it were now the most important thing in her life she went to the desk in the salon. Using the wallet of keys she opened the centre drawer. The passport lay on top of a pile of papers. For this soft pale cover with its red cross she had passed the night.

She found she alternated between surges of almost manic energy and almost complete exhaustion. Each time she forced herself to move she became aware of a dry sobbing deep in her chest, far from tears. Again the image in the mirror shocked her. She knew that unless she washed off his blood, the blood of both of them, she was in danger of complete collapse. The thought steadied her. She walked carefully, one foot placed in front of the other, into the bathroom.

She had showered the blood from her and wrapped herself in a thick bath towel when the knock came at the door. She looked at herself slowly in the long mirror as her grandmother's voice called her from outside. She looked, she thought, almost unharmed by the violence of the night. Most of the stripes from the cane were now covered by the towel. Her face was pale and the jaw from some angles, swollen. Her hands too were lacerated as she had tried to defend herself from the cane.

She felt a century older. For a few moments she stood utterly still, drawing deep breaths while the voice of Bernadette pleaded outside. Then she walked slowly to the door and opened it.

Her grandmother's face smiled up at her eagerly. 'Did you get it?'

Nan Luc's hand rose to hit her, but she had no strength to spare. She opened wider the door and gestured to where she had left the passport. With a squeal of pleasure Bernadette crossed the room and snatched it up. Pressing it to her lips, she slid it into the waistband of her black peasant dress and turned to her grand-daughter. 'He's not still here, is he?' she said, dropping her voice.

Nan gestured to the open bedroom door. 'No need to whisper. He can't hear you,' she said.

'He's gone? Good. Monsieur Quatch can keep ahead of any police force.'

She stopped. Then came forward and laid her hand on Nan's arm. 'Was it perhaps not too bad, chérie?'

'Not too bad,' Nan Luc said, throwing off her grandmother's hand.

Bernadette's excitement blinded her to the disgust in Nan's gesture. 'I know he's not an . . . easy man,' she smiled brightly. 'No, not an easy man. Your cheek's a little swollen I see.' Nan Luc turned away. 'What you did for me last night, chérie, will never be forgotten. However far away . . .'

'Stop,' Nan Luc screamed. 'Stop, for God's sake.'

'But we're family. We've proved to each other that we're family again. Listen, I must get out of these peasant clothes. I must get dressed and made up. Important figures in the International Red Cross do not wear clothes like this.' She walked into the bedroom, stopped in shock. Then she went in, closing the door behind her.

Nan Luc turned and walked out into the hallway. In the kitchen she heated a pot and made tea. Her mind seemed to be circling the small core of sanity left to her. She leaned back against the stove and drank the tea. Behind her closed eyes she saw rushing, spurting blood. Only when she jerked open her eyes did she realise Bernadette was in the room beside her. She had chosen a black suit with velvet collar, high heels, and a pale trenchcoat which she wore round her shoulders.

'You have my word, chérie,' she said. 'He had talked about it often, but I swear I never believed it was more than a flight of fancy. He's still breathing. Just. I'll telephone to the clinic from the airport.' She looked into Nan Luc's glazed eyes. 'The edge of the grave,' she said. 'He had always boasted that he would have the company of a beautiful woman to the very edge of the grave.'

Nan Luc walked ahead of her from the kitchen. 'Find me some clothes,' she said.

Her grandmother followed her. 'Upstairs,' she said, 'you have the choice of my whole wardrobe. I must leave you, chérie, for my new life.'

'Not yet.' Nan's voice was unlike any woman's voice Bernadette had heard before. It had a new steely quality that made Bernadette turn her head sharply. 'We have some unfinished business.'

'I have no time to talk,' Bernadette said.

'You must find time,' Nan said. 'You are not leaving this apartment until we have talked.'

'About what?'

'About my father.' Bernadette made a petulant gesture of impatience. 'About my father,' Nan repeated.

'I've nothing to add to what I told you. I know next to nothing about him.'

'You know more than you told me.'

'No.'

'You even made it clear at the time. I want the answers before you go. Who was he?'

'An American newsman.' She looked from Nan to the standing clock and back again.

'I must know. Did he try to get me out of Saigon after my mother died?'

Bernadette took up the one valise she had packed. 'Everybody was trying to get someone out of Saigon.'

'But did my father try to get me out?'

'Why is this so important to you now, so many years later?'

'I want to know,' Nan Luc said. 'If he was a good man I want to know.'

'To play at loving him?' Bernadette laughed bitterly. 'To pretend to love someone you don't even know?'

'To honour him. If he was a good man, to honour him as a father.' Nan Luc was holding her against the wall.

Bernadette dropped her valise. 'Believe me. I know only that after the American war Quatch met him in Europe. From that time on he began to send sums of money to Quatch from America. That's all I know,' Bernadette said savagely. 'Let me go.'

Nan Luc blocked the door. 'The birth certificate. Where is it?'

For a moment Bernadette looked at her. 'You're chasing the west wind, Nan Luc. The birth certificate is upstairs in my secretaire. Go and get it and burn it and forget you ever had an American father. What will it ever matter to you what sort of man he was?'

'One more thing,' Nan Luc said. 'The German, Peter Benning, why was he killed?'

'He was interfering in Monsieur Quatch's business arrangements, that's all I know.'

'What business arrangements?'

Bernadette stopped suddenly. 'If Quatch lives, there'll still be a trial. I'm saying this for your sake, Nan Luc. The less you know the safer you'll be. You have a life here in this benighted Communist paradise. Make it easy for yourself. Know nothing. Ask nothing. Look beautiful. Marry Van Khoa. Now I must go.' She came forward and held Nan tightly. 'Let me go now, chérie.'

Half an hour after her grandmother left, Nan Luc made her way slowly down the stairs in the dark well of the apartment building. She knew her strange feeling of elation came as much from exhaustion and pain as from anything else. But there was also something else. What Bernadette had said about her father brought surges of pleasure to her as she thought about it. Why had he sent Quatch money from America?

There was no other possible answer.

In the belief, however misplaced, that he could trust Quatch to use his influence on her behalf, to take her under his protection.

8

In the dressing room of his house at Piebald, on the outskirts of Meyerick City, Cy Stevenson hummed to himself as he fixed his black tie. He had been told by some self-elected arbiter of gentlemen's fashion that nothing less a full butterfly bow tie was acceptable with a dinner jacket. No clip-ons, no Slim Jims, no racy plaids. A black, deep-winged butterfly and nothing less.

He had heard the phone ringing and was adjusting the final balance of the two wings of the bow tie when Sunny called up that George Savary was on the line.

He looked again in the mirror. He was pleased with the result, looking forward to the evening ahead. Sunny's sister, Mary, and Fin, her husband, were dull enough but tonight they had invited friends from Mary's schooldays in Paris, the woman, a bright, very flirty Parisienne, Cy particularly liked on first meeting. He picked up the phone.

'Cy,' an agitated voice said. 'This is George Savary. I wanted to catch you before you went out.'

'What is it, George? Fund business?'

'I'm sorry to call you at this time, Cy . . .'

'That's OK, George,' Cy said testily. 'But listen, if it's going to take some time, call me tomorrow morning at Fin and Mary's place. We're staying overnight there.'

'I just wanted to know if you had the *New York Times* for yesterday.'

'I guess so,' Cy said. 'Is it worth pulling it out of the garbage?'

'There's a small item on page three,' Savary said, reacting to Cy's tone. 'Your Vietnamese contact, Quatch, has been arrested.'

Cy felt his knees buckle. 'Arrested?'

'It appears he tried to kill himself, but failed. The Vietnamese authorities are bringing him to trial.'

'What is he to be charged with?' Cy forced the panic from his voice.

'Corruption,' Savary said. 'The accusation is that large sums of money are involved.'

Two days later on the morning of the Meyerick Fund luncheon, Mary Page Butler and her younger sister Sunny Stevenson drove through a summer rainstorm towards the Meyerick Country Club. They drove for the most part in silence, sitting high in Mary's immaculate white Range Rover, frowning at the leaping crowns of water on the road ahead of them.

Their mother's death when Sunny was five had left Mary, herself just twenty years old, effectively responsible for raising her sister. Their father, wealthy, preoccupied and often away from home was content to let Mary decide. In a real sense Sunny, named for her outwardly bland, equable disposition, became Mary's daughter. Inevitably their love for each other was more like that between mother and daughter than between older and younger sister. At the same time their relationship had also been built on a strange, competitive tension. Both, beneath their easy-going exteriors, were firm, stubborn, even competitive. Mary's standards, based on an America which had all but disappeared, were, for Sunny, a source of mixed amusement and respect.

But her relationship with Sunny was not the most important thing in Mary's life. Nor, any longer, was her relationship with her husband, Fin Butler. Several times she had considered divorce. But although she had long ago realised that she did not love her husband, she nevertheless still felt friendship and affection for his bumbling way through life. And divorce seemed to Mary's essential kindliness, too harsh a comment on their admittedly not very satisfactory life together. For Mary, Fin Butler remained an adjunct, sometimes embarrassing, sometimes convenient, a man she shared her bedroom but not her thoughts with, a figure of no vital importance in her life.

Nor was money of any importance to Mary Page Butler. She was not really rich, at least not super-rich, but she had had, all her life, sufficient money to do what she wanted. Five generations of Pages of Meyerick County had seen to that. Her great-grandfather had built railroads in South America; her grandfather had been a banker; her father had speculated in property.

Her aspirations were not high: the eight-bedroom old Rectory in the favoured southern part of Meyerick County; a few dozen acres, paddock and stables; two or three hunters and a groom to look after them. Nothing more than what she already had.

No, Mary Butler's overwhelming concern was now different. It was age. She had been an attractive womanly woman since her early twenties, well shaped, not too tall, with pleasant features and thick brown hair. Not a showy looking woman, but distinctively well dressed all the same with clothes from New York and London, rather than Paris and Rome.

But she was now entering her fiftieth year. She exercised regularly in her own small gym and at the club pool – she had grown up to consider it vulgar to have a pool of one's own. She still commanded the occasional appreciative glance of younger men. But she knew that she was now of an age when very soon it would be possible only to be thin or fat. The rounded slenderness, the aura of sensual warmth she had always exuded, was now on the way to being lost for ever. She was, in every way, ripe for an affair. Furthermore she was already pretty sure who it would be with.

Her sister, almost as if she were following Mary's thoughts, touched her arm. 'You're looking great today,' she said. 'You'll be the prettiest geriatric at the luncheon, darling.'

Mary glanced sideways at her, grimacing. Yet Sunny was not trying to be cruel, she knew that. It was simply a category Sunny liked to place her in. Not just her elder sister. A different generation. At the age of thirty-four Sunny Stevenson still looked on Mary as more a mother than a sister.

'Geriatric? Not very kind, Sunny,' Mary said mildly. And by God, she thought with a guilty start, after last Thursday evening, not very true either.

Sunny slid down lazily in her seat belt and watched the rain storm clearing over the rolling downland ahead. 'So you've decided to resign from the Fund committee?'

'I was a founder member, you know,' Mary said, her eyes on the road. 'Nearly twenty years. It's enough.'

'Cy won't be pleased.'

'I don't see why not.'

'You've always been a loyal supporter.'

'Not an uncritical one at times,' Mary said with a hint of sharpness. She hated the idea of being taken for a pushover.

'Who's going to take your place,' Sunny asked, not really interested.

Mary sideglanced her. 'We need young blood. Not another geriatric.'

'Sorry.'

Mary smiled. 'Just evening the score. How about you?'

'For the committee?'

'Why not?'

'To be candid it bores me.'

Mary drew in her breath, sharply disapproving. Sunny shrugged, reached over and patted Mary's hand. 'What I love about you, Mary, is that you have inherited the old Page conscience. Enough for both of us.'

Was that it? Mary wondered. Was that why she couldn't quite feel towards her sister as she should, because of that smug, myopic certainty which made her incapable of realising that life could deliver blows, that fortunes could be lost, people she loved or at least liked mangled in car accidents? Perhaps the simple truth was, Mary told herself, that Sunny just wasn't very bright. Or was maybe just plain lazy about the way she thought of others, about the way she took them for granted. Perhaps Mary should have handed her out a few sharp lessons years ago.

Of course it was too late now. A sharp lesson. A shock.

It would be if she knew! Mary felt a thrill of excitement pass through her as the image of that brief, improbable moment on Thursday night again invaded her thoughts. A thrill of excitement and a flush of guilt.

They drove on in silence until they breasted the last hill and the Meyerick Country Club lay below them, its low building and stone tourette set in well-kept lawns and gardens, with yew hedges discreetly surrounding shale tennis courts and swimming pools. Even from the hill the parking lot was barely visible behind the line of pine trees that acted as a shield.

Mary waved her hand towards the valley. 'Don't you ever feel slightly uneasy about all this, Sunny?'

Her sister's eyes were closed. 'About what?' she said without opening her eyes.

A surge of anger passed through Mary. 'About having all this. About having life so easy.'

Sunny opened one eye and grunted a negative. 'Not when my husband's charging them two hundred and fifty dollars a plate for this lunch.' She struggled upright in her seat. 'And at least that much for the tombola unless they want to look cheap.'

They drove into the parking lot and found a place beside Fin Butler's green Jaguar.

Sunny slipped her seat belt. 'God,' she said, 'I hope there are not going to be too many drunken speeches. Or too many drunks.'

'Keep an eye on Fin for me,' Mary said as they walked across the gravel to the striped awning.

'Why?' Sunny asked laconically. 'Who will you be keeping an eye on?'

Did she mean that?

They gained the shade of the awning and were welcomed by the Irish doorman. 'Some party today, ladies! And the prizes for the tombola are enough to make your eyes pop.'

They smiled politely and moved into the main clubroom. The long room was set with tables in a squared off U-shape. The sunlight shafts touched the glasses and cutlery and deepened the wine red upholstery of the chairs. Maids in black skirts and white blouses moved back and forth across the room. Vic Impari and his red-coated bar staff clustered round the side table from which the selected wine would be served: an old dry Amontillado sherry would accompany the lobster bisque; a Château Rabaut Promis, a Sauterne, was, in the new French manner, to accompany the *foie gras*; and a 1982 La Lagune claret had been chosen for the quail. There would be one of the newly acquired Burgundies for the cheese and a vintage champagne to finish the lunch. None of this, Vic Impari was thinking, included the whiskies, martinis and gin and tonics which would prepare the guests for their gastronomic ordeal. Vic Impari swallowed his resentment.

As the old bell from the long demolished Meyerick court house began to toll in its new resting place high in the tourette, the club members and their guests came in to take their places. There was much banter and a mock jostle for position. What had been for deadly real were the struggles over the last few weeks of each member to make certain he or she was sitting beside someone they wanted to sit with. Now it was the time among the ladies of the club for low, whispered comment or a show of surprise as they were led to their places.

Mary, between Colonel George Savary and a New York bond salesman from the north end of the county, was content enough. Her husband, Fin, was not yet in his place. But sitting there at the top end of the table between the wife of a State senator and a modestly successful actress from New York, Cy Stevenson looked good. A handsome figure.

Other Fund committee members were placed at intervals around the table. The Reverend Hector Hand sat next to a very old lady who told him several times between the lobster bisque and the dessert that there had been less than twenty-five members when she had joined the club and that girls playing tennis wore sensible straw hats and skirts to their ankles.

The two Anderson brothers had achieved places no more than one seat between them so they could lean forward and communicate with their inscrutable smiles. The recently widowed Anita Simpson sat next to Finlay Butler, or rather the place he would occupy when he came from the locker room.

Mrs Helen Rose, deeply disapproving of a luncheon which cost two hundred and fifty dollars, however good the cause, sat frostily between Oliver Digweed and her son, Jason, counting the glasses of Amontillado the Chairman of the Fund trustees had taken while *waiting* for the lobster bisque.

Finlay Butler arrived just as the soup plates were being served. After twenty years of marriage to him Mary still wondered if he timed these entrances. He no longer managed to draw all eyes to him as he crossed the room, bending to shake hands with a man or kiss a woman on the cheek. Mary now saw him as an old rogue no longer with the looks to impress the girls, all his stories of Prince Charles and Windsor Castle long ago told and retold. Nice enough, but sad.

Cy Stevenson was making the rounds. It was his day and everybody recognised it. He moved along the table, shaking hands or kissing cheeks. Mrs Rose and her son Jason, Anita Simpson and her escort Dr John Harker.

'Have you decided on the date for the special meeting yet, Cy?' Savary asked him. 'I see it as a matter of urgency.'

'I'll be calling everybody tomorrow morning,' Cy said. 'Don't worry, I haven't been idle. I've been checking around so that the fullest possible information can be put before the trustees.'

'Fullest possible information on what?' Mary asked.

'Today is playtime,' Cy said. 'Business tomorrow.'

He moved on a place. One arm on the back of Mary's chair he bent over to kiss Mary briefly on the cheek. 'How's my glamorous sister-in-law today?'

'Very well,' Mary turned smiling. She decided to reply in kind. 'And how's my handsome brother-in-law?'

His lips touched her cheek. 'Horny,' he whispered.

She felt herself blush, wondered if George Savary could possibly have heard anything, wondered if Sunny could see from the far end of the table, decided there was nothing to worry about there, and with a smile at her bond salesman neighbour lifted her spoon to try the lobster bisque which had been set before her. She tasted nothing as she slowly spooned the soup. Her thoughts were on last Thursday evening and the strange exhilarating few moments, the memory of which made her tremble.

Sunny and Cy had come over for supper, with Jacques and Josette Picard, friends from the year she had studied at the Sorbonne. In the certainty that Cy and perhaps even Sunny would drink too much she had asked them to stay over. Looking back on it as she had done a dozen times since, she was astonished at the unexpectedness of what had happened. She was equally astonished that it seemed to have a sort of inevitability. She knew that she liked Cy but with reservations. Reservations about his bounce, his brashness, his overwhelming self-confidence. What she did like was what she and the world first saw of Cy Stevenson. A good-looking young man, a little over forty, light-hearted, competent, free with his compliments.

Last Thursday night, she remembered, he had been particularly free with his compliments to her. He had not even come on to Josette Picard as she had expected him to.

Her mind drifted, savouring that extraordinary moment. Around about midnight on the evening of the dinner party, after the Picards had left, Sunny had gone to take a shower. Fin was in a familiar slumped condition, close to sleep in the library. Mary herself was checking one of the guest bedrooms and Cy was nowhere to be seen.

She had made sure the windows were open as Sunny insisted and she was staring down at the bed wondering whether Sunny would want a lighter blanket when she was aware of someone in the room with her.

She glanced over her shoulder. 'Hullo, Cy.' She looked back at the bed. 'I'm wondering whether Sunny is going to need a lighter blanket.'

'Uhuh,' he said, standing behind her.

'OK, you're not interested.'

'That's not strictly true,' his voice said.

She frowned. Something had brushed the seat of her black skirt. It took one astonishing moment to realise it was the palm of his hand. She breathed in, pretending to be considering the question of the blanket, pretending to be unaware of his touch. This time the palms of both his hands brushed lightly up and down. And stayed.

They both knew there was room for her to step forward a pace. That he'd laugh and make a joke and it would be over. Instead, she pressed back slightly into his hands.

Her eyes were on the bathroom door. Behind that door Sunny was taking a shower; or was cleaning her teeth; or was just slipping on a bathrobe. She kept her eyes on the bathroom door handle as she pressed backwards.

'That you, Cy?' Sunny's voice called through the bathroom door.

'Sure, you almost finished?'

'Just coming out,' Sunny's voice said. 'Listen, you're not going to spend half the night boozing with Fin.'

Now Cy had come forward, pressing against her. Mary seemed to stop breathing. Lust, heightened by drink and an appalling sense of guilt, flooded her. She reached back and took Cy's hands, guiding them to her waist and then up underneath until he cupped her breast under the silk of her evening blouse. For a moment they stood together as a sharp exquisite feeling surged through her. Then the door handle turned and Cy stepped backwards.

Sunny came out of the bathroom wrapped in a robe, drying

her hair with a towel. 'It's not good for you,' she said to Cy. Mary looked at her helplessly. 'It's not good for him, this non-stop drinking. Don't let Fin encourage him for God's sake, Mary.'

'Myself, I'm going to bed,' Cy said. 'Now.'

Sunny looked up at her sister. Then: 'Hey, you've got a hot flush.'

'I was just wondering whether you'd want a lighter blanket.'

'No, what I really want is for you to get some air conditioning into this house. But of course, you'd consider that vulgar.'

'If that blanket's all right then . . .' Mary murmured moving towards the door, 'I'll say goodnight to you both.'

Sunny stopped drying her hair and frowned. 'I didn't say anything to offend you, did I?'

'No, of course not.' The words came out much more sharply than she had intended.

'Menopausal impatience,' Sunny announced. 'I think you've reached that time of life.'

'Menopausal impatience.' She turned away angrily. Catching Cy's eye in the mirror she stopped at the door. Menopausal impatience? Could it be? 'Goodnight, Cy,' she said. 'Goodnight, Sunny.'

At the luncheon, conversation with the bond salesman on her left was proving difficult. With Colonel Savary on her right it was almost impossible. He was preoccupied and remote. Every time she decided on a line of polite small-talk, the word Cy just drifted through her mind. She found she savoured it. She drank wine to complement it. At the end of lunch she smoked a small cheroot to accompany it.

Cy had remembered. And had wanted her to know that.

The lunch was protracted, the speeches were, by all except Cy himself, tedious and overlong. Beside her George Savary had reacted grudgingly to the generous compliment Cy had paid him for his courage in accepting 'a role on a committee that's bound to be unpopular when it charges two hundred and fifty dollars for lunch'. When she asked him if he was already regretting it she told her that at first when Helen Rose had proposed him, he had thought Cy reluctant to countersign her proposal. He realised he was an outsider, a newcomer to Meyerick County, but he had been at Yale with Helen Rose's husband, Philip. Even as a soldier, he said, he had come to look upon the Vietnamese war as different from other wars. He intended no lack of patriotism but when young Jason Rose was blinded – he had served with the Colonel's unit near Da Nang – he confessed he had begun to think seriously about what the US was doing there.

'Cy says,' Mary moved cautiously, 'that our understanding of the Vietnamese was zero. I don't know.'

'I think news reporters sometimes get closer to what's going on than the soldiers on the spot. The mystery is they don't seem able to tell what they know.'

So he wasn't all service stories and well-cut suits, Mary reflected. A bit huffy perhaps, but a good man. A man who, like many veterans of all ranks, had even now not stopped thinking about Vietnam even in the aftermath of victory in the Gulf.

As she talked to George Savary she could feel her brother-in-law's eyes on her. She found, to her annoyance, that she was stuttering and slightly incoherent. She was a fifty-year-old woman, she reminded herself. There was only one legitimate reason now for her to get hot flushes.

'You heard me mention to Cy an emergency meeting of trustees,' Savary said, when the speeches and toasts were over. 'I feel it's my duty to press Cy on this. There have been some important developments in Saigon in the last few days.'

She had no wish to think about developments in Ho Chi Minh City. 'What does Cy say?' she asked, her eyes ranging across the tables.

'Cy says he's looking into it,' Savary said.

'That's all right, then.' Mary smiled full-face at the colonel before he could go on. 'Now I'm going to ask you to help me run the tombola, George. Let's concentrate on the thing in hand. As Cy says, today's playday. But there are still some good dollars to be extracted from our unsuspecting guests.' She took his hand and drew him, reluctant, to his feet.

Out on the terrace Cy walked with his arm locked in Sunny's. His free hand was gesturing expansively but his face was drawn tight with anger. 'She can't resign, for Christ's sake,' he said.

'She's drafting a letter to Oliver tomorrow.'

'She can't do it,' he snarled. 'Not now.'

She pulled away from him. 'You mean now that Quatch has been arrested?'

He stopped, smiled easily at Hector and Sarah Hand as they passed by and returned a cold glance to Sunny. 'Who told you?'

'Colonel Savary told me. Apparently there was an item in the *New York Times*,' she said.

'For God's sake, you must see Mary can't resign now. This trial spells trouble for the Fund.'

'It spells trouble for you, Cy, doesn't it?'

He began to walk beside her. 'What are you getting at, Sunny?'

She looked at him angrily. 'I know you, Cy. Not well, not the way a wife should know her husband. But well enough to know that there's something not quite above board about this Quatch deal. I've felt it for a long time. What are you doing,' she said with a casual bitterness, 'syphoning some of it?'

'Is that what Mary said?'

'Of course not. If Mary believed that she would have called the cops long ago. She's just uneasy about this money being paid. She's not alone, you know that.'

'I need the family's support now more than ever.'

They had reached the end of the terrace. She turned, shaking her head. 'I don't know what you're up to, Cy,' Sunny said wearily. 'But better she resigns now than vote against you on committee.'

The tombola raised several thousand dollars as club members paid sky-high prices for tickets to win goods supplied free by other club members. For a chaste kiss from the Anderson brothers a wild auction raised seven hundred dollars from an angry Anita Simpson. She had been caught holding the last bid, certain that her friend Marsha Shaw would take the bidding up further. She paid up with obvious reluctance and took her prize in the most perfunctory manner.

At some time during the proceedings it was clear that Fin Butler was not just drunk, but very drunk. When the dancing on the terrace began, Sunny came over to Mary. 'Listen,' she said, 'Cy is going to have to be here until the last drunk can't get another word out.'

'You want to stay at Page Corner tonight? It saves twenty minutes' drive.'

'Sure. I want out of here. I thought I'd take your keys and drive Fin back. He's had too much already. Cy can drive you back when the shindig ends.'

'OK,' Mary said, a warm excitement flowing through her. 'OK. We'll be along later.'

In the Rectory living room, Fin Butler sat slumped in a chair. Sunny had made him coffee but he had left it untouched. A bottle of whisky stood on the low table beside him.

'Fin,' Sunny said, irritated that Cy and her sister were still not back, 'I'm going to take this whisky away. You understand me. I'm taking the whisky away.' She reached for the bottle but he looked up at her with a pale, sickly look that made her stop her hand before it grasped the neck of the bottle.

She straightened up. 'For God's sake, Fin, you've had enough.' She cast around for some threat to offer. 'If you don't stop now and drink some coffee I'm going to call Dr Harker.'

Where in God's name was Mary? Sunny poured more coffee and fed some to Fin. Then she took the whisky bottle with her across the room to the telephone. He barely noticed.

She punched the number of the club and waited for the long tones to summon someone to the reception area. It was Vic Impari who answered.

'Vic,' Sunny said. 'Has my sister left yet? Sunny Stevenson here,' she added quickly as an afterthought.

'Oh hullo, Mrs Stevenson. Yes, your sister left with Mr Stevenson about an hour ago. Nothing wrong, I hope.'

'No, nothing,' Sunny said shortly. 'OK, thank you.'

She put down the phone and turned back to Fin. He was slumped forward. Alarmed, she took his shoulders and pulled him back in the chair. She poured herself a drink and sipped it, watching Fin. Was he conscious? His eyes opened from time to time but he only stared fixedly at the carpet before closing his eyes again.

She thought again about calling Dr Harker. But Dr Harker gossiped too much about his patients. No, she would wait for Mary.

And then one of the most curious feelings she had ever experienced came into her mind. Her sister . . . And Cy.

Sunny stood upright and caught a glimpse of herself in the Italian mirror over the mantelpiece. She could see the tense, suspicious look on her face. She shook her head. She had told herself a hundred times that she wouldn't care if Cy started an affair. But with her sister. With Mary!

She tried to force a dismissive smile. But the muscles around her mouth would not respond. Again, as unbidden as the first thought a few seconds earlier, the image came into her mind of the time last week she and Cy had stayed in this house. That moment when she had come out of the bathroom drying her hair. Cy was already moving backwards, away from Mary, she remembered that.

Strangely, she seemed to retain a complete picture in her mind. Cy, his hands raised. Her sister's flushed face.

9

'I have a file to pick up from the office,' Cy said. 'OK if we make the detour?'

In the passenger seat beside him Mary had nodded without turning her head. She was saying to herself: this is the most absurdly dangerous thing I have ever done in my life.

Through the trees she could see the lights of Page Corner, the house she had lived in since she was a child. The house where Sunny was waiting for her. She shook her head. No, Fin would be out cold and Sunny would be watching TV and thinking of an early night.

Through the corner of his eye Cy had caught the slight shake of her head. Waiting until they had swung past Page Corner and were travelling the straight road towards Meyerick, he reached out and touched her knee, walking his fingers slowly back towards her thigh.

She put the palm of her hand on the back of his and pressed down, exerting a slight pressure towards the inside of her leg. They droved like that to Meyerick.

The offices of the Meyerick Fund had been chosen by Cy in his first year as president. In that year the city had announced plans for the refurbishment of the old commercial waterfront, a half-mile or so of crumbling warehouses intersected by two stagnant canals. On behalf of the Fund Cy had bought a large loft in a neo-Gothic warehouse, its gable inscribed 1885 and its timbers saturated with soft, oriental odours. He had acted, as he often did, without too much consultation. Oliver Digweed had been informed and had apparently agreed. By the next trustee meeting the loft belonged to the Meyerick Fund. Within six months everybody agreed it was an inspired buy.

Cy's Mercedes moved along the waterfront under the ornate

cast iron lamps which the developers had retained. The river gleamed in the yellow lights. He pulled the car to a stop, switched off the engine and turned slowly in his seat.

'What about your file?' she said.

He reached out so that his hand was along her shoulder, touching the back of her neck. She made no effort to move away. His arm moved further round her shoulder. Drawing her towards him, he kissed her, plunging his tongue into her mouth as she fumbled desperately for him.

She could not believe the fire in her, the heat surging from face to loins, the trembling of her arms and legs, the fierce, palpitating heartbeat.

He drew back from her. 'The lady's hot,' he said. She didn't like that. But he had not understood. 'The lady's very hot,' he said.

She could not control her trembling limbs. 'May I have a cigarette?' she said.

'Sure. But you don't usually smoke.'

'Tonight I do.'

'OK,' he said. 'But we don't have to smoke here. I've got a nice wide sofa up in my office . . .'

'The one Sunny used to speak so highly of?'

'Mistake, Mary.' He handed her a cigarette and lit it for her. 'Don't hold it against me. These things happen,' he said.

She drew on the cigarette. 'The mistake's mine, Cy,' she said. She exhaled fiercely. 'I must be mad to be here.'

'Mad?' He shrugged. 'I don't think so, Mary. I think this is something we've both thought about for a long time. I think it's something we've both wanted for a long time.' She shook her head, partly to conceal the shiver of excitement that passed through her. Had he watched her, had dreams about her as she had had about him?

'For me it goes back a long way,' he said. 'Strangely enough I remember the very evening. I guess you hadn't been too pleased about Sunny's marriage. Saw me as something of an interloper, a boy gold-digger even.' She flinched. 'Something like that, uh? Anyway, the evening I'm talking about, we all went over to the Rose house. You remember, Jason Rose was giving a winter garden roast to introduce Ruth to the gentry of Meyerick. You remember that night?'

'I remember,' she said.

'I remember too,' he said. 'Because you and me were the only ones who didn't laugh at the snide "blind man" jokes about "maybe he hasn't found out what colour she is yet?" '

'Not the only ones,' she said.

'OK, maybe not the only ones. But suddenly we were kind of allies for an hour or two.' She nodded, drawing on the cigarette. 'Strange thing about a moment like that between two people. You notice things that you'd always known of course, but it hadn't really hit where it hurts.'

'What sort of things?'

'Like what a pretty woman you are.'

'That hurts?'

'Sometimes,' he said.

'I'm sorry, Cy. I didn't mean to be smart.'

He reached his arm around her shoulders. For a moment she hesitated, then yielded to the faint pressure of his arm. As she turned towards him, she felt his free hand slide under her silk jacket, his palm opening slowly to enclose her breast. 'Just stay like that,' he said. 'Just relax a few moments, and we'll go back.' He made no attempt to kiss her. No attempt beyond the faintest movement of his hand to caress her breast.

But she could feel herself melting towards him. *I am Sunny's sister*, she said to herself. *This man is Sunny's husband. His hand beneath my jacket, moving now, sliding below the scooped front of my dress.* 'No,' she said, as the tips of his fingers fanned across her bare flesh. 'No, Cy. Take me home. Take me home now, Cy.'

He withdrew his hand slowly. 'You're sure, Mary. You're sure you want to go back?'

All she felt now was a sort of numb fatigue. 'Yes,' she said. 'Please, Cy.'

He leaned across and kissed her on the forehead. 'Give me one minute,' he said. 'I've got something to pick up from the office.'

He was away a few minutes. Enough for her to repeat to herself four or five times: there's no justification for the risk. It's not love, it's lust. There's no justification. But she was still hoping he'd say something more.

A few moments later he climbed back into the car and threw something on to the rear seat. 'OK,' he said, with a quick smile towards her. 'Let's go back and see the folks.'

Sunny stood in the big living room alone. She could hear the crunch of gravel outside as Cy's car drew up. It seemed to her a long time before the car doors slammed and footsteps approached the house. She hurried through to the hall, flicked on all the lights in the chandelier and pulled open the door.

Mary, her foot on the bottom step, and Cy staring up at her, caught in the blaze of light. 'Has something happened?' Mary said. She was looking across to Harker's car, seeing it for the first time. 'Sunny,' she looked at her sister's grim face. 'Is that Dr Harker's car?'

Sunny nodded, mouth clamped tight.

Mary hurried past her into the house. 'Has something happened to Fin?' She swung round. 'Tell me, for goodness' sake.'

Behind her Sunny exploded. 'And where were you if something had happened?'

'He's all right? Fin's all right?' Cy said gripping her arm.

Sunny nodded. 'He looked bad for a while,' her anger was subsiding slowly. 'He was breathing strangely. I thought maybe he was having a heart attack. Where were you?' There was less of a note of accusation in her voice.

'We drove into Meyerick,' Mary said.

'Had to pick up something from the office.' Cy waved the file. 'How is he now?'

Dr Harker was coming down the stairs. 'False alarm, this time, Mary,' he said.

'I'll go up and see him.' Mary walked past Harker towards the foot of the stairs.

'No point now,' Harker said. 'Leave him to sleep a little. He's vomited most of the alcohol. He'll be OK now.'

'I phoned the club an hour ago,' Sunny said grimly. 'Vic Impari told me you'd already left.'

Mary put her hand out to her sister. 'Slow down, Sunny,' she said. 'I didn't know Fin was that bad.' She found she was experiencing a real sense of virtue, as if it were her decision, not the chance mention of the sofa, that had prevented anything happening in Meyerick. Perhaps something showed in her voice.

Suddenly Sunny's face softened. 'I was worried. I guess I panicked.'

'OK, Sunny.' Cy came forward and put his arm round her. 'Our fault for leaving you alone.' He turned to Harker. 'We're grateful to you for coming over, John,' Cy said. 'It would have been too much for Sunny alone.'

'I *was* alone,' Sunny said, 'for the best part of two hours.' She watched the faint flush climb her sister's cheek and the same ugly suspicions came back to her. Was it possible? Was it even remotely possible? Her sister, the steady, conventional Mary Page Butler. Was it possible she had spent the last hour screwing her brother-in-law on the office sofa?

Dr Harker was going. 'I'll call in tomorrow. I want him to go for a complete medical, everything. But I know Fin. By tomorrow he'll be asking you what all the hassle is about.'

'I'll make sure he doesn't,' Mary said. 'I know it's important.' She took him to the door and thanked him again.

'I've had a rough night,' she heard Sunny say to Cy. 'Are you coming to bed?'

'Sure,' Cy said casually. 'I'll be up.'

'I mean like now,' Sunny snapped.

When they had gone upstairs Mary went up to check on Fin. He was sleeping peacefully enough, snoring gently, his face relaxed and youthful. She felt a rush of emotion for him. Not really love perhaps, but a great surge of friendliness. Bending forward she kissed him on the forehead, the first time her lips had touched him in more than a year. Then she returned downstairs and walked through the house into the kitchen and made herself coffee.

Did Sunny suspect? But suspect what? After all nothing had happened. She sipped the hot coffee. She was trembling again. She wanted to run upstairs and shake Sunny and tell her nothing had happened. And that nothing ever would. *Ever.*

But of course she couldn't do that. First because it would confirm any suspicions Sunny might have. And second because she didn't know if it was true.

10

Seated in the Thai Airlines short-haul from Bangkok, Max Benning could see below him the tiny shapes of fishing boats on the grey-blue sea. They had already begun the long shallow descent on Ho Chi Minh City's Tan Son Nhut airport. As they banked lower he could see that the fishing fleets were distinguished by different sails, a slack heavy red sail in the boats to starboard, a dull white a few miles ahead and closest to the coast a strangely shaped black sail, a wind-filled rhomboid of canvas.

As the undercarriage thumped down for the landing, Max looked out across the paddy fields and blue hills fleeing away behind his line of sight. A dusty single-track road built high on an embankment cut across the paddies and headed for the hills. He found himself already overwhelmed by the sadness of the country and by the sense that the dead on both sides, East and West were somehow present in this strangely forlorn landscape.

Did Max feel this because he knew his father had felt these things? His mother had given him a small pack of his father's letters before he left. He remembered by heart the lines of a letter Peter Benning had written to his wife during the French war from a foxhole at Dien Bien Phu: 'We shall certainly be defeated here – that is as it should be. We are trying to destroy an ancient tradition. There will be no peace for either side until the end of the century.'

The wheels hit the ground and the pilot put the engines into reverse thrust. His father wrote with a strange apocalyptic foresight. Peace still evaded the tortured people of this land. And the memory of the war was still not effaced from the life of millions of Americans. But it now seemed the Vietnamese government was about to make the first stumbling overtures towards the West. Their leaders had watched the Soviet empire crumble in Europe.

Without Western aid they saw the writing on the wall for themselves.

The letter Max had received from Ho Chi Minh City had been remarkably frank: 'We are aware of the dangers of corruption among some provincial officials. The trial of Quatch will be open to Western journalists. It will prove once and for all that the government is striving towards an open, democratic Vietnam.' For Max a postscript had been added to the letter sent to other journalists. For his work in tracing and rescuing Vietnamese antiquities during the war, Peter Benning was to be posthumously decorated with the Ho Chi Minh Star. Max was asked to be present to accept it.

Leaving the air conditioning of the plane Max stepped into air like a thick soup. Widely travelled as he was, he had not experienced this degree of heat and humidity outside a sauna. A big Australian journalist behind him said: 'Up in the jungle it's different. Worse. My name's Hunter.'

Max indicated the card pinned to his shirt. 'Benning,' he said. They shook hands.

Around them milled a group of Western journalists carrying cameras and camera bags. They stood together for a moment on the oil-stained concrete apron. A long fascia board across low concrete buildings read: TAN SON NHUT AIRPORT, and underneath: WELCOME TO HO CHI MINH CITY.

'They're a very courteous nation,' Hunter said. 'Don't take it personally.'

From the airport bus, old and bouncing on its springs, Max looked out at the former city of Saigon spread before them under cloud seeping from the sky over the shoulders of a north-east monsoon. From ground level the interminable paddy fields, pocket handkerchiefs of flooded land between green embankments, looked desolate and uncared for. A freshly painted American tank, its turret half blown away, stood by the roadside in a square of neat whitened rope.

At a hotel in the city outskirts, the bus stopped. Duffel bag hooked over his shoulder, Max stood in line waiting to get off. As he reached the doorway he stepped down on to the hotel forecourt and stopped, looking towards the hotel. The man behind him eased him aside. Max grunted an apology. He was looking at a group of Vietnamese standing in the doorway of the hotel. Mostly he was looking at the remarkable Amerasian girl in a sleeveless pink high-necked blouse. As he watched, the leader of the Vietnamese welcoming party crossed towards the visiting journalists filing off the bus and began introducing himself and his assistant interpreters.

'Mr Benning,' Nan Luc said. 'Welcome to Vietnam.' He watched the muscles flicker up the olive-smooth arm as she held out her hand to him. Her face was composed, blank. 'I'm Nan Luc,' she said. 'I've been assigned to look after you during your stay.'

The possibility of seeing her again was certainly in his mind when he accepted the Vietnamese government invitation, but he had never dreamed it would happen like this, moments after arriving in Saigon. He looked at her, remembering the impression she had made on him in Paris, seeing her as you might a hologram, flickering from Asian to Westerner at the slightest movement of her head. He shook her hand. It was long-fingered, with carefully shaped, polished nails.

She led him towards the hotel. 'What happened in Paris?' he said, as soon as they were out of earshot of the others. 'Did I cause trouble for you?'

Nan smiled a greeting to another of the interpreters as they passed. 'My grandmother had me recalled,' Nan said. 'She was afraid, for Quatch's sake, of reviving interest in your father.'

'Are you saying Quatch was responsible for my father's death?'

She shook her head. 'That's not a charge at the trial. Nevertheless I think the Chief Prosecutor, Van Khoa, believes it's so.'

They were entering the hotel. 'Will we get a chance to talk?' he asked her.

'Later,' she said. 'You'll want to take a shower. I'll show you to your room. Then maybe you would like to meet in the bar. Trin Lo is a kilometre or two from here.'

'Trin Lo?'

She looked up at him. 'Trin Lo is the village where the monument has been erected in honour of your father,' she said.

'A monument?'

'He was an extraordinary man,' Nan Luc said.

'So I'm beginning to understand.'

'During the worst fighting at Hue he entered the old Imperial library and brought out many hundreds of kilos of historical documents and artifacts. Vietnam is indebted to him.'

After Max had taken a cold shower and changed, Nan Luc met him in the bar. There was no barman and the room, like the rooms above, showed damp patches on the ceiling and curling leaves of paint coming off the walls. The other newsmen were just arriving in groups or with their various assigned interpreters. Hunter, the Australian, detached himself and brought his drink over to the table with Nan Luc and Max.

'Tell us about you, Nan Luc,' Hunter said. He looked like a huge, lecherous schoolboy.

'That would not be helpful,' she said firmly. 'Mr Benning and myself have a visit to make before supper. There is little time.' She turned to Max. 'We have a jeep outside,' she said. 'When you're ready, Mr Benning.'

Outside the hotel they got into the jeep. He waited until she pulled the vehicle out of the courtyard before he spoke. 'After Paris I always hoped we'd meet again. It seemed pretty unlikely.'

'I believed we would.' He looked at her in surprise. Perhaps she had surprised herself with the vehemence with which she had said it. 'So much is changing in Vietnam,' she added quickly. 'Men like Van Khoa are coming to the top. He is not like Quatch. He is an honest man.'

She drove the jeep carefully through the massed bicycles and velo taxis out along the boulevard towards the suburb of Cholon. Decaying French colonial villas were set back from the road. Many seemed gutted and empty, others were the homes of a dozen families whose children played in the puddles of the drive or hauled bundles of firewood cut from the overgrown gardens.

She pointed to a large, decaying building set back behind iron railings, a typical nineteenth-century French barrack building. 'That's where I grew up,' she said. 'Orphanage Number 7.'

'Were your family all killed in the war?' he asked her. 'Except your grandmother?'

'My mother was killed. I believe I have an aunt in the United States.' He noticed she made no mention of her father. For a few moments they drove in silence. 'I'm happy to be the one to take you to this place,' Nan Luc said. 'For us such a monument is a great honour.'

The wind, bouncing off the jeep's windshield lifted her hair behind her neck. He wondered who *her* father was.

'For me it's not quite the same,' he said. 'Since I've no memory of my father.'

She glanced at him quickly before turning her eyes back to the road. 'But you *know* about him,' she said. 'Perhaps you have no recollection of him, but you have something at least, even if only the recollection of others.'

He knew by the way she spoke that she was talking about herself. 'Your own father,' he said, cautiously, 'do you know if he's still alive?'

She turned the jeep past some chickens pecking in the roadway. 'Perhaps, some day,' she said, 'I will find out.'

Max steadied himself with a hand on the top of the windshield as she made a wide turn on to a dirt road wet with leaves and slush. The grey sky pressed low on the treetops on either side of the track. Somewhere ahead he could see figures moving before a cooking fire and a jumble of outbuildings that had been extended by corrugated tin roofs and packing-case walls.

'This is Trin Lo,' Nan said. 'It's still called a village but really it's just another part of the city.' She stopped the jeep suddenly, slewing left across the mud and leaves. 'I'm sorry,' she said, her smile illuminating the mournful surroundings. 'I must call the headman.' She hit the horn several times until a procession of children, some carrying lanterns on sticks, walked sedately from the shanty village at the end of the track. Behind them came a group of men in shorts and shirts.

Nan Luc introduced them by name. The headman she said was Mr Ky. He stepped forward and extended his hand. 'Honour to the son of Peter Benning,' he said.

'You knew my father, Mr Ky?' Max asked him as they shook hands.

'I regret no,' Ky said. 'Most of the war I commanded a company in the Da Nang sector. Your father served the revolution in what was then Saigon.' Ky gestured towards the trees by the side of the road. 'Please come this way, Mr Benning.'

A wide path had been hacked through the bushes. Max and

Nan Luc followed Ky and his delegation and were in turn followed by the children squelching barefoot along the path. After about twenty or thirty yards Ky stopped. Gravel had been strewn to the depth of an inch or two across a broad rectangle of cleared ground by the side of the track. In the centre of the rectangle lay a plain slab of reddish stone on which were incised the name, Peter Benning, the dates, 1930–1975, and a line in Vietnamese.

'It says,' Nan Luc stepped forward, 'An honoured comrade of the War of Independence.'

Max nodded and walked to the side of the stone. He had no way of telling whether the emotion rippling through him was real or not. He raised his eyes past the red stone. The outline of a house was just visible through the trees. Even in the dusk he could see, from the black holes where the windows had once been, that it had been gutted by fire.

'The house,' he pointed to the burnt out villa. 'Who lived there?'

'For some years your father lived there,' Ky said.

'Alone?'

'The village people say that from time to time they saw a companion. But your father was not often at the house.'

'Can I go and see it?'

'Sadly there is now no trace of his occupation. But there are plans to make of it a small museum to his memory. For the present there will be a ceremony here beside the grave. There will be an honour guard and photograph for the international press.'

Max looked from Ky's face to the stone and back to the leathered expressionless features of the headman. Then he turned to Nan Luc. 'What does this inscription on the side say?'

'In English it sounds odd,' she said in some confusion. 'Perhaps a little flowery.'

'That's OK,' he said.

'It reads: A true hero of the people who delivered the Vietnamese past from the hands of the convicted traitor Quatch.'

Max stared at the flowing writing on the stone. The *convicted traitor* Quatch! Before Quatch is even brought to trial? He turned to face her. 'I think you believe that in the West we were all born yesterday.'

'I don't understand,' she said in alarm.

'Thank you, Mr Ky.' Max nodded brusquely to the headman and strode back towards the jeep.

Nan followed quickly after him. He swung himself up and stood in the seat well as she got up behind the wheel. 'Let's find somewhere we can get a drink,' he said. 'Not the hotel.'

'You're angry.'

'Of course I'm angry,' he said. 'I get the feeling that the purpose of that monument has not much to do with my father and a lot to do with underlining Quatch's guilt. What happened to Van Khoa's fair trial? Maybe Quatch is guilty of all he's charged with and more. But when the state orders a stonemason to chip out the verdict before the trial even begins, I wonder what the hell all these Western newsmen are doing here. I'll pass that on to the newsmen. Perhaps you'll pass it on to Van Khoa?'

They sat in a narrow courtyard. Under a bamboo awning bare-bulb lights threw shadows across their faces. An old woman served them two mugs of weak coffee.

He felt the sudden icy chill in her voice. 'Perhaps you believe that all the charges against Quatch are fabricated for political reasons, Mr Benning?'

'What the hell do I know?' he said. 'I just thought that guilt or innocence was a matter to be decided by trial.'

'Listen,' she said carefully. 'Corruption has been part of Vietnamese life for centuries. The French took it over from the emperors, the Americans took it over from the French. Some people in this government, people like Van Khoa, believe it must be eradicated.'

'However doubtful the means?'

'Be more forgiving, Mr Benning. What you've just seen is a blunder of a primitive system of justice. But I can promise you, I know Van Khoa. He aims at justice.'

'OK,' he shrugged doubtfully.

'Van Khoa is convinced Quatch is guilty of the charges against him.'

'Are you?'

She met his eyes. 'I believe Quatch capable of any crime you can imagine.'

'Is that what your grandmother told you?'

'No.'

He hesitated. 'You mean you know that from your own experience?'

'Yes.'

He looked into her wide eyes, knowing that she had entrusted him with a confidence which, however little understood, bound them together.

11

In the heavy early morning rain the gleaming ancient green Paris
single decker looked misleadingly new. It was more than half full
of foreign journalists as Max got in outside the hotel. The Americans settled down to play cards at the back of the bus; Hunter and
a British cameraman talked about cricket; the French discussed the
dinner they had been subjected to the night before and Max sat
alone in a front seat. The interpreters and the two men from the
Vietnam Press Agency had left by separate bus an hour before.

The first part of the journey south-west, crossing the Mekong
estuaries to Can Tho, perhaps a hundred and fifty kilometres in
all, took ten hours. Though most of the narrow-laned highway
was asphalted, they were obliged, for reasons no one even tried to
explain, to take hour-long detours. Off the highway the slashing,
incessant rain turned the single-track, boarded roads into quag-
mires as yellow mud was forced up between the split logs of the
road surface by the weight of the bus. Slithering dangerously from
side to side they drove between patchwork fields, or thin stunted
woods, the blue black humps of the hills always to the north.

At midday when they were given sandwiches and a can of beer,
Max looked up to see a broad-shouldered, middle-aged American
reporter standing next to his seat.

'Mind if I join you?' the man said. 'My name's Bolson. Hal
Bolson. You're Max Benning, aren't you?'

Max moved his bag aside. 'Sit down,' he said.

Bolson slumped into the seat and peered across Max out of the
window. 'Never really thought I'd be here again,' he said.

For a few moments they talked in a desultory way about Saigon
in the last violent glittering months of the war, the cafés, the
hotels and bars the journalists used. 'I came across your father a
few times before the end,' Bolson said. Max looked at him in

surprise. 'Nothing strange about it,' Bolson said. 'I didn't know him well but we all used the same places, newsmen, hustlers, Vietcong agents. We were parasites, Max. Not your father. But the rest of us lived off each other.'

'What was he like, my father?'

'Big good-looking guy like you. But very, very tough. Not like you I'd guess.'

'No,' Max smiled, 'not like me.'

'He did crazy things. No wonder the Viets are giving him a monument. He pulled half their history out of the ruins.'

Max smiled. 'I take it there's a degree of exaggeration there.'

'A degree,' Bolson conceded. 'I knew Quatch too,' he added casually.

'Do you think he killed my father?'

'Probably. Your father pursued him to Paris, and that was the only way out for Quatch.'

'Did you like him?'

'Your father? He wasn't an easy man, you understand. There was almost a religious sense of purpose about him. He could drink any of us under the table, but he'd still have an ear open for a clue to a manuscript or piece of statuary he was tracking.' Bolson pushed himself up out of his seat. 'We'll be seeing more of each other, Max,' he said and made his way back down the aisle.

At Can Tho they stayed the night in a long palm-thatched schoolroom on the outskirts of the town. Here US Army cots had been provided and clean sheets and blankets. Dinner in the teachers' room met the qualified approval of even the French. There were a few bottles of wine and even some whisky. It was, altogether, a more comfortable night than the one before.

Dawn the next morning saw them climbing back into the bus under a cloudless sky. The road was now straight and asphalted and travelling west they reached the border of Cahn Roc province in less than two hours.

The night before, at dinner, Nan Luc had explained the geography of the region. Cahn Roc was a small, poor province on both sides of the Cahn Roc River. The road they would be following ran alongside the river through mango swamps until they reached higher ground. This was the most prosperous part of Cahn Roc, a plateau where mining and timber were the principal occupations. From this plateau they would be able to see, on the coast, the small port and provincial capital, Cahn Roc, and beyond it the Gulf of Thailand.

Arriving at the provincial capital they drove through the outskirts of the tiny town, mostly through narrow roads awash with floodwater from the days or months before. The houses were a shambles of small French administrators' villas and more recent rusted tin structures. There seemed to be cultivated strips and patches between every building from which women with conical straw hats looked up, shielding their eyes from the rays of the setting sun.

They swung round on a cobbled road through the port with its mass of fishing boats being prepared for the night's fishing and stopped in the main square of solid colonial buildings. Each was easily identifiable: an old Catholic convent or monastery, perhaps; the Palais de Justice, now the People's Court; and along one side of the square a barracks, damaged by shellfire, windowless but with washing hanging from strings across the gaping holes. A gigantic puddle filled a large part of the centre of the paved square and the palm trees outside the courthouse looked bowed and battered by the rains.

The bus pulled up outside the hotel building which occupied the fourth side of the square. There had been no attempt to change the French name. It was still the Grand Hotel. Its yellow stucco walls were peeling in large patches, its balcony ironwork was red with rust. On a side wall a barely legible painted advertisement promoted the aperitif 'Suze'.

'Let's ask them if they can get this trial through before the weekend,' Hunter said, surveying the square with a horrified grimace. A sudden rain squall struck them and he dragged his duffel bag and equipment into the Grand Hotel with Max behind him.

'Listen,' one of the British newsmen was saying in the hotel lobby to Nan Luc, 'I thought this trial was taking place in Saigon.'

'Quatch was administrator in Cahn Roc,' she told him. 'It seemed more appropriate to hold it here.'

'There's not much going on in Cahn Roc at night?'

'Oh plenty,' Max heard Nan Luc say.

'Music, clubs?'

'Political discussions,' Nan said with mock seriousness, 'diamat lectures.'

'What do *you* do in the evening?' the journalist pressed.

'I get ready for the next day, monsieur.' She turned away. As she walked past Max a faint wry smile, aimed only at him, touched her lips. He followed her out into the *place*.

Dusk was falling and the old French lamps threw a thin yellow light through the palm trees on to the flooded square. He felt as if they were walking round the edges of a Chinese lake, the fountain in the middle rising from the water, the peeling neglect of all the surrounding buildings hidden by the darkness.

'Do you live here, in Cahn Roc?' Max asked her.

'I live down by the port. I have a room in the old harbour-master's tower.'

'Sounds very picturesque.'

She put her face to one side and smiled. 'It will be a long time before Vietnam can afford to indulge the picturesque.'

'The war was over fifteen years ago,' he said. 'That's a long time.'

She stopped, her head down, looking into the reflections in the still water. What she said so echoed his father's letter that he turned his head in surprise. 'It will take more than this century,' she said, 'to bring peace to the people of Vietnam.' He knew that by peace she didn't just mean the absence of war.

They continued on slowly round the *place*. They were opposite the Grand Hotel now, looking back on the lighted windows and the figures of the journalists moving behind them.

'Is it true that New York is a dirty city? That garbage blows through the streets?' she asked.

'It's a year or two since I was there but I don't think things have changed too much.'

'And the roads are pitted and pot-holed like the roads of Saigon?'

'Some of them.'

'And black Americans are discriminated against?'

'There's discrimination, sure.'

'There's discrimination here too,' she said. 'Against people of Chinese descent. Against anyone with European or American blood.'

'How old were you when the Americans left?'

'I was six years old.'

'You remember nothing at all of the American past?'

She shrugged. 'Perhaps I have memories, I don't know. Children fabricate the past to suit themselves.'

Max had a strong sense of trespassing into another human being's dream. They walked on in silence until he nodded to the road running down to the harbour, the Rue du Port. 'Are you going home now?'

'Yes.'

'Let me walk you back.' They began to walk down the steep, cobbled road towards the port.

'I hope you will be satisfied by the trial,' she said. 'Van Khoa has put a lot into preparing it.'

'Does it matter if I'm satisfied?'

'To me it does.'

She almost slipped on the glistening cobbles and he put out a hand to catch her arm, holding her a moment longer than was necessary.

They walked on, the red moon tingeing the sea the deep dark colour of blood. 'I mean that I hope you'll be satisfied that justice will be done to your father's memory.'

'Like I told you. I don't have any memory of my father,' he said. 'Of course I want to see justice done. But in court. Not in Van Khoa's office a week before the trial. You understand that.'

She nodded, her eyes on the reflections on the cobblestones. In front of them there were a few lights and the movement of small boats across the harbour. She was frowning in an effort to understand. Her face turned towards the *lune rousse*. 'What could be more important than justice done to your father's memory?' she said. She had slowed to a stop.

Equally baffled he stood opposite her on the edge of the quayside. He could see the harbourmaster's tower rising from the end of the jetty. 'I told you. I've no memory of my father. I never knew him.'

'But what difference does that make? You can honour him as your father, surely. You will not be able to imitate his acts. But you can still honour him.'

'The West is different,' Max said. 'More prosaic. We want to know what the acts of the father were before we honour them.'

'Perhaps I understand you,' she said. 'But for us justice is necessary because it brings revenge. And revenge is necessary because it brings peace.' She pointed up to the tower. 'Thank you for walking me home.'

'I'll see you tomorrow,' he said. 'You'll be in court?'

'Of course.' She turned and walked along the jetty, swaying as if she were walking in a light wind. When she reached the tower she turned and saw he was still there. Then she opened the door and disappeared inside.

He stood for a moment until the gleam of a lamp appeared in one of the windows high in the tower. He wasn't unaware of the poetry, of the fabled princess in the Gothic tower. But he had never imagined he would have to come halfway round the world to find her.

12

Mary Page Butler watched the hot summer road slipping away under the tyres of Cy's Mercedes. He had not spoken since he picked her up at Page Corner. Despite her own efforts she had received little more than a few grunts in response.

'Sunny's visiting with the Kellermans this weekend, isn't she?' Mary said.

He nodded absently and Mary retreated into her own thoughts as Cy drove, far too fast, towards the club.

She had been confident he would be pleased she called. Of course she knew Sunny was away. Obviously, at least to her, she was making some movement towards him. She was saying: Well, maybe I did shut the door the night of the Fund luncheon but it's not locked and barred. She frowned angrily at her own coy imagery. She was a middle-aged woman, she could face facts. What she was telling Cy by this morning's phone call was that she wanted him to take up where he had left off. Slowly. Not at a speed she couldn't handle. A mild flirtation. Nothing more.

But he wasn't interested. He had grunted agreement to picking her up for the meeting at the club but there had been not the slightest indication that he saw it as anything but a chore. A chore imposed upon him by his sister-in-law.

Anger rose in her. 'You're driving too fast, Cy,' she said as they swerved past a small pick-up truck and swept along the grass verge on the wrong side.

'You want to get to this meeting?'

She decided to forgo the obvious rejoinder. What was wrong with him? Was he angry about the night outside his office? He hadn't seemed angry before. Or was he feeling that she was blowing hot and cold, a sort of tease. Of course she knew what sort of tease she was talking about but she kept the word out of

her head. In any case the idea of a middle-aged woman being that
sort of tease was faintly ridiculous.

She decided to ask him. 'All right, Cy,' she said, lighting a
cigarette, 'what is it?'

'What's what?'

'What have I done to offend you?'

'Nothing, as far as I know.'

'Then why the grim looks, the driving on the wrong side of the
road . . . ? Was it because I sent Fin off to play polo this weekend?'

It was so long before he answered that she thought he had
relapsed into another prolonged silence. 'Fin's away playing polo?'
he said finally.

'I already told you.'

'Light me a cigarette, will you, Mary?' he said in his friendliest
tone so far.

She lit him a cigarette and handed it to him. As he inhaled she
felt the car slow. This was better. 'So what are you angry about,
Cy?'

'Not angry.'

'What then?'

'Oliver called this morning and told me you were resigning
from the committee.'

'I've been thinking about it for a long time.' She looked at him.
'Is that what was upsetting you?'

He shrugged. 'I suppose I thought it was because of what
happened after the club luncheon.'

'No,' she said carefully. 'I'd been thinking about it for months.'

'Because I promise you, Mary, I won't step out of line again.'

She felt a flare of panic. This was not a promise she was looking
for. 'What's a mild flirtation among old friends,' she said lightly.
Old friends, not brother- and sister-in-law.

'It's a hell of a time to be resigning.' Cy reverted to the subject.
'There are some tough moments on the horizon. We're going to
be facing some of the problems this morning.'

She decided not to get side-tracked about the agenda. 'My note
to Oliver was just an informal warning that I was thinking it was
time I left,' she said. 'If you think this is a bad time, I've no
objection to staying on for a month or two.'

'I have a feeling I'm going to need all the support I can get, Mary. If you'd put the resignation on hold . . .'

She touched his arm. 'For a month or two. OK?'

'OK.' He turned to her and grinned. But, to Mary, his mouth was tight with the effort he made. Not as it was the night he had kissed her. Not as it was the night he had plunged his tongue deep into her mouth.

Driving fast through the club gates he swung into the parking lot. As he got out of the driver's seat to open the car door for her she weighed the possibility of one more effort. Fin didn't play polo and Sunny didn't visit with friends every weekend. She let her skirt ride like a twenty-year-old as he opened her door but Cy was looking across at the club entrance. Mrs Rose and her son Jason were standing under the awning talking to Colonel Savary.

Cy waved to them. Mary pulled down her skirt and got out of the car. Standing in the sunlight she could feel his impatience to start towards the entrance.

In the tourette room the members of the Meyerick Fund Committee took their cue from Cy Stevenson's worried, abstracted expression. While they waited for the Reverend Hector Hand to arrive, Cy stood alone at the window, hands deep in his pockets. The moment Hector Hand entered the room Cy swung round and moved towards his seat. The reverend raised a palm in greeting, received no response and with mumbled apologies sat down.

There was a scraping of chair legs on the polished plank floor. As it faded into silence Cy said: 'Emergency meeting of the Meyerick Fund is in session.'

'I think this is the first emergency meeting we've had since my husband founded the society,' Mrs Rose said. 'He was, as you know, a very organised person. I think he felt generally that emergency meetings were a bad thing.'

'He was a careful man,' Hector Hand said. 'Careful as well as caring.'

'I've called you together,' Cy said, 'because of the very serious situation that has developed. I think by now you probably all know the nature of the problem.'

Mary looked blankly at him. The others, she was aware, seemed to be nodding in agreement. 'What is the problem, Cy?' She frowned. Why hadn't Cy said anything in the car?

'Quatch has been arrested and brought to trial.'

'What are the charges?' Mrs Rose asked.

'We're dealing with a totalitarian state,' Cy said. 'I don't imagine the precise charges matter a lot.'

'They might,' George Savary said. His presence was heavy in the room, his eyes seldom seemed to leave Cy's face. 'I must remind you, Cy, that there'll be Western journalists there.'

'Exactly,' Cy said. 'It's a show trial. Quatch has been accused of a whole bag of crimes. That's the way a government like this operates. Plenty of foul weather cover.'

'It would help to know the precise charges,' Mary said. 'If you know them, that is, Cy.' She kept her voice low and unhurried but she was wondering how long he had known about this development.

'The charges,' Cy said, 'would, I guess, fill several pages. I don't have access to that information. All I know from a limited newspaper piece and a few enquiries is that the principal charges relate to various offences described as abuse of power.'

'In other words, corruption,' Savary said.

Cy nodded briskly. 'Corruption.'

'So what are we faced with?' Hector Hand asked. He was considering his reputation.

'We're faced with the trial of Quatch,' Cy said, pouring himself a glass of water. 'We're faced with the fact that he will undoubtedly admit that he received payments from an American fund. Possibly, even probably, our fund will be mentioned in court.'

'This is serious,' Hand said. 'Will Quatch say that the payments were passed on to the coastguard and the like to facilitate the escape of refugees?'

'What do you think, Hector?' Cy said, tipping back on his chair. 'In Vietnam today, you're better off accepting the rap for pure corruption – dollars in a Swiss bank – than a political offence. Treason.'

'It will seem therefore that we are paying this Mr Quatch for no visible reason,' Mrs Rose said. 'Surely nobody on either side will believe that.'

'No,' Cy said slowly. 'My guess is that in order to keep it

personal, in order to avoid a capital sentence for treason, Quatch will claim the money was being paid to him for other reasons.'

'What sort of other reasons, Cy?' Mary said, watching him carefully.

'We can't tell at the moment. Could be any wild story, Mary. And now,' Cy got up and lifted the phone, 'I don't know about the rest of you but I could use a drink.'

'My husband specifically ruled out drinks during a trust session,' Mrs Rose said sharply. 'A celebration like last time, he considered outside the basic rule. But essentially he believed that alcohol blunts the judgement.'

'Since this is an emergency session I guess the formal rules don't apply,' Jason Rose said. 'Why don't you just order yourself up a drink, Cy?'

Cy spun in his chair. 'Anybody else?'

'Sure, I'll take a scotch and water,' Jason said. His mother subsided in her chair.

'OK.' Cy gave his orders over the phone and sat down.

'I don't mind telling you I'm worried, Cy. Concerned,' Hector Hand said.

'I think we all are,' Jason said. 'We all appreciate we could be in for some pretty ugly publicity.'

'As of this moment,' Cy said, 'we don't even know whether the Meyerick Fund will be mentioned by name. But in the meantime I've given our bank orders to despatch nothing more to Switzerland.'

Mrs Rose fixed Cy with her withering look. 'What do we do now?'

'We wait,' Cy said. 'We wait until we discover what wild accusations Quatch is going to bring against us.'

'You anticipate wild accusations?' Savary said.

'I do,' Cy said briskly. 'For the reasons I've given.'

'Can you guess what sort of wild accusations?' Savary was making it obvious to everybody round the table that he was probing.

'I'm not a Vietnamese politician,' Cy snapped.

A knock on the door broke the silence. Vic Impari entered and served Cy and Jason with their drinks.

Pausing until Impari had left, Cy let his eyes move across the faces of the trustees. 'No point in trying to disguise the fact that we're about to enter heavy waters.'

'And when that happens?' Savary said.

'When that happens,' Cy finished his drink in a final mouthful, 'we close ranks and refute any Vietnamese allegations. *We* all know what the money was given for.'

Mary found herself nodding vigorously. Her eyes came to rest on George Savary, angrily hunched forward. 'I agree,' Mary said firmly. 'This is the time for everybody on this committee to give Cy our full support.' She turned back to Oliver Digweed. 'I want you to destroy the letter I sent you, Oliver. This is no time for committee resignations.'

'Quite a meeting,' Cy said.

Mary stood on the veranda in her tennis skirt, a white sweater knotted round her shoulders. 'Quite a meeting,' she said, sipping a long glass of iced fresh orange.

'I didn't get a chance to say thank you for your vote,' Cy said.

'It's not really a matter of thanks.'

'Sure,' he said, 'but . . . I'd like to do something. Maybe drive up to Woodstock, buy you lunch.'

'That *would* start the tongues wagging,' she laughed.

'What the eye doesn't see the tongue can't wag about.'

She felt her neck flushing. She was desperately tempted. 'No,' she said. 'It wouldn't be right, Cy.'

His blue eyes opened wide. 'Of course it wouldn't. Otherwise we'd be talking about having lunch here. In plain sight.'

Her legs seemed to be trembling. 'You're not talking about lunch.'

'Not just lunch.'

'Oh my God,' she said involuntarily. It was of course why she had encouraged Fin to go away for the weekend. But now that the moment had come she found herself as off-balance as any teenager.

'Oh my God yes. Or, oh my God no?' Cy lifted his eyebrows.

She took a deep breath. 'No, Cy. Definitely oh my God, no.'

13

In the wide, ornate courtroom of Cahn Roc, the trial of Monsieur Quatch opened at midday. The invited journalists sat behind a rail in an enclosed area on the left which may have been the jury box in the distant past. Among them interpreters were arranged at intervals. As the court assembled Max watched from his corner seat in the railed box as Nan Luc entered by the rear swing doors.

She was wearing a high necked dark green shirt and black linen trousers that outlined her legs as she walked. Reaching the rail she ducked under it and took the seat beside him, then she turned and without speaking raised her eyebrows to him in greeting.

'Hi,' he said. 'I was wondering where you were going to be sitting.'

'Next to Mr Benning,' she said, 'for however long the trial lasts, I'm afraid.'

There were no spectators. When the three judges had taken their seats and Van Khoa and his assistant prosecutors and the recording clerks were in position, the courtroom still seemed empty. For the moment no one seemed prepared to begin the proceedings then, from the corner of his eye, Max saw a movement at the back of the court. A small man, tieless, in a pale suit and with thinning grey hair, gave a brisk nod of his head. Professor Cao, the presiding judge, seemed to acknowledge it. He cleared his throat and lifted his head importantly. 'The court is in session,' he intoned. 'Bring in the prisoner.'

Max sat hunched forward over his notebook. The rain which had started again during the night now beat incessantly on the court-room windows. Within the high ceilinged room an expectant silence directed all faces towards the tall double panelled door at the side of the judges' bench. Max turned his head to Nan Luc beside him but her eyes too were fixed on the door.

'Members of the Western press,' Professor Cao said. 'It has been decided, for your benefit, that his trial shall be conducted as much as possible in English. The reason for this is simple. In the climate of calumny and distortion that surrounds every peace-loving act of the Vietnamese Republic, the government wishes it to be clear that the prisoner Quatch is receiving a fair trial. We rely on you, distinguished members of the Western press, to report a fair trial fairly.'

Pleased with his short speech, the Professor called again: 'Bring in the prisoner.'

For a moment the rain stopped beating against the windows, the sudden quiet compounding the silence in the courtroom. Foot-steps on flagstones in a distant corridor announced the approach of the prisoner. The panelled door now opened and a young Vietnamese police officer entered the courtroom. A long thin chain swooped from a hook on his belt through the open doorway. Brought to a halt as the chain tightened, the young policeman turned with a peremptory high-pitched order and jerked hard twice on the chain.

Vo Tran Quatch stumbled forward, regained his balance and shuffled to the judges' bench. He was chained at the ankles and wrists. His cheeks, no longer plump, hung below the jawline in folds of loose flesh. He wore no jacket or tie but his white shirt was clean, the collar barely concealing the knotted scars that ran like a line of medallions round his throat.

Nan Luc's face was fixed with a look of loathing. For a moment it seemed as if the burden of hatred was too much for her and with a sudden movement she dropped her head and stared at the planked floor at her feet.

The presiding judge was leaning forward, whispering to Quatch and writing details as Quatch answered in an equally low voice. When Quatch was led away to stand behind the single, waist-high rail, the president said almost carelessly: 'The People's Court of Cahn Roc Province states that the prisoner Quatch pleads *guilty* to the charges of corruption and betrayal of the interests of the revolution.' Quatch stood at the bar flanked by two police-men. At the judge's words his mouth moved and he seemed to incline his head in agreement.

Van Khoa had risen to his feet. Reading from a script, his

laboured English contrasting with the fervour with which he spoke, he denounced Quatch for bringing disgrace and dishonour to the Republic of Vietnam, of abusing the authority vested in him, and, for good measure, of being responsible for the scurrilous news stories in the Western press accusing the Vietnamese government of condoning the corrupt practices of provincial officials.

Max had met Van Khoa the night before at the Grand Hotel. With Nan Luc's translations supplementing his limited English he had seemed to Max to be one of those tough, resilient cadres who had formed the backbone of the Vietcong during the past war. Now, in the echoing courtroom, he found it difficult to reconcile the Van Khoa of the night before with the ranting figure in the well of the court.

'God knows how long we've got of this,' Hunter muttered, 'and not a decent looking woman in sight. Except one, of course.' He nodded almost imperceptibly in the direction of Nan Luc. 'And she's spoken for.'

'Spoken for? Who by?' Max's voice was loud enough to cause Cao, the president, to lift his eyes towards the press section. 'Who by?' Max leaned close to Hunter.

'By the State Prosecutor of course.' Hunter kept his voice low. 'Did you see the way he acted towards the girl? Very polite.'

'So?'

'In this part of the world the men of power are even less deferential than where we come from. No, he's laying her. And he's enjoying it. Which,' Hunter added, 'comes as no surprise to anyone. She's delicious. Bad luck, sport.'

Van Khoa's opening denunciation lasted almost two hours. From what seemed a mass of speculation and abstractions, Max distilled the charges of betrayal of the revolution by the export and sale abroad of the nation's cultural heritage. There was no respite. After a short break in the early afternoon when tea and a hard, sour-tasting biscuit was served, the prosecution's denunciation of Quatch continued for another three hours, empty assertions unsupported by evidence. By now Van Khoa was alternating with his principal assistant, a small and unusually bald headed man in white shirt and grey shorts. His sandals clacking across the tiled courtroom floor he would run forward to hurl abuse at Quatch, then step quickly back as you might from a chained Doberman.

'Day One,' Hunter growled in Max's ear, 'and it's already looking more like a farce than anything else.' One of the judges hissed in Hunter's direction and he acknowledged the rebuke with a surly nod.

Van Khoa now occupied the well of the court. 'You have heard the charges described,' he said, addressing the judges. 'In the following days I will bring proof of Quatch's betrayal of the ideals of our revolution. For the moment, as Chief Prosecutor, I must state the penalty which the prosecution believes would be fitting. . .'

'Death,' Hunter intoned in a low rumble.

Van Khoa turned his back on the Westerners. 'It is our belief that men are not criminal in themselves,' he said. 'It is our belief that society is the criminal. In particular it is foreign society which has corrupted Quatch. In view of this belief,' Van Khoa turned to face Quatch, 'the prosecution asks the court for a sentence of seven years' re-education.'

Max felt Nan Luc move beside him and a stir of anger pass through her, but when he looked her face showed no emotion. He glanced quickly in the direction she was looking. A faint smile had appeared on Quatch's lips. He bowed his head to the court. To Max it was as if the court had just confirmed its side of a bargain. At six in the evening the president called the session at a close.

'My guess is that Quatch is very pleased with what the prosecution is asking for,' Hal Bolson said to Max as the foreign press filed out of the courtroom. 'In a closed session these charges would have carried death.'

'So why the leniency,' Max asked, 'if Quatch is guilty of all he's being charged with and more?'

Bolson hunched his shoulders. 'Because I guess this trial isn't really about Vo Tran Quatch. It's about Vietnam trying to make a good impression on the world. A modest degree of corruption uncovered, brought to open trial and punished with restraint.'

'You think Van Khoa wrote the scenario?'

'Van Khoa and the little grey-haired guy in the baggy cream suit at the back of the court. I think what we're seeing is a carefully contained version of the new Vietnamese justice. I hope you're impressed, young Max.'

The correspondents stood outside the courthouse under the dripping, broken fronds of the palm trees and looked with distaste across at the Grand Hotel.

'A mate of mine, who was here last year,' Hunter said, 'told me there's a sort of unofficial knocking shop in Can Tho.'

'What's a knocking shop?' a Frenchman asked.

'A bordello,' Max told him. 'A cat-house, a knocking shop.'

'Praise be to God,' the Frenchman said.

'They sell vodka for dollars, this mate of mine claimed,' Hunter told them.

'Can Tho must be a hundred K from here,' Hal Bolson said. 'Too far.'

'So we start now,' Hunter urged. 'We get back by dawn and we sleep it off in court.'

'Something tells me we're not going to miss a lot tomorrow,' someone put in from the back.

Max moved away from the group. Nan Luc was leaving the courtroom with Van Khoa. He watched them as they crossed the square towards the hotel. What signs, he wondered, would two Vietnamese give, that they were lovers?

He spent only a few minutes with her that evening. She had stopped him on the stairs just before dinner, a worried look on her face. 'One of the kitchen boys tells me the bus has gone,' she said anxiously.

Max nodded. 'Yes. It seems I'm dining alone tonight.'

'But the driver of the bus is still here,' she said, perplexed.

'When I saw it leave,' Max said as gently as possible, 'the Australian, Hunter, was driving it.'

She looked blank. 'But who authorised it? Colonel Khoa?'

'Does someone have to authorise it?' She was silent. 'Guests of the Vietnamese people,' he suggested. 'Gone for a night out. That's all.'

'Do you know where they've gone, Monsieur Benning?'

He considered the possibility that Van Khoa would send someone to bring them back, decided they had too long a start and said: 'I think they took the Can Tho road.'

'Can Tho?'

He nodded. 'Will this cause you trouble, Nan Luc?'

It was the first time he had used her name and she looked up at him, then quickly down at her short black skirt and sandalled feet. 'No,' she said. 'I am only responsible for you.'

'Then the rest have gone to Can Tho but I'm still here . . . what the hell?'

She looked up at him, saw he was smiling and burst into delighted laughter. 'All right, Monsieur Benning. What the hell!'

She was not in the dining room that evening and after an imitation French meal Max went up to his room. He had brought with him the slim pack of his father's letters given to him by his mother. Crossing to the window he looked out over the courthouse. He found it hard to accept that his father's murder would receive no mention in this trial. He began to riffle through the letters.

There was very little news in any of them. Some were written from captivity and described Peter Benning's growing devotion to the Vietnamese past. In the third or fourth letter Max paused. He had read the sentences before but they had had less of an impact. Now, re-reading, he came to believe that they actually summed up the essence of this mysterious man.

'Only by an irrational act,' Peter Benning had written, 'can the human being define himself. It can be an act of the utmost savagery or an act of love. It can be an act of apparent importance or of utter triviality. But only when the human being has fully committed himself to this act, will all others know him. And only then will he know himself.'

Max got up and paced the room. A total commitment, his father argued, to a woman, a people, a culture, a tree or a river, was the essence of being human. A single definitive act. His spine tingled and the hair on his neck seemed to rise. Throughout his life he had avoided commitment, had used freedom from commitment as an excuse. But in some way he knew now that he responded to his father's mad notion.

He had no doubt that he was already thinking ahead, thinking forward to when this trial ended, to the moment he would be faced with leaving Nan Luc.

An earsplitting thudding on the door jerked him upright. Outside in the corridor he heard shouts and running footsteps, whoops and deep laughter.

The newsmen had returned.

14

In the pillared entrance of the courthouse the next morning, Max stood on the top step and watched the silent, pale-faced journalists labour up the steps and into the entrance hall. He had not seen Nan Luc approach. She stopped and stood next to him on the courthouse steps.

'Do the Vietnamese drink?' Max asked her.

She nodded vigorously. 'A village celebration can be a very drunken affair.'

'What do they drink?'

'Mostly a locally brewed spirit called Lua Moi. Very strong.'

For a moment she watched the Westerners. 'Why didn't you go?' she asked suddenly.

'Shall I tell the truth?'

'Why not?'

'I didn't go because I'd hoped I might spend the evening with you.'

'This is not Paris, Mr Benning,' she said quietly. They stood for a moment looking at each other. Then Nan Luc turned sharply away. He moved to touch her arm but she shook her head. 'Not Paris, not New York or London. This is Cahn Roc, Mr Benning.' He had come to recognise her anxiety to cut short any moment growing between them. She looked towards the journalists.

'What do you think of this appalling sight?' Max asked lightly. 'The wages of sin, would you say?'

Suddenly she was laughing, grateful to him for having changed the mood. She stretched up, her hand on his arm. 'What I would say, Monsieur Benning,' she whispered in his ear, 'is *what the hell!*'

For Max the morning in court had a nightmare quality of repetition and irrelevance. Van Khoa's assistant prosecutor who delivered most of the morning's statements spent at least an hour on Quatch's Paris finances, establishing that his allowance from the then North Vietnamese was extremely modest. Against this he read from details of what he claimed were Quatch's bank account at the Crédit Marseillais. What might have been established in ten minutes, that Quatch had an extra source of income while he was in Paris, took over three hours. Throughout these statements Quatch sat on a small cane chair, his manacled hands in his lap, his expression unchanged from one of vague detached boredom. To Max it seemed as if he already considered the trial over.

Only after lunch was the froth of rhetoric suddenly blown away. 'The case of former comrade Quatch is a revolutionary tragedy.' Van Khoa suddenly reverted to normal tones. 'He was sent to Paris as a man of honour. Among the many tasks entrusted to him was to attempt to recover from museums and even private collectors as many as possible of the Vietnamese works of art which had been stolen from us during the period of French colonialism.' Van Khoa glanced towards Quatch, his mouth turning down. 'But the corruption of the West was already working on Quatch. He began to abandon the simple precepts of Ho Chi Minh. He began to dress in the finest Western clothes. To eat at the celebrated restaurants of Paris. To escort his concubine to the Opera or the horse races at Longchamps. He began to seek out even more dubious pleasures.'

Van Khoa turned his back on Quatch. 'But the corrupt life had to be paid for. And how was this to be done? A Paris museum had agreed to the return to us of an *objet d'art* of great beauty, an ivory screen from the Imperial Palace at Hue.' Van Khoa stopped. 'Through a certain antiquaire of the seventeenth arrondissement, Paris, a convicted receiver of stolen goods, Quatch disposed of the screen for his own profit. It was broken into individual pieces, comrades, this screen which was unique in Sino-Vietnamese history, and sold throughout the Western world. It was the first of many dealings Quatch was to have with this criminal Frenchman.'

'Were any of the prisoner's illegal profits brought back to this country?' one of the judges asked.

'When we searched the administrator's apartment on Avenue

Giap and his summer house on the river we recovered twenty-thousand US dollars,' Van Khoa said. 'The prisoner's claim is that this is all that remains of the considerable sums he made from the sale of antiquities in Paris.'

Before he could continue the court's attention was deflected by the low hiss of voices at the panelled door as an official was reluctantly allowed past by the soldiers. Crossing to Van Khoa he handed him a note. The court watched while the prosecutor read it and, with a long glance at Quatch, approached the president of the judges. An adjournment was immediately announced. Longer than the standard ten minutes, it stretched to twenty, then half an hour. A further announcement was then made. The newsmen were free to leave the court. The adjournment would last for a further hour. A new witness was to be called.

Outside in the square, Max sought out Nan Luc. She came towards him, biting her lip anxiously. 'Van Khoa has just told me that they have found my grandmother.'

'I thought she was in Paris?'

'Her Red Cross passport was out of date. At the last moment she discovered that Quatch had failed to renew it. It would amuse him of course. My grandmother has been living in a village in the Delta, bribing people to look after her. When her money ran out they turned her over to the police.'

'Why does Van Khoa need your grandmother? Doesn't he have all the evidence he needs anyway?'

She hesitated. 'Van Khoa has always believed that Quatch still has money hidden in Europe. Perhaps my grandmother will confirm this.'

When the court reassembled Van Khoa announced that there had been certain developments concerning a witness he had been seeking for some weeks. Suddenly Max felt a tingle of electricity pass through the courtroom. Quatch, for the first time, seemed disturbed, his hands fluttering in his lap. The newsmen were leaning forward trying to make out what was happening.

'I wish to call,' the prosecutor said, 'Bernadette Hyn. Prostitute. Mistress of former administrator Quatch.'

Nan Luc was watching Quatch. His sense of shock was palpable. He had thought Bernadette was already in Paris, beyond reach of Van Khoa's questions. His mouth had tightened. His thin

jowls were tucked into his collar. He turned in his seat, his manacles clinking lightly on his wrists.

Bernadette was led from the same door at which Quatch had
appeared. She was greatly changed from the last time Nan Luc
had seen her. Her hair hung about her thin face and her grey
prison clothes made of her a shapeless, shuffling form. Staring at
her grandmother, Nan felt a numbness, a cold absence of emotion.
In the past weeks when she had imagined Bernadette in Paris, safe
and rich and uncaring, Nan Luc had experienced sharp shafts of
bitterness at the idea that her grandmother should triumph so
effortlessly once again. Then, when a few minutes ago Van Khoa
had told her that Bernadette had been found, Nan Luc imagined
she might feel something approaching pity for her. But now,
watching the shuffling figure, she felt more apprehension than
pity.

Bernadette offered her one cold glance as she took her place in
the witness box and Nan Luc knew, from that glance alone, that
her grandmother had somehow contrived to sell herself yet again.
From his wary expression Quatch knew it too.

'I first met Monsieur Quatch,' she said, in answer to the first
question, 'in 1965 in what was then known as Saigon. Later he
asked me to work with him in Paris. Mistakenly, I agreed. I
was already completely under his influence.' She glanced brazenly
across the courtroom. 'Monsieur Quatch delights in submission.'

'He forced you to do things against your will?'

'He beat me regularly.'

Nan Luc studied the face of Quatch. He had recovered from
the shock of seeing Bernadette in court and now pretended to be
watching the scene before him with no great interest. A smile
touched his lips as Bernadette continued, but whether it was
intended as a smile of contempt for the treachery of his mistress,
or of pleasure at a memory he relived, it was impossible to say.

'Tell the court about these beatings,' the president said.

'These beatings were part of the sexual act,' Bernadette continued. 'He would also take me up to the Bastille area in Paris.
There the streetwalkers gave beatings for money. Quatch would
pay them to beat me.'

Van Khoa nodded. 'After your return from Paris did he continue
to beat you?'

'From time to time.'

'Why did you not leave him?'

Bernadette smiled. 'He was also very generous.'

'He gave you a place to live, food and wine . . .'

'More than that. He gave me a passport, a Red Cross passport, so that when the time came I could leave for the West with him.'

'He intended to defect?'

'Of course,' she said slowly. 'That's where all his money was. Here, he only had a few thousand dollars left. The money you found at the summer house.'

Van Khoa let the moment sink in. 'The prisoner Quatch has bank accounts in the West?'

Quatch's reptilian eyes slid back and forth across the courtroom.

'In recent years, yes. . .'

Van Khoa flipped his hair back with the stump of his hand, a look of bewilderment on his face. 'In recent years? In recent years?' he repeated. 'How can that be? How can Vo Tran Quatch still be trading in antiquities?'

Bernadette laughed theatrically at his puzzlement. 'Still trading in antiquities? Who's talking about antiquities? Today Monsieur Quatch earns his money by blackmail!' Her voice rose to a screech. 'By blackmailing his own partner in crime.'

'This is not among the charges,' Quatch shouted hoarsely.

'Monsieur Quatch's business in Paris was antiquities,' Bernadette said rapidly. 'But his pleasure was pornography. Movies made here, specially commissioned in the corrupt city of Saigon. Long after he returned from Paris, a year or two ago, he met the film maker, his old supplier of filth, at a conference in Geneva. The blackmail began then.'

The newsmen saw from Quatch's evident agitation that this was no part of the set-piece. The manacles on his hands rattled. He was trying to stand, turning towards the judges, one arm raised, dragging the other with it.

'Let the prisoner remain seated,' the presiding judge said.

Quatch shrugged off the restraining hand of one of the guards. 'I wish to make a statement, monsieur le president. I wish to make a statement on the introduction of the subject of these Western bank accounts.'

'Let the prisoner be seated,' the president said again. He looked desperately towards the man in the rumpled cream suit at the back of the court. 'If this money exists, unadmitted by the prisoner, the Chief Prosecutor will no doubt be requesting the court to change very dramatically the sentence he was asking for.' He turned to the newsmen. 'You see,' he said excitedly, 'this is the democratic process at work. Further crimes are being unearthed as the trial continues. Greater sentences will be demanded.'

'I insist on my right to make a statement,' Quatch said, his voice rising.

From the back of the court there was a movement. The man in the cream suit stood abruptly. Heads swivelled in that direction.

The small grey haired man made a dismissive gesture with his right hand.

'There will be no statement,' said the judge.

Quatch was on his feet, the manacles trailing from his wrists. 'I insist that the part played by the American be brought out into the open,' he cried out in his high voice.

Among the journalists there was uproar. Quatch turned towards them, spreading his manacled arms. 'Yes, messieurs, there is also an American involved. I see no reason now why his role should not be revealed.'

'The prisoner must be silent,' the judge shouted. 'The court is adjourned!'

'The prosecutor has betrayed the terms of our agreement.' Quatch raised his voice above the din.

'What agreement?' Hunter roared from the press box.

The court erupted into chaos. Hunter jumped the barrier and reached Quatch's side. Two other journalists were a step or two behind. Quatch screamed over his shoulder as the guards dragged him from the court: 'If further charges are to be preferred the American pornographer should be named now!'

'What American pornographer, for Christ's sake?' one of the newsmen bawled at Quatch. More guards had run into the court, rifles pointing at Hunter and the journalists.

'The trial is adjourned,' the presiding judge shouted above the scuffling figures. 'Adjourned!'

In the confusion, the high screams of the guards, the deeper voices of the angry Westerners demanding to know the name of the American, Max turned towards Nan Luc. She was standing, her face drained of colour. For a moment he thought she was about to faint. 'Nan Luc,' he shouted above the din.

But she heard nothing. She had taken several steps forward so that she faced the witness stand. She was staring into the face of her grandmother. 'Is this true?' Max heard her say. 'Tell me, for God's sake, is this true?'

Then Bernadette too was dragged away and a line of guards began prodding rifles at the Westerners to drive them towards the wide double doors at the back of the courtroom.

From his position on the edge of the square Max watched Nan Luc come running down the courtroom steps. Perhaps she saw him, but she ran past, her sandals clicking on the sidewalk as she made for the Rue du Port.

For a moment he hesitated, still shocked by the horror he had seen on her face as she turned on her grandmother in the courtroom. Then behind him he heard a step.

'Leave it, Max,' Hal Bolson's voice rumbled deeply. 'Come on I'll buy you a drink.'

Max turned to Bolson, nodding. 'Sure,' he said. 'I could use one.'

Together they walked across the paved square between the huge puddles. The humidity forced Bolson to slow his step. Sweat poured from him, staining great black patches on the chest of his khaki shirt.

'Do you think this American exists?' Max said.

'Maybe,' Bolson shrugged. 'Maybe not.' They reached the Grand Hotel and entered, standing for a moment under the ancient revolving fan in the roof of the hall. 'All we really know is that there was a pre-trial deal. The old lady blew it. Deliberately let the cat out of the bag about an American involvement. *That* wasn't part of the deal. My guess is she's signed Quatch's death warrant.'

They approached the hotel in silence, Max's thoughts on the way Nan Luc had faced her grandmother. And the words, what were they? 'Tell me, for God's sake, is this true?'

In the hotel bar most of the journalists were drinking beer or thin sugary orange drinks. Hunter alone seemed to be drinking liquor. He greeted them with a grimace. 'Have you heard the news? We're all off to Saigon for a five-day drunk.'

'What happened?' Max looked round at the angry faces of the journalists.

'What happened,' Hunter said, 'is that without any explanation they've ended the trial. Van Khoa was just here to give us the news.'

'The trial's over?' Max said. 'It's hardly begun.'

Hunter nodded. 'Seems we were wrong.'

'So we all go home?' Max said. 'Just like that?'

'Anybody who wants to,' Hunter rasped, 'can come back in five days for the inevitable verdict – guilty on all counts, you bet your sweet life.'

15

The river carried them forward. There was no sense of motion unless he lifted his eyes to look past the rim of the boat at the overhanging branches of huge mango trees. In the prow of the sampan, shaded by a woven reed canopy he lay among cushions while Nan Luc, in a pale cotton dress, barefoot on the wet planking, guided the boat with the bamboo punt pole. Two old bicycles, one a rusting US Army foldaway, lay in the belly of the boat.

She turned the sampan from the middle of the river, against the pull of the tide so that it moved towards the bank. Almost reluctantly, Max lifted himself on to one elbow. He could see now that they were approaching a small township, a square with low yellow rendered buildings of which the river itself formed the fourth side. The square itself was unpaved and empty except for a few figures spreading nets to dry in the afternoon sun. Along the bank women in conical hats were bringing long branches while men stood in the water, chest deep, weaving a cage of bamboo about ten feet from the bank.

'They throw food inside.' Nan Luc followed Max's curious glance. 'When a big fish swims in they block the entrance and fish him out.'

'And the nets?' He looked towards the square.

'Oh they're for birds,' she said. 'The peasants stretch them between two mango trees and beat drums and blow whistles to drive the birds into the nets.'

'And what then?'

She laughed. 'They cook them and eat them.'

'Why are we pulling in?'

'For lunch. Aren't you hungry?'

'What sort of birds?' he asked uncertainly.

'This is a breast of duck,' Nan Luc said a few minutes later as an old woman handed them pieces of meat on a skewer. 'I promise you.'

It seemed to Max that the whole village had turned out to examine him as he sat on a rough bench next to Nan Luc and watched the old women manipulate the fire. One small boy marched up and down wearing what was for him a vast US Army helmet. Young girls peeped shyly from behind a sampan beached on blocks for repair. A few black hogs squelched in the mud of the river bank and a transistor radio played a strange selection of Western and oriental music. To Max almost every fourth or fifth song seemed to be a strangely haunting gloat of Vietnamese triumph: 'Hue, Saigon, Hanoi'.

Max looked around him as more duck was roasted and Nan Luc chattered rapidly with the old women. For the first time now he noticed the huge ponds of green water that lay behind the river bank, craters from the bombing during the war. Looking from face to face, the young man with only one arm, the young girls dancing together between the sampans, Max realised that the Englishman, Kipling, had been wrong. East and West *had* met. On the battlefields of Vietnam. A unique meeting which had affected both worlds. He looked back towards Nan Luc, her face animated and laughing. It was beginning to affect his world too.

After lunch Max sat on the bank with Nan Luc watching the incredible activity of the river, the painted rice barges hung with rubber tyres; the bustling sampans, crossing and recrossing with loads of timber or ducks and hogs; and once or twice a lone oarsman in a skiff flying across the water with the grace of a swan about to take off.

'Was it a great surprise to see your grandmother in court yesterday?' he asked her. They had not yet talked about yesterday afternoon. Each time Max had started on the subject he had felt Nan Luc's reluctance to talk.

'It was a surprise,' Nan conceded. 'I thought she had escaped to Paris.'

'There's no love lost between you and your grandmother, is there?'

'I wish her no harm,' Nan Luc said shortly.

'What about the American pornographer, was that a red herring?'

He could see Nan Luc's face change shape and colour. 'I'm not sure what a red herring means,' she said carefully. 'But I believe my grandmother was lying. I believe there was no American pornographer. Perhaps an American who paid sums of money to Quatch for services in Vietnam he wished him to render. But that is all.'

He leaned on his elbow looking up at her. Her eyes were fixed on the far bank. He knew that if he pursued the subject of her grandmother's evidence that he was in danger of breaking something, some trust that had developed between them. 'Perhaps sometime you will tell me something of your life in the West,' she said matter of factly.

'Now?'

'If you like.'

'What would you like to know?'

'Do you have a big family?' He shook his head smiling. 'You're laughing at me,' she said uneasily. 'Have I said something wrong?'

'No.' He leaned back on one arm. 'It's just such a Vietnamese first question. The family.' He paused. 'I have a mother who's very sick. She lives in London. I have uncles and aunts and cousins in the United States.'

'In New York?' she asked at length.

'Some of them. But mostly Philadelphia. And a scattering in California.' He paused. 'They're all pretty remote from my life, I guess. Except my mother. Mostly families don't mean the same in the West.'

She nodded, waiting for him to go on. 'You are not married then, Mr Benning.'

'I was. No longer.'

A sampan floated by. Nan Luc seemed to be concentrating on the monkey leaping across its cargo of cut reeds. 'Was your wife an American woman?'

'No,' Max said. 'She's German. The sister of my best friend.' It seemed to him he continued without hesitating. 'We divorced last year.'

'Because you no longer loved each other?'

'I don't know,' he said. 'I guess so.'

'What other reason could there be?' she asked, her eyes wide and candid.

This time he knew he hesitated. 'There was a child. Four years old now. Katey.'

'You still see her.'

Max looked up at the sharpness of her tone. 'Yes, I still see her.' He stopped, uncertain whether to go on. 'She's not my child, Nan Luc,' he said quickly. 'We'd been married a year. I had no reason to believe there was anyone else in Monika's life. Naturally I thought Katey was my child.' He felt a sudden rush of relief that he had said it out loud. And then surprise, astonishment almost, that he had said it to this girl, virtually a stranger. She sat beside him waiting, not pressing him, yet saying nothing that would break the thread if he chose to take it up.

'We had been married a few months. We were both pretty young and things weren't quite what either of us expected, I guess. You understand what I mean?'

'It happens here too.'

'Sure.' He paused. 'Mostly it was my fault. I was away constantly with my work. Monika had left her job in Germany to come to London. She didn't speak English too well at that time. She was bored.'

'And you?'

'I came to believe I'd married Monika for no better reason than she was my best friend's sister. I came back from my next trip, another long one to Brazil, to find she was pregnant. That seemed to solve all the problems.'

A group of men had arrived on the far bank. Each carried a short-handled axe with a huge heavy head. Their voices carried chattering across the river.

'A long time afterwards, when Katey was nearly two, I learnt by chance that she was not my child.'

She was looking out across the river as the woodsmen selected a tree. 'Do you know who was the father?'

'Someone I was at school with in Germany. He'd come to stay a week or two in London after I left for the long trip to Brazil. He and Monika had a few drinks together. They'd known each other a long time too. I guess she cried on his shoulder. It happens. Mostly there's no pregnancy to follow.' The sounds of frenetic wood chopping carried across the river. 'I've no right to tell you all this,' he said. She was biting on her bottom lip. He stood up and offered her a hand. 'My only excuse is that I wanted to.'

'Ah . . .' She released her lip and he saw that her white teeth were flecked with blood. 'And now?'

'Monika married Katey's father a few months after we were divorced. I see them whenever I go to Munich or they come to London. I think it's working out.'

She stood up. He could feel the agitation in her movements, not hostile, not distancing herself from him.

'Have you ever thought of leaving Vietnam?' he asked her as they began to walk along the river bank.

'Perhaps sometime it will be possible,' she said. 'Not yet.'

'Would you go to America?'

'Yes. I would want to find my father.' He was silent. She glanced towards him. 'You're thinking there are many American fathers who don't wish to see their Vietnamese children. Who might wish to put the past behind them.'

'I wouldn't like to see you hurt,' he said.

'You're wrong.' She spoke with certainty. 'Somehow I know you're wrong.'

'It's easy to romanticise the idea of America, Nan Luc.'

She shook her head. 'You must understand, Max, I believe I have the right to know my father. It's the right of all Vietnamese.'

They walked along the river path in silence. At a bend in the river Max looked across at a long low white pavilion, terraced and balconied below a delicate oriental roof. In the creek beside it a freshly painted white launch was moored.

'Who the hell lives there?' Max asked her.

She seemed to flinch. 'It was once the summer pavilion of Vo Tran Quatch,' she said. 'Before his arrest.'

He reached out and put his arm round her shoulders, turning her from the pavilion. After a few steps he felt her hesitate, then she wriggled her right arm free and placed it round his waist. 'No two lives run parallel,' she said as they walked slowly, leaning on each other. 'But at some points ours almost touch.'

As the sun began to go down behind the giant trees they left the village and bicycled back along the dusty track to Cahn Roc. The river was tidal for the first few miles and it was not possible, Nan Luc explained, to punt a sampan against the tide down to

Cahn Roc. When the tide changed the villagers had agreed to return the boat, a service included in the few coins which was the price of lunch.

From time to time they met another cyclist or a walker going in the opposite direction and each time bicycles were stopped and elaborate greetings were exchanged. Riding along the narrow roads behind the girl in the pale dress it was, to Max Benning, as if he were playing a role in an idyll where no time existed, in an incredible landscape of giant trees and sudden breathtaking vistas of the river.

16

She had said no, standing there on the terrace. No to lunch in Woodstock. No to a hotel room afterwards. No.

She had left well before seven and driven her white Range Rover along the side roads back towards Page Corner. It was a drive she loved in the early summer when cowslips carpeted the rolling meadows and poppies lined the hedgerows. Through the open window she drew in the smells of a countryside she loved.

She had slowed almost to a halt when she realised Cy's Mercedes was following her. With a touch of acceleration he overtook her and braked, forcing her to a stop.

Perhaps her real mistake had been to get out of the car as he walked towards her.

'Hi,' he said. 'At the club I couldn't tell you how sexy you look in a tennis skirt.'

She found herself immensely flattered. 'I'm your very grown-up sister-in-law,' she rebuked him.

'And I'm just a kid off the Detroit assembly line,' he said.

'Detroit?' She frowned.

He took her hand. 'Over lunch I could tell you the story of my life. The real story. The one not even Sunny knows.' With his free hand he ran his fingers up the inside of her arm until he pressed gently but deep into her armpit.

She stepped back, away from him. Her back rested against the side of the Range Rover. He moved forward until they were inches apart. 'I want you, Mary,' he said, matter of factly, 'and I think you want me.' She swallowed hard. Her eyes widened but she found it impossible to speak.

He reached and slid his arms round her. She found she was kissing him and struggling at the same time. As his hand passed up her bare thigh, she melted.

She had arrived home later that evening in a state of shock. She had taken a shower and gulped down a brandy and she was still trembling. What in God's name had happened to her? Had she taken leave of her senses? Had she totally forgotten who she was? She had allowed Cy Stevenson to have sex with her on a grass bank by the roadside like any highway trucker's harlot. Mary Page Butler had allowed that!

At just before noon on Monday, two days after the trial of Quatch had been suddenly concluded, Cy Stevenson received a telephone call from New York. A gentleman from Ho Chi Minh City named Van Khoa (the girl had carefully spelt out the name) would like to meet Mr Stevenson at the Swiss consulate at two o'clock. If necessary he would wait.

Not Saigon. Ho Chi Minh City.

Cy drove badly, his arms affected by a loose, slow trembling. One hand on the wheel he found was not enough. He was unable to light a cigarette without pulling to the side of the road. His imagination ran a constant newsreel of his past. Of the years growing up in Detroit, of the grandmother who had been as brutal as her frailty allowed. Of the day, aged fifteen, he had hit her. Had she died? He never knew. He had moved neighbourhoods, worked on an assembly line, attracted more trouble because trouble seemed to stick to him. Moved on again. East.

He was a good-looking young man, Steven Wokalski. He lived with a woman in a quiet suburb of Boston in an apartment overlooking the Charles River. But the woman was over sixty. Before he moved on she gave him money for a new identity. In Roxbury he had met a man. He supplied everything, a new name, a background, burial details of parents, recollections of high school friends. The complete service. Steve Wokalski walked through one door and young Cy Stevenson emerged through another. Thirteen thousand dollars and English great-grand-parents thrown in. The right, give or take a generation, to wear a Greenjacket tie.

A few stumbling steps. Then, through a woman again, a job as a news reporter. And his first trip to Vietnam and the girls and booze and booze and girls. Stronger than any drug. That feeling in Saigon in the late sixties that you could do *anything*.

Home flew the hero. More or less a hero and to no real home. But with enough dollars to rent an apartment in Meyerick, sixty miles from New York, and look at what the future might bring. And a few weeks later Sunny Page is what it brought. At a party in the same apartment block. A contrived meeting. Cy was good at that sort of thing. Unable to join the party because of an engagement in New York. Just stay long enough for one drink and your telephone number.

Sunny Page's elder sister was like a mother. Nearly twenty years older, intelligent, cautious, a fairly amiable snob. Cy knew she could be serious opposition. Charm didn't work on her. From the day he married Sunny he had known that he might have to find out if anything else did.

Against Mary's opposition, implied rather than stated, he married Sunny and one half of the Page inheritance. The need for a gentleman's pursuit led him in the direction of the Meyerick-Vietnam Fund, headless since its founder, Philip Rose, had died a few years before.

The world was treating Cy Stevenson well but he was aware that his sister-in-law's eyes continued to follow him across the room, speculative, yes, but also distrustful, uncertain, permanently suspicious. And interested?

That evening in Geneva had looked as if it was going to shatter his dream-life. A reception at God knows what charity organisation. Heads of a lot of Western charity funds. Drinks, excellent food, the promise of some girls later. But also some Vietnamese 'meeting friends of new Vietnam'. Quatch. Unmistakable in a perfectly cut pearl-grey suit. Yellow eyes like boiled sweets. Bull's-eyes the kids called them on Soden Avenue. Quatch smiling, Quatch remembering.

His price for silence was at first not unmanageable. Fifty thousand dollars to be paid into a Swiss numbered account. The next year the figure rose.

In the waiting room of the Swiss Consulate a slender man with a shock of black hair falling over his forehead stood up as Stevenson entered and proffered his left hand. The right, Cy saw, was not much more than a scarred stump.

They walked into a private office and the Vietnamese indicated a chair. 'I'm sure you understand why I'm here, Mr Stevenson,'

Van Khoa said in an English, well enough pronounced, but bereft of its normal intonation.

'No,' Cy said. 'No, I don't, Mr Van Khoa.'

'Yet you drove in to New York immediately you got my message.'

'I was coming in anyway,' Cy said casually. 'Mondays I often leave it late. New York morning traffic tails right back to nowhere.'

'I am the officer responsible for the trial of a man named Quatch, former chief administrator of the province of Cahn Roc.'

'I know the area,' Cy said. 'The river's very pretty down in Cahn Roc.'

'You also know Quatch.'

There was a long pause. 'Yes,' Cy said after a moment, 'I remember Quatch. Used to see him a lot in Saigon at one time. He was in the sugar business, if I remember. Learnt afterwards he was a leading political officer of the Vietcong.'

Van Khoa nodded slowly, took a pack of Chesterfields from his pocket, opened it and knocked out a cigarette on his torn hand. 'We know that you began paying money to Quatch after a chance meeting in Geneva in 1987.' Cy got up and poured himself a glass of water. He raised it, watching Van Khoa across the lip of the glass. 'We know that you returned to the United States and arranged for large sums of money to be transferred to the Banque Helvétie in Switzerland. A numbered account belonging to Quatch.'

'Go on, Mr Van Khoa, please.'

'We know that the source of the money is the Meyerick-Vietnam Fund which you took over as president when the founder, Mr Philip Rose, died.'

'Where does this lead us, Mr Van Khoa? Where are we going?'

'The trial of Quatch is concluded.'

'Already?' Cy looked at him in bewilderment. 'Reporters were invited. I expected to read something about it in the Western press.'

Van Khoa inclined his head. 'I think now it will be a small story. My government has taken a decision at the highest level.'

A tiny nodule of hope was growing inside Cy Stevenson. 'Your government changed its mind about a show trial?'

'It decided that, in the last resort, it would not be in the national interest to disclose too many of these facts. I was unaware of the scope of the matter when the trial began.'

'Having decided what would *not* be in the national interest, have you decided what would be?' Cy said cautiously.

'Yes.'

'That is?'

'That the payments from the Meyerick-Vietnam Fund should continue to be lodged at the same numbered account in Switzerland.'

'The same account.'

'Vietnam is desperately short of dollars, Mr Stevenson. The US went back on its promise of economic aid after the war. The sum your fund pays is not great, but it is not insignificant.'

'There will be no revelations?'

The self-disgust showed in Van Khoa's face. 'No.'

'No names named?'

'No. You simply continue paying as before.'

A great wave of relief swept over Cy Stevenson. 'We should shake hands on this.' He extended his hand and looked down, recoiling. 'I'm sorry.'

Van Khoa's black eyes fumed hate. 'Don't be,' he said and thrust his ugly stump into Cy's hand.

The phone rang in Fin and Mary Butler's house, its monotone sounding through the empty drawing room, up the imported English stairwell along the deserted landings and into the south bedroom where the former Steve Wokalski of Soden Avenue, Detroit, straddled the mistress of the house, Mary Page Butler.

'Leave it,' she said. 'For God's sake leave it.'

He pressed into her, leaning across her body. 'It could be good news,' he said, picking up the phone.

She stared up at him, horrified as she made out the sound of Sunny's voice on the end of the line. Without speaking he handed the phone down to Mary. By now Sunny's voice was shrill. 'Mary, is that you?' she was repeating.

'It's Mary,' her sister-in-law managed to gasp.

'What the hell are you doing?'

'I'm out of breath, that's all,' Mary said, an elder sister's impatience coming to her rescue. 'I just ran in from the garden.'

'Is Cy there? I called home. He should be back from New York by now. I'm dying to know what his meeting with the Viets was about.'

'No,' Mary said. 'Sorry, Sunny. I'll get him to call you if he drops by.' She waited for Sunny to ring off then gave the phone to Cy who, still straddling her, reached over and dropped it on the rest. 'What meeting?' she said.

'Later.'

'Get off me, Cy. What meeting?'

'Very good news,' he said. 'One in the eye for George Savary. The trial of Quatch has been concluded without evidence of corruption even being offered.' He lifted her thigh and with a quick shift in his own weight, entered her.

'For God's sake, Cy!'

'All they want,' he said, riding gently back and forth, 'is for us to continue paying the money for the same service. But this time it's better. We pay direct to the Vietnamese government. Even Savary can't object to that.'

She tried to wriggle up but he held her hips strongly, pulling her down on him. 'Cy, please. Secret payments to the Vietnamese government? You're getting in too deep.'

They both stopped as she laughed, realising what she had said. He bent forward and kissed her nose.

'OK,' she groaned. 'Go now – talk later.'

17

Max stood on his balcony looking out across the square. By this time of the evening it was almost empty of bicycles. The low yellow buildings of the hospital opposite were touched with gold as the sun went down. Long fingers of shadow stretched between the stone arches of the old French building. He supposed, from the cross that rose above the main doorway and the niches filled with the effigies of saints, that it had once been a hospital run by monks or nuns. For a few moments he watched the figure walking through the arches, a Bhuddist monk, his robes glowing cream-yellow and gold as he emerged on to the square.

Max turned back into his room. Most of the journalists had already left. One or two had gone to spend the waiting period in Ho Chi Minh City. He knew the reason he was staying on had nothing to do with the outcome of the trial.

Leaving the room he went down to the ground floor. The lobby was deserted. Walking quickly through it he came out in the square. He knew where he was going. Passing the corner of the courtroom he went on down the sloping Rue du Port towards the long wharf where the fishing boats were hauling up their sails.

He could see the harbour tower at the end of the steep street and behind it the backing of an empty sea. Walking slowly down he passed stilted, thatched-roof fishermen's huts, a roper's shop with thick coils of hemp displayed on iron hooks and painted plank coffins stacked outside a coffin maker's.

He knew that he had never before been touched by a girl in this way. He felt he was beginning to understand her, slowly learning how to look beyond her obvious beauty to what he sensed was a woman of great softness and great strength.

His father's ideas of commitment, of a definitive act passed through his mind. He smiled to himself and walked on, responding as the coffin maker raised his hand in greeting.

Nan Luc was disturbed. What troubled her was that she could not be sure *how much* she was disturbed. She had tried throughout the day to identify the feeling but that had proved impossible. It was a feeling akin to embarrassment. Yet at the same time a feeling of deep pleasure. And again a feeling of intense self-criticism.

She could go on but each attempt to analyse the feeling brought her back to the same place: all these currents of introspection, pleasure, and self-examination were intensified in the company of Max Benning.

She was aware that a Westerner might say that she was falling in love. But that to Nan Luc and to many Vietnamese girls was an experience only possible after a long gestation period. In that private core of self which she had defended from her teachers at the orphanage, from her grandmother and even, that appalling night, from Quatch, she was angry at the thought of love. At least of love after a few hours together, of love based on physical attraction. She thought about that for a few moments. A physical attraction. Clearly he was unlike Van Khoa for example. He was taller by seven or eight inches. He had fair hair and eyes of a blue-grey colour. Yes, she conceded, he possessed physical attraction. More than Van Khoa.

In her room in the harbour tower it was growing dark. She got up to light her kerosene lamp, amused at herself. In the orphanage fifteen-year-old girls had fallen in love with their instructors and endlessly recited a litany of their physical attractions. Is that what she was doing? No. She put the match to the wick and watched it flare before replacing the glass. No, she was doing something different. She was exorcising the possibility of succumbing to that Western trivialisation of love. That's what she was doing.

Her fingers stung as the match burned down. Good. An appropriate reminder. She must do some washing and later she should read some of the depositions in a village trial she would have to conduct.

The knock on the door startled her. She had had barely a dozen visitors since she had come to Cahn Roc. Sometimes the children of the family that lived downstairs came up to sit with her as she read or wrote reports. She crossed to the door and opened it.

'Perhaps it's not done to call on you,' Max said.

She opened the door wider. 'Please come in.'

He came forward and closed the door. All those feelings she had tried to analyse surged through. One, sheer embarrassment, predominated.

He stood in the middle of the room. 'I wondered if I could ask you to come for a walk with me.'

'If there are things about the trial you wish to discuss . . .' she said, aware, even when she turned to pick up her jacket, that his eyes were on her.

'No, just a walk. Like the day you took me on the river. Not to discuss anything. Nothing special anyway. I just came to ask you to go for a walk.'

She laughed, feeling suddenly more confident. 'You came because you couldn't stand another evening playing poker with your comrades in the Grand Hotel when they get back tonight.'

'Maybe.' He thrust his hands deep into the pockets of his leather jacket. 'I'm not really a poker player.'

She turned out the lamp and they left the room. They groped their way down the dark, spiral staircase, their bodies touching momentarily.

Along the empty quayside they walked towards the town square, talking about America, about how Americans feel about Vietnam, about how the Vietnamese in America are making out.

'Let's talk about you,' Max said after a while.

'You know most of what there is to know.'

'Will you tell me why you hate Quatch?' Max asked her. He felt her start violently. They continued walking on past the coffin makers. The tops of the buildings in the square were visible to them.

'I should have answered you,' she said, after a long silence. 'But for a moment it was impossible.' She paused. 'I can answer you now. I have reason to hate Quatch. Perhaps, even, I would kill him if I could before he is sentenced tomorrow.'

'Listen, Nan Luc,' Max said, 'I want you to understand. We come from two worlds far part. If I ask questions you think are intrusive, you just tell me. OK?'

She shook her head, her eyes on the cobbled road. 'You are right to ask me,' she said.

At the point where the Rue de Port joined the square they stopped, standing together in the shadows beside the old Hôpital St Hubert. 'We can walk in the gardens of the hospital, if you like.'

They turned in through an arched doorway. Kerosene lamps lit a stone cloister surrounding a square of green. 'I often come in here,' Nan Luc said.

'I can understand that,' Max said, not adding that he could understand that the cloister was an escape from the peeling blandness of Cahn Roc.

She walked in silence, a pace or two from him, through the old monastery hospital buildings.

'What are you thinking about, Nan Luc?' he asked her as they completed the circle of the cloister.

She stopped and leaned against a stone pillar in the yellow lights from the hanging lamps. 'I am thinking that what is happening to you and me, Monsieur Benning,' she said, 'is that we're falling just a little in love.' He leaned back against the wall. A surge passed through his body. 'I've read books by Americans,' she said. 'I know Westerners think Vietnamese women are all too shy to talk about their feelings.' She looked up at him. 'It's not true.' She smiled. 'In fact we talk very candidly about falling in love in our culture. There is no shame in it. I suspect it's the West that thinks there is.'

'Is that what you think,' he said, 'that we're falling in love?'

'If we are,' she said softly, 'then it must be stopped.'

'Why, why must it be stopped?'

'Because we're both too young. We are both half-formed.'

'Too young.' He came off the wall. 'I'm thirty years old, Nan. Thirty-year-old men in the United States have wives and children, run big businesses.'

'Don't be angry, Monsieur Benning.'

'Will you call me, Max, for God's sake. We're talking about whether or not we're falling in love with each other, you can't go on calling me Monsieur Benning.'

She laughed. 'OK, I'll call you, Max.'

'All right.' He wanted to reach out and touch her but he sensed that would be a mistake. 'Why must it be stopped?'

'I meant only that we still have a long way to go separately. Down our own paths. I am a half-American living in the land of the other half of my being. I have to make a choice between the two.' She stopped and moved along the cloister. 'And you too, Max. You have choices to make, too. That's what I meant when I said we were both half-formed.'

'I'm amazed how much you know about me in a matter of days.'

'Don't be,' she said laughing. 'I've been studying you seven hours a day.'

'Would you ever think of going to the West,' he said, 'if there were someone waiting for you there?'

'I've thought about it,' she said quickly. 'Often. But if I went to the West it would be first to find my father. After that . . .'

They turned through another arch and came to a long corridor that took them towards the square. He had thought she might pause for a moment in the shadow but she stepped out into the square. 'Thank you, Monsieur Benning,' she said, 'Max, I mean.' She held out her hand. 'I've enjoyed our talk.'

He took her hand. 'Let me walk you back to the port. We've still got a lot more to say.'

She shook her head. 'No. We've talked. That's enough.'

'*You*'ve talked.'

'Yes, I've talked. Goodnight, Max.'

'I would like to kiss you,' he said. 'Is that permitted in Vietnam?'

Her eyes widened. 'You should have stopped in the shadow before we came into the square,' she said, smiling.

'It's not too late to turn back,' he said.

She stepped backwards into the shadow. 'For you and me, Max, we must always make sure,' she said, fitting her body to his, 'that it is never too late to turn back.'

Sometime in the middle of the night Max awoke, aware that the sheet under him was wet with sweat. He had been dreaming the most garishly savage dreams of his life. They centred of course, in that vague dreamlike way, on a dozen versions of Nan Luc and Quatch and the bloodied bed.

She had left out no detail. She had spared herself neither the nightmare nor the humiliation. In a voice which was as low and matter-of-fact as she could make it she had recounted every moment from her arrival at Avenue Giap to the moment she had woken in the bloodstained bed. For a Vietnamese girl it was a piece of extraordinary candour. It was a night that would be with her for ever. It was a night that would now stay with him for ever.

His head thumped painfully in time with his heartbeat. He had sat alone in his room late into the night. He had drunk perhaps three or four whiskies.

He got out of bed and stood unsteadily by the window. The bus which had taken the newsmen into Ho Chi Minh City last week now stood at its own slight angle on the square below him. Somewhere in the hotel he could hear voices speaking in English. He looked at his watch, registering slowly that the others had returned, wondering vaguely what sort of time they had had. The watch face showed two in the morning.

The night air on his body now seemed uncomfortably cold and he was aware that he was trembling. He turned back into his room and sat naked on the bed, the top sheet pulled half over his shoulders. The trembling seemed if anything to be worse. And yet he was not really cold.

He got up and poured himself a small whisky. The pain in his head surged forward and receded in a rhythm of its own but syncopated all the time by the beat of his heart.

He put on his robe and sat in the cane chair beside the table piled with trial notes. His face seemed to blaze with a heat of its own while his body shivered beneath the thin robe. He got up and stumbled to the bed. The damp seeped from the sheets through the robe. He could hear the fast rhythm of his breath soughing between his teeth.

As the fever deepened Max faded in and out of sleep, barely able to distinguish moments of wakefulness. Brief dreams of the courtroom and the trial were erased by other, more sickly images of Nan Luc, images in which he was no longer a spectator at her humiliation and fear but was the perpetrator himself rolling with her in the sheets of that bloodied bed.

At 7.30 a.m. Harold Bolson stood before him. 'You can't go to the court today,' Bolson said. 'For God's sake you can hardly stand up.'

Max sat on the edge of the bed. He felt drained of energy but purged too, as if the fever was necessary to clear his mind. 'How was the Big Apple?'

'Quiet compared to the last time I was here. But we found a few places. Listen Max, take a shower and I'll get someone to change the bed. Give today's session a miss.'

'I'm OK,' Max said. 'The fever's passed.'

Bolson shrugged. 'So what did you learn about the trial?' he said, collapsing into the creaking cane chair by the table. 'What did Nan Luc have to tell you?'

'Nothing.'

'You mean you spent five days with her and you didn't ask her?'

'No.'

Bolson raised his eyebrows in silent disbelief.

Within an hour the fever came surging back. When Bolson came to collect him for the sentencing session, which was to take place at the end of the afternoon, he stopped in the door.

Max looked up from his chair. 'What is it?'

'You,' Bolson said. 'I'm getting a doctor. Better than that, I'm taking you across to the hospital. They've still got a French priest there who did medicine at the Sorbonne.'

'I can't get across there,' Max said, wiping sweat from his face with a towel. 'Just let me rest here.'

'They call this lotus fever,' Bolson said. 'It's like everything else in Vietnam. Treacherous.'

18

'Basically,' Cy said, 'a storm in a teacup.'

In the tourette room of the Meyerick Club George Savary eyed the fund president across the table. 'I can't agree,' he said. 'I can't agree to continuing payments. I never liked the payments when I first heard about them . . .'

Cy held up his hand. His face was set. 'I hope you take what I'm going to say as it's intended, George. Perhaps you don't appreciate the suffering of many millions of Vietnamese, oppressed by the regime. We should not be misled by any recent apparent liberalisation.'

'Hear, hear,' Hector Hand said loudly.

'As from today,' Cy said, 'we can buy at source. Straight from the Vietnamese government.'

'And what, in your view, are we buying?'

'A secure passage from Cahn Roc for thousands of boat people. What we're getting for our dollar is hope and opportunity.'

'That's not the issue,' Savary said angrily. 'The issue is whether or not a private charity should be making a deal of this nature.'

'I think the rest of the committee is basically agreed,' Cy said dismissively.

Savary shook his head. 'I'd have to ask for a vote on that,' he said. The trustees looked from Cy to George Savary. There was a long silence as Cy kept his eyes down on the papers before him. 'I'd go further, Mr President,' Savary said with deliberate formality. 'I'd have to inform the committee that I would consider this a resignation issue.'

Cy's head came up. He shuffled his papers brusquely. 'OK, we'll take a vote. I'm bound to say this will be the first vote of this committee which has not been a formality.'

'Perhaps, Mr President, too much has gone by on the nod.'

The Anderson brothers permitted themselves a sharp intake of breath. Mary kept her eyes down on the table. She found her heart was thumping heavily.

'Before I ask members to speak on this matter,' Cy said, 'I would like to remind you, George, that a resignation does not free you to speak publicly about our deliberations.'

'I'm aware that that was one of the terms of my acceptance,' Savary said. 'I never for a moment thought the issue would arise.'

'Maybe it won't,' Cy smiled spectrally, 'if the vote goes your way.' He sat back, his elbows on the arms of his chair, his fingertips interlocked under his chin. 'I'd like to hear other members of the committee on this,' he said.

'You're in favour of going ahead dealing with Hanoi?' Arne Anderson said.

'I am,' Cy said decisively. 'I'm not prepared to let these people stew.' The Andersons nodded.

'I feel very much that on something like this we should support our president,' Mrs Rose said. 'But I appreciate the colonel's concerns. Surely this is an opportunity to get out of the distasteful end of the business. Of course I understand its purpose in the past and I have agreed. But now I would prefer to see us spending the splendid amounts Cy has raised in, well, a more conventional manner.'

The Anderson brothers pursed their lips.

'Fin?' Cy said.

'It's flakey,' he said. 'I think I'm for staying clear. Let's get back to basics. Let's spend the money here in the United States.'

Cy was counting. The committee at full strength numbered ten. Today, with Jason Rose absent, there were nine voting. No proxies, no abstentions, was a rule established by the founder. So a decision was inevitable. In favour: himself, Oliver Digweed and Hector Hand certainly. Three. And against: Savary, Mrs Rose, Fin. Three. That left the Anderson brothers and Mary. He looked towards the Anderson brothers but neither of them spoke.

'OK,' he said slowly, looking towards Oliver Digweed. 'Let it be recorded in the minutes of the emergency meeting that a vote was taken on the president's proposal. I'll take your vote in turn. Colonel?'

'Against.'

'Fin?'

'Against. Sorry, Cy.'

'Helen?'

'Against,' Mrs Rose said. 'With great reluctance.'

Cy nodded. 'Oliver?'

'For.'

'Hector?'

'Very definitely for.' Cy lifted his head to the Andersons.

'Against,' one said.

'For,' the other said at almost the same moment. Cy smiled grimly. Four in favour of this motion. Four against.

'Mary?'

She had locked her hands together on the table before her but found herself still unable to prevent her arms and shoulders from trembling.

'I'm sorry, Mary,' Cy said. 'You seem to have the deciding vote.'

Her heart was thumping outrageously, worse even than when he was on top of her, inside her. She brushed the intrusive image away with an impatient movement of her hand, which Mrs Rose interpreted as being aimed at Cy.

'Give me a moment,' Mary said. She knew perfectly well that a month ago she would have voted with Colonel Savary. She had never felt comfortable with so much donated money being used as it had been. 'This is, I suppose,' she said carefully, 'an opportunity to review the situation.'

'I'm sorry, Mary. We're taking the vote. For or against?' Cy's voice was soft, insistent, not pleading, though Mary knew that if she voted with Savary it would be the end of Cy's presidency.

'In favour,' she said with a rush of colour to her cheeks. 'I vote for Cy's proposal.'

Mrs Rose sideglanced her almost savagely. Colonel Savary closed the folder before him with an air of finality. Cy rose from his place. His eye caught Mary's for the briefest moment. 'The proposal is carried,' he said. He turned his attention to George Savary, fighting to keep the triumph from his voice. 'I think I can speak for all of us when I say we're sorry to lose you, George.'

Savary lifted his eyes to Cy. His jaw was set. 'I'm not resigning, Mr President.'

'Perhaps I misunderstood,' Cy said. 'I thought you spoke of a resignation issue.'

'I did.' Savary's lips were set. 'But when I spoke of a resignation I meant yours. Not mine.'

'You're staying on despite your disagreement with trust policy?'

'Because of it,' Savary said. 'I see it as my duty to fight you on this.'

'Even though the majority of this committee is clearly against you?'

'A majority of one.' Savary looked at Mary and then back to Cy. 'I understand that Philip Rose's original constitution laid down an annual election for president.'

'It did,' Mrs Rose said firmly.

'And this clause has been adhered to?' Savary asked, his glance passing round the table.

Oliver Digweed cleared his throat. 'I think I can honestly answer yes to that question. Since Cy became president it's true that the annual vote passed on the nod, so to speak. But at each Christmas Eve meeting it has been a recorded vote.'

'I see,' Savary said slowly. 'Christmas Eve you say.'

'What are you getting at?' Cy said.

'I'm simply giving fair warning that at this coming Christmas meeting, the election for president will not pass through on the nod.'

Cy sat back. 'Frankly, colonel, I would have said the honourable move would have been to step down.'

Savary's face was white. 'I suspected for some time, Mr Stevenson,' he said, 'that you and I are likely to disagree on what the honourable move might be. I repeat, I don't plan to step out of the ring. I'm going to persuade the trustees here today that your policy is deeply wrong. And at the Christmas election I'm going to call for your resignation.' He paused. 'And furthermore I think I'm going to get it.'

19

'Aspirin and boiled water,' the French priest said. 'Not an extensive armoury with which to fight disease, but it's all we have.'

'Did you train in Paris?' Max asked him.

'As a priest. Not as a doctor. But I'm tolerated here for the little hit and miss medical knowledge I've acquired along the way.'

In the bright second-floor room cooled by a slowly moving wooden ceiling fan, Max lay back in clean rough linen sheets, his head slowly clearing. As the priest moved towards the door, he raised himself on his elbow.

'When I get back to London, is there anything I can send you?'

The priest shook his head. 'Nothing that would reach me. All modern medical supplies are allocated to the military. And to our masters.' He crossed to the side of the bed and held out his hand. 'I have to go up-country tomorrow. Goodbye, Mr Benning.'

'Thank you again for what you've done, Father.' Max shook his hand.

The priest smiled down at him. 'In such fevers,' he said, 'nursing assumes more importance than the efforts of a priest turned doctor.'

The fever was now sudsiding as quickly as it had come upon him. When the priest left Max pulled himself up in the wide iron bed. Feeling his cheeks and forehead for a feverish dampness he found his skin now dry and cool. He got out of bed and opened the briefcase Hal Bolson had brought across from the hotel. He registered that the case seemed unusually heavy and that his legs shook. But his head felt steady, his mind clear.

He considered for a moment going across to the courtroom for the sentencing. Bolson had said it would probably consist of a two- or three-hour abject plea from Quatch before he received the court's judgement. Most likely, the newsmen thought, a long spell in a hard labour reconstruction camp. Or death.

Max sat on the side of his bed and thought about opening the briefcase of notes. But the wave of fatigue that came across him was dissuasive enough. Changing his mind he swung his legs back on to the bed.

He awoke from a deep sleep to hear the commotion out on the square. Voices in English were raised; angry Vietnamese voices rose above them.

Max pulled back the sheet and stood up beside the bed. His cotton pyjamas were dry and his face cool. But the earlier weakness in the legs was still there. He felt, somehow, always on the edge of another surge of fever.

He stepped forward two or three paces and stood by the long open window. Below in the square Vietnamese police, thirty or forty of them, were holding back the newsmen. Among shouts of outrage the Westerners were trying to push close enough to the courtroom doors to point their cameras.

Running footsteps along the stone corridor outside made Max turn from the window. Before the door burst open he knew it was Nan Luc. She stopped just inside the door, tears streaming down her face. Then she moved quickly across to the window and looked down.

'Nan, what is it for God's sake?'

She was trembling as violently as he had been earlier. She pointed down to the courtroom steps. Quatch was emerging from the darkened hall.

'The court,' Nan Luc hissed in hatred, 'have found Quatch *not guilty*.'

20

She was ashamed to be so utterly inexperienced, so utterly inhibited in her lovemaking.

'The East,' Cy said, 'takes these things seriously. They see nothing wrong with the pursuit of pleasure for pleasure's sake.'

The day after the Meyerick Fund meeting they had lunched together on the covered terrace behind Cy's house. Sunny, gardener, and their new maid Mrs Hammet were away all day, Cy assured Mary.

She had drunk a lot. A lot for her, perhaps the best part of a whole bottle of champagne. In the warm sunlight they had danced on the terrace and kissed and fondled until he drew her by the hand, into the house and up the stairs.

She had no qualms about rolling half naked on Sunny's bed. All that was far behind her now. After only two or three sessions of lovemaking she had come to realise she had fewer and fewer qualms about anything.

Did she love him? Not uncritically, she told herself. She was still aware of something almost piratical about him, something far from her own, and Meyerick County's, way of looking at the world.

'Relax,' he was whispering, 'relax and enjoy it.' He was kneeling over her, pressing himself forward.

'I've never, never in my life . . .'

'Even contemplated . . .'

'Of course not.'

'But now?'

'I don't know, Cy.'

'Everybody does it.'

She lifted her eyes up towards his face. He was frowning.

Listening. Then she heard it too. The crackle of wheels over gravel. Terror swamped her. 'Sunny,' she hissed, rising.

His palm pushed down flat on her breast-bone as he leapt across the bed and stood at the window. 'It's not Sunny's car,' he said.

'For God's sake, who is it?' she scrambled up to stand next to him, shaking uncontrollably.

A Chrysler sports had pulled up in the drive below. A girl in her mid-twenties got out of the car. Under the black cap of hair Mary could see that her features were oriental, Vietnamese. She wore a cheap imitation fur, high heels and carried a boxy leatherette case.

Cy was slipping on his robe. 'Who is she?' Mary said.

'Get back into bed. I'll deal with it,' he said.

Still shivering, she got into the bed and sat, the sheet pulled up to her shoulders. She heard the bell, the girl's voice, then Cy's. A salesgirl perhaps. Cosmetics. The voices continued. Then the door closed. Listening hard she heard Cy coming up the stairs. And behind him the click of heels! With a sudden intake of breath she realised he was bringing the girl up to the bedroom.

The door opened. Cy's head appeared. He was smiling. 'A little surprise for you,' he said.

'What's happening, Cy?' Mary's voice was low, a harsh whisper. 'What's happening for God's sake?'

He came into the room. 'A little surprise for you, Mary. Something to relax you.'

She was angry and afraid in about equal proportions. 'What in God's name are you talking about?'

He came forward and sat on the edge of the bed. 'Listen,' he said, taking her hand, 'couples do this all the time in Vietnam.'

'Do *what* all the time?'

'Call in a professional.' He turned to the door. 'A masseuse. Come in, honey,' he called.

'I'm getting dressed,' Mary said.

The girl was in the room now. She wore a neat white nurse's dress. Placing the black square box on Sunny's dressing table, she smiled apologetically. 'Good afternoon, ma'am,' she said politely.

She was not a threat. Mary felt the alarm drain from her. 'Cy,' she said sharply. 'I don't think this is at all wise.'

'It's not meant to be wise,' he said. 'It's meant to be fun.'

'I don't like it, Cy,' she said, less convincingly. 'I'm not sure it's at all the sort of thing . . .' Her voice trailed away. Perhaps it was the white uniform dress. Perhaps the girl's youth or her apologetic smile. 'What's in the box?' she asked.

'A sun lamp,' Cy said laughing. He turned to the girl. 'This is my wife's first Saigon massage,' he said. 'I think she's a little alarmed.'

The girl smiled at Mary. 'If you turn over please. It's important not to look towards the light source.'

Mary felt somehow excited. She dropped back to rest on one elbow. 'You could have warned me, Cy,' she grumbled, turning to lie on her stomach.

'You would never have agreed,' Cy said. He was standing to the side, still in his robe.

Mary rested her face on her crossed arm. She heard the machine click on and felt her body flooded with warm light. Cy had seated himself on the side of the bed. 'In principle I like massage,' Mary said.

'Relax, just relax.' Cy reached out to stroke the back of her head.

Sandalwood spices surrounded her. The Vietnamese girl's small hands kneaded Mary's shoulders and massaged her back . . . her legs and thighs. Slowly Mary could feel the tension leaving her.

'Turn over, darling,' Cy's voice said. 'Careful of the light. Eyes closed.'

Mary turned, sleepily. The sandalwood oil exploded warm on her stomach, the fierce energy of the small hands traced her hips and rounded her breasts.

'After this,' Cy's voice whispered in her ear, 'you'll feel so relaxed, you'll take on anything.'

'This is incredibly decadent, Cy.' She stretched out a hand towards him. 'Incredibly decadent.' The girl's hands worked her stomach, smoothing, furrowing. 'No!' Mary sat up, pushing the girl's hands away. 'No!'

Her eyes were open. For a brief moment she didn't realise, didn't see the change, didn't realise that the girl who knelt over her was naked. That her white coat lay crumpled on the floor.

'Get her out of here,' she screamed at Cy. 'For God's sake get her out of here!'

'Mary,' Cy's voice was charged with emotion. 'Mary, believe me. In Saigon . . .'

'We're not in Saigon,' Mary said.

'Just listen a moment. In Saigon married couples have the masseuse over, it's considered normal.' She shook her head. 'Will you believe how sorry I am?' They were standing just inside the front doorway.

'I don't know what to think.' She shrugged, angry at him; furious at herself. 'I over-reacted, I suppose.'

He bent to kiss her but she pulled away. 'I'll go now, Cy.'

'When will I see you?'

'I don't know. I'll call you in a day or two.'

'Be sure to.'

She nodded and walked past him to the door. He opened it for her and watched her cross to her Range Rover and get in. She looked round once and raised a hand. Cy raised a hand in return and closed the door as the white vehicle swept down the curving drive. As he turned back into the house he was smiling, well pleased with his afternoon's work.

In Mary Page Butler's garden, Fitzgerald was lifting plants for transferring to Sunny's greenhouse. Her hands deep in the pockets of her full yellow skirt, Sunny watched Fitz and her sister working together waiting for the undercurrent of hostility, with which Mary always treated Fitz, to emerge.

'Can you afford being just a gardener, Fitz?' Mary said.

'I can afford it because I enjoy it.'

'But don't you want to settle down, have children?'

'Yes.'

'Then how will you afford that?' He grinned at Sunny and she raised her eyebrows in embarrassment. 'Well?' Mary demanded.

'I guess the Lord will provide,' Fitz said.

'You mean something will come up.'

'That's what I mean, Mrs Butler. Now I'd like to wrap all these plants in wet newsprint for the trip across to Sunny's place.'

'In the kitchen,' Mary said. 'Lucy will show you where to find it.' For a few moments Mary watched Fitz as he walked towards the house. Then she gave her attention to the herb garden.

In jeans and an old T-shirt, a straw hat balanced on the back of her head, Sunny thought, surely Mary Page Butler looked like any middle-aged lady living within a ten-mile radius of Page Corner. But as she stood up, her sister noticed, her breasts rose firmly, her neck was smooth and unwrinkled; she moved easily along the gravel path, stopped and rested her hands on her hips. The movements of a young woman. But there was something matronly about her too. She was still a middle-aged woman, Sunny told herself. A middle-aged woman. Ten years older than Cy.

Sunny stood up and walked down the gravel path, stopping where she cast a shadow across her sister's work. Mary came up off one knee. 'Don't let me disturb you,' Sunny said.

'You're in my light, dear.' Mary pulled at her straw hat. 'My eyes are so bad these days I'm afraid to do the weeding in anything but bright sunlight.'

'What are you growing there?' Sunny gestured towards the rows of herbs. 'Tarragon, basil, all that stuff?'

Her sister frowned. 'I think that's the first time since you were a child that you've ever asked me a single question about gardening.'

'Maybe,' Sunny said. 'Always a first time.'

'Walk with me back to the house.' Mary took her sister's arm. 'No, I always imagined you rather despised the gardener's art. Thought it was trivial or time-wasting or something when you can buy such good produce in the Thursday market.'

'You garden if you like gardening, I guess,' Sunny said shortly.

Her sister sideglanced her wryly. 'I like it,' she said. 'I still suspect you don't. That's why you hire that hippie.'

'I didn't come out to talk about Fitz,' Sunny said.

'What did you come out here to talk about?' Mary released her arm to bend over to pick off a dead head.

Sunny walked on a pace and stopped. Looking towards the house she agonised about her next words. Was she about to make a monumental fool of herself? 'I came out to ask you what you thought of Cy,' she said before she could stop herself. Her sister found another dead head and twisted it off its stalk. Turning to look at her Sunny saw that she was still bending, searching for more withered flowers. 'For God's sake, Mary,' she said. 'Will you stop that pretence of gardening.'

Mary stood up. 'Pretence of gardening?' she said mildly. 'There, you don't think much of it. Don't deny it.'

She looked Sunny straight in the eyes. 'You know what I think about Cy,' she said. 'I told you when you first decided to marry him. I thought he was fast, racy, not entirely well-bred. You know that I'm an appalling snob at heart. I haven't changed my opinion of Cy very much in eight years. Have you?'

Sunny shrugged, disconcerted by her sister's answer, desperately uncertain of her ground. 'I think perhaps Cy's having an affair,' she said.

Mary's grey eyes rose slowly to Sunny's face. 'Do you mind?'

'That's a pretty strange thing to say – do you mind?'

'Strange?'

'Most people would want to know who with?'

Mary shrugged. 'I'm concerned about you, I suppose. OK,' she said slowly, 'who with?'

Sunny watched her, all but shaking in disbelief. Not Mary. Not her old, old, elder sister. Cy would go for something different surely, an actress, a showgirl. Not Mary.

Mary reached for a dead bud, stopped her hand in mid-movement and walked on to place her sister just behind her. 'Do you have any ideas, Sunny?'

While Sunny struggled to decide on her answer, her sister turned slowly to face her. Her cheeks, Sunny noticed, were flushed. Her eyes were brimming at the corners. Was it the brightness of the sun or an acute, heart-stopping guilt? Poised between believing the two reasons, ready to burst into apologies, Sunny said: 'Yes. I have some idea.'

Mary knew her next few sentences were crucial. She frowned very slowly, holding the intense silence between them. Both were aware of birds fluttering from branch to branch, of a distant car taking the Page corner at speed. 'Someone from the club?'

Her sister stood, biting her lip. 'Anita,' she said, on the spur of the moment.

She watched Mary gasp in breath. 'Anita? Anita Simpson, for God's sake! She's too . . .'

'Old,' Sunny supplied the word.

'I was going to say unattractive. Her age is beside the point.

No, I don't believe it,' Mary said with finality. 'Cy loves you. And on reflection, you're right. Anita is too old. Far too old.'

Anita and Mary had been born in the same year, the same month. Sunny looked at Mary's frank, honest face and misconstrued her anger. Relief flooded her body. She was on the edge of apologies, of confession of her suspicions. Then a movement made her look down. Her sister was still holding a gardening trowel; it was being shaken violently by the trembling of her hand.

As soon as Sunny had left, Mary walked into the house. She felt more drained, more frightened than she had ever felt in her life. Those moments of confrontation in the garden had brought home to her more powerfully than anything else could, the appalling risks she was running. She didn't love Cy, she was fairly sure of that. She enjoyed being with him; she was excited by the sex they shared. Even the shock of the Vietnamese masseuse had faded quickly. That was what was so frightening: everything with Cy was so easy to accept. Even the risk of discovery. Except when it had nearly happened as she stood in front of her younger sister in the garden a moment or two ago.

She knew she was poised on the brink. She knew her very first impressions of Cy had been the right ones. She had been a fool, allowed herself to be flattered into adultery with her own brother-in-law. For him it was adventure. She stopped pacing the long room. The deeper shadow that had crossed her mind was that for him it was *not* an adventure. For him it was a means of securing her vote!

She found she had nearly gagged on the thought. She pushed it away. But her anger was rising.

In the back of her consciousness she had heard Fin's car draw up, the door slam, voices. Despite her anger she experienced a moment's hope that it might be Cy with Fin, but when the door opened it was the older, modulated voice of George Savary that was greeting her. They shook hands while Mary apologised for her gardening clothes.

'Good to see you looking so well, Mary. Like you I'm an enthusiastic gardener.' He waved his hand towards the French doors and the garden beyond. 'Unlike you I have no overview of what a garden should look like. But that's a criticism of the military, I suppose. Lacks imagination.'

'I wouldn't say any of us on the committee could accuse you of a lack of imagination, George,' Fin said clumsily. 'I think you've opened a lot of people's eyes to a very unsatisfactory situation. I asked George over,' he turned to Mary, 'to have a word with you about how you stand.'

Mary felt her fists clench involuntarily. 'I think you might have consulted me first, Fin,' she said angrily. 'But in any case, I think which way we vote is something for each of us to decide individually.'

'According to our own estimate of the situation,' Savary said, nodding. 'According to our own conscience.'

'Indeed,' Mary said. 'Now I don't want to be impolite, George, but I'm going to take a shower while you and Fin talk over whatever it is you two want to talk about. And afterwards I'll come down and we'll all have a drink together.' She forced a smile. 'How would that be?'

'It's for you to say, Mary,' George Savary said, inclining his head.

Upstairs Mary lay back against the glass wall of the shower while water coursed over her body. Inevitably the sensual impact of the warm water conjured up memories of Cy. But whole afternoons were spent these days resting on a hoe in the garden, with a book slipping from her lap in the conservatory, dreaming. Recreating those fierce excitements which had never come her way before.

She dried herself and dressed slowly. When she arrived downstairs again it was nearly an hour later. She was not sorry to see that George Savary had left. To Fin she affected mild disappointment.

'He decided to walk back across the fields,' Fin said. 'I don't think he felt very welcome.'

'Are you surprised?'

Fin shrugged apologetically. 'Not tactful. OK, sorry.'

'It's not important.' Mary dropped into a sofa and reached for a magazine.

'George says it is,' Fin said with a rare show of persistence. 'George says the way we each vote is damned important.'

'Fin, I am not going to be canvassed. Do you understand? I'm going to make up my own mind.'

'If that's what's happening, fine.' Mary brought her head up slowly from the magazine. 'I wouldn't like to see anybody make a fool of you, Mary.' He paused. 'We're old friends. We can say these things.' He looked at his watch, mimicked surprise. 'My goodness. I'm going to be unforgivably late if I don't hurry. Don't wait up for me.' She never did.

Long after he had left she sat motionless on the sofa. The sensation of vertigo was as real as if a physical abyss was opening at her feet. Her husband knew . . . something at least. Her sister teetered on the edge of suspicion. While she herself, Mary Page Butler, fought to keep at arm's length the thought that all Cy Stevenson's attention, flattery, compliments and caresses were devoted to the single aim of buying her vote.

She hurled the magazine across the room, fury possessing her as even he had never possessed her. Water poured from an upturned flower vase. The magazine skidded to a slow stop across the carpet. The sound of her scream of anger came back to her as an echo memory.

While the resolution was still with her she picked up the phone. It would be late in Paris but not too late. Fin, she told Josette Picard on the phone, was planning a business trip. Could she come over to Paris to stay for a few weeks while he was away?

When that was settled she made another call, this time to Cannes and after that a call to the Marbella Club in southern Spain. By the arrangements she made she had ensured that she would be away from Meyerick until late into the autumn.

21

The fever returned as night fell. In the white vaulted hospital room lit by a single kerosene lamp, Nan Luc sat beside Max's bed feeding him trickles of water and washing the heat from his body.

For Max the night was another agony of strange dreams; of intolerable heat; and the sounds of torrential rain raking the long windows of the hospital room, gurgling along zinc gutters and spurting from downpipes. But it was also a night when he was aware of Nan Luc next to him, aware of holding her hands and talking to her, feverish repetitions of his wish for them to stay together.

Waking before dawn, he found Nan Luc lying awake on the bed beside him. Her face had an extraordinary, almost translucent pallor like the transulence of her teeth between the slightly parted lips. She lay on her side, facing him. Her legs were drawn up towards him, not quite evenly, so that he could reach out and touch the smoothness of the inside of her thigh.

She smiled at him. 'You're feeling better.'

'I must be.' He leaned over and kissed her lips. 'I feel as if I've been talking to you all night.'

She smiled. 'You have.'

'Was it gibberish? Nonsense?'

'Not nonsense,' she said.

'I'm not leaving without you, Nan Luc.' He stopped. 'Did I say that already?'

'Many times last night,' she said. 'That and a lot of other things.'

He heaved himself on to one elbow. 'I don't know how it came out but I meant it all,' he said. 'I want to marry you, Nan.'

'You said that, too.'

'And what did you say?'

'I said I wanted to marry you.'

'If we were married here in Vietnam, is there any chance the government would let you leave?'

She sat up on the edge of the bed, her face turned towards the window. 'We must stop talking like this, Max,' she said after a moment. 'It hurts and it does no good. Even if the French priest would marry us, the administration would never recognise it. Much less let us leave together. You know, you've seen it. The party line is that nobody has any wish to leave Vietnam, even while hundreds of boat people each day are risking everything on the high seas.' She got up and fetched the water bowl and a cloth from the wooden table and began to bathe his hands and arms.

'If I found a way, another way,' he said, 'would you come with me?'

'There's no time to find another way.'

'If we could make time, would you take the risk?'

'It's not just a risk for me, Max. You would have to be very sure yourself.'

'You think all this is just the fever talking.'

She shrugged uncertainly. 'You're a long way from the West, you meet a girl . . .'

'I was sure back in Paris,' he said. 'From the moment I realised you were not going to make it to the café.'

'Is that true?'

'It's true.'

She knelt on the bed, resting her forehead against the side of his head. 'If you're sure,' she said, 'I'll take any risk. Any risk for us just to be together.'

'Forget about her, Max,' Harold Bolson said. 'Every second American who comes here falls for one of these girls. Usually it's not something that lasts. In any case you can't put her in your duffel bag and smuggle her from Saigon. It's over. Be smart about it.'

Max stood unsteadily in Bolson's hotel room. 'Sometimes it pays not to be too smart,' he said.

'Tell me when,' Bolson said. 'Listen, I'm thinking of Nan Luc.

Van Khoa's a decent man. He can give her the protection she needs here.'

'And if she doesn't want to marry Van Khoa?'

Bolson shrugged. 'You're still pretty sick. I guess they just might let you stay on a few days. Settle for that, Max.'

Max shook his head. 'They've made it clear we all leave together.'

'Then what the hell have you got Hunter running round trying to buy black market jerry cans of fuel for? Even if you can heist a jeep and make a run for the Cambodian border you'll be no safer there. The whole central and southern part of the country is controlled by a pro-Vietnamese government. To the north you risk falling into the hands of the crazy goons of the Khmer Rouge. Like I said, Max, forget about her. It's best for both of you.'

Outside, a small party of Vietnamese had been assembled by Van Khoa to see off the foreign journalists: some of the court officials, the hotel management, the interpreters and Van Khoa himself. Max's eyes never left Nan Luc as Van Khoa made a brief speech from the bottom step of the bus.

'What has been important in your visit is the demonstration that Vietnam has a system of effective, revolutionary justice,' Van Khoa said, reading rapidly in barely comprehensible English. 'Comrade Quatch was faced with serious charges. The court was quickly able to determine that these charges were malicious and false. Accordingly the verdict was *not guilty* on all counts.'

'You're saying there was *no* corruption?' Hunter called from the back. 'You're saying there was no American associate in Geneva?'

Van Khoa consulted his watch. 'Regrettably we have no time for questions before the bus leaves. Good luck, gentlemen.' He bent his head to his script again. 'And let us hope you will feel able, as the judge said in his opening words, let us hope that you will feel able to report a fair trial, fairly.'

Van Khoa came forward to shake hands with Hal Bolson. One or two journalists said goodbyes to the interpreters they had worked with. Max and Nan Luc were no more than four yards apart. He walked slowly towards her and she extended her hand.

'I love you,' he said quietly as they shook hands.

'What difference can that make to us now?' she said, her eyes brimming with tears.

'You meant what you said about the risk?'

'Yes.'

'Meet me on the river path. As close to midnight as you can make it.'

She looked towards the bus where some of the journalists were already climbing aboard. 'But they're taking you straight back to Saigon.'

'Please, Miss Hyn,' Van Khoa's voice called. 'The bus is leaving.'

'I'll be waiting for you,' he said. 'Where the river bends.' And releasing her hand he turned away and mounted the steps to join the other Westerners on the crowded open platform at the back of the old bus.

'And so we say farewell to the earthly paradise of Cahn Roc,' Hunter intoned to the waving Vietnamese. 'A city famed throughout the orient as a legendary seat of Marxist justice.'

Max forced his way to where Hunter stood at the rail. He looked down. Nan Luc's face was lifted towards his. 'Did you get it?' he said to the Australian.

'It'll be where you asked for it. Five jerry-cans. It's just cost you two hundred dollars, sport,' he said. He, too, was looking down at Nan Luc. 'But if I were asked I'd say it was worth every brass farthing.'

A low pink moon faded in and out behind a ragged mass of black cloud. From the reeds on the dark river bank a million frogs croaked and chortled. Fish flickered like quicksilver and splashed back into the water.

From where he stood in the deep shadow of the exposed roots of a mango, Max could see the outline of the city of Cahn Roc not half a mile away where the river formed a tiny Mekong Delta of its own as it broadened out in dozens of separate channels towards the sea.

So far it had gone smoothly. After telling the bus driver that he needed to get off to be sick, Max had plunged into the deep forest by the roadside and run until even the sound of Hunter singing 'Waltzing Matilda' as he blocked the driver's way had faded into a mass of buzzing, trilling insects around his head. He knew the fever had not yet completely left him but as he had walked all afternoon through the dank, dripping forest paths, he had felt buoyed by what he was doing, by the prospect of escape with Nan Luc.

It had taken longer than he had thought to reach the river. No forest path ran straight and steering by the sun was not always possible in the green half-darkness of the afternoon. But by early evening he had heard voices and moving carefully forward, he was able to see a group of men stripped to their torn, muddy shorts, building a fish trap on the river bank.

It was dark by the time he had reached the point on the river where it bent back on itself towards the delta. Now, as his watch said ten minutes after midnight, he was already beginning to worry.

Another ten minutes elapsed before he heard a low crackling of bicycle wheels across the twigs and leaves on the path and saw the moonlit outline of Nan Luc riding towards him along the river bank. When he emerged from under the dome of mango roots she stopped and let the bicycle fall from her. He saw that, tied across her back, she carried a flat canvas pouch and felt a lump rise in his throat at the thought that this sack was enough to carry all her possessions.

'Some fishermen were unloading on the river road,' she said. 'I had to wait until they were through.'

He took her hands and drew her into the shadow of the tree roots. 'You've had time to think,' he said. 'You can still turn back.'

She shook her head. 'The Cambodian border is less than ten miles from here,' she said briskly. 'Are you hoping we can cross it tonight?'

'No,' he said. 'Cambodia's too dangerous. I think we can get away by sea.'

She shook her head. 'There's a coastguard cutter permanently stationed at Cahn Roc. In any case it would take weeks of planning to buy a boat. And then more waiting for a moonless night.'

'We already have a boat,' he said. 'Fast enough to outrun the coastguard in a full moon.'

*

Deep in the shadowed creek the sharp white prow of Quatch's launch gleamed in the moonlight. Behind it, across the lawns, the curved roofs and balconied windows of the administrator's summer pavilion were visible among the great trees. Watching from the thick reeds Nan Luc and Max could see no lights in the house, no sign of guards in the grounds.

It had been a long bitter journey, struggling through the reeds and tree roots of the river bank, each dragging two five gallon jerry cans of fuel which Hunter had had hidden at a point where the river almost touched the road. It was obvious to Nan Luc that Max's fever was barely being kept at bay. She had taken the lead, wading through the shallows, trying to choose a path where the floating roots were least tangled with the sharp bladed water grasses. Inexorably their rests had become more and more frequent until every five or ten minutes Max would slump forward across the top of a jerry can gasping for breath as the sweat poured down his face.

'It's three o'clock,' he said. 'If we can't get under way in half an hour we'll have to wait up until tomorrow night.'

She was kneeling in the shallow water beside him, watchful as the moon emerged from the ragged rain clouds. It was then that she had seen it. First as a hazy white fairy palace and then in sharper detail as Quatch's shuttered summer pavilion, with the moored launch riding unattended in the creek.

Max knew that he was close to the end of his strength, at times even close to losing consciousness. As they dragged the heavy fuel cans the last hundred yards along the bank of the creek his pulse was thudding in his head and the burning salt from his own sweat blurred his vision to near blindness.

Beside the smooth whiteness of the launch they stopped to listen. Fighting the waves of weakness that came over him, Max sought to concentrate on the night sounds, the frogs and insects, the screech of birds and monkeys in the high trees.

'Is it possible the whole place has been left unguarded?' he whispered to Nan as they loaded the fuel into the boat.

She came to stand next to him, half supporting him. 'In the country,' she said, 'there's no real need for guards.'

'What about servants? Would they have all been dismissed when Quatch was arrested?'

'Perhaps. Or perhaps all but one or two.'

'OK,' he said. 'We take our first big risk. If there's a servant still at the house he'll hear the engine start. I guess a phone call ahead to the coastguard at Cahn Roc is all he'd need to do.'

'If we don't start the engine, it won't be heard.' She crossed quickly to the bank and slid into the water. Standing up to her shoulders she looked up at him. 'Throw me down the rope,' she said.

'You can't haul this thing alone.' He slipped the mooring. 'If we're going to get out of here we're going to do it together,' he said and slid down the bank into the water beside her.

There was still no sign from the house, no voices of guards, no barking of dogs. Inch by inch they dragged the launch along the creek, Nan Luc hauling on the bow rope, Max, part pushing, part guiding the sharp edge of the prow through the white tentacles of roots that reached out from the bank.

For Nan Luc it was no less a nightmare than it was for Max. Every few steps she picked through the tangle of roots and weeds on the river bed, every time she turned to haul on the rope, she was confronted by Max's face, drawn, dark-eyed, exhausted almost beyond endurance, his teeth clamped against the waves of shivering that swept over him. But they both knew there was no stopping now. In half an hour the first dawn light would make it out of the question to run for the open sea. Hauling on the rope, watching the bow ease forward another foot or two, turning to see Max struggling for his balance, almost slipping below the black water, the nightmare continued.

For Max the anaesthesia of fever had already taken over. Each time he felt the launch move he gripped and pushed on the slippery woodwork. But he was no longer able to feel the ache in his legs or the sharpness of the broken roots as they flailed his shoulders. If he thought of anything his mind was drifting back to afternoons on the Charles River, rowing against Yale or Princeton, conscious of nothing but the numbed pain of the last few rhythmic strokes of a tight finish.

When he heard Nan Luc's voice it was through what seemed a swirling fog, the words repeated twice before he understood. 'We're here, Max. We're at the mouth of the creek.'

Resting his back against the bank, he forced his eyes to focus.

From shoulder level the great width of the open river spread away into the darkness.

She held the launch close to the bank while he climbed through the tangle of roots and scrambled aboard. Moments later they were standing together in the well of the boat, the water streaming from them to form a gleaming puddle on the polished planking.

Running at half throttle before the river's flow, the launch cut easily through the water, its powerful engine a muffled throb. It had proved easy enough to start, relocking the fuel line and short circuiting the ignition. Summers spent on Cape Cod had provided the little expertise necessary. The fuel tank had been, as he expected, virtually empty. But the twenty gallons of gasoline they had dragged along the river bank would, if all went well, be just enough to carry them first to the open sea and then to a landfall just inside the Thai coastline. If all went well.

'Two hundred kilometres,' Nan Luc said, kneeling on the wheel seat beside him. 'Out at full speed past Phu Quoc Island and then north to the Thai coast opposite Ko Kut. We're going to make it.'

'Do many boat people make it from Cahn Roc?'

'Not sailing straight past the lighthouse,' she said. 'But then not many people think of hiring the ex-administrator's boat for the day.'

He found himself lifted by her confidence. By one of the unpredictable changes in the course of the fever, he was feeling better again, clearer headed. In his nostrils he could smell the open sea, now no more than a mile ahead. The cloud had thickened too, reducing the moon to a faint pink glow in the sky. Before them the river was beginning to widen, the channels of the delta like the fingers of a hand spread flat on the landscape.

The searchlight hit them from out of the darkness of the channel ahead. As Max wrenched his head from the path of the blinding white light he pulled on the throttle and felt the launch surge forward. Blinded from the front, he turned the launch in a tight half circle. Then from the bank somewhere behind them another searchlight flared. Held in the cross-lights they ducked below the gunwale as they heard the thud of a heavy machine gun and saw the edge of the sprayshield shatter above their heads.

They lay together in the well of the boat as another burst of fire splintered woodwork and ricocheted howling into the night. Then the firing stopped and a voice, high-pitched even through the loud-hailer, called to them in Vietnamese.

'They are ordering us to cut the engine,' Nan Luc said. 'Then to stand up with our hands in the air.'

'I'll put the boat towards the bank,' he said. 'When I cut the engine, you roll over the side. The launch will cover you as you swim for it.'

'You'll come too, Max,' she said fiercely. 'This doesn't have to be the end.'

'This is not the end,' he said. 'Somehow, I'll be back.'

She held him to her. 'If ever . . .' she said.

The loud-hailer voice rose in pitch. As Max reached up to cut the engine, the launch was already drifting towards the bank. For a moment he held Nan Luc's hand tightly, then releasing her, he stood up in the full glare of the searchlight, slowly raising his hands above his head.

Behind him he heard a faint splash, like the fall of a flying fish.

It had been raining since first light, a rattling percussion on an overturned oil drum in the courtyard beyond the barred window of his cell. Max sat on the frame bed, his head hanging forward, somewhere between sleep and waking. He was fairly sure that Nan Luc had made it clear away. The soldiers, young boys in their late teens under an older sergeant, had triumphantly hustled their Westerner back to the courthouse at Cahn Roc. They had no more than a few words of English or French, not enough to put questions to their prisoner. And none of them seemed to have considered the possibility that he had not been alone.

As the cell lightened Max had become aware of a sound from across the corridor, less than a man snoring, a deep inhalation and exhalation of breath. For ten minutes or so he had accepted it into the rhythm of his own breathing until, briefly emerging from his nodding half-sleep, he had become aware that the sound had stopped.

Lifting his head with effort, he looked across the corridor into the deep darkness of the windowless cell opposite.

'You are the young man who was sitting next to Nan Luc in court each day,' a voice said in French-accented English.

Max got to his feet and stood at the barred door of his cell. 'Who are you?' he said, straining his eyes into the darkness.

A white shape approached the bars of the cell opposite. 'Vo Tran Quatch,' the voice said. 'Found *not guilty*, for what it's worth.' He lifted his shoulders. 'In any event I shall be dead by tonight.' On the floor above they could hear the excited chattering of voices. 'They've realised their mistake,' Quatch said, his tiny mouth twisted in amusement. 'They should never have put us together.'

'What did you mean, you'll be dead by tonight?'

'In Vietnam,' Quatch said, 'the difference between *guilty* and *not guilty* is semantic. That's to say, something to be ignored by honest men or the state.'

Sandalled feet clattered lightly down the winding stair. 'Who was the American?' Max asked him. 'The American you met in Geneva?'

Three soldiers ran shouting along the corridor. The grille to Quatch's cell was unlocked and he was dragged out.

'Stevenson,' Quatch said, as he was borne away by the guards. 'Nan Luc's father, Cy Stevenson . . .'

Van Khoa's face was drawn, as pale as his olive skin could become. 'I have no need to ask you who was with you on the launch,' he said.

Max sat on the frame bed looking up at him as the last of the rain dripped and pinged against the oil drum in the courtyard. 'That part of the incident can be considered closed,' Van Khoa added in a voice little above a whisper.

Max turned towards him. 'You mean you will not be pursuing what you call that part of the incident?' he said cautiously.

'For what purpose?' Max shrugged. 'I mentioned it to reassure you, Mr Benning. To reassure you that no one will suffer unnecessarily.'

'You're an unusual policeman, Mr Van Khoa.'

Van Khoa smiled wryly. 'Hear me to the end,' he said. 'Somebody made a blunder.'

'When they put me in a cell opposite Quatch?'

Van Khoa nodded slowly. He walked across the cell and stood at the window, smoothing the arm of his khaki uniform with his mutilated hand. 'You will be put upon a plane from Saigon this afternoon,' he said. 'There will be no further investigation of this incident. You left Vietnam a day after the other journalists because you were too sick to travel. Do you accept my terms?'

'No further investigation as long as I write exactly the same account of the trial as the other journalists?'

'Let's put it in clear, Mr Benning. No action will be taken against Nan Luc unless you publicise anything Vo Tran Quatch might or might not have said to you across this corridor.'

They faced each other.

'I accept,' said Max.

22

In her room Nan Luc made no attempt to light the lamp. For a few moments she stood by the open window looking out over the dark sea. Nothing, she thought, compares with the emptiness of the sound of the tide washing along the shore. Nothing invokes loneliness like the incessant heaving of the black waters. She turned away from the window and sank down on to the sleeping mat, her back against the wall, her knees drawn up before her.

Above the low rumble of the sea she heard a door open and close somewhere in the building. For a moment she listened. Outside on the stone landing she heard a step.

'This isn't the end,' Max had said.

The footsteps continued up the stone stairs. A flood of hope brought her scrambling from the sleeping mat. Then the door opened and Van Khoa stood shadowed in the doorway.

She stood before him without greeting him then stepped back to allow him in. 'The American flew to Bangkok this afternoon,' he said. She watched him, not speaking. 'He is unharmed.'

'You came to tell me that?'

'I am returning to Ho Chi Minh City, tomorrow,' he said. 'I came to say goodbye.'

She turned away from him and lit the kerosene lamp. Now that she knew Max was safe she felt no fear of him. 'So you were only here in Cahn Roc for the trial,' she said. 'To make sure the trial went as you wished.'

'It's over now.'

'I know you are an important man,' she said bitterly. 'A senior officer in the Ministry of State Security. Why should we need you now that justice has been done in Cahn Roc?'

The warm yellow light spread across her face. Van Khoa moved round the table until he was again facing her. 'Quatch is dead,' he said. 'Isn't that the justice you require?'

'Dead?'

'He was taken out to the forest this morning. He was shot by a firing squad.'

'An innocent man,' she taunted him.

'May I sit down?'

She nodded towards a chair. 'I will make tea.' She filled and lit the US Army field cooker. Van Khoa sat staring down where the lamplight fell on his hands, one unmarked, one crippled. It was the first time he had come to her room.

She stood opposite him. 'What sort of verdict was that?' she asked him, emboldened by anger and grief.

'Often there are political reasons,' he said, 'which we find hard to understand.'

'How can there be such injustice in the republic you fought for? How do you allow it?' He looked across to the window. She came forward. 'Is this why thousands want to leave our country? Hundreds of thousands?'

'Quatch is not representative of our revolution, Nan Luc,' he said fiercely. 'You know that.'

'But he was guilty.'

'Of many things.'

'Of the murder of Peter Benning?'

'Responsible, yes, I've no doubt.'

'And guilty of corruption?'

'Yes.'

Her anger made her reckless. 'What happened?' she asked. 'Did other provincial governors, as corrupt as Quatch, object to a verdict of guilty?'

He looked down at the bubbling field cooker. 'There were reasons of state.' He lapsed into silence. 'I don't approve,' he said, 'but I obey.'

She busied herself with the tea. Kneeling, with her back to him, she said: 'The American, Quatch mentioned. Does he exist?' She stood up and handed Van Khoa his tea. 'Does he really exist?'

Van Khoa put down his tea. 'You have a right to know,' he said softly.

'What right do I have more than any other Vietnamese?'

He had begun the long series of fumbling movements with his damaged hand which would draw a cigarette from a pack and light it. He brought the lighter up to the cigarette and squinted at the glowing tip. 'There is no doubt of Quatch's corruption,' he said. 'Of his degeneracy.' She waited. 'He was a collector of a certain type of literature, pornography of course. And movies. Pornographic movies. Films that reflected his own obscene interests. He was wealthy enough to write his own scenarios and to have them made here, in what was then Saigon.'

'There were such studios in Saigon?'

'Where better to make such films? During the war there were many women prepared to make such films. The results were distributed throughout the world.' Van Khoa inhaled on his cigarette. He was watching her, as if considering how much more to say.

'Who was the American who made the movies here in Saigon?'

'Your grandmother tells me that you already know.'

She shook her head in panic. 'I don't believe it. There were thousands of Americans in Saigon, tens of thousands . . .'

He drew heavily on his cigarette. 'Listen to me, Nan Luc. Years after Quatch bought pornography from the American, they met again at a conference in Geneva. By now the American was himself rich and had access to even greater riches. Quatch still had some of the films. He used them to blackmail the American.'

'No.'

'Believe me, Nan Luc. I am not telling you these things to pain you, but you must know the truth. You must stare it in the face. Your father is an evil man, a degenerate as bad or worse than Quatch.'

Nan Luc covered her face with her hands. 'Go now, please go.'

He stood. 'You know,' he said quietly, 'that I would still wish to marry you, Nan Luc. I can offer much. But I know there's no chance of your agreement until you have finally turned your face against America. Against your father.'

For a long time she sat silently, the light from the kerosene lamp gleaming yellow on her dark hair. 'The American's name was Stevenson?' she said at last.

'Yes.'

'How could my mother love a pornographer?'

'That is not for me to explain.'

'How could my mother love a pornographer?' her voice rose. He reached into his pocket with his mangled hand and hooked a set of keys on his one good finger.

'The keys to my office,' he said. 'And to the safe.' He dropped them on the sleeping mat beside her. 'In the safe is the evidence I never used. The evidence Quatch used to blackmail the American, your father.'

Leaving the harbourmaster's tower Nan hurried up the steep Rue de Port, her mind in turmoil. Max was safe. No effort could make her accept that it was only this morning she had last seen him. The sheer misery of the intervening hours had agonisingly stretched every moment. It seemed to her that since she had regained the safety of her room, everything had slowed, even the rhythm of the sun's progress across the sky, the lengthening of the shadows of dusk and the pace of nightfall itself.

What she now knew about her father only magnified the scale of her loss. And added to it an overwhelming sense of apprehension. For a moment she stopped on the steps of the People's Court, grasping Van Khoa's keys in her hand. The image, the single image, she had of her mother came vividly to mind. Something in her stirred, some unexplained chill passed up her spine. She knew she was terrified of the evidence she would find in Van Khoa's safe.

Climbing the stairs past the courtroom she entered and let herself in to the prosecutor's office. Documents stood in neat piles on the desk, blue evidence files, red prosecution folders.

The safe stood on a concrete block in a corner of the room. In it, it now seemed possible, was the answer to the questions which had tantalised and confused her as she had struggled to make sense of the fears and memories she had carried with her since childhood.

Outside in the square the lorry bus from Can Tho pulled in under the weak street lamps flanking the courthouse. There were few passengers: a pair of soldiers on demobilisation leave; a peasant or two with wooden hoes or sickles bartered for handfuls of rice in Can Tho market; a fisherman and his wife returning from a family funeral.

The lorry shuddered into silence as the engine was switched off and the passengers stood obediently waiting for the driver to lower the tailgate. A few moments later they all stood on the sidewalk about to take their leave of each other.

It was then, they would later recount to their families, that the woman's screams came tearing from the courthouse. On the sidewalk the lorry bus passengers stood unmoving, staring up at the lighted window, listening while the screams ebbed into a distraught, heart-rending sobbing.

A man on a bicycle, passing through the square, paused, his face turned upwards. Then in ones and twos the bus passengers began to shuffle away, aware that none of their number had the courage to approach the courthouse door.

PART TWO

Via Gulanga

23

'I have telephoned Cahn Roc,' said the guide in the lobby of Ho Chi Minh City's Independence Hotel, 'and there is no such person working in the People's Court at Cahn Roc.' She smiled a mouth full of teeth as if to a child dismissing nonsense fears of ghosts.

Max Benning faced the uniformed Vietnamese girl across the counter. 'When did she leave?' He was trying hard to control the desperation rising inside him.

'There is no such woman,' the guide repeated.

'There *was* such a woman. I met her two months ago,' Max said.

The guide shook her head authoritatively. 'Some other woman,' she said. 'You have made a mistake, Mr Benning. It sometimes happens,' she added generously.

'No.' Max placed his hands flat on the table between them. 'Nan Luc Hyn was senior investigating clerk at the People's Court in Cahn Roc.'

The guide shook her head, smiling toothily. 'Not so.'

Max stared at her until her smile faded. 'OK,' he said. 'If you say so.' He turned to go, then swung back towards her. 'This morning's tour,' he said, 'is to Prahat?'

She nodded happily, her point won. 'Prahat and the Mekong temples,' she said.

'I'll take it.' He walked across the lobby and took the elevator to his floor. Leaving the lift he checked that he had both Vietnamese money and dollars then walked on past his room to the emergency stairs.

It was only three flights down and he could see the tour bus in the forecourt from the landing windows. At the bottom of the concrete staircase a swing door led out into a small courtyard where an old woman was pushing a trolley of bedsheets. Beyond the first courtyard was another, a parking lot for vans supplying the hotel.

He crossed quickly, ducking behind the vehicles so that the attendant on the rear gate could not see him. In the street behind the hotel he walked towards the Cathedral Square. Yesterday, with the sort of wrench that left him breathless, he had seen a lorry bus stopping there with Cahn Roc painted on its side.

In the streets of Saigon a Western face no longer excited any great interest. Tours were encouraged by a Vietnamese government desperately short of hard currency and, on his earlier trip, Max had seen the first American veterans making organised visits to the areas in which they had served.

But on the back of a lorry bus to Cahn Roc the tall young man in the safari jacket, already sweat-stained above the pockets, was an object of anxious curiosity to the twenty or so peasant men and women travelling with him. They took his offered cigarettes and sat back to whisper tensely among themselves. Max spoke nothing but phrasebook Vietnamese; the peasants spoke neither English nor French.

He had no real plan beyond seeing Nan Luc again. He had found that he had missed her unendurably in the two months they had been separated. Even so, there were times he wondered if he wasn't crazy, pursuing the sort of dream that is best left where it ended.

Max sat on the slatted bench, his back jolting against the side of the truck, and let the persistent excitement of Nan Luc's aura wash over him. He was not a fool. He knew the dangers of constantly exposing himself to his memories of Nan Luc but every day, every night since he had been parted from her, he had struggled to recreate that extraordinary femininity, the softness and the strength, the East and West in everything she did, the way she walked, stood, laughed.

He had told his mother in the London clinic that he was going back to Vietnam and she had waved her now emaciated hand in the air, a gesture of contemptuous dismissal. 'Like father . . .' she had said, then dropped her hand, too weak to finish the line.

'I'll be back inside a fortnight,' he said. 'That's all my visa allows.'

'Let's hope *my* visa runs a little past that,' she said without self-pity. 'It's a woman of course.'

'Yes.'

'Ah. And your father, the scholar adventurer, did he have a girl?'

'I don't know.' He pressed his mother's wrist. 'I'll be back in a couple of weeks,' he had said.

It was dark when the lorry bus bucked and rattled into the square at Cahn Roc. Most of the peasants had got off at villages or road crossings on the way. An old man and his wife slept intermittently opposite Max; a young soldier, perhaps home on leave, was stretched out the length of the tailgate drunk on Lua Moi.

As the old US Army truck came to a halt Max jumped off the back and walked quickly across the square past the People's Court towards the hospital. He had wondered if the guide at the hotel in Saigon might phone ahead, suspecting he was making for Cahn Roc. But then he had realised that that is not the way the mind, schooled in a closed system, works. She would have reported his absence from the tour of Prahat, that's all. Anything more would be to assume too much involvement and thus responsibility for what was happening.

On the hospital side of the square he turned into the Rue du Vieux Port. In the narrow street, lights chinked through shuttered windows and the high Vietnamese voices and cooking smells floated in the night. He could see the gulf now, a shimmering stretch of blackness broken by the faint lights of fishing boats, like stars in a black firmament.

The harbour tower stood a lighter coloured stone than the building around it. Two or three oil lamps glowed at the windows. Nan Luc's room, he remembered, was up on the top floor. He walked on past the arched entrance and looked up. He was flooded with relief to see a shadow cast by an oil lamp moving across the window and retraced his steps quickly to the entrance to the tower.

He had time, standing in the strangely vaulted lobby, to register that his breathing was shallow and fast, almost as if he were trembling after some physical effort. As he climbed the stone steps the longing to see her, the need to touch her and talk to her and lie beside her drained energy from him.

On the top landing her door burst open. A tiny Vietnamese boy, naked, fat-bellied, ran for the stairs pursued by an elder sister. Scooping the child up and hugging him the teenage girl suddenly became aware of Max standing in the shadows. Her mouth dropped open and the child came close to sliding out of her arms. She ran for the open door and slammed it behind her.

He stood sickened by the glimpse he had through the open door. In place of the rolled sleeping mat, the travelling chest, the neatly piled books, he saw a family's quarters, a jumble of pots around a small floor stove, a string of washing from wall to wall and people, four or five Vietnamese, looking at him in astonishment.

The door opened slowly. A middle-aged man wearing a jungle green T-shirt and jean shorts stood in the doorway. There was no welcome on his creased, tanned face.

'What do you want here?' he said in French.

'I'm looking for Nan Luc Hyn. She used to live here.' The man's expression did not change. 'Do you know her?' The Vietnamese shook his head briefly and began to close the door. 'An investigating clerk at the People's Court here at Cahn Roc.' Max had moved his foot to stop the door closing. The man gave two brief shakes of his head and looked down at Max's shoe.

'You took over the room from her,' Max said, digging into his pocket. He pulled out a wad of Vietnamese notes and thrust them into the startled man's hand. 'Tell me what happened to her,' Max said. 'Is she still at the People's Court?'

The Vietnamese crossed to the head of the stairs and peered down, his hand lifted, enjoining silence. Then, clutching the money, he came back and opened the door to the room. 'Please, monsieur . . .' he said, gesturing for Max to enter.

Max went in. Two women were grilling fish over the floor stove. The teenage girl still held the child. Another child was asleep on a mat in the corner.

The door closed behind him. The Vietnamese inclined his head. 'Duong Tran Tron,' he said. 'This is my family.'

'Can you help me find Nan Luc?' Max looked into the hard, weatherbeaten face.

'Perhaps,' Duong said.

'How long have you and your family had this room?'

'We moved here last week.'

'And Nan Luc?'

'She is no longer here,' Duong said. 'She left after the trial of the provincial administrator Quatch.'

'She went to Saigon?'

The Vietnamese hung his head. 'Her father was American,' he said at length. 'Perhaps she went to America.'

A turmoil of feeling combined with the heavy smells of cooking in the room to make his stomach heave. 'She became a refugee?'

Again the man's head hung and Max realised he was expressing his shame. 'She bought a fishing boat from one of the villages up the coast,' he said. 'She left with other refugees by night.'

'You're sure of this.'

The small face nodded slowly. 'She had an American face,' he said, seeking an explanation which would satisfy him. 'Perhaps she left to look for her father.'

Through the split crust of faded posters the double doors of the Eros Bar still showed a dusty red. The wide windows, past which a generation of GIs had drifted, staring at the girls and good times within, were now crudely boarded up and layered with their own thick coat of government announcements.

For a few moments Max stood before the building and tried to conjure a picture of the Eros as it had once been, throbbing with rock music, alive with the shouts of GIs and the giggling laughter of the bar girls.

When the woman's voice spoke from the balcony above, Max stepped back, startled. 'One moment, monsieur,' the voice repeated in French, 'I'll come down and let you in.'

He could hear her voice as she descended the stairs, urging him not to go away. Then the door opened and a grey head of hair was thrust out. 'You men are all such romantics,' Bernadette said. 'But then when I was young, men would have crossed the seas for me too.' She pulled the door wide. 'Come upstairs. I'll give you tea.'

She moved with agility across the broken glass which still littered the floor and began to mount the winding staircase. Following her, Max breathed in the dank smells of the abandoned bar room. A few broken metal chairs were all that was left of the furnishings. Curtains had been torn down, glasses and bottles smashed or carried away, the bar itself splintered and torn out for firewood.

The room above was different, small, neatly kept. There was no cupboard or box. On a wooden board Bernadette's possessions were for all to see: a pile of carefully folded clothes of rough linen; a few cooking pans; an old French primus stove; a teapot and bowls.

She waved her hand. 'How are the mighty fallen, you're saying to yourself.'

Max shook his head. 'Have you lived here since the trial?'

'Van Khoa allows me. He is not a vindictive man. And of course he's still in love with Nan Luc. It's better than a labour camp, but I've no future beyond this room. Thanks to Quatch.'

'You seem to know me,' Max said.

'Of course. I saw you at the trial. Afterwards, briefly, I spoke to Nan Luc about you. You've come to look for her and she's already gone.'

'I know that.'

'It's a dangerous journey, monsieur. Sit down while I make tea.'

'Where would she head for?' Max asked as Bernadette pumped the stove and lit it.

'If they left from Cahn Roc, mostly to Thailand. If they left further south, perhaps even to Hong Kong. Mostly it would be chance. Winds, storms, the charts they were able to procure, the quantity of gasoline . . .' He was silent, watching her. 'I notice,' she said, 'that you haven't asked me why she decided to leave.'

'No.' Max sat down on a bent metal chair rescued from the bar downstairs. 'I've no need to ask you that.'

She smiled, filtered a few tea leaves through her fingers into the teapot and poured in a tiny amount of boiling water. 'Why then, I wonder, did you accept my invitation to drink tea?'

Max paused for a moment, watching her add water to the brew. 'My father was murdered in your apartment in Paris.'

She nodded a casual assent and smiled at his angry intake of breath. 'You can't be surprised still at the way we Vietnamese look on death. What can it mean to you, the death of a father you had never even seen?'

'He was a husband too.'

She pouted dismissively. 'His love was Vietnam.'

'Do you know how he died?'

She placed a bowl of tea on the board next to him. 'Of course. He had traced many of the pieces of the great Hue screen which Quatch had had broken up to sell separately. He was about to denounce us to our government. A young man was selected. A few francs. Unfortunately the hothead did it in my apartment.'

Max looked at her unbelievingly. 'That's all? Unfortunately the hothead did it in your apartment! That's all you have to say?'

'You want me to say I'm sorry? Drink your tea, monsieur, it's you who's the hypocrite. Not me.'

'Later, when Nan Luc went to Paris herself, did she know you were involved?'

'Of course not. And in fact I was barely involved.'

'An accessory.'

'If you like. I knew it was to happen, but it was Monsieur Quatch of course who organised it. We suffered a few days of worry, but by then our forces were marching into Saigon and the French government had no wish to be gratuitously unfriendly.'

Max stood up. 'I'll go now. I made a mistake. I shouldn't have come up.'

'You haven't drunk your tea, monsieur. More hypocrisy.' She paused. 'And so you believe she undertook this highly dangerous passage to the West to find *you*?' The old woman emitted a sudden shriek of laughter. A chill struck him. Bernadette lifted her bowl of tea and sipped. 'Van Khoa was jealous,' she said softly. 'Of you, of America . . . He believed she could never be his while she remained poised between East and West. He believed her dreams of America had led her away from him. To you.' She sucked tea from the bowl and set it down on the board. 'He told me this just before he released me from custody. He regrets what he did. He felt powerless, you see, unable to combat these dreams of America, an American family, an American father.'

'Go on . . .'

'But, you see, he knew about her father. And he knew that what she had heard in the trial she refused to believe. So Van

Khoa came to a decision. To tell her everything about her father. By the harsh method he chose, he forced the truth upon her.'

'You're telling me she left to find her father?'

She grinned triumphantly. 'To find her father – to find vengeance!'

24

After three weeks at sea Nan Luc had only her sense of outrage to sustain her. Thoughts of Max were thoughts of another time in her life, too warm, too disturbing, too creative of a sense of irreparable loss.

It was easier to think of her father, to nurse the hate, to let his ultimate betrayal fester inside her. She knew with a total certainty that her father's betrayal had to be avenged. She knew also that she was the only one who could do it.

At night on the prow of the ship, looking out over the unmoving sea, she indulged the vastness of her hate. By day she was captain of the ship, controller of the commissary, doctor and sustainer of morale. Three of the women were dangerously sick; an old man had died. The ration was necessarily much smaller than planned: the rice the refugees had been sold had been mixed with white beach sand, reducing the edible portion of a sack by half. The water, taken from the clear streams around Cahn Roc, had turned brackish and bitter in the mouth. Only the fruits were enough to maintain a meagre ration.

In their second week out they had suffered a sudden and terrifying storm which had left arms broken and planks torn from the high side of the boat so that the menace of shipping water existed in everything but a calm sea.

There had been pirates too, amateurs, Thai fishermen who lacked the commitment to attack when she shouted across the water that they had cholera aboard. And there had been the sad and human quarrelling on the fishing boat itself about the distribution of rations or the allotment of sleeping places.

But against these setbacks, overwhelming them, her will burnt like a magnesium flare, stoking her determination to survive. To reach America.

Her leadership was never questioned. They looked to her for their orders, they clung to her decisions and to her own icy certainty that they would survive. Kim Hoang appointed himself her deputy, interpreting and explaining her orders to the others. They had first met as children at the orphanage. And again later, when he had come to write upbeat stories for the Cahn Roc provincial newspaper. Memories of their orphanage days enabled him to trust her: first with stories of petty corruption or disobedience, later with the names of people he met as a provincial journalist, people who were still prepared to risk their lives to escape what amounted to life in Vietnam in the early 1990s.

At nights Nan Luc slept on the prow of the fishing boat, a blanket over her, an empty rice sack for a pillow. Most nights she dreamed of Max Benning, then woke angry with herself. She had come to think that to dream of him, even to think of him, weakened the resolve which she knew must drive her through this next part of her life. She knew she had been touched by a man as she never would be again. She knew that whatever happened to her in the future she would be loyal to him as the man she loved. But she had no hope that she would see him again. As a Vietnamese woman she was certain that a life of love for this one man did not accord with her destiny. That had been set long ago in her life. The fulfilment of destiny was to reach America. To find her father. To dream and dream of Max Benning softened her, diluted the vital force that must give her the energy to succeed in her task.

The second moon of their voyage lighted a glittering sea. If lying there she sometimes let thoughts of Max come into her mind, she forced herself to think without longing. To think of him as an incident in her past, like a candle at the back of the temple, the priests said, whose flame fades each step we take from it, but whose brightness we know remains undimmed.

They had expected by now to be in the main lanes for merchant shipping but they had seen nothing but a huge ghostly oil tanker gliding across the night sea several miles ahead. They had lit their lantern and shouted and banged gongs but without real hope. That had been more than ten days ago.

Sitting on the prow of the fishing boat Nan Luc tried to analyse their position. They had been eating fish only for the last week or more but the difficulty of catching enough for over twenty people had reduced them all to a level close to starvation. Water was more serious. One US Army jerry-can was all that remained. The fishing boat itself was solid in calm conditions but in another storm it could very easily capsize. They must sight a ship in the next few days.

As dawn broke behind the boat, she lay on her stomach, her hands locked under her chin, peering into the still dark western sky. The motion of the fishing boat was easy across the slight swell. The splashing of the bow wave lulled her into thoughts of Max. She was still more than half asleep but the candle of light ahead was not disappearing. Every step you take, the priests said, every week, every year . . . She shook her head and a second later scrambled to her feet calling to the watch.

At sea the eyes play strange tricks. She found she was unable to decide whether it was moving right or left across their bow. It seemed almost as if the distant ship were stationary. A fishing vessel perhaps. But fishing vessels did not carry generators to produce a light like this. And yet this light, if the ship were moving towards them, grew no stronger.

Then, as they lit the lanterns she began to understand. The ship was moving towards them, but the lightening sky behind them cancelled what would have been, at night, the growing brightness of the deck lights.

She found her own excitement difficult to sustain now. If the vessel stayed on course it was bound to see them. It was surely even bound by now to have picked them up on radar. Or finally, if all else failed, would they not be bound to see against the pale lemon aureola of the rising sun the silhouette of the black-sailed fishing boat?

As the sun rose and the bright bow lights before them faded, it became easier to make out the lines of the approaching ship. By its speed and superstructure it was clearly a warship. As the angle of approach slightly changed Nan saw the American flag fluttering from its stern.

'The captain's on the bridge, miss,' the lieutenant said. 'We're on Fleet Manoeuvres. We're authorised to give you food, water, medical attention and even temporary repairs. But we can only take the sick on board. We cannot deviate or change course.'

'Please let me see the captain,' Nan Luc repeated. She had heard on the radio from Saigon that refugees were no longer welcome in Malaysia, Singapore and Hong Kong. She had heard from Van Khoa that at one time 50,000 boat people a month were asking for asylum. But she had never believed the US Navy would turn them away.

'I'm sorry, miss,' the American said. 'I really am.'

She stepped back to the polished wooden rail where the cutter waited below. 'I will go back,' she said, 'and arrange for the sick to be transferred to you. Where will you take them?'

'They will be treated on board, miss. As I explained we are on Fleet Manoeuvres. We won't be seeing land for five or six weeks.'

'I understand, lieutenant,' Nan Luc said.

The lieutenant nodded, relieved. 'I'm giving orders for the food and medical stores to be brought up now.' He paused. 'Look, miss,' he said, 'you must head for Gulanga Island.'

'How far is that?'

'About three hundred miles due south. There's a United Nations Camp there. I can provide you with a chart.'

'Thank you.' She started down the rope ladder to the cutter. 'The problem is, lieutenant, we have nobody on board who can read a chart.'

The lieutenant leaned on the rail watching the cutter move alongside the listing fishing boat as Nan Luc climbed on to the deck. He felt bad. The girl was an American. Or at least very nearly. He had offered, on the grounds of her having an American father, to let her stay on the destroyer, but she had refused. A very tough and a very beautiful girl.

He straightened up and saluted as Commodore Brompton came down the accommodation ladder. 'A melancholy business,' Brompton said.

'The girl's half American,' the lieutenant told him. 'It seems to make it worse, sir. I know it shouldn't, but it does.'

'You offered medical supplies and repairs if necessary?'

'She's arranging for the sick to be transferred.'

Brompton nodded. Across the fifty yards of water he watched the refugees coming up on deck. They waved, most of them, as they came out on the deck house. Brompton lifted his hand to shield his eyes from the low angled sun.

'That's the girl, sir,' the lieutenant said. 'The one that's hustling them all up on deck.' He looked round and was puzzled to see that the captain was smiling to himself. As he looked back it took him a moment or two to realise that something was different. He looked again, harder this time. The angle of that strange sail was different. He checked the level of the deck. The bow was angled strangely upwards. 'Good God,' he said. 'She's sinking.'

He saw the captain smile again. 'Get another boat out there and swing the nets down,' Brompton ordered.

It was an operation carried out with consummate efficiency. Women and children were handed down to the cutter as the stern of the fishing boat settled in the water. Then the men jumped from the low rail and started swimming towards the warship. Nan Luc left last, diving from the rising prow.

From the destroyer's deck the captain watched her cut through the water then swim slowly back and forth behind the swimming refugees, shepherding her charges as they reached for the nets being lowered down the ship's side.

She was the last to come aboard, almost tipped from the net at his feet, Ed Brompton thought, like a rare, beautiful object from the deep. She got to her feet.

'Of course,' he said holding out his hand. 'It's obvious, when you think about it. Sink your own ship. You could almost call it the Nelson touch.'

Nan Luc turned to the rail. Less than fifty yards away the oddly shaped black sail of *Cahn Roc* listed sharply and slid into the water.

'Now hear this,' Edward Brompton's voice came over the ship's loudspeakers. 'I have just received a signal from the Admiral's flagship. It reads: "Special commendation to F flotilla, Commodore Brompton and officers and crews of his ships. Exercise Peking Duck ends as of now." '

Nan Luc was leaning on the deck rail looking out across the slow swell of the ocean when Ed Brompton came down the accommodation ladder. She had grown to like the man with his easy white-toothed smile, his close-cropped hair and the gold-rimmed spectacles that gave him almost an academic air.

'Congratulations,' Nan Luc smiled. 'That's what a special commendation for F flotilla means, isn't it?'

He nodded. 'You're learning Navy ways, Nan.' For a moment he stood looking at her.

'What happens now?' she said.

'Now we put you ashore and sail for home.' He paused again. 'Six weeks is a long time, Nan. I'm going to miss having you on board. The whole crew is,' he added hurriedly.

'They've been wonderful,' she said. 'I feel like writing my own commendation to the Navy Department.'

He grinned. 'That could be going too far. My orders now are to put you ashore at the UN reception island of Gulanga. It's technically Indonesian territory but administered by the UN.'

'Is it far from here?'

'No. Only five or six hours' sailing.'

'And then what?'

'And then your applications are processed.'

'I can't believe it's all going to happen.'

He gripped the rail. 'Sometimes it doesn't just happen like that,' he said. 'Not everybody gets accepted. I don't know how they decide these things but it's not always plain sailing.'

'One step at a time,' she said. 'It's plain sailing as far as Gulanga Island.'

'Just point the bow and let wind and wave do the rest.'

She touched his hand. 'I can never thank you enough,' she said.

He looked at her, indecisive for almost the first time in his life. She was not yet twenty-five. He was more than twenty years older. He looked from her face out over the grey swell beyond the rail. 'It's been easy,' he said, 'all too easy.'

Nan Luc stood on the white concrete quayside. Around the bay the thickly wooded hills rose blue and strangely pinnacled with rock. A half-mile out the USS *John C. Hunter* was raising anchor. The little group of refugees around Nan watched and waved.

The sun glistened on the bridge glazing and Nan Luc too lifted her hand, sure, even though she could not see him, that Ed Brompton was standing there. Then she turned and led the group of refugees towards the registry and the barrage of signs and directions for the reception of refugees.

At the door a man in khaki shirt and shorts was emerging. He was a thin, sandy-haired man with a beach towel thrown over his shoulder and some snorkelling equipment under one arm. He looked at the long straggle of refugees coming up the steps. Lifting his free hand he said in a carefully enunciated English accent, 'The registry is closed for today. Temporary accommodation will be provided until it reopens on Monday morning.'

'It's Thursday midday,' Nan said. 'What do we do until Monday?'

The Englishman shrugged. 'Get to know the island,' he suggested impatiently. 'Lovely views.'

'We need to register,' Nan Luc said. 'We need to feel our applications are at least in the machine.'

The UN officer looked contemptuously at her. He shifted his snorkelling equipment from one arm to another. 'The registry is only one part of the work that goes on here,' the Englishman said severely. 'The business of Gulanga can't be stopped to process the reception of two dozen new refugees.'

'I thought that was the business of Gulanga,' Nan said.

The Englishman turned his eyes on her. They were a pale, almost colourless green. 'You would be advised,' he said, 'to appreciate that you are not an American yet.'

25

'Nan Luc, come here.' The Australian woman's voice rose peremptorily. Freda O'Keefe appeared in the doorway of the kitchen, small, thin-faced, not yet thirty years old. 'I said I wanted the breakfast things cleared first. Your English is good enough to know what that means.' She paused to give weight to the words. 'It means I damn well want the breakfast things cleared first.'

Nan Luc rose from the floor where she was kneeling. 'One of the children broke a glass, Mrs O'Keefe,' she said calmly. 'I thought I should clear that up first.'

Freda O'Keefe turned away. 'Just do what you're told when you're told. If I'm wanted I'm down at the beach.'

Nan Luc stood at the window and watched the woman follow the path down to where her car was parked in the dusty road between the two rows of identical UN staff bungalows. Beyond, she could see the stretch of white sand speckled with the coloured umbrellas of UN staff families spending Sunday on the beach.

On the point, the headland which took up a quarter of the island and almost all its habitable land, was the gigantic shanty town of tents and boxwood huts which the Vietnamese refugees called bitterly, New Saigon. Some of them had been on Gulanga Island for over two years; some had already chosen to be returned to Vietnam. Many, like Nan Luc herself, were deep in the process of interviews and 'verifications' which might, at some point, lead them to Australia or the United States. But the process was heartbreakingly slow and only the strongest refugees endured it without scars.

It was three months since Nan Luc had left Cahn Roc. After their time aboard the USS *John C. Hunter* the contrast in their treatment on Gulanga was immediate and painful. Here on the island a mostly unimpressive selection of the world's civil servants exercised a haughty authority over the refugees in their power. They were encouraged by the fact that the newspapers and television companies of the West no longer found the plight of the boat people particularly newsworthy.

Nan Luc thought back to the day when she had been interviewed at the registry by a Belgian reception officer. She had sat in a small room in a wood and tarpaper hut with a huge fan lifting papers on the desk and causing the ash in a full Ricard ashtray to drift across the room.

The man behind the desk had nodded to her as she came in. 'Nan Luc Hyn.' He pushed a paper towards her. 'Please verify the spelling. Please check the date of birth and date of arrival at Gulanga UN camp. You understand,' he intoned by heart, 'that your acceptance and registration at this camp in no way entitles you to claim rights to visas from member states of the United Nations and that, furthermore, registration here implies no United Nations responsibility for accident or loss during your period of stay.'

Nan glanced at the paper. 'The spelling, date of birth and date of arrival are correct,' she said crisply.

The Belgian looked up. He smiled. For a brief moment the determined self-contained manner of the beautiful girl in front of him made him pause. Then he thought of all the other confident, beautiful girls who had arrived at the camp in the past. She would be worn down by the system as they all were. Worn down by the impossibility of resettling a refugee people nobody wanted. He looked down. 'Your papers say you are making a claim to US citizenship. Correct?'

'Yes.'

'Based on part American parentage.'

'Yes.'

'Father's name?'

'Stevenson,' Nan said. 'C. Stevenson of New York City.'

'Will your father accept responsibility for your maintenance? Will he act as guarantor?'

Nan hesitated. 'Of course,' she said firmly.

The Belgian looked up, his eyes hooded with disbelief. 'OK, Miss Hyn. From here on you'll go through a verification process.'

'How long will it take?'

'Don't hold your breath,' the Belgian said, pleased with his use of American idiom. He looked up into a pair of steely eyes. 'It could take maybe a month or two. Maybe longer,' he added apologetically.

On that day Nan Luc became one of the army of displaced persons the twentieth century has created. Jews, Poles, Palestinians, Tartars, Germans, Kurds, Ukranians, Ugandans . . . among nearly fifty peoples displaced by force or choice the Vietnamese boat people were only the most recent. Now on this South China Sea island of thick forest and huge wild flowers the Vietnamese girl lived a strange, unreal life. Her home was shared with twenty others, a single boarded room with a tarpaper roof. Her daily work was scrubbing floors and cleaning house for the tyrannical wife of one of the UN officers. Her spare time was spent as a leading member of the refugee committee appointed by the administrators to deal with refugee complaints.

Small children grew up knowing only the camp as their home. Young couples married; old people died. And all the while only a dribble of people ever left Gulanga Island.

Young single men and women were required to work for the small UN allowance they received. The men worked on land clearing and ever more necessary water and sanitation projects and the young women worked as cooks and kitchen hands in the vast canteens or as maids to the wives of UN administrators.

Freda O'Keefe had not chosen Nan Luc. The Vietnamese girl was too tall, too imposing a figure for her. The assignment had been made by the camp domestic staff officer. Mrs O'Keefe had a deep, gnawing suspicion that her husband had been behind the assignment. Each day a tiny piece of theatre was played out between them when Freda O'Keefe tried to get her husband to comment on the Vietnamese girl's attractions.

'You mean to say you never noticed the figure on that girl?' John O'Keefe would grunt into the papers he was working on. 'Does that mean yes you do notice or no you don't?'

'It means yes, she's got a good figure.'

'You notice these things.'

'Every man notices these things. It's not important.'

'I only have your word for that.'

'True.' John O'Keefe got up to pour himself more coffee. He

had already decided on a divorce as soon as they got back to Sydney. For the present he just wanted to avoid the questions. Of course he'd noticed what an incredible looking girl their maid was. He also knew she was intelligent, pleasant and thoughtful with the children. It was because of them that O'Keefe was desperately anxious to avoid open warfare with his wife.

'If you want to get another girl, that's OK with me, Freda,' he said pouring coffee.

'I'll get rid of her when I'm good and ready,' Freda O'Keefe said. 'Meanwhile I'll keep her here where I know more or less what she's doing all day.'

'You decide,' he said. 'It means nothing to me either way.'

She seethed with anger as he collected up his papers and walked into his office. She too knew their marriage was over.

To John O'Keefe it was another tiny battle won. A victory which meant Nan Luc would continue to be in and out of the house all day, moving before his eyes, laughing with the children, occasionally even speaking directly to O'Keefe himself. Within a week he had found himself wildly in love with her. A generally cool-headed, balanced civil servant, he had been astounded at the impact the Vietnamese girl had had on him. And it was an impact which grew daily, which caused him to entertain, even luxuriate, in impossible dreams; to do things he could not imagine contemplating before.

To be with her just a few moments while she worked he would walk half a mile in the humid midday heat to collect a file from the bungalow that he had deliberately left that morning. He had twice altered appointments with the Nigerian camp administrator in order not to miss Nan Luc with the children at the beach.

But most of all he had done the unforgivable. The idea that she might receive a US visa before his own term of service expired, was intolerable to John O'Keefe. Haunted with guilt about it he had nevertheless removed her name from the central registry computer. He would replace it, he promised himself, as soon as his own term expired in two months. He would replace it and add a glowing employer's recommendation. She would lose barely a month's seniority. Perhaps not even that.

The system had a rough and ready fairness. Refugees were required to fill in questionnaires as soon as they arrived and once cleared for international criminal records their names placed on the register. It was from that point the complexities began. Applicants could be moved forward or backward on the basis of categorisation as political or economic refugees. Most damning of all was to have a camp offence recorded against you – theft, assault, prostitution.

Thinking of the incredible young woman who had unwittingly entered his dreams, John O'Keefe was confident his wife's suspicions could be held at bay until he could file for a divorce back in Sydney.

26

'You want to marry this girl?' the English policeman said.

Max looked out over the cramped skyscrapers of Hong Kong. 'Yes,' he said patiently. 'I am making enquiries because I want to find her and I want to marry her.'

Inspector Ottenshaw lifted an eyebrow. Surprise. Disapproval. Something of each, Max thought.

'You know for certain that she's a refugee?'

'Yes.'

'In Hong Kong?'

'No. I know she left Cahn Roc over a month ago. I'm told they could either have sailed north to Thailand or round the Mekong Delta and headed for Hong Kong.'

The inspector was a balding red-faced man, his heavy blond-haired arms were crossed on the desk in front of him. 'It's a needle in a haystack,' he said, not unkindly. 'But if the needle's there, there'll be some record of it.' He turned in his seat and tapped the keyboard on the L section of his desk. 'No,' he said, watching the screen, 'she's not reported landing in Thailand either. You don't know the names of any of the people with her, of course?'

'No.'

'Let's try the other first reception countries.' Again he tapped. Sat back, shaking his head and tapped again. 'No. No luck in Malaysia, Singapore, any of them.'

'There must be other possibilities.'

The inspector nodded, tapping his keyboard. 'Some UN reception camps, Lutha Bol, Gulanga . . . no, I'm getting negatives from there too, I'm afraid.'

Max got up from his seat in front of the desk. He suddenly felt fear pressing down on him. A claustrophobic fear in this tiny office overpopulated by one fat Englishman and hemmed in by white high-rise buildings all around him. 'She must have landed somewhere,' he said desperately. 'A month at sea isn't possible, is it?'

He was willing the inspector to reassure him and the policeman knew it. He paused, looking up at Max. 'Sit down, Mr Benning,' he said. Max left the window and sat down again. 'Now I could tell you what you want to hear. Or I could tell you the way it is. What do you want?'

'I'll take the truth.'

The inspector swung round in his leather armchair and pulled out invisible creases in his white uniform shirt. 'At any time,' he said, 'thousands of Vietnamese boat people are in the Gulf of Thailand or the South China Sea. Some have compasses and navigation equipment; some have nothing. Some have engines, some have a few shreds of sail. Some have food and more important, water; some have very little . . .'

'The girl I'm asking about would not have left unless she were well prepared. I'm sure of that.'

'OK. Well prepared against sudden, violent storms? Well prepared against Vietnamese coastguard cutters? Well prepared against bounty hunters and pirates?'

'Oh Christ.'

'Mr Benning. A short time ago five thousand Vietnamese were landing per week in Hong Kong alone. Does that mean that ninety per cent of those who left Vietnam made it? Or eighty per cent? Or just fifty per cent?' He looked down at his tanned arms. 'We just don't know, sir. We have no means of finding out. But we interview refugees. We hear their stories.'

'What's your estimate?'

The Englishman shrugged. 'I don't have one. But it's a long and very dangerous journey. A lot of people don't make it. I think you've got to face that fact.' The inspector got up and took a bottle of whisky and a single glass from a cupboard. 'The sun's very nearly over the yardarm,' he said. 'It'll do you good.'

Max took the whisky the inspector had poured. 'These journeys,' he said, 'how long do they take on average?'

'It depends on a dozen different factors. If the weather's bad you can double the time.'

'But the average?' Max pressed.

The inspector replaced the whisky in the cupboard without pouring himself a drink. 'Much less than six weeks, I'm afraid,' he said. 'Much, much less.' Max put his drink on the desk. 'You can't believe it,' the inspector nodded, echoing Max's thoughts. 'Go back to London and get your life going again. I'll run her name through the UN listings for the next couple of weeks. If she comes up I'll let you know. But she won't, Mr Benning. Not now, not six weeks later.'

A few minutes later Max left the Seaguard police station and walked down the wharf. He knew the English policeman was right. As he walked slowly past the row of blue and white police launches he was thinking of the last evening he had spent in Ho Chi Minh City. Stopping now at the edge of the wharf, perhaps it was the lapping of the water against the jetty that brought to mind that first glimpse of the Eros Bar. The hotel building in the old French style with its balconies and shutters relieving a dull, rendered façade; the neon sign, long defunct, tracing out the name Eros, the thin glass tubes outlining a girl, hand on hip, head thrown back; the slogan posters thick on the door and windows. Before Bernadette had called down to him he had stood there beside the front door finding it had required little effort of the imagination to bring the Eros back to life, to see a bright, invitingly red door, to hear to the music, to watch the child Nan Luc run up the worn stone steps, as innocently at home at the Eros as her schoolfriends were in other houses, in other parts of Saigon. Standing there in the street he had been filled with the belief, more than that, the certainty, that he would find Nan Luc in Bangkok or Hong Kong. Storms, starvation, pirates in the South China Sea he had read about but applied to others. The idea that Nan Luc would not survive the voyage had simply not been allowed to engage his thoughts.

He lifted his head and saw at a second floor office window Inspector Ottenshaw watching him. Embarrassed at being seen, the inspector shrugged a clumsy gesture of regret and turned away.

There was something totally final in the gesture. Six weeks, it said, is far too long to prolong hope. Go back to London, the gesture said. Go back and start your life.

*

When Jill Borota of the registry phoned her friend Freda O'Keefe
it was with intriguing news. 'Freda honey,' she said, 'I've got news
for you.'

'What about?'

'Your preposterously beautiful Viet, Nan Luc Hyn . . .'

'What now?' Freda drained her glass.

'Somebody's taken her name off the main register.'

Freda's hand slowly brought the phone down. She was aware
of having trouble grasping the significance of what her friend
was breathlessly trying to tell her. She sat, the phone in her
lap, squinting at the empty glass which she held at eye
level.

'You there, honey?' Jill Borota's voice was far away. 'You heard
what I said?'

Freda brought the phone to her ear. 'You're saying someone
took her name off deliberately. Slowed her passage.'

'You got it.'

'You're sure of this? It's deliberate?'

'Couldn't be more so. Someone's even cut the reinstatement
signal.'

'Johnny.'

'He runs the office.'

'Thanks Jill.' Freda put the phone down.

Her instincts had been right. She had known it. Her husband
was cheating on her. With the Vietnamese slut. You could buy
them for nothing. She poured and drank a gin and tonic in one
long draught. She felt as if the spirit was spreading through all
the vital channels of her body. She heard Nan Luc coming down
the stairs. Very quickly she poured another drink. No ice, very
little tonic. Mostly gin.

Nan Luc came into the kitchen. 'Good morning, Mrs O'Keefe,'
she said in her superior way. Why didn't she have a heavy accent
like the other Viets? She had an accent of course, but light, as if
she were French.

'It's time you and me had a talk,' Freda O'Keefe said. Nan Luc
looked at her without speaking. 'You're having an affair with
him.' She finished her drink in one gulp.

'I don't understand you, Mrs O'Keefe.'

'You understand me. I'm talking about my husband. The man you're having an affair with.'

'No,' Nan Luc said. 'I would be sorry if you thought that.'

'You'd be sorry?' Freda O'Keefe fumed.

'I'd be sorry if you thought that because it's not true.'

'You're lying. He's paying you. He's probably promised you a visa.'

'In the time I've been here, Mrs O'Keefe,' Nan Luc said evenly, 'I've learnt enough to know that Mr O'Keefe alone can't get me a US visa.'

'You're not answering my question, for Christ's sake. He's giving it to you.'

'There's nothing to answer, Mrs O'Keefe,' Nan Luc said. 'You're making a mistake.'

'You're lying.' Mrs O'Keefe's voice rose. 'It's happening to all my friends with Viet maids. PX and promise we call it. Goes straight to the heart of every Vietnamese slut.'

Nan Luc turned away. At the kitchen door she stopped. 'I'll apply for another job,' she said calmly. 'The registry say they're still short of English-speaking girls.'

'You'll do what I tell you to,' Freda O'Keefe said. She came forward; in her high heels she was on a level with Nan's eyes.

The Vietnamese girl shook her head. 'No. I'll go to the registry now,' she said.

A wave of rage overtook the other woman. 'I hire you, I fire you,' she screamed at Nan Luc. 'You come when I call. You go when I tell you. Understand?'

'No, I don't, Mrs O'Keefe. I'm going now.'

Nan Luc turned into an open palmed slap in the face. She stood there, her cheek stinging, her eyes watering.

'I knew it from the day you started,' the Australian woman said. 'From the day he chose you.' Freda O'Keefe reached out to grab her arms, shaking her until the shoulder of her cotton shirt came away with a sharp ripping sound. 'Get to work,' she hissed. 'You work your ass off for me, not for him. D'you hear me?' Her hand rose again.

Nan Luc hit her with the same open hand slap to the side of the cheek that Mrs O'Keefe was halfway towards delivering. But it was a blow struck with that lethal coolness that she had learnt in a childhood of self-defence lessons at the orphanage. It propelled Freda O'Keefe across the room and left her tumbled on the sofa, blood bubbling in one nostril.

27

From his ship steaming towards its home port of San Diego, Ed Brompton wrote:

Dear Nan

I will not make this a long letter. I have made some enquiries in the last month and discovered that not only are you still at Gulanga but that on the stand-in-line system you are likely to be there for many months yet. In the present climate no one in the so called countries of final reception seems anxious to speed up the processes. The boat people have assumed the proportions of an 'intractable problem' which is just another way of saying our solutions are going to have to be devious.

In the light of all this I have come to a serious decision. I have been a widower for over ten years and my daughter, as you know, is now grown up and living in Europe. I know you are well aware of what I feel about you and I'm realist enough to know that it is not reciprocated in the same way.

Despite this I want to ask you to marry me. The first benefit to you is obvious enough. As the wife of a US citizen you can leave Gulanga immediately. Other benefits may follow. Who knows? But if you want a 'marriage of convenience', OK. If you want a divorce as soon as it can legally be obtained, so be it.

For my part I don't need to tell you that I've missed you like hell.

Ed.

In Hong Kong Inspector Bert Ottenshaw stood at his office window and watched the big jets taking off out across the ocean.

It was too early for a drink, too early to go home to his empty apartment with its empty view of sea and sky. Young Benning would soon be on one of those planes. Better in a way. These East-West marriages seldom worked out. His hadn't.

Ottenshaw sat down at his computer and began to play variants of H-Y-N. There were Hyns and Hyn variants at all the camps but no one to fit the age, sex, date of arrival profile of Nan Luc. He tried Gulanga again because elements of the US fleet had been steaming in off their Peking Duck exercise over the last few weeks.

The screen flashed an immediate negative.

He was a man who tried to keep a strict eye on his drinking, knew he had to. His solution was to invest in the best malt whisky he knew. Swinging in his chair, he bent and took his bottle of Glenmorangie and a glass from the bottom drawer of his desk. Pouring himself a drink he sat, swinging from side to side, while the negative flashed at him from the screen. He lifted his glass. This was the modern epitaph for thousands of Vietnamese today. A flashing negative on a screen.

The malt whisky was like velvet. A different drink from the commercial blend he offered his visitors. He sat rocking back and forth. His wife, Ping, had been a Chinese refugee, one of those that didn't die on the swim across. Ottenshaw had been the first to tap in her name. Pretty, quiet, unassuming, but what a bitch! Ran her own chain of restaurant bars now. But it was no secret that food wasn't what the company made its money from.

He poured himself another carefully calculated Glenmorangie. To wrench his mind away from Ping he accessed the lists he would have to work on tomorrow. Under last month's agreement, Hong Kong, or the British on Hong Kong's behalf, had agreed to accept refugee felony categories from three UN camps.

Give me your starving millions! Ottenshaw sipped whisky and thought how much he hated politicians. Everybody round that negotiating table had known that Hong Kong couldn't take any more boat people. Everybody knew that what it would finally come to was a nasty dawn repatriation of desperate refugees, screaming or silent in their grief or hopelessness. A $50 bill in their pocket to ease the conscience of the repatriators.

He glanced at category A felons. Serious crimes of murder or assault. A hundred or more that he'd have to find detention space for from Hong Kong alone. Two or three from each of the other camps.

He poured what would definitely be his last drink. Category B. Petty theft, prostitution. Of course it was rife in the camps, but middle-class morality couldn't condone it, turn a blind eye even. Dozens of women, old, young, beautiful, ugly. HYN, NAN LUC. He thumped his glass down on the desk. HYN, NAN LUC, AGED TWENTY-FIVE, FORMER RECORDING CLERK, CAHN ROC PEOPLE'S COURT. ACCUSATION: MRS FREDA L. O'KEEFE. MRS JILL BOROTA.

Bert Ottenshaw looked up as a plane climbed in steep take-off across the island. He lifted the phone and asked to be connected to the information desk at the airport. The thoughts tumbled through his mind. Prostitution. Hell, it was second nature to some of these girls. Look at the way Ping made her millions. The trouble was, behind those smiles you could never really know what they were thinking. Nobody could. Not Bert Ottenshaw. Not young Benning.

The phone rang on his desk. Nobody could know what they were thinking. So clever some of them. So quick if it was in their own interest. So ready with the glib hard-luck story. No . . . with the best will in the world you just couldn't really know what they were thinking.

Methodically, while the phone rang on, he put away the Glenmorangie and wiped the glass with his handkerchief. East is east and west is west . . . Kipling knew a bloody thing or two about these matters. He straightened up. Let his mind slip to his wife Ping in those first weeks he had known her. Gave one last glance at the phone as he put the glass away in the drawer.

As Inspector Ottenshaw took his uniform cap from the stand and walked out into the corridor the call from the information desk at Hong Kong Airport ceased ringing.

On the evening she received Ed Brompton's letter Nan Luc walked up the headland where a stone monument had been erected in memory of Dutch and Australian soldiers of some distant war. Sitting on the stone step at the foot of the monument Nan Luc looked out to sea.

'We are not a court of law,' the Dutch administrator had said that morning. 'But these are serious allegations, made by two responsible women. I have no choice but to place the accusation of prostitution on your file.'

Thus, casually, she had been handed a sentence to remain on Gulanga for ever. Or perhaps to be deported to a detention centre in Hong Kong. The Dutchman had said that she would naturally be informed at the earliest possible moment.

In the pocket of the US Navy anorak she wore, Nan moved her thumb slowly back and forth across the surface of Ed Brompton's letter. Acceptance of his offer of marriage meant the loss of Max for ever. Any hope that one day their lives would link up again would have to be trampled on until it no longer had the power of pain. As a memory, a dream, he could occupy some recess of her being. But she was well aware of the difference between the memory and the hope.

He had told her that he spent a good deal of time in the United States. Within weeks she could be living there. But there must be no attempt to make contact, no phone call, no letter. If she accepted Ed Brompton's offer she was bound by her sense of honour to make every effort to create a marriage. She could not use a man like Ed in any other way.

Or she could return to Gulanga after her period of detention in Hong Kong. Hope and struggle one day to be granted a visa. But then, though Max Benning would not perhaps be lost to her for ever, the task she set herself, the finding of her father, would have to be abandoned for months, even for years. And nothing in her would tolerate that. She must take what was generously offered.

She looked out to where moonlight gleamed on the sea like a thin stream running across a flat black landscape. She remembered standing at the rail of the American warship on that first night of their salvation. She had looked out across the same flat sea and watched the black sail of *Cahn Roc* list sharply and glide like a shark's fin into the glistening water.

In that moment, now it seemed so long ago, Nan Luc had experienced an orgasmic thrill of triumph. Max Benning had stood somehow securely in her distant future. America, and her father, lay immediately before her.

But that was when she still believed that what she had fought for she could grasp with both hands. Before she understood that the Western world was sick of refugees. Before she understood that she would be forced to choose between the hope of Max Benning and the revenge she needed to make her whole again. Before she decided she must accept what Ed Brompton's letter offered her.

Max Benning crossed the concourse at Hong Kong international airport, his eyes scanning the gate numbers, but his real attention confined to the unending flight calls and requests for passengers to proceed to departure gates.

It was not anything as positive as hope, perhaps even it was closer to despair, but the fantasy haunted him of a call from Ottenshaw, sparked by a last-minute discovery on his screen of Nan Luc's name, tucked away in some small, so far unsearched, reception centre. Every name called over the loudspeaker system only slowly registered as being *not* his name.

He shook his head in anger. His flight was already boarding. The girl's voice, softly Chinese accented, was requesting someone to go to the Central Information Desk. The name was muffled by the liquidity of her accent. Had she said Benning?

Max stopped on the concourse streaming with small, neatly suited Hong Kong businessmen. He was a few yards from the information desk. He started forward. He could see the girl in the blue uniform lean into her microphone. 'Will Mr Henson, British Airways passenger to London, please come to the information desk. Mr Roger Henson, please.'

The surge of hope died. The sharp image he had held of Nan Luc's face, suddenly alight with astonishment, faded. Max turned and walked back to the departure gates. Through a glass panel he could see a British Airways 747 and two long streams of passengers boarding.

PART THREE

To New York

28

It was a brilliant winter afternoon. The fog had lifted early. From the long orangery terrace of Ed Brompton's low built Spanish house the view was across North Island, the city of San Diego and the bay. A green and black tanker moved slowly out towards the ocean led by an escort of madcap seagulls. From island to shore, ferries and tugs criss-crossed the pale water.

'After Ellie died,' the woman in the pale green picture hat said, 'I would have bet anything on Ed staying single. But this one, I have to admit, is gorgeous.'

Ed Brompton's sister Susan, standing beside the woman in the green hat, looked towards Nan Luc who stood among a group of Navy men at the far end of the orangery. 'I like her,' Susan said. 'She's very frank about the gulf between the life they've both led up to now. But when she said, "I will" I think she meant it.'

'They were actually married in the boat people's camp, she told me,' Susan's friend Kate Morgan said.

Susan shrugged. 'So what? I was married in a tented camp in Kenya.'

'That was romantic and your own choice,' Kate said. 'Don't try to pretend that this isn't different.'

Susan laughed. 'Ed's too old for romance.' She paused. 'He's got a nice, prosaic, unruffled mind. Just perfect for a quiet middle-aged marriage. I hope that's never a problem between them.'

From the double doors leading from the house Ed Brompton looked down the length of the orangery and out over the broad lawn, liberally sprinkled with people in the sort of clothes they might have chosen for a Washington spring garden party. Even for the bay it was a period of freak weather, the sun warm, the ocean heavy with a lazy, almost summer swell that belied the calendar reading. He could pick out Nan Luc's plain yellow dress among the Navy uniforms and for a moment or two he leaned back against the door jamb and let himself catch his breath.

She had said yes. That was, to Ed Brompton, the staggering, amazing fact he had still to absorb. She had made no secret of the conditions at Gulanga, of the near impossibility of escape without an American guarantor or proof of verifiable political refugee status. How had she put it? He had remembered the words for Susan when they got back from Gulanga. 'Yes, to me, means yes. I accept my responsibility in making the marriage work.'

She had insisted on returning with him to San Diego for their honeymoon and while he had been at sea for the month that followed she had found herself a job among the large Vietnamese population of Southern California. Somehow the nature of her work slightly embarrassed Ed. Perhaps he felt it reflected in some way on his own marriage.

'A marriage broker?' Susan had exclaimed nervously when she first heard of what Nan Luc was doing. 'What's a marriage broker do in the twentieth century?'

Nan Luc smiled. 'Roughly what they've been doing for a couple of dozen centuries before it. They don't operate as a dating agency, if that's what you're thinking. In Vietnam they are brought in at the next stage, when a marriage contract has to be drawn up.'

'You mean terms and conditions are laid down,' Susan's husband Garrard had said. 'And the two parties sign up.'

'The two families sign up,' Nan Luc told him. 'I started drawing up contracts in Vietnam. It was part of my job in the villages. In the camp at Gulanga I just carried right on. Lots of girls got pregnant, marriages were agreed but dowries and settlements were difficult. Most families didn't know where they were going to be in a month's time. I promise you, Susan, there's nothing you couldn't tell your grandmother about it.' Nan smiled. 'Or I, mine.'

After supper at two long tables in the Spanish barn, Ed's brother stood up to propose the toast of the couple. Although it was some weeks since the marriage, everybody recognised that this was the wedding party.

The guests' comments on Ed's new wife flowed as freely as the champagne.

'Adorable creature.'

'Lucky Edward.'

'I'll drink to that.'

'*Tall* for a Vietnamese girl.'

'Some sort of marriage counsellor, apparently.'

'Hope she never needs her own advice.'

'Will it last?'

'*Can* it last?'

'How long do you give her?'

'Superb looking woman.'

'Lucky Edward.'

'I'll drink to that.'

When the last cars had gone Ed and Nan walked together back down the drive and on to the covered terrace. Across the bay, lights sparkled through the thin mist.

'Let me pour you a drink,' Nan said. 'I have something to talk to you about.'

He lifted his head towards her. He had an irrational hope that she was going to tell him that she was pregnant, but her expression presaged something else. 'OK,' he said. 'Say I have a Scotch. Is it something serious?'

'Yes.' She poured an inch of whisky and lifted it towards him.

He nodded. 'How serious?'

A cold chill was creeping through him. He had known, or perhaps just feared, that the simple happiness he had known with Nan Luc could not last. He watched her as she crossed the terrace, put the drink on the table in front of him and sat down in the garden chair opposite.

'How serious?' he asked again.

'I want to go to New York, Ed.'

'OK,' he said uncertainly. 'As soon as I have time free . . .'

'Alone,' she said.

'Alone?'

'Yes.' He waited, his finger circling the rim of the glass. 'I'm coming back, Ed. As soon as I've found him.'

He nodded slowly. 'Look Nan,' he said after a moment. 'Why not just leave it as it is. He was a lousy father from what you say, abandoned you there in Saigon. Why the need to confront him?' He could see her body tense although her expression was unchanging. He tried to fill the gap that was opening between them. 'C. Stevenson, a businessman who once lived in New York City, is not much to go on. The private investigator got nowhere.'

'I must try myself. I've already asked for enquiries to be made about my aunt, Louise. I'm sure she's living in New York somewhere. She could know where to find my father.'

'The PI had her name too, Nan.'

'But the detective wasn't Vietnamese,' Nan said carefully. 'He didn't speak the language, didn't have access to the Vietnamese community in New York.'

'Nan, listen to me.' He leaned forward across the table. 'He was a bad father. After your mother's death he deserted you at the worst possible time. At a time you really needed him. But what's the point of looking for him? What's the point of finding him? What are you going to do? Tell him what a lousy human being he is? Or maybe even just was. He was probably some boy soldier in his teens, or early twenties . . .'

'Don't try to dissuade me, Ed. Try to understand. I can't be at peace until I've found him.'

'And then what?'

'Don't, Ed, please. I know this makes no sense to you.' She reached out a hand and covered his. 'I've got to try, Ed. I can't explain. It's part of being Vietnamese, part of the way we think of the family. Let me do this and I'll come back and we can take up the thread of our life together.'

Through one of the open orangery windows a wind came off the ocean and he shivered. New York. He had never liked the city. Now he felt something like a sick, jealous hatred for it. But there was nothing he could do. He had known from the beginning that at one point she would go to look for her father. She had never really told him what drove her. Or what she wanted to say to him when she found him. But Ed Brompton knew it was something he had agreed to when they were married. It had never been a spoken condition on Nan's part. Never overt, like one of the contacts she drew up for her Vietnamese clients. But it had been there all the same. Something she would do as soon as she herself had earned the money to do it. Something she was driven to do by her extraordinary will, by some depth of feeling about her father that he could not begin to understand.

'How long will you be gone?' he asked reluctantly.

'A month perhaps. I'm not sure. But I will be back. You must have no doubts about that. As long as you want me, I will be back.'

He shook his head slowly. He was a naval officer, instinct had never meant a lot in his life and he wasn't sure that it was instinct that was worrying him now. But the cold chill of presentiment would not leave him. He stood up, his whisky undrunk. 'Let's go in,' he said, 'I'm finding it cold out here.'

In the Meyerick Fund offices on Constitution Wharf, Meyerick City, Cy Stevenson shook hands with General Brogan and walked with him to the elevator. 'Good of you to take an interest in what we do,' Cy said.

'It's more than an interest in what you do, Cy. A lot of us feel we'd like to do something to help. You may not believe it but a lot of retired military feel like that. Those that served there. No apologies, you understand.'

'I understand that.'

'I guess it's a feeling,' the general said, 'of a job left uncompleted. I think a lot of Americans feel that way about Vietnam.'

'I think they do,' Cy said.

He pressed the button to open the elevator door. 'You've been very generous, general.'

'I'm sure we will be able to meet that commitment. We're an informal body as I explained to you. Some people think the name we chose, "Alumni of the Vietnam War" is a little pretentious.'

The door slid open. 'Pretentious or not, general,' Cy said. 'That's what a lot of us were.'

'It certainly taught me the difference between my ass and my elbow.'

'It taught a lot of us that.' Cy held the door open.

'We all live on this planet together, Cy.'

Stevenson nodded, felt the door kick against his hand and pressed it back again. He thought that if the general wanted to indulge in a little homespun philosophy they should have done it over a drink in his office.

'The same planet,' the general repeated to himself. Then, as if shaking himself free of such ideas, he walked briskly into the elevator.

Cy released the door. Compressed air hissed.

'You'll get your donation, Cy. I personally guarantee it.'

When the door had hushed closed Cy walked back through the main office. He stopped at his secretary's desk. She looked up enquiringly.

'He promised a hundred thousand dollars by Christmas.' Her mouth turned down appreciatively. 'Putty in my hands,' he smiled.

'Aren't we all, Mr Stevenson?'

He took out a cigarette. 'I thought he'd never go.'

'You're not through yet,' she said. 'Someone's due at five.'

'I have another appointment?'

'It's in the book. Somebody looking for a donation from us this time. She's from the Masterman Pope Project in New York City. They're planning to build a hostel for girls, teenage girls.'

'And they're raising money.'

'And they think Meyerick might help.'

'Well, why not?' Cy said expansively. 'Nothing political there, no cross lines as far as you can see?' Cy lit his cigarette and drew on it.

'No,' the girl said. 'Looks OK. The girls are young Vietnamese. Some of them very beautiful I'm told.'

'You've sold me.' Cy strolled towards his office door. 'We'll get through this in a few minutes. I'll agree the donation subject to the usual guarantees and checks.'

'Quick decision. How much will you give?'

'I'll have to clear it with a few calls to the other trustees but I guess we can go to twenty-five thousand dollars. Show them straight in.'

'Just one,' the girl said. 'A Mrs Louise Cartwright.'

Cy poured himself a Scotch and sat at his desk. Things were looking good. Lazily he thought back a few months to the appalling worries of Quatch's arrest and trial. He had been lucky. Very, very lucky. And that last vote at the fund had been close. But Mary had come through. Without pressure. Or at least without too much. He still had the Christmas vote to handle, but Mary would be back by then and he calculated things would have quietened down enough for him to be able to hold on to his core support: Fin, Hector, Ollie Digweed, Mary.

All in all he had come through. Again.

He concluded his brief review of life as it was for Cy Stevenson with a cursory thought for Sunny. His wife seemed to be in a strange mood lately. Strangely on edge. Was it possible she was having an affair? But who with? Fitz, the gardener? He drank his Scotch. No, Sunny was too straitlaced. Her family upbringing didn't allow for affairs. But then a few months ago he would have said the same about Mary. He drew on his cigar, smiling. It had worked: she had felt bad about it maybe. She had known in her heart why she voted for him. But she had voted.

It was just before five o'clock. The Vietnamese girl would be here in a few minutes. Time for another drink. He took the bottle of Scotch and poured a liberal inch. The Vietnamese. He wondered what she would look like. Even now, fifteen years later, he had not got over his obsession with Vietnamese women.

His secretary rang the bell. He put down his untouched Scotch and crossed to open the door.

Cy Stevenson and the woman he had known in the Eros Bar as Louise Hyn looked at each other in undisguised horror.

For a moment he thought the Vietnamese woman was about to turn and run. He leaned forward and took her clumsily by the forearm. 'Come in, come in,' he muttered, drawing her into the room. 'Come in.' He swung the door closed with a bang. For a moment they stood facing each other. 'What are you doing here, for God's sake?' he said.

'I'm looking for funds . . . a donation.'

He looked at her suspiciously. 'What is this? What sort of donation?'

'Please,' the Vietnamese woman said desperately, 'the past is the past.'

'What's that supposed to mean?'

'I mean that I'm no more anxious than you are to relive Saigon.'

His suspicion began to ebb. 'You really are from the Masterman Pope Project?'

'Of course. You don't think I knew who I was coming to see?'

He picked up his drink and took a mouthful. 'Your English is a lot better,' he said.

'In fifteen years, what would you expect?'

He shrugged. 'A drink?'

She shook her head. 'I'll stay for a moment or two then go. It will look strange if I leave straight away.'

'Sure.' He stood staring at her for a moment as if recovering a memory of many years ago. 'You got out of Saigon before the roof fell in. A few weeks before if I remember?'

'Yes.'

He nodded slowly. 'Did you marry your MP?'

'Yes. He's still a cop. In NYPD now.'

He was silent trying to phrase what he wanted to say. 'The past's dead and gone then.'

'They were terrible days, Mr Stevenson. Nobody wants to think about Saigon any more.'

'Yuh. We did some crazy things,' Cy said cautiously.

'I'm married to a good man. A man who knows nothing of what happened at the Eros Bar. I'm not here to stir up the past. I plan to keep it buried.'

'Me too. I've become a solid citizen. A pillar of the community. I like it.'

For a long time she looked down at the floor. 'And my sister's child, she stayed in Saigon?'

He looked at the black glossy head she presented him, willing her to bring her face up so that he could see her expression. 'Yuh. There was nothing I could do. Those last days were chaos.' He walked back to his desk. 'You never heard anything of her?' She shook her head, looking up at him now. 'You can guess what it was like in those days,' he said. 'Once I'd lost touch there was nothing I could do.'

'No.'

He felt a weight lift from him. She was moving towards the door. 'I owe you,' he said.

She shook her head vigorously. 'Not me.'

'For you it must be a lot of money.'

'I want nothing to do with it.'

'OK. I'll pitch it in as a donation. How about that?' She shrugged. 'Leave the details with my secretary. We'll arrange a donation,' he said.

She nodded, running her tongue across her lower lip. 'They were bad, bad times, Mr Stevenson. We did many bad things.'

'We're going to forget all that, Louise. If ever I meet you again you're going to be Mrs Cartwright of the Masterman Pope. I didn't even know Louise the bar-girl.'

He could see her agitation in the trembling hand that reached for the door. 'And you didn't know me either. OK?' he said. 'Except now, as a trustee of the Meyerick Fund.'

She nodded, turning the door handle.

'Still got a very pretty ass there, Louise,' he whispered as she stood, her hand shaking on the door handle. Her mouth tightened. Cy grinned. 'Just kidding.' His voice rose from the whisper. 'Goodbye, Mrs Cartwright. Nice meeting you. I'll have my secretary look into the details and let you know.'

29

Fear is a distorting mirror.

It was the first time Nan Luc had been in New York and the city, at this end of Manhattan Island, was neon signs and rubbish in battered shop doorways; grafitti and Hispanic voices; sauntering black youths in parti-coloured anoraks and white trainers; lights and music on wide, run-down boulevards and empty demolition lots in the dark streets behind.

And fear. Fear that she might be unable to fight back, as she had been unable to fight back against Quatch. Fear brought to the surface that she was, in the last resort, too timorous, that she lacked the savagery to avenge her family.

The taxi had dropped her too soon. She knew that, at least, by the street numbers. She had asked directions from a man who had stumbled past without answering and a pale-faced girl who seemed to think she was here buying crack.

She turned at the next intersection. Cars cruised along it but there were, quite suddenly, no people. She moved on quickly, checking until she saw with despair the number she wanted was a burnt out bakery. She stopped. A cold blast of wind rattled dark windows above her head. Snow, like salt, was driven through the pools of light below the streetlights.

She walked on quickly. Her heels clicked echoingly between the tattered shop fronts. She knew how totally female a sound was that. She took a left and then a right down a short narrow street between high buildings decorated with fire escapes. Under a street lamp a human bundle lay on a doorstep, defended by a rampart of old cloth bags. Steam rose through the street lights.

Nan Luc stopped. The old woman was awake, smiling. 'Excuse me, do you know a restaurant near here called Saigon-Hue?'

'A restaurant?' The old woman puckered her grimy brows.

'A Vietnamese restaurant.'

'There's a diner a block away. You can get sum'un to eat there.'

'No, I'm looking for one special restaurant,' Nan Luc said carefully. 'The Saigon-Hue on Dixon Street.'

'Dixon Street?'

'You know it?' The old lady shook her head. 'Do you know where I can get a taxi?' Nan Luc said urgently.

'A taxi,' the old woman cackled. She raised herself on her elbow. 'There's a subway down there.'

Nan Luc shook her head. 'I'm lost. I need a taxi. I need to get back to Lennox Avenue to find a taxi.'

The old lady thought hard. 'I'm from New Jersey myself,' she said finally. 'South Amboy. You know it?'

Two men were approaching on the other side of the street. Their faces under the street light were dark, not black. One of them wore a wide brimmed hat, tipped back. It was their sauntering walk that made her afraid.

She knelt down quickly beside the old lady. 'My folks was travellers,' the old lady said. 'But at the last, they said, you've got to settle. When we came to Jersey I stayed around a while then moved on.'

The men's footsteps were close now, almost level with the doorway. She crouched lower. More than anything she was fearful that they would see her legs.

'Hey, lady,' one of the men called, stopping on the sidewalk opposite.

She stood up. The subway. She began walking rapidly in the direction the old lady had pointed. Only after a hundred yards or so, did she look round. The two men were behind her, approaching, their sauntering walk speeded. 'Hey lady,' she heard again.

The subway station was cast iron, boarded, unused. She circled it once looking for an entrance. The man in the wide hat played peek-a-boo round the side of it. 'Hey lady,' he said and pulled back out of sight, laughing. 'The bag lady say you're looking for the Saigon-Hue?' He pointed. 'Just across the street there, lady.'

On the street corner a flicker of neon stuttered Saigon-Hue. From a clutch of Chinese lanterns light shone from the one remaining bulb down on to the dark green and red painted entrance door.

Nan moved warily to pass him. The man in the wide brimmed hat stepped aside. 'I like it Chinese, too,' he whispered in her ear as she passed him.

Reaching the restaurant she pressed her face close to the glass pane. Through a bamboo screen on the window Nan Luc could see candle-lit tables, mostly unoccupied. She pushed open the door and a young Vietnamese in jeans and an expensive black silk shirt emerged from the shadows.

'This is a private club,' he said in English. 'You know someone here?'

'Kim Hoang sent me. To see Kiet Vo Tron.' The young man's manner changed, relaxed. 'I'm an old friend of Kim's,' Nan said. 'Now he's away on assignment, I'm borrowing his apartment.'

'OK,' the boy said. 'You're Nan Luc, right? We know all about you. He called this morning. He's covering the election in Atlantic City. Will the Vietnamese vote for a black mayor? I could tell him now, no way.' The boy reminded her of some of the Ricains in Independence Square, desperately aping a streetwise American style.

'Is Mr Tron here?' Nan asked.

'Sure.' He was leading the way towards a red painted, bolted iron staircase. 'The way Kim Hoang told it,' he clattered down the stairs, 'I thought you'd be older. He said you led him and twenty or thirty others out of Vietnam.' He had paused looking up at her from the angle of the red iron stair. 'Right?'

'I set it up.' Nan followed him down. 'But we all did it together.'

'OK,' he grinned over his shoulder as he jumped down the last steps. 'Then you won't be upset by this.' He was pointing to a thick purple curtain which obscured the rest of the basement.

She frowned, aware, beyond the curtain, of a breathing silence broken by a sound like many pairs of chopsticks. The boy pulled the curtain. The basement was vast, dimly lit at the edges. Fifty, a hundred Vietnamese men crouched round one pool of light. An abacus clicked as dark figures came silently forward and placed bills in one of the two boxes.

The young man led Nan forward and stopped. She stood, looking over the shadowed heads to the area of light. Two red-combed cocks, the spurs of their yellow feet elongated by sharpened steel picks, circled each other with slow, deliberate paces. Nan watched in fascination as one of the cocks took the centre of the ring, threw back its head and crowed its challenge. The other cock, shuffling long black, green-sheened feathers, stood, its eyes on the challenger. Then in a cloud of dust and feather they were locked together, pecking and clawing, scattering blood over the front rows of no longer silent men.

'It is an honour for Kiet Vo Tron to be of service to you.' An old man in jeans and T-shirt and a sort of light bathrobe had moved silently to stand beside Nan Luc. 'You have seen this sport before, of course.'

Nan shook her head. 'At home it is no longer allowed,' she said. 'I'm sure you still find it in the villages but officially gambling is prohibited.'

The old man smiled, his tongue visible through broken teeth. 'Come this way, Nan Luc. We have much to talk about.'

Seated in a small boarded room opposite the old man, Nan accepted tea and waited.

'You're young to be dealing in such things, Nan Luc.'

'We are no longer at home,' she said. 'In America we must make our way as we must.'

'You're a journalist like my kinsman, Kim Hoang.'

'No.'

'You are not thinking of entering this evil trade yourself.'

'No. I'm looking for someone of great importance to me.'

'I read your eyes. You mean him ill.'

'I have a duty to perform.'

He inclined his head. 'Kim Hoang says I can trust you absolutely.'

'You can.'

The old man shuffled in his seat. 'I accept his word. And yours.' He paused. 'My business is only in the soft end, you understand. The boys and girls who work for me do it voluntarily. For the money.' She nodded. 'The men who buy, the clients, call themselves collectors. They are prepared to pay well for classic material.' The old man waved his hand dismissively. 'You've heard stories of items using big Hollywood stars when they were young and reckless. Garbo before she left Sweden. Monroe of course. There are more stories of her black pictures than there are of sunken treasure. No doubt some of these things exist. But mostly they exist only in the mind and greed of collectors. It's chasing moonbeams, Nan Luc.'

'I'm talking about classics,' she said. 'Classics that do exist.'

'For instance?'

'Eros Films, for instance.'

'Ah,' the old man's eyes never left her. 'Eros. Specialist interests. I have never seen any Eros material. I know it's old. Goes back to the last days of Saigon. They say the prints are bad.'

'Even so.'

'It is a dangerous area to deal in, Nan Luc.' Tron's thin jowls wagged loose and yellow.

'My thought was to trace the man Stevenson who made the Eros movies.'

Tron shook his head slowly. 'I can be of no help there. I had not even known his name.'

Nan waited, her excitement rising. She watched Tron's eyes roam the blank wall above her head. She had begun to suspect he knew something. It was characteristic of an older generation of Vietnamese to spend time building the problem before demonstrating the solution. 'I see no easy answer,' she said.

He shook his head, poking his tongue through his gapped teeth. 'But because Kim Hoang asked me to do everything in my power . . .' He let the sentence trail.

Nan lifted her teacup.

'I have a family obligation to point you in a helpful direction,' Tron said sombrely, but he was fighting a small smile of triumph. 'I can give you a name. Formerly a stud.' His hazy yellow eyes met hers. 'You must go see my colleague, Charlie Mandrake.'

30

In London's Hyde Park it was a cold, clear December morning. The little girl, dressed in a pale blue anorak and red woollen hat, skipped along the edge of the lake and sang nursery rhymes oblivious of the amused glances she was attracting.

A few yards behind her mother, Monika, watched while she opened her bag of crusts and threw bread to the ducks, then turned to see the figure of her ex-husband walking quickly along the asphalt path towards them. The child, absorbed in the antics of the ducks had not seen him.

Monika walked a few paces towards him and stopped. She could see the expression on his face. He nodded. It was more an affirmation than a greeting.

'An hour ago,' he said, 'she was more or less conscious. Not in pain.'

'I'm glad of that at least,' Monika said. 'You got the answer-phone message we'd be here?'

'Yes.' Max tensed as the child stepped too close to the water's edge.

'She won't fall in,' Monika said. 'Relax. You can now.'

He shrugged. 'There's no point in pretending she was a likeable woman, you know that. She was stiff with pride, selfish mostly. Now she's dead I don't think I feel anything much.'

'I suppose there's a lot for you to do now.'

He nodded. 'My mother had more bank accounts than W. C. Fields. I've already been warned by her solicitor that he doesn't know the full extent of her estate. He's optimistic, he says. He thinks it'll take no more than ten years. That's what passes for English legal humour.'

'Have you thought about the funeral?'

'That was decided weeks ago. By her. Putney Vale Cemetery. I guess it'll be Wednesday or Thursday.'

'Katey and I won't come.'

'No. Better that way.' He paused. 'Katey's going to be a rich little girl now. Or in a few years anyway.'

Monika's face was white. 'I think I was afraid of that. It doesn't seem fair.'

'As far as my mother was concerned, Katey was her grandchild. She doesn't come into the first bunch of money until she's eighteen. It'll work out OK.'

They walked in silence.

'I heard about the Vietnamese girl,' Monika said. 'I'm sorry, Max.' He grunted, his breath streaming into the cold air. 'Is there nothing more you can do?'

'No. Nothing more.' Max shoved his hands deep into his pockets.

They walked on, following the progress of the child in the red hat along the edge of the lake as she threw handfuls of bread to the ducks that arrowed towards her across the flat water.

In New York it was colder. The wind from the East River bit at her cheeks and set her hair streaming behind her. From where she paid off the cab Nan Luc could see the wooden pier pushing into the river and the jumble of clapboard, cinder block and rusting tin under which, on the older supporting brickwork, was painted: Center for 21st Century Arts. Welcome All!

Nan pushed at the door and found herself in a wide passageway lined with perhaps fifty or sixty rusting bicycles. Mostly the wheels had gone or the spokes rotted away so that each machine stood tipped forward on its front forks. The makes were from all over the world: a BSA, a Sunbeam, a heavy early century aluminium Peugeot. Music thudded from above. A corkboard, brightly painted, carried the name Charles Mandrake and pinned to the board a glove with a worn index finger pointing into the dark end of the passageway. Threading her way through to the base of a staircase Nan Luc climbed the cement stairs to the floor above.

The music got louder. Light flashed in blue segments through the glass transom above the single door. There seemed to be no point in knocking. She pushed the door open and stood squinting into the buzzing flashes of acetylene light.

'Yo!' a voice called and screwing up her eyes she saw, as the flashing light stopped, a figure lifting a face shield from his eyes. The man who casually threw aside the acetylene torch and eased the shield off his head was into his early forties, his black jeans torn below the right knee, his denim shirt, sleeveless, and his grey-blond hair long and worn in bunches. His straight toothed smile in his unshaven face was friendly. He waved the face shield in welcome.

'Hi,' he said. 'Charlie Mandrake. Girls like you don't visit me every day any more so I guess you must be Nan Luc. Old Mr Tron tells me he owes you a favour. No offence but that could make him one hell of a lucky guy. What can I do for you, Nan Luc?'

Nan looked at the huge structure of old bicycles welded into something resembling a prehistoric animal. 'Mr Tron didn't tell me you were an artist.'

'What did he say I was?'

'Someone who could help me with a problem.'

Mandrake took her elbow. The view was across the river to the end of the La Guardia runway. 'You want coffee, a drink . . .?'

She shook her head and he released her arm and went across to an open fronted cupboard where instant coffee, a milk carton and packet sugar stood beside a bottle of whisky. 'Old Tron says you're looking for information on old Eros numbers. Is that true?'

'You're familiar with them?'

Charlie smiled. 'I know some of them are gelignite to handle.' He poured himself a drink. 'You're not looking to buy? If you are it's not my trade, darling.'

She shook her head. 'Information, that's all.'

'OK.' he said. 'I'm making it clear, right? Mr Tron sent you over here because I once played stud in some of the early Eros numbers, but that's when me and Eros parted company. Early days, understand? A boy, a girl and a bed. Before Stevenson started taking special orders.'

She found it difficult not to react to the sound of the name, not to ply him with questions, but she nodded calmly. 'OK' she said, 'I understand. Early numbers.'

He relaxed. 'There was nothing to it,' he said. 'Stevenson had the camera equipment, Vietnam had the girls and there were a few hundred crazy young deserters like me running around in Saigon trying to earn a dollar. When Steve offered us work we thought we were in paradise. When he told us what work it was we knew we were.'

'Just good fun.'

'Believe me,' he said. 'Ver' straight. We were making them for the guys out there in the bamboo. They were one step from sex education.'

'And then?'

'Then the numbers started becoming heavier. Scenarist stuff, you know what that is?' Her eyes on him, she shook her head. 'It's when the customer gets to write the scenario, get it? That's when the crazies move in. That's when the producer also starts to make big bucks. But sometimes the crazies are very crazy. They like very crazy things up there on the silver screen. You get me?'

'Who were these customers?'

'In Saigon, anybody. An American general, a Swedish aid administrator, a British diplomat, a Frenchman, an Australian . . .'

'And Vietnamese?'

'Sure. Ministers, police chiefs . . . they all paid a small fortune to write up their own private little fantasies. But it was rough, rough stuff Nan. Not long before Steve asked me would I do a snuff. You know what that is? You kill the girl under you, the girl you're humping. Every second script was asking for it. Men are just wonderful. I said no. Definitely no. I wasn't going to throttle any girl for some crazy to get off on.'

'What did he say to that?'

'He didn't like it. He came on strong about them only being bar-girls, short shelf life. He was crazier than the guys who wrote the scenarios.'

She nodded, wishing she'd asked for a drink to quell her uneasy stomach.

'I got out when he put it to me straight. Either I snuffed the next girl on camera or he'd hand me over to the MPs. I was so scared I gave myself up. Naturally I wasn't telling anybody I'd spent my time over the wall making art movies. I served three years in Leavenworth and came back home to New York a much wiser man.'

'And Stevenson?'

'Never saw him again.' He grimaced. 'I'd like to. If only to wrap him in a blanket and drop him deep in the East River. For all those young Viet chicks . . .' He stopped. 'No offence. Somehow, you look different.'

'What was Stevenson's name?' she said. 'His first name?'

Charlie Mandrake shrugged. 'We called him Steve. Never thought about a first name.'

'What was he, a newsman?'

'He was a sort of hustler. I think he was into whatever made him some money. He came over as a freelance newsman, but he never got near the bamboo.' Charlie swigged hard at his Scotch. 'Old Tron warned me you could be interested in something other than collector's items. What is it? Stevenson himself?'

She nodded. 'Stevenson himself,' she said. 'What was he like?'

Charlie strolled across the big room. 'A bucket of charm. When he laughed the world laughed with him.'

'And when it didn't?'

Charlie swung round savagely. 'The guy made snuff movies, for Christ's sake. Real snuff movies. Doesn't that say it all?'

'Are you going to help me, Charlie?'

'You want him? Right?'

'I want him.'

He stood looking down at her, twisting his tumbler in his hand, until her relentless stare made him turn away. 'OK, Nan Luc,' he said. 'I won't ask what happens when you find him.'

She waited while he poured himself another Scotch. 'Did you ever use the Eros Bar?' she asked him.

He came across the room, his drink in his hand. 'Not a lot. The MPs swept it pretty regular. Guys like me, deserters, we mostly stayed way over in Cholon.'

'Did you know a girl named Louise at the Eros?'

'Louise Hyn? She worked on camera couple of times with me. We knew each other, yes.' He laughed. 'Then she got herself an MP and a ticket to New York.'

'I think she lives in New York now?'

He swung himself up to sit on the window shelf. 'What's Louise to you?'

'Louise Hyn is my aunt. She could help me find Stevenson.'

'Her husband's a cop.' Nan Luc shrugged. 'Even now my life's open to interpretation, Nan. I don't want cops around me.'

'Is it possible Louise kept contact with Stevenson?'

'It's possible.' He hesitated. 'OK, I used to see a girl named Mai Su. Vietnamese married to an Italian guy. Years ago, when I just came out of the stockade. I needed money and she offered me a few days' work on camera. Needs must . . . She and I did a few numbers together. The earth didn't move for the producer so he found himself another couple. I hadn't seen Mai Bassano for years until a couple of months ago. Then I saw her twice.' Nan waited. 'Riding in an old convertible in the Bronx. I was over there a few mornings later looking over a property and I saw her again. This time she's got my old co-star, Louise, in the passenger seat. They're held at a stop light on the Grand Concourse.'

'Did you speak to them?'

'I was two floors up. I yelled down hullo to Mai Su, hullo to Louise. Mai Su waves. Louise looks up and I've known guys owe me money more pleased to see me.'

'You don't know where she lives?' He shook his head. 'Where can I find Mai Bassano?'

'I've got nothing against Mai. I wouldn't like to be married to her but I got nothing against her.'

'Nor have I, Charlie,' Nan said. 'Nothing against Louise either.'

'Just Stevenson.'

'Just Stevenson.'

He nodded, taking a deep breath. 'When I knew Mai her husband's family ran a place called the Palermo Luncheonette over in the Italian neighbourhood, Belmont.'

The trees masking the parking lot at the Meyerick County Club were sparse and leafless. The wind that came off the Meyerick Hills brought the threat of snow. Local stations warned of only twenty-three shopping days to Christmas.

Every time the warm voice of DJ Artie Sandella reduced the shopping days by one, Cy's stomach turned over. Twenty-three shopping days to Christmas. Twenty-two shopping days to the fund vote that could tear his life apart.

He was finding it more and more difficult now to read the thoughts of the fund trustees when he met them at the club or at one of the cocktail parties which were a feature of the long run up to Christmas in Meyerick County. Oliver Digweed was rock solid. But the Anderson brothers were as unpredictable as ever. And, most of all, Mary was not yet back from Europe.

Across the parking lot he saw the Reverend Hector Hand approach. 'Hullo, Cy, hullo,' he called from a few yards away. Then he dropped his voice conspiratorially, 'I came down specially to see you,' he said.

'Let's go in and have a drink, then,' Cy steered him by the elbow towards the entrance to the club.

'No, I won't go in,' Hector said. 'I've got lunch in Meyerick. Let's just talk out here.'

'If that's what you want. What's on your mind, Hector?' They began to pace the parking lot.

'The annual meeting, Cy. Christmas Eve.'

'What's the problem, Hector? Savary is going to bleat a little more, Mrs Rose will look disapproving and we'll be voted through.'

'I saw George Savary last night. He came over to the church. We sat alone there and prayed for guidance.' Cy pulled a face. 'Guidance is what we need at the moment, Cy.'

'Sure. What did Savary have to say?'

'He said the course you were taking was both immoral and illegal.'

Cy pursed his lips. 'Strong words.'

'He says if it were not for people like myself and Mary Butler having voted for you last time, he would have gone to the police.' Cy stopped pacing. 'George Savary isn't going to let this one go, Cy,' Hector said anxiously.

'Savary's threatening you, Hector. You're not the sort of man that takes threats.'

'Of course not.' Cy looked at the red face. He could read the honest uncertainty in the man's expression. 'Maybe we should put a moratorium on the clandestine donations.'

'We decided to continue on down the road,' Cy said. 'It's a course we chose together.'

'Listen, Cy, this is what Savary plans to do. At the Christmas Eve meeting he is going to propose Fin Butler for president.'

'Fin? Has he agreed?'

'Apparently, yes.'

Cy put out a hand to steady himself against the top of a car. He knew now he was in desperate trouble. If Fin became president, if the flow of dollars stopped, the Vietnamese wouldn't just sit back and accept the cut-off. If he couldn't deliver, he would be exposed. The first thing anybody learnt about the Vietnamese was that they were utterly implacable.

'George Savary's talking to each member in private,' Hector Hand said. 'He says he thinks Mary will vote against you this time.'

'Mary's in Europe.'

'She got back the beginning of the week.'

And didn't call him.

'What are we going to do, Cy? I don't like Savary's talk of a scandal. He puts it in pretty strong terms. Not an accusation, you understand, but he thinks it's scandalous to be paying Hanoi. Supporting them, he calls it. And frankly I couldn't afford to be caught up in a scandal of any sort.'

'What are you saying, Hector?'

'I'm not being disloyal, Cy, but I guess what I'm saying is that talk of illegalities, of scandals, that sort of talk carries a lot of weight.'

'A lot of weight,' Cy agreed. 'But if we don't panic, this thing will go through smoothly enough. And next year maybe we'll start reducing contributions, slowly phasing them out. How about that approach?'

'It's no good, Cy. We won't carry the vote,' Hector said, 'unless Mary casts as she did last time.'

'Hector,' Cy put his arm round him, 'I'm going to personally guarantee, and you can pass this on to our supporters, that Mary Butler will be voting for us.'

'Even against her husband?'

'Even against her husband.'

There was no sign of Fin Butler's car in the drive but the garage doors stood open and the heavy grille of Mary's Range Rover was visible.

Cy pulled up outside the house, scattering gravel. Getting out of the car he walked slowly towards the shallow flight of steps that led to the door. It was already opening as he approached.

Mary Butler stood in the doorway. A dark blue dress set off a deep tan. Her smile, Cy noticed, was not unfriendly, but tentative, uncertain.

'You didn't let me know you were back,' he said.

She opened the door wider for him to come in. He stopped in the hall beside her. 'Come to think of it, you didn't even let me know that you'd gone.'

Without answering she led the way into the sitting room.

'It's good to see you, Mary. I've missed you.'

She indicated the drinks table. 'Help yourself, Cy.'

'And for you?'

'Nothing for me.'

She stood watching him as he poured whisky for himself. 'I'd like to go on from here, Cy, as if nothing had ever happened between us,' she said to his back.

He turned slowly, drink in hand. 'That's a pretty tall order, Mary. Something *did* happen between us. Turning back the pages, that's something people find pretty difficult,' he said carefully.

'Being away has made it all a lot clearer.' With a gesture of impatience at herself she crossed to the table and poured herself a drink. She was alarmed at how affected she found herself by his presence. His presence and those precise, sometimes exhilarating, memories of their past. In the South of France, three thousand miles away from him, she had seen it all differently. As a rather crude *affaire*. Josette Picard had been excited by the details, of course, those details she had been told. But then she was French. It was a way of life for women like her, living in Antibes. One night they had even allowed themselves to be picked up in a restaurant and had accepted an invitation on to a yacht. But Mary had balked at the last moment, with the Italian's hand unzipping her dress. She had felt like a schoolgirl. Absurd, when she had set out to prove to herself that she could accept a lover other than Cy. The young Italian had been frightfully offended, especially when Josette was already moaning in ecstasy with her own young man on the other side of the wheelhouse.

The Italians were crew members, of course. As they escorted them back to shore, Josette's young man had even intimated to her that he was not averse to being paid. The one pleasurable moment for Mary in a disastrous evening.

Cy was smiling as if he were shadowing her thoughts. 'Far away things always seem clearer, Mary. But we don't lead our everyday lives far away. We lead them here, in Meyerick. Where you and I see each other two, three times a week as a matter of course.'

'Cy, we were criminally stupid. What happened was not just an affair. It was something which could have destroyed both our marriages. Destroyed our whole lives here in Meyerick. Thank God I realised before it was too late.'

He nodded. 'OK, I'll be going.' He put down his half-finished glass. 'Just dropped in to say hullo.'

'Finish your drink,' she said, shocked at the speed of his leaving.

He drained his glass. 'Finished.' He walked towards the door.

When he had left she stood shaking in the hallway. She had expected him to make a fuss. Why hadn't he? She thought back to yesterday seeing Anita Simpson at Henri's. Something between a smile and a smirk on her face. And she remembered now, that day in the garden before she left for Europe, Sunny had thought of Anita Simpson. Was it possible? She shook her head in a half-hearted answer. In any case, what Cy was doing now was nothing to do with her any longer. Her mind was made up. It was just that it had been so much easier than she expected. Easy? Except that he seemed even more attractive than ever. She walked slowly back into the sitting room, exploding a short bitter laugh. Just her luck that he was also her brother-in-law.

The doorbell rang a sharp single blast. With a frown she turned back to open it. It was Cy.

'One thing I forgot to say,' he said, his voice subdued. 'I forgot to say I still love you. That's not going to change.'

She felt herself tense as waves of confused feeling passed through her. Maddened by the effect he still had on her, she set her face angrily.

'I didn't want to make you mad, Mary,' he said. 'But it was something I just needed to say, that's all.'

She opened the door wider. 'You'd better come in,' she said, stiffly. He slipped his arm round her waist as she closed the door. She felt herself move towards him and with an effort mostly inspired by anger at herself, she pulled away.

'Cy,' she said. 'You say you love me. But I'm trying to tell whether that's the way you really feel or not, you have no right to say it any more.'

He looked pained. 'Mary, of course it's the way I feel.'

She walked ahead of him back into the room. 'Whether you chose to have an affair with me because you loved me or just wanted to bed me, I don't know. Either way we've come to the end, Cy.'

'OK, Mary, perhaps first of all I just wanted you in bed. But that changed into something more, pretty quickly.'

'The answer's still the same, Cy.'

'Give it a few days. Time to think it over.'

'I thought it over while I was in Europe.'

He shrugged lightly. 'We remain friends?'

'Of course.'

'Friends. Comrades-in-arms through life's battles to come?'

Her expression tightened. 'Are you talking about George Savary. About the vote on Christmas Eve?'

He nodded. 'Christmas Eve is going to be quite a battle.'

'What's that got to do with what we've been talking about?'

'It's pretty important to me, Mary. You know that.'

She could feel the blood drain from her face. 'For God's sake, Cy, I said it's over. It's all over. Everything. Do you understand me now?'

'Maybe not,' he said slowly. 'Leastways, I hope maybe not.'

She walked past him out of the room. 'Wait here,' she said, over her shoulder.

He crossed to the table and poured himself another drink, and stood listening to her rapid footsteps on the landing above. The glass held at chest level, he watched her come down the stairs. 'I didn't tell you, Mary. You're looking beautiful,' he said. 'That's a terrific tan.'

She was carrying an unsealed letter. Without speaking she crossed the room and handed him the letter.

Unhurriedly he took a pull at his drink and set down the glass. 'What's this? A "Dear John"?'

'You can think of it that way if you want.'

He clucked his tongue at her and opened the letter. Her resignation.

'Mary darling,' he said, sliding the letter back into the envelope. 'You know this could destroy me.'

'I understand it means, in effect, you're unlikely to remain president of the fund. That's hardly destroying you.'

'Losing to George Savary on this issue amounts to the same thing. That man is conducting a vendetta against me. You know that. And yet you're resigning, opening the gates to him. What's happening for Christ's sake? Are you laying *him* now?'

She slapped him with a force that astonished herself.

'I thought you kept that tiger streak for bedfellows.'

'Jesus God.' She turned away from him. 'Five minutes ago you were telling me you loved me. Five minutes ago I was halfway believing you.'

'Take this back, Mary,' he said softly, waving the envelope slowly in the air.

'No, Cy. OK, I'm sorry I slapped you.'

'Our first fight,' he said. 'Making up's going to be fun.'

'It's over, Cy. Over, over, over. Understand that. Understand too, that I'm resigning as a trustee. With Fin standing I cannot *possibly* vote for you.'

'You can.' Slowly he tore up the letter.

'Are you mad?'

'No,' he said reaching into his inside pocket. 'You showed me yours. I'll show you mine.' He handed Mary a buff business envelope. She took it from him, saw it had already been opened and flashed him one quick anxious glance. 'Go ahead,' he said encouragingly.

She drew from the brown envelope a pack of photographs wrapped in a bill. The bill read: Received from Mrs Mary Page Butler, two hundred dollars for massage services. Mary fanned open the photographs. Of herself, Mary Page Butler, writhing naked on a bed with an equally naked Vietnamese girl doing indescribable things to her.

'The sunlamp was a camera, of course,' Cy said jovially. 'Keep the pictures, Mary. The negatives are all I need.' She faced him too shocked to move. 'It's a matter of principle,' Cy said. 'You tell everybody you feel so strongly about the way I see things that you even have to vote against your husband, dear old Fin.'

'I'll buy the negatives from you,' she said.

He smiled. 'You're buying them now, Mary darling, even as we speak.' He leaned forward and pressed the torn pieces of the resignation letter into her hand.

31

Four-thirty in the afternoon was a down-time for the Palermo Luncheonette a few dozen yards from the corner of Belmont Avenue and 187th Street. Its marbled pink plastic tables were empty. Two young men sat at the end of the long matching pink counter. A young Vietnamese woman, carefully made up, stood flirting openly with them.

As Nan took a place in the centre of the pink bar the Vietnamese girl glanced up at her, registered a mild, fleeting interest in their common race and turned back towards the young men.

From behind a large Gaggia coffee machine a woman's voice with a strong Italian accent said. 'You going serve this customer, Mai? Or you want I do as well as make the lasagne and clean tables and sweep floors?'

Mai Su turned, hands on hips, a parody of Hollywood in the fifties. 'What can I get you?' she said to Nan with a toss of her head.

'Cappucino. And maybe a slice of that pastry.'

Nan watched the Vietnamese girl saunter towards the Gaggia and fill and fit the metal cup. She could see now the Italian woman, sixty or seventy years old, short, dumpy, grey-haired.

'Remember what Julio say,' the old lady hissed. 'The customer come first.'

Mai Su Bassano treated her mother-in-law to an exhausted sigh. 'The boys are customers,' she said. 'They're in here every day.'

'What they come in here for they get for free,' the old woman said fiercely looking Mai up and down. 'Remember who you are. You're Julio's wife.'

'I'm not likely to forget it, am I?' The Vietnamese girl ran the steam into the milk and slopped it into the coffee.

She came back down the counter and Nan leaned forward to

see that the old lady had pulled back somewhere into the room behind. 'When did you leave Saigon?' she asked Mai in Vietnamese.

Mai handed her the coffee. 'I speak English,' she said. 'All that other stuff I've forgotten, so long I've been here.'

'You're Mai Su Bassano, am I right?' Nan said.

'How d'you know who I am?'

'I'm trying to contact one of my family. Her name was Louise Hyn before her marriage.'

'I don't know any Louise.'

The two boys got up from their corner seat and sauntered along the bar. 'Keep well, Mai. Be in tomorrow,' one of them said.

Mai Su drew herself up to smile.

'Louise Hyn,' Nan said. '

The Vietnamese girl's head turned back to her. Something in her customer's tone spoke authority. Or the authorities. 'I told you I don't know any Louise Hyn.'

'You drive her to work some days in a black Ford convertible.'

The electric wall clock with the Mickey Mouse face pinged four-forty-five. 'Hey, my break,' Mai Su said. 'Mama'll take the money. I don't answer questions on my own time.'

As the Vietnamese girl disappeared the Italian woman shuffled forward. She jerked a flour covered thumb to the sound of her daughter-in-law's high heels clacking up the stairs. 'My son Julio's in hospital. Automobile accident. Every night this one goes out.'

'With Louise Hyn?'

'No. Louise is a good person. Married to a cop.'

'Why won't Mai Su admit she knows her?'

'Because she's afraid.'

'Afraid?'

'Of any questions about the past.' The old woman threw her arms in the air. 'Why ask questions about her past? What you see in the present tells you all you want to know. Did she give you the pastry?'

Nan shook her head. 'Coffee's fine. Do you know where Louise lives?'

'No.'

'Her married name?'

'Just Louise to me. They're not really friends. Louise is a decent girl.'

'Where does Mai Su take her to?'

'Eh . . . eh,' the old woman slapped her own cheek, transferring flour. 'Mai Su ran her into work a few times a while back when Louise was without no car. The project. The Vietnamese Project down around 152nd Street. Masterman Pope, they call it. Don't tell Mai Su,' the old woman said. 'She'll scream at me for a week.'

Under London's dark December skies, Bert Ottenshaw, bulky in a dark raglan topcoat, his hands deep in his pockets, passed the Park Lane Hilton and turned up Curzon Street. He had a clear two hours before his train took him north, to the three unmarried sisters to whom he was the admired younger brother, policing exotic and dangerous corners of the world.

A week or two of this admiration round the tea-table was all Ottenshaw could stand. The rest of his leave he usually took in Amsterdam where a Chinese girl in the red-light district would spend a week with him for a thousand US dollars. He insisted she spoke only in Chinese, although he spoke very little himself, but the language and her light movements round the hotel room enabled him to lie in bed and imagine he was still married to Ping.

The thought of Ping was strong with him today. Amazing that she had remembered this was his last home leave before he left Hong Kong for ever. Amazing she should have sent that note. An offer of the job as manager of her three bars in Singapore. Good salary. And with his pension. Ottenshaw smiled. The letter had transformed his life. With a job like this he could stay in the East. In a way, he told himself, you could say Ping had come up trumps in the end.

He turned under the arch from Curzon Street into Shepherd Market, then continued on through one of the narrow alleys to the south side. The pub was just ahead of him. He would do what he had to do then walk along Piccadilly to Gerard Street and get himself a Chinese dinner in Wong's.

He entered the pub. Max Benning was standing at the bar. They shook hands. Ottenshaw ordered a pint.

'I don't quite know how to say this, Benning,' Ottenshaw stood awkwardly at the bar, 'but I've had a sort of change of mind since I last saw you. Not unconnected with a rather pleasant gesture my ex-wife just made, I'll admit.'

'Has something come up?' Max pressed him. It was the morning of his mother's funeral. He wore a black overcoat and black tie. 'Have you got news of Nan Luc?'

'I shouldn't have done it. I know that now. You can't play God, can you?' Ottenshaw said. 'None of us can.'

Max handed him his pint of bitter. 'Shouldn't have done what? I haven't got much time, inspector.'

'I know.' Ottenshaw supped heavily. 'The truth is, Benning,' he said uncomfortably, 'I have an apology to make to you.'

'The Masterman Pope Project for Vietnamese immigrants is the hard end of the business,' the cab driver said. 'Their prestige international offices are located just there.'

Across the vacant lot the low clapboard hut stood on a cracked concrete apron. Hard packed brick and mortar formed its drive; colour washed graffiti covered every wall section between doors and wire-mesh windows. The tar-paper roof was torn in several places. A few cars were parked haphazardly on the cement pad in front of the building. A sign-board, remarkably new and still undamaged, read Masterman Pope Project in black on bright white.

Paying off the cab, Nan Luc crossed the oil-stained cement pad to the double swing doors. A confused hubbub of voices seemed to penetrate the clapboard walls of the hut.

She pushed on one side of the doorway and found herself staring into a room in which about ten desks and their occupants were almost swamped by the drifting crowd of people. Some of the desks bore cardboard signs in Vietnamese and these seemed to collect a line of people, Vietnamese, young and old, ill-dressed and hopeless.

A young Vietnamese with a German shepherd dog came towards Nan as she entered the big room. 'What you want here?' he asked, letting his dog to within inches of Nan's leg. 'Masterman Pope is for poor people,' he said. 'No black, no Hispanic, no rich. Only poor Vietnamese people.'

'I have business with Louise,' Nan said coolly.

'Louise Cartwright?'

'Yes.'

'You need appointment,' he said, looking at her silk shirt and cashmere sweater. 'Or you a friend?'

'A friend,' Nan said. 'Where can I find her?'

The Vietnamese looked again at Nan, then turned. Pointing to a half-open door at the back of the hut, he dragged at the dog and turned away as if whoever entered the building was none of his business. Nan walked across the room. Knocking briefly, she pushed the door.

The Vietnamese woman in her late-thirties pushed a few files into her desk drawer. 'Hi,' she said, glancing up. Nan watched the colour drain from Louise's cheeks. She stopped dead; to her astonishment she saw fear play across her aunt's face. For a moment the older woman's mouth gaped. Then with a visible effort of self-control she stood up. 'Enquiries are dealt with at the appropriate desk in the main room,' she said. She forced a smile. 'I take over after they've run out of ideas.'

'You must know me,' Nan said.

'No, I don't know you.' She spoke with too much finality.

'Nan Luc,' Nan said. 'I'm Nan Luc, Pham's daughter.'

Louise had no strength left. She leaned back against the window sill behind her.

'You recognise me now,' Nan Luc said. 'Even after all these years.'

Louise nodded silently.

32

There had been no embraces, no sign of pleasure on Louise's part. 'I'm happy for you,' Nan Luc said. 'You married an American. In Vietnam today life is harsh.'

'You escaped, too,' Louise said.

There was no relaxation between them. No sign of a family reunited. Nan Luc watched the signs of caution in her aunt's face change to fear.

'When did you leave Saigon?' she asked Louise in English.

'I got away a few weeks before the evacuation. It was already chaos. Everybody knew it was a matter of time before the soldiers from the north arrived.'

'Was my mother still alive?'

'A few months later I heard from some other refugees here in New York that your mother had come back to Saigon looking for you. They said when she didn't find you she killed herself. Listen, Nan, I'm not going to be held responsible.'

'Why didn't my mother find me when she came back?'

'You'd already been taken to an orphanage I guess.'

'She had left me in your care?'

'In anybody's care!' Louise exploded. 'You don't understand what those days were like.'

'Tell me,' Nan said.

'I'm not reliving all that again,' Louise said angrily. 'Your mother should have stayed and looked after you in Saigon. Girls like us worked in bars. There was nothing else. That or the Army. In the Army she had the luxury of being respectable.'

'Perhaps,' Nan Luc said.

'She thought she was better than she was,' Louise said bitterly. 'She could have worked in the bar like I did. She had no right to expect me to look after her child.' Louise sat behind her desk, pale-faced and tense.

'What happened to me?' Nan Luc said carefully. 'After you left.'

'I don't feel guilty about it,' Louise said. 'I'm not going to let you do that to me. OK, I left you there. In the Eros. I'm not proud of it but I was eighteen, for God's sake. I'd met a good man. I had a chance to live. I took it.'

'I'm not blaming you, Louise. I was too young. I don't remember enough of those times. I grew up in an orphanage. OK, it wasn't that bad.'

'Where was Bernadette?'

'She came back from Paris when the north took over Saigon.'

'And she left you in the orphanage?'

Nan Luc shrugged. 'She knew I was there. I wouldn't expect her to have wanted me out.'

'We're in America now. Forget the past, Nan. It can ruin you.'

The silence in the room hung heavily. Through the door voices from the reception area came in waves of bird-like chatter. From where Nan Luc sat she could see a police patrol car bump across the rubble-strewn grass to pull up outside the tenement blocks opposite.

'Why did you come?' Louise broke the silence. 'You live in California. San Diego. You didn't come all the way to New York to look up your mother's sister, someone you barely remember.'

'I came to ask you about my father.' She watched her aunt's eyes. 'There's no one else I can ask.'

'I never knew your father,' Louise said. 'You were already three or four years old when your mother found me at the Eros. I hadn't seen her for five or six years since we all left Hanoi.' She stood stiffly, her back to the window of her office. Behind her head Nan Luc could see the grey layer of cloud hanging over a line of broken tenements.

'But you know who my father was.' She shook her head. 'His name, at least.'

'I know nothing, Nan Luc,' Louise said, facing her with finality. 'Your mother was my elder sister, four or five years older. Most of the time we were apart. In any case she was different from me. She kept her own secrets. You don't understand perhaps. She wasn't like the rest of us. People respected her. They knew better than to ask Pham questions like that. As far as we all knew you never had a father.'

Nan came forward. 'Let's go out and get coffee somewhere, Louise,' she said. 'There are things I must know.'

'Some other time, Nan Luc. When you're next in New York maybe.' She pointed to the outer office. 'You can see what it's like out there. People need help, attention, advice. I've no time for coffee.'

'You're afraid, Louise,' Nan Luc said. 'What of?'

Louise was shaking her head. 'Listen, Nan Luc,' she said, her voice rising, 'try to understand. The past could ruin me. If my husband guessed I'd worked a bar . . .' Nan Luc watched her silently. 'It was the times, Nan,' Louise said. 'Everybody was crazy. Crazy for sex, drugs, drink, blood. Times when soldiers went about with peace bandannas round their helmets and used their rifle barrels for smoking dope.'

Nan Luc came forward and stood opposite her aunt, her clear green eyes dramatic in a frame of dark hair. 'What are you saying?'

'I'm saying that you *have* no father. We were all at constant risk of pregnancy. Yes, even your mother. GIs passed through. Any girl could get pregnant and never know who . . .'

'My mother too, you say?'

'For God's sake,' Louise said wildly, 'try to understand what I'm saying. I'm still Vietnamese enough to remember what a family, a father, should mean. But it's too late, Nan. You'll never find your father. His name died with your mother. It's as if he doesn't exist.'

Outside, behind Louise's head, a group of young black boys came racing down the concrete staircase of one of the tenements and burst out across the vacant lot. Behind them two uniformed policemen gave up the pursuit and stood on the bottom steps staring after the disappearing boys before climbing into their car.

Louise began to gather things from her desk drawers, her head down, refusing to look at her niece, aware of the younger woman's intimidating silence. 'I have work to do, Nan,' she said. She brought her head up. 'I've nothing more to tell you.'

'Bernadette knew him.' Nan's voice was harsh. 'She said he was an American named Stevenson.' Louise recoiled in shock. Pencils and a spiral notepad spilled from her hands and rattled on the desktop. Nan watched her as Louise fought to suppress the fear in her face. 'You knew him too, Louise. You knew he was no passing GI.'

Louise rounded the desk and pulled open the door. 'Get out of my life, Nan Luc,' her voice rose in panic. Heads in the outer room turned towards the door. 'I want nothing more to do with the past. People scratch about in the past, they always find things they're better off not knowing. You want a family, go back to your rich husband in California and make one of your own!'

33

The big rooms of the Belgravia apartment were suddenly almost empty of people. Standing at the door Max shook hands with old friends of his mother, people barely known to him, men and women in late middle-age, dressed in expensive black. It had been, he reflected, an occasion which had brought out the crêpe de Chine, the jet Victorian mourning jewellery.

He closed the door on the last mourners. A butler and two maids hired for the occasion were already clearing glasses and sherry bottles from the drawing room. Max looked at his watch. His taxi to London Airport would arrive in less than half an hour.

Taking a drink with him he went into his mother's bedroom where he had left his duffel bag. Quickly he changed out of his dark suit and into light slacks and a leather jacket. On the bed lay his black topcoat. It would be cold in New York this time of year.

Ever since he had spoken to Ottenshaw his mind had operated on two separate levels. On one level he had gone through the offered condolences and the grim drive to Putney Vale Crematorium in a black limousine at the head of a column of other black limousines. On the other level his consciousness was totally occupied with the fact that Nan Luc was still alive. It was a fact that he couldn't dismiss from his mind for a moment, couldn't even push entirely to the back of his mind as the cortege swept through the stone-capped gates of Putney Vale.

In the last hour, greeting near strangers, thanking them for coming, he had acted like a robot, but a robot always aware of the ticket to New York tucked into his passport in his briefcase. And the single piece of information (apart from the details of the preposterous accusation) that Ottenshaw had been able to give him: the name of Nan Luc's guarantor in the United States, Commodore Edward P. Brompton, of San Diego, California.

He took his drink and sipped it as he looked around the room. He felt himself to be on the edge of a new life with Nan Luc, time to pack off to the auction rooms all these dozens of expensive trinkets, miniature bronzes and porcelain figures. It all represented a style of life he had never been comfortable with, a style which had divided him from his mother since his early teens.

As the butler's staff rattled the dishes in the main part of the flat his mind moved to his father and the curious feeling that he had found out now all there was to know, by the simple fact of the death of everybody who had anything to tell.

He took another pull at his drink. It was a huge old room, crammed with furniture. All these cupboards and drawers and bureaux and secretaires would have to be cleared, his mother's clothes disposed of, her jewellery sorted, her papers read. Looking from locked drawer to locked drawer it had seemed a monstrous invasion to use the bunch of keys she had pressed into his hand the morning of her death. The keys lay on her writing table now. He picked them up, juggling them in the palm of his hand.

He checked his watch. Still fifteen minutes before the cab arrived. He walked across to the secretaire, sipping his drink as he poked first one and then another key into the lock. The third key lifted a lever within the lock and turned it in a smooth, oiled two-hundred-year-old movement. He opened the desk. A bank of perfectly made mahogany drawers faced him, each containing some minor privacy in his mother's life.

He pulled the brass knob of one of the drawers. A small photographic album lay inside. Visits to the Côte d'Azur, 1970–75. A letter in a flowing hand regretted her decision not to have lunch with him at the Negresco. It was signed, Paul. Max replaced the letter in the album. He knew he would have to do it some day but he had no relish for delving into the lost opportunities in his mother's life.

He pushed the slender drawer closed and pulled open the main central drawer. A framed picture of his father looked up at him, in crude hand-painted colour, a lean face with a wry smile on the lips beneath a red French para's beret. Max put the framed picture

aside. Underneath there were letters tied with blue tape, yellow
military documents in French.

'Excuse me, sir.' Max turned to find one of the maids in the
doorway. 'Did you call for a cab?'

Max thanked her, pushed the centre drawer and slid home the
runners to close the hinged top lid. At the last moment he hesitated. Opening the drawer again he took out the packet of letters
and documents beneath the framed photograph. Closing up the
desk and locking it, he put the papers in his briefcase, picked up
his coat and duffel bag and left to catch the plane to New York.

'Meet me,' Cy said on the phone, 'at the motel at nine this
evening.'

'I'll be there.' Louise Cartwright's voice was low, barely above
a whisper.

'You're sure you can find it? About an hour's drive from the
city.'

'I can find it.'

'What about your husband? Won't he wonder where you are?'

She glanced up the stairs and moved the phone to the other
ear. 'He's on shift tonight,' she said. 'He's sleeping now.'

'OK, Louise,' Cy said. 'I'll see you later. In the meantime I'll
do a lot of thinking.'

Louise hung up and went into the kitchen. With methodical,
unthinking movements she prepared French fries, peppered a steak
from the refrigerator and made salad. At six o'clock she woke her
husband, Ben, and went downstairs again. She had just finished
cooking as he came down showered and crisp in his uniform.
'That was a really great sleep,' he said. It was what he said every
day. There were few worries to trouble the big, good-natured
Irishman with the red hair and very pale, blue eyes.

Louise moved silently about the kitchen while he ate and talked
about work and the chances of promotion to a desk job in nar-
cotics.

When he had finished he stood up and put an arm round her.
'What is it?' he asked. 'You've hardly said a word.'

'You were talking too much,' she said lightly. 'Anyway, I was
interested.'

He nodded, not believing her. 'Nothing you want to say to me?'

She hesitated. She felt an intense urge to tell him. Not by any means everything. Just a hint at some sort of past in Saigon before he came on the scene. But she knew, in parallel with the thought, that it would be immensely dangerous. He was a cop. By temperament and training he would want the whole story.

He raised his pale eyebrows towards her. 'We talk, remember?' he said. 'When we have a problem, we talk.'

'It's work,' she said finally. 'Every day, so many ruined kids, so many broken people. My own people. Sometimes it gets to you.'

'It gets to you that much,' he said, 'maybe it's time to change jobs.'

'No.' She walked out into the hall and came back with his cap and belt. 'Just sometimes I feel so lucky to have you. And all this.'

'It's no palace,' he said. 'It's the Bronx.'

'Almost Riverdale. And I'm very happy here,' Louise said firmly.

He held her face in both hands. 'You have a strange way of showing it, sometimes.'

'Go to work,' she said, forcing a smile. 'Catch criminals. Clean up New York.'

34

'I asked you to come,' Louise said, across a corner table in the Palermo Luncheonette, 'because I have something to tell you.'

Nan Luc waited until Mai Bassano had put two cups of coffee on the table and passed a few words with Louise. The excitement building inside her was almost suffocating. As soon as Mai had turned away she leaned forward towards Louise. 'Before you tell me anything,' she said to Louise, 'I want you to know I understand what your new life means to you in America. The past is safe with me.'

'Just listen to what I have to tell you,' Louise said.

The chill in her tone was clearly conveyed to Nan Luc. Whatever she was about to say, Nan Luc knew, was with reluctance, under some form of duress. Or possibly even a construction, a red herring to lead her away from her father. Tense, slightly sick to her stomach, Nan Luc waited.

'In the last days before the evacuation,' Louise said, 'everybody was desperate to leave Saigon. There were rumours of massacres, mass rapes, robbing and pillaging.'

'I can believe that,' Nan Luc said. 'Instead it was poverty, hunger.'

'In the spring of 1975,' Louise said, 'everybody used whatever money and influence they had to get a plane out.' She paused. 'Your mother guessed what the new world would be. She understood that a child like you, half Vietnamese, half American could only expect a life of deprivation.'

'Did she talk about these things?'

Louise nodded. 'We all recognised she was not like us. She could have worked the bars for hundreds of dollars a week. But she preferred working in a field hospital. Your grandmother thought she was mad.'

'I can imagine.'

'Pham believed everybody who fought against the Vietcong would be sent to work camps in the north. When she realised the end was near, she asked me to choose an American to help.'

'Choose him to do what?'

'To stand in as your father. To take you back to America.'

Nan drew in her breath slowly. In the corner of her eye she could see Mai Bassano standing, hands on hips, behind the counter.

'Understand what was happening. The whole city was mad with excitement, a sort of suppressed panic. From the medical unit Pham sent back money to get you to America.'

'Then what?'

'I had no time for anything, Nan. I was leading a double life.'

'What sort of double life?'

'I was a bar-girl at the Eros, for God's sake . . .'

'And your MP thought you worked at a store.'

'Whatever. My main problem was what to do with you. I still had to find an American to take you out. I was desperate. I knew an ordinary GI wouldn't get a pass in time, so I went to Stevenson. I offered him the five thousand dollars your mother had given me. Stevenson said why not. At the same time Ben had asked me to marry him. I raced over to Saigon Town Hall and bribed a clerk to alter your birth certificate, to put a name in the slot where the father's name should go.'

'There was no name before that?' Louise shook her head. Nan Luc's eyes blazed from her pale face. 'And then? Then what happened?'

'The deal was Stevenson would deliver you to someone who would be waiting in Los Angeles.'

'Who?'

'Nan, it's a world ago. I had a name on a piece of paper. I barely spoke more than bar-girl English. It didn't mean a thing to me.'

A rapid pulse was beating in Nan's throat. 'Go on,' she said. 'You left Saigon . . .'

'I was married and left the same day. Ben's officer arranged everything.' Louise pushed aside her coffee cup. 'I'm not proud of my part in all this, Nan Luc. But the money was paid to Stevenson.'

Nan Luc reached out and gripped her wrist. 'You expect me to believe this story?' she said fiercely.

'Believe it because it's true.'

'Where do I find him?'

'You don't.' Nan stiffened. 'Stevenson asked me to meet you. He's prepared to pay you the five thousand dollars Pham gave him. And another five on top. He recognises that he never earned the money.'

The door swung open with a blast of cold air. A group of four or five young girls came in and clattered on high heels up to the counter. For a moment their laughter and greetings to Mai Bassano filled the long narrow room.

'He recognises,' Nan Luc said slowly, 'that he never earned the moeny. Is that really so?'

'Don't be a fool, Nan Luc,' Louise said, picking up on her tone. 'Ten grand is a lot of money. No way you could force him to return it, and he's doing it without being asked.'

'I want to know where to find him, Louise. Tell me that.'

'For Christ's sake, ten thousand dollars he's offering you.'

'His address,' Nan Luc said. 'That's all I want.'

Louise stood up. 'You're crazy, Nan Luc. I'm having nothing to do with this. You're off your head. What other Vietnamese girl can come to New York and get offered this kind of money? Just tell me what to tell him. You take the money or not?'

'You tell him I want to meet him.'

'The life there makes people crazy,' Louise said. 'Always did. What d'you want to meet him for? He's not your father. I see why he doesn't want anything to do with you. He's got a wife. Kids maybe.'

'He's afraid, Louise.'

'Like me.'

'Not like you, Louise,' Nan Luc said quietly. 'Do you know how my mother died?' she asked after a moment.

'She had nothing to live for, I guess that's what she felt. Plenty of South Vietnamese did in those days. She killed herself.'

'Or to put it another way,' Nan Luc said harshly. 'Stevenson killed her.' Louise stared at her wildly. 'With his pornographic movies, Stevenson killed her. This is the man you're defending, Louise.'

'It's myself I'm defending,' Louise said. 'I don't know what Stevenson did. I don't want to know. It may be wicked but I don't care any more. He's not your father, Nan. Put the past behind you, for God's sake. It was full of horrors. But we survived. That's all we have left. That's all that matters now.' Her voice rose desperately. 'Leave me alone, Nan Luc. You've got money. I can see how you're dressed. You've survived.'

'Is that all it's about?'

'The past is dead, Nan. Don't become another victim of it after all this time.'

Nan Luc nodded slowly. 'You're asking me to forget what he did? The answer's no, Louise. By me it will never be forgotten. Or forgiven.' She paused. 'Tell him that.'

As the afternoon Lufthansa flight to Kennedy lifted over London's far western suburbs and headed out across the Midlands to leave the coast of the British Isles north of Glasgow, Max settled back with a glass of wine, his mind lulled by the low throb of the engines, his thoughts on Nan Luc.

He opened his briefcase and looked down at the papers he had scooped quickly from his mother's desk. Some, he saw, went back to his father's childhood in Germany. Photographs of a family picnic beside a river in the 1920s; of family holidays in Italy. Medical certificates from Heidelberg belonging to his grandfather, Doctor Rolf Lutz Benning. Pictures of a blonde-haired, middle-aged woman, his grandmother, sketching in the mountains with a small boy, Max's father, posed intently watching beside her. The few remaining traces of a family his mother had always claimed to know absolutely nothing about.

She had never really relented. Even on her deathbed she had given him only the barest facts. He thought for a moment of how much she must have hated his father. Or loved him.

He opened a grey cardboard fold with a French Police Judiciaire stamp on the front cover. A letter addressed to his mother said, without further explanation, that, at the conclusion of police investigations, the writer was forwarding the enclosed material to her as the next of kin of Peter Lutz Benning.

Photographs. Of his father holding up a large ivory statue as a fisherman might proudly display a fish. Of his father and a Vietnamese woman in uniform . . . The powerful current of dismay passed through him like an electric shock.

'Is anything wrong?' the flight attendant was asking.

He shook his head and looked back down at the photograph. He was looking at the smiling face of the woman and the small Amerasian girl, slightly out of focus, but unmistakably Nan Luc, running towards his father's outstretched arms.

35

In San Diego it was a cold, brilliantly sunny afternoon. Edward Brompton had invited his sister and brother-in-law and their family over. The descent of his sister Susan and the Garrat family for lunch was always something he dreaded in anticipation and enjoyed when the time came round. Four children under twelve years old were never likely to provide a quiet afternoon.

By the time he had arrived back from the dockyard Susan and her family were already in occupation. Children ran screaming along the terraces and through the house. As Ed got out of his car he had to remind himself that this was his own place.

But now lunch in the long terrace room was going well. The children, Edward reflected, were at last reaching a tolerable age, or a tolerable level of exhaustion.

His sister could never long conceal her curiosity about Nan Luc. Before the Vietnamese maid had cleared the first course, Susan had steered the conversation in the direction of her always intriguing sister-in-law. 'So tell us about Nan Luc,' she said. 'What's she doing in New York?'

Edward surrendered his plate to the maid. 'You know her obsession with finding her father. She's in New York to see if there's more to be found out there.'

'Even though she's no memories of him as a child?' Garrat said.

'The Vietnamese don't have that same casual view of ancestry most of the West has today,' Edward said. 'Knowledge of your ancestors, particularly honour of your father is part of your birth-right.'

'She feels it's been taken away from her. That seems reasonable,' Susan Garrat said, 'given the premise.'

'I suppose so,' Edward said. 'I'm just sorry it takes up so much of her time.'

Susan sat up straight. 'Talking of Nan Luc,' she said, 'someone called for her before you got back.'

'Who was that?'

'A young man named Max Benning.'

Edward placed his knife and fork carefully on his plate. 'Was he calling from here, San Diego?'

'New York City. I wrote down the number of his hotel on the pad. I said you'd pass it on to Nan next time you called her.'

'Thank you.' He reached forward and poured Garrat some wine. 'What did he sound like, this young man?' he asked feeling sick with apprehension.

'Very charming. Very anxious to get hold of Nan Luc. He'd met her in Vietnam, apparently.' She paused. 'He seemed to think you were her American guarantor.'

Ed nodded. 'I was, of course.'

'I mean,' Susan said patiently, 'that he didn't seem aware you were also her husband.'

'Did you tell him?'

'No. Should I have? Nor did I tell him Garrat is my husband, that I have four impossible but talented children and that, though of mature years, I'm still capable of creating a sensation in the La Scala lobby. Or would be if ever I got there.'

'Do you know him?' Garrat asked Ed. 'This young man who called?'

Edward shook his head. 'Never met him of course. Nan Luc mentioned him once or twice, that's all.'

The room was green and gold: the walls a drab ivy green, the carpet a worn nylon gold. The curtains, bedcover and lampshades were also either green or gold. In the room next door a man and woman could be heard. The deeper rumbling of his voice was punctuated every now and again with a shriek of her laughter.

Louise stood with her back to the French doors, her hands deep in the pockets of her short coat. She detested the seediness of the room, the obviousness of it. The green candlewick was stained in three or four places. She knew the stiff stain of semen. She had seen it too many times in her life.

Her fury at Nan Luc rose. It was her doing. It was Nan Luc who was responsible for her being here. Waiting in a seamy motel off Sawmill River Parkway, determined to protect the happiness she had had in the last twenty years, determined to protect her family, her American family, Ben and the boys, from the truth about her past. Just as suddenly the anger flowed out of her. Was Nan Luc right? In the Eros there were rumours that Cy Stevenson was into all sorts of things. Was it possible?

The door opened and Cy came into the room. He nodded to her and closed the door behind him. His eyes wandered round from curtains to bed. 'Pretty crummy place,' he said. She nodded. 'I didn't realise. I should have suggested a bar somewhere.'

'This is better,' she said. 'Cops visit bars. I wouldn't want to be seen by friends of my husband.'

'No.' He was trembling. He sat on the edge of the bed. Excitement overwhelmed him. He found it hard not to laugh. If Nan Luc presented herself at Meyerick, he was lost. The laughter rose in him again, drunken hysteria. He rubbed hard at his face and looked up at Louise, controlling himself. 'I brought the money.' He reached into his inside pocket. His hand froze as he saw the expression on her face.

'She doesn't want the money,' Louise said. 'She won't take it.'

'Ten thousand dollars. You told her I owe it to her?'

'She doesn't believe it.'

'Jesus.'

'She knows Pham wasn't a bar-girl. She knows her father wasn't a passing lay.'

'What else?' he asked carefully.

Louise looked at him with that strange indifferent loathing he had seen on so many Vietnamese women's faces. 'What else? She believes you're responsible for her mother's death.' He went pale. 'She still thinks you're her father.'

Beads of sweat formed on his forehead. 'What can she do?'

'If she finds you, she'll kill you, Mr Stevenson,' Louise said. 'You have to understand. She's here to kill you.'

He was brought up short. 'The bitch, she will,' he said.

He looked up at Louise. Her face was impassive, not like a real face. He stood up. She seemed as small as a child beside him. Like a doll, the soldiers always said about Vietnamese girls.

The whisky he had drunk thumped in his head. The sweat rolled and broke on his eyebrows. 'Tell me,' he said, swallowing to control his nausea. 'When Nan Luc came to see you at the Project . . .' His mouth was dry with fear.

'Yes?'

'How did she find you?'

'By chance. Someone had seen me driving in to work.'

It all seemed so long ago. He was a kid then, barely older than the boy soldiers the US had sent to fight the Vietcong. He sat, looking down at the gold carpet, thinking of the Eros and the noise and the girls wrapped around soldiers they had met five minutes before. Vietnamese were different. He had seen so many of them die. So many of them suffer with that mute acceptance that drove Americans crazy. He had seen what they did to other Vietnamese too. He had seen split bellies and heads thrown like footballs into the village bamboo thicket. Torture, maiming. Every sort of sexual abuse. They were past masters. They had taught a lot of Americans the game.

He looked at the woman opposite him. Denim skirt, sling-back heels. Cloth coat. A civilised veneer. Underneath she was just another Indo-Chinese. Running for her life, from the day she was born.

'What the hell we going to do?' he muttered to himself.

She made no attempt to answer. In the heavy silence, beneath his gaze, she shifted uncomfortably. Through the curtained windows he could hear the roar of the trucks on the highway.

From the car Nan Luc watched the motel front. A light rain began to fall and the thrumming of the vehicles on the highway took on a softer swishing sound. The red neon flashed like a slow pulse beat. There was no sign of Louise.

She had followed Louise from the Palermo diner to the motel. She knew that people under stress do things, sometimes stupid things, to relieve the pressure. It looked to Nan Luc as if Louise was doing just that.

She had pulled up across the road when Louise had turned her Jeep Wagoneer into the motel parking lot. She had watched Louise get out and go into the lobby. And minutes later walk down the side of the building until she disappeared through the lighted archway. She knew it was only a matter of minutes before he arrived.

Five, ten minutes later she had seen a tall light-haired man appear, walking from round the bend in the road. He had passed in front of her and turned to cross the hotel parking lot. She had been surprised at the obvious mud stains on the knees of his well-cut suit.

Looking at him she had felt her throat tighten. A man still young, fitting the image of those earlier dreams, when she had believed in him. Young enough to have been on the prow of a boatful of partying people. The commanding figure in a board-room, maybe. The father watching his children run with the sleek dogs across the lawn. Any of these men. Any of the men plucked out of a lifetime of fantasy. A fantasy which had changed one evening in Cahn Roc.

As his face caught the light she swept Louise's story behind her; she watched in the absolute certainty it was her father. She watched in the grip of hatred which threatened to strangle her. She had imagined the moment a thousand times in the last months. As a moment of burning, stifling anger. Now she was unprepared for the coldness of her feelings. Unprepared even after all her carefully nurtured resolution, for the determination she now felt to end his life.

Less than half an hour had passed. It was raining more heavily now, the drops drumming on the roof of the hire car and merging to flow down the windshield.

Nan Luc sat upright in her seat and switched on the windshield wipers. The man emerging from the lighted archway opposite stood for a moment in the rain. She saw no more than fifty yards away, close enough to see his wet hair plastered across his forehead. When he moved it was forward, it was not back towards the motel check-in but down the grassy slope.

Alarm gripped her. She turned on the engine. He had broken into a run across the parking lot and towards the dark scrub and bushes on the far side.

Moving the car up towards the bend in the road she could see the man running down the road away from her. Then suddenly he turned towards the bushes beside him. Perhaps, she thought, he had turned in response to someone calling but the drumming of the rain on the roof of the car prevented her from hearing anything at that distance. Or perhaps he had realised he was being followed.

As the man disappeared into the bushes Nan Luc braked and flung open the driver's door. Jumping out she raced across the road and through a gap in the broken shrubs. She could see a car now on the ramp leading on to the highway and she could see the man stumble and slip as he mounted the slope. By the time she had reached the foot of the slope a car door had slammed closed above her head. In a second, headlights were sweeping across the top of the bushes lining the ramp.

She scrambled out of the bushes and jumped the steel retaining rail on to the ramp. A dark Mercedes, black, royal blue even, was pulling away fast. She stood for a second in furious desperation. Then, suddenly aware that she was picked out in the headlights of a vehicle coming up the ramp behind her, she swung round and waved her arms, a few feet from the driver's face.

An old pick-up truck belonging to the Bronx & Bronx Garage Company swept past her. Two more cars ignored her as she frantically flagged them down. The fourth car stopped. The window wheeled down and a small bald head was stuck out into the rain. 'You want a lift?' His eyes twinkled lasciviously.

The Mercedes was out of sight beyond the top of the ramp. She shook her head and turned back, climbed the rail and slid and scrambled down the slope.

Her hair was wet and the knees of her jeans were stained with mud from sliding down the steep bank, as his had been when he made his way to the motel.

Returning to the hire car Nan Luc poured herself a cup of black coffee from the flask and sat, the car door half open, looking towards the Jeep Wagoneer still parked on the crown of the sloping lot. She could not be sure why she was shaking. The sight of her father? That was the easy explanation. But was it fear, anger, hatred or memory that made the paper cup in her hand spill black drops of coffee at her lips to run warm down her chin?

What to do now? She could go into the motel and confront Louise. But why would she tell her anything more than she had told her this morning. To follow her now would be pointless. The man, Stevenson, her father, had gone. Louise would be leaving for home.

The extraordinary acuity of her emotion at seeing her father had muddled her thoughts. But she knew that if Louise were to lead her to him it would have to be another day.

For a last time she looked towards the motel lights sparkling in the thin rain. Feeling sick at her failure, she slammed the car door closed, started the engine and cruised past the lot and the silent Jeep Wagoneer.

36

Nan Luc sat in a yellow bathrobe in her room in the Greenwich village apartment Kim Hoang had lent her. Across the room she could see herself in the long mirror, her bare legs stretched out before her, her hair tumbled across her shoulders.

Although she could not see it in the reflection across a room lit only by city lights outside, she willed that there was something else visible in that mirror.

She wanted it to be hate.

She stood up quickly, unable to bear the thought that other things showed in her face. Doubt. The doubt that Louise had sown with her story of the five thousand dollars. Was it possible he was not her father? Was it possible she was wrong? She shook off the idea angrily and crossed the room and in the half darkness poured herself some mineral water. Dropping ice and lime into the glass she walked barefoot back to stand in front of the window.

She had arrived home half an hour ago, wet, tired, bitterly angry with herself at the opportunity she had missed. She had taken a shower and put on the lemon yellow bathrobe. Standing at the window she looked out at the lights of the city flickering through floating banks of rain-laden mist.

She turned slowly, still in the half dark, and punched the button to see if Edward had called. She listened to his easy voice, relaxed, asking her to hurry through her business and get back out West. She sipped her mineral water and listened to his voice as he told her Susan and the family were there. 'So that's the West Coast news and weather, Nan.' He paused and she detected a faint change of tone. 'Yes, one more thing. Max Benning called. Staying at the Chelverton Hotel, West 44th Street. Wants you to get in touch with him there. Hurry back, Nan. I miss you.'

The telephone stood on a low cream coloured table beside her now. She knew she had only to pick up the phone. But she also knew Max, and Max alone, could come between her and her duty. Her duty to Edward. Her duty to herself.

She turned to the mirror and stared at her face. It was moments before she realised she was crying.

She threw herself back into the armchair. Her drink spilled forward between the folds of her robe. She almost cried aloud as the cold liquid rolled down her thigh.

She did not ask herself why he was in New York. At this moment she didn't care. The simple idea that Max was sitting in a bar or restaurant or hotel room within a mile or two of where she was affected her with such intensity that it was almost enough for the moment.

She let her mind slide back into the past, fuzzing the edges of the images like a waking dream. She knew they shared memories not because she believed he had been affected in the same way by each event in their time together, but because it had been so short a time, there had been so few events.

She drifted with the sampan down the river and felt the extra-ordinary glow that warmed her body by the knowledge that this one man was watching her every movement. She relived the hypnotic effect of the sunlight through the great overhanging trees. And she felt again that exclusive surrender which she had not allowed herself since Max had left Saigon.

In a fever almost equal to that Max had suffered, she relived the night in bed beside him, his hot, shivering body, the strangeness of his eyes as he slipped back into consciousness and realised she was naked against him. She raised in her mind the shadowed image of his unshaven cheek, the whiteness of his teeth, the smudges below his eyes.

Would she love him when he walked quickly, no longer bowed with fever, across the lobby of a New York hotel and stopped in front of her?

Her body answered her. She could feel that she was trembling slightly and she sat forward and shook her head. She remembered with a smile that Edward had told her that young British and American boys, in the sort of private school he had attended, were recommended a brisk cold shower when thoughts of the opposite sex became too disturbing. She also remembered he said it was very much a short-term solution.

She got up and switched on lights.

She had given Edward her word. He had not bribed her into marriage. She had been totally candid about it. She had told him about Max. Told him that she loved Max. In turn, when he had offered marriage as a solution, he had told her she could take it as a simple facility offered by a friend, one that would enable her to escape from Gulanga. But as soon as they met in Gulanga, even before the marriage had taken place, she had made it clear what she intended. She would not use marriage to him as a device to become an American citizen. She had accepted his offer of marriage and would be a full partner in the marriage. She would share his burdens and successes as he would share hers. She would share his bed. She would stay with him as long as he wanted her.

She took her drink to the window and stood leaning against it, peering down into the half-lit darkness of the street. Did she have the strength to meet Max? Just once more?

The rain, which had been falling in large drops, flickering in the streetlights like a million fireflies, had almost stopped.

Nan Luc turned back to the telephone. She had decided.

Schmidt's laid no claim to modernity. A long bar faced the entrance; a line of booths ran along both side walls, booths with red plush seats and heavy brass rails from which at one time curtains could be drawn for privacy. The tables were covered with white cloths and the boarded floor had not yet been carpeted or tiled. Germans had always come here, Emil Jannings once, Marlene Dietrich several times. Now young Germans came, diplomatic, business and advertising men and women visiting New York from Hamburg and Frankfurt and Berlin. This year it was one of New York's in places, to the surprise of its elderly waiters and the third Schmidt in line to have owned it.

Max knew most of the staff from earlier visits to New York and used the restaurant like a club. But he had chosen Schmidt's for other reasons, reasons attached in some way to the idea of a meeting on emotionally neutral ground. Now that the moment had come to tell her, he felt the pit of his stomach falling away, a fierce turmoil in him that rose in a flush to the face and forehead.

He had not yet adapted to the idea of seeing her against anything but a Vietnamese backdrop, the courthouse, the stone harbourmaster's tower, the Cahn Roc River.

She was of course married. The woman he had spoken to, Edward Brompton's sister, had not said so in so many words. But she had said enough. She had said too, casually, not knowing its significance that Nan Luc was in New York, in New York City trying to trace her father. He must tell her. And here at Schmidt's was a better place than most, a gentler place, a survivor from another age.

Max watched her push open the door and hesitate. She had seen him before he stood up. She did not smile. As he came forward she walked towards him. She was wearing jeans and a polo-shirt and a short suede jacket. Somehow in all his dreams about her he had only seen her in black trousers and a white Mao jacket.

She found him greatly changed. As she crossed the room he rose from his seat, a young fair-haired man in a dark linen suit. But his eyes were dark, his smile almost anguished. She wanted to throw her arms round him, to ask him what was wrong. But she felt now, at this moment of seeing him, desperately nervous, as if all the Western experiences of the last months had fallen away from her. She was, she realised, as so many people young and not so young have realised before, made infinitely shy by love.

She stopped a pace from him. 'Max,' she said in a voice little above a whisper.

He took her arm and guided her to the booth, barely trusting himself to speak. When they were sitting down he reached out and held her hands across the white tablecloth. Then withdrew them quickly. 'Just give me a moment to catch my breath.'

She smiled, a soft unhurried smile. 'Take your time,' she said. 'I don't want to move from here, ever.'

He shook his head. 'Ask me something, some ordinary question to wake me up.'

'All right. How did you find me?'

'I went back to Vietnam, to Cahn Roc. An English policeman in Hong Kong . . . It's a long story.'

Pain shadowed her face. 'You went back to Cahn Roc?'

'You must have known I would.'

'So you knew I'd gone to the West.'

'I knew you'd tried. I went to Bangkok and Hong Kong.' He stopped.

'I was at Gulanga.'

He nodded. 'I know. I discovered. Too late.'

For a long time she said nothing, looking at him, her face pale, her eyes full of tears. 'I'm sorry, Max,' she said at last.

'You mustn't be, Nan.'

'I'm married, Max.'

'Mrs Nan Brompton, San Diego?'

'Yes.'

She watched his eyes, dark and troubled. He reached out and held her hands again. 'I've a lot to talk to you about, Nan.'

She nodded slowly. 'Order me some wine,' she said, 'and we'll talk.'

He signalled to a waiter and ordered a bottle of Riesling.

'First tell me why you're here, Max.'

'I don't want to try to answer that question,' he said carefully. 'Not yet.'

'I could ask you a thousand questions,' she said. 'But only one really interests me.' He nodded for her to go on. 'I'm married,' she said. 'I have no right, but I need to know how you feel.'

'I have no right to say so but the answer is, the same.' She swallowed hard. Her eyes closed. 'And you?' he said.

'The same, Max. Always the same.'

The waiter came and placed the long-necked bottle and two glasses before them. When he made to pour the wine, Max thanked him in German and took the bottle from him. 'Why are you here in New York, Nan?' he said, filling her glass.

'The story's too long, too full of hatred.' She touched his face. 'You have no part in it.'

'Your father,' he said. She withdrew her hand. 'Have you found him?'

'I'm close.'

Max nodded slowly. 'In Ho Chi Minh City I went to the Eros Hotel. Just to see it. I found your grandmother, Bernadette, living among the rubble.'

'Bernadette . . .' Nan Luc said the name slowly. 'It seems a lifetime ago.'

'She told me why you left.' Nan looked at Max without speaking. 'She told me you believe he was responsible for your mother's death.'

'Then you understand why I had to come to America.'

'If this man Stevenson is guilty, you can leave him to the law.'

Her head came up, hurling the hair from her face. '*The law*? You think he could ever be found guilty of something that happened fifteen years ago? In what's now virtually an enemy country? I've seen the American system, Max. Even in the few months I've lived here I've watched lawyer cross with lawyer over tiny, unreal points, I've watched trials prolonged and guilty men, even *murderers*, walk free.' She caught her breath. 'If that happened to him, I would kill myself.'

'Let's go,' Max said brusquely. They stood and he dropped money on the table next to the untouched bottle of wine. 'I've something to tell you.'

She stood up slowly. 'Something about my father?'

He hesitated. 'Yes, Nan. Something about your father.'

In the street outside he made no attempt to put his arm round her. He walked with slow, heavy paces, both hands deep in his trouser pockets.

Beside him Nan Luc walked flooded with unhappiness. Since Cahn Roc she had carefully compartmented her life – Edward – the search for her father – her memory of Max. But now all that was important to her had been thrust together, every decision had been made to overlap.

'What right have you to take revenge,' Max said, looking down at the sidewalk, 'if he is *not* your father?'

'Are you telling me what my aunt, Louise, tried to tell me? That my father's name died when my mother died?'

He shook his head. 'I'm not telling you that, Nan. I'm asking you if you'd feel the same way if he were not your father.'

'Don't say that, Max. Please don't say that.'

'He could still be brought to justice.'

'No,' she said bitterly. 'You still don't understand, Max. For me, justice is only justice. Justice is not enough.'

In the darkened lobby of the Chelverton Hotel they sat, both leaning forward towards each other, both holding cups of coffee in their hands.

'I wanted it to be so different,' she said, 'if we ever met again.'

'I dreamed of a different ending, too.'

'So tell me,' she said.

'You want more coffee?' She nodded. He lifted the pot and poured a thin trickle into her cup. She touched his arm. 'Forget the coffee,' she said.

'OK.' He took a deep breath. 'I told you in Cahn Roc that my mother was sick, beyond all hope of recovery.'

'I remember.'

'Last week she died. In her desk was a file of my father's papers.'

'From his time in Vietnam?'

He paused. 'Some of the papers belonged to your mother,' he said.

A shudder passed through her. 'What papers?'

'Details of her service record with the Field Hospital.' His eyes never leaving her face, Max reached into his pocket. 'And this.' He laid the photograph on the table between them. 'The man,' he said, 'is my father.'

She stared down at it. He could see the fear grow on her face. 'What does it mean, Max?'

'Look at them, Nan,' he said gently. 'Look at their faces. I think you know what it means. What it must mean.'

'No.' She fought to control her voice. 'They knew each other perhaps. They were friends, that's all.' Her hands rose to cover her face.

He reached out and held her wrist. 'We have to face the possibility that it's more than that, Nan.'

'No,' Nan Luc whispered through her fingers. 'No, I don't believe it . . . I won't believe it. If that's what you want to think, it's your decision, Max.' She dropped her hands. 'Is that what you want to believe?'

'If it saves you from ruining your life, if it saves you from a twenty-year jail sentence for murder,' Max said. '*Yes.*'

She ran because it seemed the only way to fill the other void inside her, ran to stop the uncontrollable tears and the pulse thundering in her temples. Ran through the wet, almost empty streets, across intersections, past night repairmen, urged on by flashes of bright neon. She had asked Max to get some more coffee and slipped from the hotel before he realised. She could hear his shouts echoing behind her now.

Swinging round a corner she saw a yellow cab cruising towards her and she waved her hands desperately. As it slowed beside her and she grabbed the handle of the still moving cab, the driver looked up into the wild blaze of her eyes, heard the man's shouts and running footsteps reach the corner.

'Oh, no lady.' He was shaking his head in alarm.

But she had already thrown herself into the back seat. 'Drive,' she ordered. 'Just drive.'

The cab pulled away past Max and swung back up West 44th Street.

In the back Nan Luc fought to control her breathing. She retched at the thought of what Max had said. In one stroke he had deprived her of everything that had kept her alive for the last year.

If Stevenson was not her father, then did she still have a right to a unique, personal revenge? Did it mean that the only course now was to bring Stevenson to justice, to a long wrangle in the courts, against clever, amoral lawyers? With the chance, the everpresent chance that he would finally, finally walk away free.

'You want me to drive all night?' the cab driver said. She gave him her Greenwich Village address.

Was it not possible that Max was mistaken? Of course it was. It was possible that her mother had met Peter Benning long after she had known Stevenson. Long after she had had Stevenson's child.

As she ran up the steps to the house, as she let herself in and ran along the corridor, her mind was desperately clawing away the idea that Peter Benning was her father.

She slammed the door of the apartment and walked slowly, deliberately, into the living room. The words were thrumming in her head. Phone Edward. Immediately. She punched out the numbers and waited. Even with the time difference he would be in bed.

His voice answered after a few moments. 'Nan,' he said, gathering his wits, 'what is it, is something wrong?'

She forced a glacial calm into her voice. 'No,' she said coolly, 'nothing wrong. Just something I had to call you about right away. If Max Benning calls you, please on no account give him my address here. Give him no information. Nothing.'

'Will you tell me why?'

'Sometime soon. Not now.'

There was a long silence. 'OK, Nan. No address, nothing. I've got it.'

When she had put down the phone she stood pouring herself a glass of wine, thinking of Edward, thinking of Max, thinking of her father. Wine spilled over the rim of the glass as the telephone rang.

She walked back into the living room. Edward. Who else at this time of the night. Not Max. He could not possibly know the number. She lifted the phone. Kim Hoang's voice said: 'Nan, I just got it on the wire service. Something dreadful's happened. Something really dreadful.'

37

She was sick with guilt. Sick with the image of Louise lying murdered in the motel room. Sick with the idea that she might somehow have prevented her death. On the phone Kim Hoang had urged Nan Luc to go to the police. But that would mean revealing everything Louise had been desperate to hide. Now she owed Louise silence, if nothing else.

Through the night, half sleeping and dreaming in a chair, Nan Luc tried to tear the veil aside, to break through into the Saigon world of only twenty years ago. A wild world, Louise had said, a world of sex and drugs and ugliness and tens of thousands of abandoned children. Was it possible that Louise was telling the truth about the money? To Nan it seemed more likely that the story of the five thousand dollars and the forging of the birth certificate was something Stevenson had forced Louise to tell her.

Where, Nan asked herself, would her mother, Pham, a South Vietnamese Army nurse get five thousand dollars? To any Vietnamese who wasn't involved in drugs or war profiteering or prostitution it would have been a gigantic sum.

She got up and walked back and forth through the length of the small apartment. Facing him, confronting him, was the only way. She was too Vietnamese to believe that a father could face his child without somehow revealing the truth. And then no police. No courts. No clever lawyers. He must never walk free.

As dawn etched the jagged outline of the rooftops opposite, she peeled off her clothes and fell naked across the bed. She lay there chasing an idea, a nagging thought through the corridors of memory. Stevenson had eluded her at the motel but something still drummed in her head. A connection which came from last night.

Something, through the curtain of drizzling rain, that had

flashed through her mind at the moment the Mercedes pulled away on the ramp.

Mary Page Butler, dressed in a plaid skirt, a black Pringle cashmere and a Bettina Hopman gold necklet, came down the stairs and turned left towards the drawing room. Through the hall windows she could see the low grey cloud which presaged snow. But beside the door she could also see her husband's three leather suitcases ready for loading into his car for his weekend in the city.

Two days, two nights by herself. Two days more she could put off telling Fin she wasn't going to resign from the fund. Worse, that she was voting for Cy at the Christmas Eve election. Would he guess? Fin, maybe no. But Sunny. And the other trustees.

Reaching for the door she heard voices in the drawing room. As if to match her thoughts, Fin's voice, Sunny's.

She pushed open the heavy panelled door. 'Hi, Sunny,' she said. 'I thought it was you.' She reached up and gave Sunny a careful kiss on the cheek. 'Drink's already?' she said, turning to Fin.

'I'm leaving in a few minutes,' Fin said. 'If I'm to mix them, and who else, you'll have to have them straightaway.'

'This is a surprise,' Mary dropped down on to the sofa, her eyes on Sunny.

'Yes,' Sunny said flatly.

'I thought maybe you had come round to hitch a lift with Fin into New York.'

'Looking like this?' Sunny said, without a smile.

Mary shrugged. It was true, Sunny looked worn and stale, as if she had passed a bad night. And of course she would never go into the city dressed in jeans.

'An early start to the day, but I always insist Saturdays don't count,' Fin Butler said, as he carried the two heavy tumblers, tinkling with ice, across to his wife and sister-in-law. 'There,' he handed a glass to Sunny, 'I'm justly renowned for the gin and tonics I make. Just a touch of bitters added. The Prince adores them.'

'Sunny knows,' Mary said, taking her own glass. 'In fact, Fin,' she added, not unkindly, '*everybody* knows.'

'Ah,' Butler threw his hands in the air. 'Repeating himself again. Old age, Mary.'

'You're not old,' she said, more sharply. 'If you're old, what does that make me?'

'Five years younger,' he said. 'Just as you've always been. Now,' he signalled he was changing the subject, 'I'm going into the city today for lunch at my club. Probably stay overnight. We've got the Argentinians over on a non-playing visit.'

'Best polo players in the world,' Sunny said.

Fin Butler smiled easily. 'Thank you, Sunny. Nearly repeated myself again, did I?' Giving each woman a peck on the cheek, Fin Butler left them alone in the room.

'He's a good man,' Sunny said after a moment's silence. They could hear Fin humming to himself as he picked up the bags the houseboy had brought down into the hall.

'I don't think you've a right to say that until you've lived with a man,' Mary said as the door slammed shut behind Fin. 'He's good enough, but only I can say whether he's really good.'

'A very raunchy remark from my rather prim elder sister.'

'I'm not prim,' Mary said irritably. 'And it wasn't intended as a raunchy remark. I wasn't talking about sex. I was talking about life.'

They listened to Fin's car start and the gravel of the drive crackle beneath the wheels.

Mary took a long drink of her gin and tonic. 'Yes,' she said, 'he makes a good gin and tonic. An excellent Martini. He can decant a bottle of vintage port better than any English butler. He can play polo with the best who, as he constantly reminds us, are Argentinians. He is an acquaintance of Prince Charles. But that's Finlay Butler. That's *all* of him.'

Sunny got up and carried her glass towards the drawing room door. 'My big sis *is* feeling scratchy today,' she said.

Mary shrugged. 'Perhaps. Where's Cy?'

With one finger Sunny pushed the door closed. For a moment she stood there, looking down, as if admiring the smooth swing of the door and the satisfying click of the lock. 'Cy?' she echoed. Her face turned back towards Mary. 'He's sleeping it off.'

'Sleeping what off?'

'Sleeping off whatever drink and debauchery he treated himself to last night, I suppose.'

'You don't know where he was?' Mary said tentatively. Debauchery. The picture of the naked Vietnamese masseuse bending over her swept through her mind. She drank some more gin. Spilt a drop or two on to the peach silk sofa.

'No,' Sunny said. 'He was too drunk to tell me. He passed out just after he got back. I found him this morning sprawled in an armchair, his suit covered with mud. Mud on his face, his hands . . . Not a pretty sight.'

'Did you wake him up?' Sunny, watching her sister carefully, shook her head. 'Perhaps he wasn't feeling well,' Mary said.

'I'd lay money on it.'

Mary put her drink on a side table. 'I don't understand you, Sunny. The way you describe it, almost anything could have happened. A car crash.'

'His car was parked outside the house. Parked erratically but undamaged.'

'Would you like me to come over with you?'

'Come over with me?'

'To help you if Cy's still unwell.'

Sunny took a cigarette from the silver box with the Page crest. 'Why should I need your help?' she said. 'I came over to Page Corner to get *away* from Cy. I'm certainly not going back on some mission of mercy.'

Mary stood and moved restlessly round the room. Sunny's tone disturbed her. 'Of course not, darling.' she said. 'If you think Cy's all right, then I'm sure that's OK. I just wondered for a moment if you'd come over for my help, that's all.'

'No,' Sunny said. 'I came over for something else altogether as a matter of fact.'

'What was that?'

'It was to give you this.'

She came forward and unclenched her fist over a mahogany table. Mary watched a small glinting object roll slowly from the palm of her sister's hand. An earring. 'Yours, I believe,' Sunny said, straightening up.

Mary looked down at the clasp. Was denial possible? Not with a Biancini piece. 'It looks like it,' she said. 'Where did you find it?' She was praying.

'In my bed,' Sunny said. 'Lodged beneath the mattress.'

They stood opposite each other in utter silence.

'So my prim and proper, puritanical, post-menopausal sister turns out to be screwing her much younger and much despised brother-in-law. How does she pull it off? No cheap pun intended, Mary darling.'

Mary's hands were over her face. 'Sunny, Sunny . . .' Her muffled voice burst through her fingers. 'Sunny darling . . . I wouldn't . . .'

Sunny grimaced angrily. 'Wouldn't hurt me for anything in the world?' she flung at her sister. 'Really? Well, you have. You've flattened me. I have a good looking, virile husband who I *know* likes 'em young and slim and pouty. I see where he looks in the street. He doesn't look at fifty-year-old women, however glossy they're dressed. He looks at twenty-year-old kids. Younger sometimes. All jeans and jumping T-shirts. So why *you*, for Christ's sake,' she screamed. 'I could take the occasional twenty-year-old. I could take the occasional thousand dollar hooker. But I can't take someone I've looked on all my life as practically my mother. It's sick.'

Mary knelt on the sofa. She felt as if all thought processes had stopped functioning.

'Then I realised.' Sunny's voice was almost a whisper. 'Then I realised why he chose you.'

'I don't know what you mean.' Mary half turned.

Sunny laughed. The edge of hysteria. 'It was either you or old Mrs Rose! What a choice!'

'Please, Sunny, I really do not know what you're talking about.'

'I'm talking about your vote, you silly bitch. That's what my husband wanted. And when you give it to him on Christmas Eve, as I'm sure you will, everybody on that committee will laugh themselves sick. Except Fin, of course.'

'It's over, Sunny,' Mary said desperately. 'I haven't been to your house since I got back from Europe. I came to my senses. All right, far too late. But it's over.'

'You mean you *are* resigning? You're not voting for Cy on Christmas Eve?'

She couldn't tell her. She couldn't tell her younger sister that she had somehow allowed herself to be touched by another woman. And that there were photographs of every disgusting moment.

'Yes or no?' Sunny spat at her. 'Are you voting for my husband or not?' Mary stared at her in silence. 'So he still has your vote.'

Sunny walked slowly to the door. 'I won't be running off to tell Fin, Mary. But then by Christmas Eve it won't be necessary to tell anybody anything.' She reached the door, opening it slowly. 'You bitch, Mary,' she said quietly. 'You poor old bitch.'

Then she walked out to her Volvo where Fitz sat at the wheel.

'You want a used car,' the cop had said who had given her directions. 'I could show you a hundred better places to buy. Some of them even in the South Bronx.'

The row of decrepit houses came to a stop opposite where she had pulled up. Half a dozen ageing automobiles leaked oil on to the forecourt. Another three or four stood under a tin-roofed awning in front of what had once been a bakehouse.

The two young men, Cubans or Puerto Ricans, looked up from the Ford they were working on as Nan Luc got out of the car. Something about her ease of manner, her clothes, alerted them. 'What you make of this?' the younger man said uncertainly.

They both straightened up and watched her cross the forecourt, baffled by the unhurried walk, the way she stopped to throw a critical glance at one of the ancient cars.

'You wanna buy a car, lady?' the older boy called incredulously.

Nan Luc walked past the two boys and stopped, looking at the battered pick-ups parked under the tin awning. 'Were either of you two driving that recovery truck last night?' she asked. She tossed her head towards the truck marked Bronx & Bronx Garage Company, parked on the far side of the awning.

The boys exchanged a wary look. 'Both of us,' the elder said. 'We got a call out an' nothing there when we showed. Bad for business. Kids call up for kicks.'

'On the way back you took the ramp up back of the Swallow Motel, is that right?'

'Maybe we took the ramp, maybe not,' the elder boy said. 'Who's asking? You're not a cop?'

Nan Luc took four twenties from her purse. 'You can help me. Perhaps you can help me.'

The boy hesitated. 'How can we help you, lady?' he said, his eyes flicking down to the money in Nan Luc's hand. 'Last night we jes' drove back home, is all.'

'Coming up the ramp you were behind a dark coloured Mercedes.'

'Nice car.' The younger boy spoke for the first time. Right, Tony?'

Nan Luc turned. 'You remember it?'

'We tucked up behind it right down nearly to the bridge,' the young boy said. 'It slipped a lane there and went way ahead.'

'So you were staring at the back end of this Mercedes for most of ten minutes.'

'We didn't get no number,' Tony said. 'New York plates is all I remember.'

'You're sure?' Nan Luc said. 'You didn't even get part of a number?' The boy shook his head. 'How about you?' Nan Luc turned to the younger boy.

He shuffled his feet. 'No . . .'

Tony turned back to Nan Luc and the twenties held just above the open neck of her purse. 'Sorry, lady. We'd really like to help.'

Nan's eyes roamed across the forecourt. 'You've got time to think.' She showed no sign of moving.

'The only thing I got,' the younger boy said, anxious to please, 'is a sticker.'

'The Mercedes carried a sticker?'

'In the rear window,' the boy said. 'Hey, what was it now? Something funny.' He stopped suddenly, looking at Nan Luc. 'Something about Vietnam.'

'Something about Vietnam?' Nan felt a sudden surge of hope.

'Something Vietnam. Place upstate we did that refrigerator truck.' He turned to the other boy.

'Meyerick,' his friend said flatly.

'It's coming.' The boy snapped his fingers. 'Meyerick Vietnam Fund. That's it, lady.'

'Where's Meyerick?'

'Upstate New York,' the other boy said. 'An hour or two's drive north and west.'

'You did a good night's work last night,' Nan Luc said. 'I'm sorry to hear you didn't get paid. How much do you calculate you lost?'

He felt the phone had been ringing since time began. As his eyes opened Cy Stevenson frowned into the darkness. He was in a chair, an armchair. Something was rolling around his feet. A bottle. Two even. And the phone was ringing. The curtained windows showed thin cracks of daylight. He had no idea what time it was.

He reached left and knocked over a lamp. His hand connected with the telephone. He picked it up. As he spoke into it the memory surged over him of last night. He could hear a woman's voice in his ear. Frantic, repetitive. 'Cy, is that you? For God's sake speak. Speak, for God's sake.'

He grunted.

'Cy, I've been trying to call you for the last hour. 'Sunny knows,' Mary's voice said. 'About us.'

He reached down for one of the rolling bottles, put the neck to his lips and let the last few drops of whisky trickle across his tongue.

'Cy, did you hear me? Sunny's left for Virginia. We have to talk. I'm coming straight over?'

He put the phone on the arm of the chair and felt about on the floor for the light. Clicking the switch he screwed up his eyes as light jumped across the pale carpet. Mary's voice was still coming from the phone. He picked up the receiver. His suit, he saw, was covered with mud.

'Listen,' he said, infinitely weary. 'Just for Christ's sake leave me alone.'

38

In the mirror behind the barman's head Hal Bolson caught sight of Max hurrying down the steps and swung round on the stool.

'Thanks for meeting me at such short notice, Hal,' Max said, shaking his hand.

Bolson grimaced. 'Now I'm retired I find I have all the time in the world. And I don't like it. On the phone you sounded like a worried man.'

'I am. Unless I can find Nan Luc in the next few hours. You said there are things you can tell me.'

'There are things I might be able to tell you,' Bolson corrected him cautiously. 'But I have to get clearance first.'

'Clearance? From the Pentagon, you mean? The CIA?'

Bolson shook his head. 'In the bars of Saigon there were more agents than there were whores. But I wasn't one of them.' He paused. 'You really think Nan Luc's going for the jugular?'

'The wrong jugular.'

'But she doesn't yet know where to find Stevenson?'

'Don't count on it.'

Bolson signalled to the barman. 'Let me buy you a drink.'

Max shook his head. 'I don't have that kind of time, Hal.'

'OK. I get the message.' Bolson pushed himself off the barstool. 'I'll do what I can.' They walked towards the stairs. Bolson took his topcoat from a hook and shrugged himself into it.

'This clearance you're going to have to get, Hal. Who is it from?'

Bolson buttoned his coat. 'A woman,' he said. 'I have to check with her first. All this could put a cannon shot through her life.'

Max stood under the plastic dome of a call point and punched the numbers for San Diego. He was looking through the clear side of the booth at the picture of the Vietnamese woman on the front page of a stack of newspapers at the newsstand on the street corner. Within seconds he heard the soft, unhurried voice of Edward Brompton.

'Mr Brompton,' Max said, not trying to disguise the urgency in his voice, 'this is Max Benning.'

'I told you, Mr Benning, that I couldn't help you with my wife's New York address.'

'Do you know who I am?' Max said carefully. 'Do you know I was a friend of your wife's in Vietnam?'

'Yes. I know who you are, Mr Benning. I'm afraid the answer's the same.'

'I have something to tell you, Mr Brompton, which I think might make a difference.'

'What's that?'

'In Vietnam Nan Luc used to say that if she ever got to America she would trace her father through her Aunt Louise whose husband she thought might be a New York cop.'

'Yes, that's probably one route she's following,' Brompton said cautiously. 'What is it you have to tell me?'

'I believe Louise has been murdered, Mr Brompton. I think it's her picture on the newsstands here in New York. Louise Cartwright, policeman's wife. Found murdered in the early hours of this morning.' He paused. 'I think there's every chance the man Nan Luc's looking for is a murderer.'

At the other end the phone was silent. Then Ed Brompton said abruptly. 'Nan Luc isn't at her apartment in Greenwich Village. I don't know where she is. You think she could be walking into danger.'

'I know she is. I'm not sure she knows it.'

'OK,' Ed Brompton said crisply. 'I'll give you the address of the apartment and arrange for the superintendent to let you in.' For the first time his voice betrayed his anxiety. 'Hell,' he said, 'maybe there's something at the apartment that can point the police to where she's gone.'

She had never seen such a restrained display of wealth. Cars, clothes, tennis courts, the furnishings of the club itself, all proclaimed a cautious Eastern Seaboard affluence.

The trick, Nan Luc thought, was to leave you in no doubt that this was a highly exclusive club and that its members were the wealthiest families in the county, all without hammering a notice on the door. Portraits, old and new, lined the long wall of the dining room. Jason Rose was seated below an eighteenth century wigged figure under which was written, 'Joshua Meyerick, Esq. Born 1699, Woodstock, Oxfordshire, England. Died 1789, Meyerick City, New York, in the United States of America.'

Jason Rose stood as she approached and stretched his hand. Only then, by the slightest miscalculation of direction did she realise he was blind. He smiled as the chair was drawn out for her. 'You're very quick, Mrs Brompton. I can usually fool most people for five minutes or so. It's a sort of childish game,' he added dismissively.

'It was good of you to ask me here, Mr Rose,' she said sitting down.

'Pure selfishness,' he assured her. 'When you told me you'd lived in Vietnam up to last year I saw my opportunity to find out what's going on in a land I loved. There are tourists now of course but I suspect that's not really for me.' She watched him move easily into his chair opposite her.

'You were wounded there?'

'Yes,' he said. 'Along with many, many others on both sides. First let's have some tea. Then we can tackle your questions. And then mine.'

From the attitude of waiters and passing members, Nan Luc quickly came to understand that Jason Rose was well liked in the Meyerick Club. The tea he ordered was overseen by Vic Impari himself.

'So what can I do to help?' Jason asked. 'I can call you Nan Luc, can't I?'

'Of course.'

'The girl at the fund office said you were looking for information.'

'In the US evacuation I was left behind,' Nan said carefully. 'My mother was already dead and my American father somehow lost me. I was barely seven years old at the time. The truth is, I don't remember it that clearly.' She was throbbing with excitement, trying to keep her voice as flat and calm as she could. But she was certain that she was at the end, or very nearly, at the end of her search. Certain that her father was known to this young man, perhaps even well known.

She knew now that she must make no mistake. She had planned this moment carefully, trimming the story she was prepared to tell Jason Rose. Her plan was to leave herself at the end of the meeting knowing where her father was to be found, without allowing Jason enough information to believe she knew. Certainly without allowing him to guess why she wanted to trace her father. Above all, she didn't want him warned in advance.

'My difficulty,' Nan Luc said, 'is that living in an orphanage in Saigon just after the war we weren't encouraged to dream about an American parent or use his name. By the time I was eight my memory of the name had been wiped.'

'I can understand that. How can I help?'

'You're membership secretary of the Meyerick Fund.'

'Yes.'

'I've been making enquiries since I've been in the United States,' Nan Luc said. 'Someone who believes he met my father once or twice in Vietnam tells me that, years later, he heard of him here in Meyerick, in connection with the fund.'

'He didn't have a name to give you?'

'No, it was some years ago. And just a casual meeting.'

'Your friend couldn't say what the connection was between the fund and your father?'

'He was said to be a member.'

'Without a name, that doesn't give us much to go on.'

'I thought perhaps if I could look at your membership list, the name might come back to me.'

'Is that likely?' Jason said, carefully locating his wine and lifting the glass. 'We have three thousand full members and associates. Do you think a name could come floating back just like that, after fifteen years or so?'

'It looks like my only chance.'

'I'm intrigued,' he said. 'A search for a missing father. I like it.' He paused, smiling. 'But, you'll forgive me for asking you. Will he?'

'You mean he might already have a family.'

'He might have had a family all along, Nan Luc.'

'I don't plan to rush into the middle of a ready made family waving my arms crying, Here I am!'

'I'm sure not.'

'But you would still prefer not to give me the list.'

He thought for a moment. 'No. I think you have the right to find your father. I know a little about Vietnam. I know how important it can be.'

'Does that mean you'll show me the list?'

He hesitated for only a moment longer. 'I can show you the regular membership list off my own bat. To let you have sight of the contributors list is a different problem. To do that I would have to have permission . . .' he gestured over his shoulder to one of the line of portraits, 'from our president, Cy Stevenson.'

Cy Stevenson. The name hit her like a thunderbolt. 'Cy Stevenson,' she said.

His sightless eyes turned towards her. 'He's the man in the portrait next to old Joshua Meyerick. Third portrait along, isn't it?'

Nan looked up at the picture. A man with blond, brushed hair, his eyes metallic blue, a good-looking combination of Slav cheekbones and a long Scandinavian jaw, stared down at her, arrogant, not humourless, but with a humour of his own, for defence against the world.

She had stood up without being aware of it. She heard Jason say something, but no words registered. The room seemed to be in movement but the frame enclosing the picture was completely still. She couldn't trust herself to speak. She reached for the edge of the table and gripped a handful of cloth. She could scream with hate. She could propel her frozen limbs forward and tear at the confident air that came off the canvas, gouge at those cold, smiling eyes. She could feel madness rising in her.

Jason Rose's hand was on her wrist. 'Sit down, Nan Luc,' he said. She sat down, exhausted by the shock wave of feeling.

'We have to talk,' Jason said. She was silent. 'Drive me to my house,' he said. 'We'll talk there.'

She nodded, working the dryness from her mouth.

They stood up. With one arm round her shoulder Jason gently turned her towards the door. 'You finally found him,' he said.

The words came. 'Yes,' Nan Luc looked back towards the portrait, 'I finally found my father.'

39

It was as old an American house as Nan Luc had ever seen. In the early evening light it was dominated by a dark horror film gable and at ground level a wide Gothic arch set off to one side signalled the oddly placed front door.

Lights shone in ground floor windows and in the stone porch itself as Nan Luc and Jason got out of her hired car and walked towards the front door.

A woman stood in the porch, a tall grey-haired woman with a face that was less hard than unrelenting. Somewhere, Nan thought to herself as she shook hands with Mrs Rose, there was a softer persona imprisoned in that rigid, straight-backed body.

'You know, of course,' Mrs Rose said, 'that the Meyerick Fund is pretty much a Rose family affair. My late husband was the founder. I was the first appointed trustee and now Jason works full time on fund raising and membership drives.'

They were walking along a wide first floor gallery, the walls panelled in oak and set with mullioned and leaded windows.

Mrs Rose gestured towards a meticulously constructed model of Meyerick City at the turn of the century which covered the surface of an enormous Victorian table. 'When I came to Meyerick as a girl . . .' Nan watched Jason's face assume a patient expression. '. . . the warehouses were full of down-river grain and up-river manufactures. Now what are they? Lofts for Wall Street yuppies and national insurance company offices.'

'The fund's offices are in one of them,' Jason reminded her.

'Cy Stevenson's choice,' she conceded. 'At least he was smart enough to buy it for the fund before the city developers could lay their hands on it.' They walked on.

'My husband and I were very much involved in the fate of the Vietnamese people during the war,' she said. 'Don't misunderstand me, Mrs Brompton, we were not marchers or protesters. Far from it. We were staunch patriots who simply saw, felt if you wish, the sufferings of a trapped civilian population.'

She stopped in front of a modern portrait of a severe looking man in about his early fifties. Nan Luc immediately recognised the shapes of Jason's face in his. 'My husband,' Mrs Rose said proudly. 'Many people thought of him, like his father before him, as an inflexible man,' she said. 'But is there anything wrong in being inflexible in pursuit of what is right?'

'No more family tours.' Jason came forward and took Nan Luc's arm. 'Come in and sit down.' He opened a door to a small sitting room, part of an apartment Jason kept in the big house. Mrs Rose smiled gauntly and left them alone.

A girl was standing in the middle of the room, a pretty, round-faced black girl in her early twenties. 'Hi,' she said, coming forward to shake Nan's hand. 'I'm Ruth Wilson. If we get a run of luck before the year's out I'll be Jason's better half.'

'Most successful young lawyer in Meyerick County,' Jason said. 'Earns a king's ransom for every case she handles.' He dropped his voice. 'But my mother's still convinced she's marrying me for the no longer existent family fortune. Or to become part of the illustrious Rose family. OK with you if Ruth stays?'

'Of course.'

'Coffee, Nan Luc?' Ruth asked her, moving towards a tray already prepared. Nan thanked her and took the seat opposite Jason.

For a moment he stood looking down at her as if he could, as anyone else might, study her expression. 'You believe Cy Stevenson is your father.'

'Yes.' The word came as a long sibillant hiss.

Ruth put coffee in front of each of them, then took the seat slightly outside the main arena of the room.

Jason sat on the arm of a chair opposite Nan Luc. 'From the first,' he said slowly, 'the list was just an excuse.'

'What I hadn't told you was that the name I was looking for was C. Stevenson,' Nan Luc said.

He pursed his lips. 'And as soon as I mentioned Cy . . .'

She nodded, taking from her purse a folded sheet of thick paper.

'My birth certificate,' she said. She leaned over and handed it to Ruth.

'The entry for father is C. Stevenson, New York City,' Ruth said to Jason.

Jason nodded. 'What's going on, Nan Luc?' he said slowly. 'I don't see but I get vibes. Whatever your reaction was at the club, you weren't overcome by joy.'

'No.'

'Why was that?'

'There's nothing romantic about my search,' Nan said. 'I had to find my father to bring him to justice for what he did.'

'What do you claim he did?' Ruth asked.

'He betrayed his family duties,' she said. 'Where I come from there is no worse crime.'

'Nan Luc,' Jason said carefully, 'such things are not necessarily serious felonies in the United States.'

'There's more than enough,' Nan Luc said. 'Even for American law.'

'You plan to go to the law?' Jason asked. 'Or is it a police matter?'

Nan's eyes dropped away from his sightless glance. 'A police matter,' she said briefly, aware that Ruth was watching her.

Ruth came forward, nursing her coffee. 'The birth certificate entry; is that your only documentary evidence that Cy Stevenson is the man you're looking for?'

'There's more.'

'You know,' Ruth said, 'Stevenson is a hell of a common name in the United States, Nan Luc. I don't know what led you to Meyerick but if it's just the existence of a Vietnamese fund, you could be barking up the wrong tree.'

'I've considered that possibility,' Nan Luc said carefully, taking back the birth certificate from Ruth. 'I came here tonight to ask Jason to help me exclude any doubt from the picture.'

'How can I do that?'

'You know Cahn Roc.'

He shrugged. 'Been back and forth through there.' He turned to Ruth. 'A small province and capital of the same name, northwest of Saigon.'

'I worked on the trial for corruption of a man named Quatch.'

'Quatch,' Jason repeated carefully.

'This man had, among other things, been blackmailing an American for large sums of money.'

'How large?' Ruth asked.

'Perhaps a million dollars or more over several years.'

'What was Quatch blackmailing the American for?' Ruth asked her.

Nan Luc hesitated. 'The American was a maker of pornographic films,' she said. 'Some of them of a monstrously perverted type.'

'And this American is now a respected family and businessman in smalltown USA?' Ruth said.

'The American is Cy Stevenson.' Jason got up off the arm of the chair and walked a familiar path across the large room. 'This is what you think, Nan Luc?'

'What I think is that these sums are too large to have been private money. What I'm asking you, Jason, is to give me the final chip that will fall into place. Has the fund been sending money to Vietnam – under whatever pretext or for whatever reason?'

Jason's face clouded. 'I'm sorry, Nan Luc,' he said. 'You're asking for the fund accounts.'

'Yes.'

'You're accusing Cy Stevenson of embezzling vast sums to pay his own blackmail.'

'I'm asking you if that's what was done, Jason.'

Jason walked back slowly down the room. 'What's my answer, Ruth?' he said, stopping in front of the black girl.

She thought for a moment. 'I guess your answer,' she said carefully, 'is to consult your colleagues on this accusation against the fund and its president.'

'I need an answer tonight,' Nan Luc said. Ruth looked at her, at the lines of determination in her face. 'I can't explain everything,' Nan said. 'But I am owed an answer.'

Jason crossed to the phone and pressed buttons. In the room no one spoke. 'Hector,' Jason said, 'can you get over here, right away? I know it's the weekend but this is more urgent than I can tell you on the phone. It concerns the fund. OK? I'll call Mary. Will you call Oliver and the Anderson brothers?' He thought for a moment. 'Fin and the colonel are out of town. For reasons I'll explain later I won't be calling Cy for the moment. Make that clear to the others.'

He put down the phone. 'It'll take maybe half an hour to organise,' he said to Nan Luc.

She nodded. 'While we wait, do you have another phone I can use?'

Cy Stevenson finished his shower and dressed in a pair of slacks, shirt and sweater. He was feeling better now. His brain was still fuzzy but the shower had done the trick. The panic that had seized him had passed. Louise was dead. Nothing connected him to her or the motel.

He stopped, his hand on the banister rail. There was his secretary, Beryl. She just might recognise a picture of Louise on TV. He shrugged. Unlikely. What had she said? 'I hate to say it, Mr Stevenson, but they all look alike to me.' That's what she'd said.

He continued on down the stairs. Where the hell was Sunny? The memory of the call from Mary suddenly hit him for the first time. Sunny knew! She knew about him and Mary! He ran down the stairs, stumbling, slightly out of breath as he reached the bottom. How had she found out? He couldn't believe Mary had told her. He stood next to the phone trying to focus his mind on Mary's call. Had she said Sunny had left? Did she say where?

He picked up the phone and called Mary's number. His head seemed to rock and yaw like a rudderless ship. He looked across at the two empty bottles next to the armchair. Why the hell was Mary not answering?

At Page Corner someone picked up the phone. It was the houseboy. Mrs Page Butler had left fifteen minutes ago. No, he had no idea where she had gone.

Cy put the phone down. Did he dare have a drink? He crossed the room and picked up the bottles. Even that act, bringing his head below waist level caused his brain to reel.

He found some cigars and lit one. Persevering past the first rush of nausea, he blew smoke across the light from the table lamp. First he had to get rid of that suit. Police laboratories could match anything now, mud, carpet fibres, cotton fluff from a bedcover. He stopped. His mind seemed to drain of all other thoughts. He had killed her. He was safe now. He had cut all possible connection with Nan Luc.

He poured himself a small drink. Somewhere up on the road he could hear a car. He stood, drink in hand, listening to it slow down and turn through the gates.

His first thought was that it was Sunny. But the weight of the vehicle over the gravel made him think again. He walked into the hall. Through the uncurtained window he saw nothing at first but the falling snow. Then the white Range Rover and Mary climbing down from it. He opened the door. Her face, he saw, was set. She stamped snow from her fur boots and walked past him into the hall.

Alarm rose slowly through him. 'How did Sunny find out?' he said.

She walked on into the living room turning on more lights. 'Forget Sunny,' she said. 'You're in worse trouble than that.'

He looked at her, her face drawn by panic. What in God's name was she talking about? She couldn't know about Louise. But all his instincts told him to move cautiously. 'Sit down, Mary,' he said. 'First, I'll get you a drink.'

'There's no time for that,' she snapped. 'A Vietnamese girl came to the club today to meet Jason.'

'So?'

'She told Jason you're her father.'

It was like a slap in the face. He knew she must have seen his reaction. 'She's lying.'

Mary shrugged. 'More important, she says you were using fund money to pay your blackmail.'

'She's lying, I tell you, Mary.'

'She was an official at the Quatch trial.'

The breath seemed to flow out of him. 'What's Jason going to do?' he said slowly.

She stood opposite him, her hands deep in her Barbour jacket, the melted snow glistening on the waxed material.

'He's called a meeting of the committee. If the girl convinces them, and she will, then they'll call the police.'

'Why are you telling me this?'

'You know why, Cy.'

'I'm going to need your help, Mary. I'm going to need money.'

He moved towards her but she stepped back, raising a hand between them. 'I want those pictures, Cy. Bring me the negatives and I'll get you money.'

'Negatives . . .' He shook his head slowly. 'You know better than that, Mary. The modern world, I could have made a million copies already. Just get me the money. Your guarantee that those pictures won't spring out of the box depends on you keeping the money flowing.'

'Please, Cy . . .' she said. 'Everything I've lived for is here in Meyerick. You can just disappear. I can't do that.'

'Go to Jason's committee meeting, Mary.' His head was clearing magically. Survival was one thing he was good at. 'That's it,' he said. 'Go to the meeting. Tell them what a bastard I must have been. I'll call you in a week or two and let you know how to make arrangements for the money. You and me are going to be partners for life, Mary.' He stepped towards her and took her cheeks between his hands, squeezing hard. 'I might even let you bring the money in person,' he said, planting a kiss on the distorted pout of her lips.

Alone in Jason's study, Nan Luc stood before the French windows and watched the snow falling outside.

For minutes she watched the soft, unhurried fall through the yellow terrace light, noticing how the flakes scurried between the flagstones, still uncertain how anything so light and fragile could build to the deep drifts she had seen in photographs.

She had found him.

She had found him. But now, could she kill him?

As the superintendent opened the door the phone was ringing inside the apartment. Running past him through the hall Max reached the living room and picked up the receiver.

Her voice was pitched low. He could hear no background noise, no music, no voices. 'Max,' she said. 'I just rang Edward. I knew you'd be there.'

He found his voice catching in this throat. 'Where are you?' he said. 'Tell me where you are.'

'It doesn't matter where. I didn't want to run away from you last night. But I had to. I knew you were trying to stop me.'

'Nan, please listen to me. You've got the wrong man.'

'I've got the right man.'

'You've found Stevenson?'

'I've found him, Max.' Her voice had a sudden metallic ring to it.

'For God's sake, Nan, Cy Stevenson is not your father. And even if he is, you've no right to do this yourself. Shattered dreams aren't reason enough.'

'Louise was murdered last night.'

'I know that, too. But don't you see what it means? It means that the moment you show yourself to Stevenson, you force him to act. He's a killer, Nan. Call the police, for God's sake.'

'No.'

'Then what in God's name are you talking to me for now?'

At the other end of the line there was a long silence. 'I want you to understand, Max. He killed my mother. As good as killed her.'

'I don't understand, Nan. You told me that your mother committed suicide. Whatever part Stevenson played in that, it's not worth you sacrificing your own life for revenge. To me it's simple. He killed Louise Cartwright. So call the cops.' He stopped. 'Or is there something else to tell, Nan. Is that right?'

'There's something else to tell,' she said flatly. 'I need you to know, Max. A film. Made by Stevenson. A made-to-order scenario written by Quatch. It's on the machine.'

'You want me to watch it?'

'Yes.'

He sensed she had said everything she wanted to say. 'Don't hang up,' he said. 'Tell me where you are.' No answer. 'Where?' Again the silence. 'Where are you, Nan?' He clenched the phone, willing her to answer.

'I'm going to hang up, Max,' she said.

'Nan, I'm pleading with you now. Nothing's worth it. Not all the insults, the dishonour. Nothing's worth taking the law into you own hands.'

He counted the seconds. Then her voice said: 'Watch the film.'

'OK. Then what?'

'Then ask yourself why my mother killed herself. Ask whether you could have gone unavenged.'

In Jason Rose's study she replaced the phone, brushing tears from her face. It was snowing harder now with heavier, thicker flakes. She stepped forward and opened the glazed door to the terrace. A blast of cold air hit her and she felt the strange, unfamiliar fingering of the snowflakes on her cheeks.

Closing the door behind her she ran along the side of the house to the drive where she had left her car.

40

An enormous pink Vietnamese moon hung in the sky.

Very slowly, as Max watched the screen, the camera pulled back across the rooftops of Saigon. Above the sound of music and laughter and squealing girls was laid a heavy, menacing heartbeat.

Over the image of the moonlit roofs the title came up in Gothic letters: *The House of Eros*. The camera's eye blinked and it was the interior of the Eros Bar. To the music of the Stones, giant American servicemen danced with slender Vietnamese partners. It was a scene of incredible noise and confusion. Groups of soldiers sat round tables loaded with bottles and glasses. Girls serving them were fondled routinely or, amid gales of laughter, pulled on to their laps. Bottles of whisky were passed from mouth to mouth. Fat, conical joints were inhaled, releasing swirling blue smoke into the already smoke-laden room. To Max everything suggested the *Götterdammerung*, the twilight of the gods, the last days of the gigantic American adventure in the East.

The camera panned a line of girls on bar stools, pretty twenty-year-olds in tight skirts and meshed stockings, their dark hair glistening, their teeth white against scarlet lipstick. Resting on each girl for a moment or two, debating, deciding, rejecting, the camera's gaze passed on.

The camera was a creature now, darting into corners with a voyeur's intensity of purpose. On a hand down the scooped out front of a girl's dress; on a much smaller hand deep in an open fly as a GI sprawled, rocked back in his seat, a bottle to his lips. Then the camera's gaze moved again. To the foot of the winding stairs, then up slowly to the balustered landing.

A six-year-old child sat there, on the top step, looking down impassively at the scene below. As beads of sweat poured from Max's forehead, Nan Luc stood up and began to climb the stairs.

her long hair hung down in a single plait over her green uniform dress. While Max watched in anguish she glanced down once more, indifferently, on the world of the adults below.

Then the heartbeat expanded above the sounds in the bar. And the camera detached itself and glided forward, stealthily following Nan Luc up the stairs.

41

Following the line of the Meyerick River Nan Luc checked the area map clipped next to the steering wheel. She had folded it into a section which covered the east of the county. Coming over the brow of a hill she could see the long silvery sweep of the Meyerick River below her and the lights of the town in the distance. The Stevenson house, Jason had told her, stood on the slopes of the river above the village of Piebald two or three miles outside Meyerick City itself.

The snow was falling more lightly now, affording views of pale hills crowned with rambling well-lit houses. At the roadside sign reading Piebald she slowed down.

On her right a line of snow-covered boats rode at anchor, unreal cardboard cutouts in the black water. To the left driveways opened up every two or three hundred yards, some marked by trees, some by stone gateposts and iron gates. Each driveway carried a named mailbox with a lamp illuminating the entrance. The third box, set beside an impressive stone entrance, carried the name she was looking for.

Backing up the Chevrolet so that it rode on the grass verge under thick overhanging bushes, she killed the lights. In the darkness she reached for her purse, took out the small Italian automatic she had brought from San Diego, checked the safety and thrust it into the waistband of her skirt.

Leaving the car she walked slowly forward to the stone arch that marked the entrance to the Stevenson residence. For a moment she stood looking up the dark drive to the brilliantly lit grey stucco house. Then she pulled back quickly at the sound of a car starting. Moments later headlights flared round the side of the house and swept down the tree-lined drive towards her. When the Mercedes stopped to make the turn into the road she was standing three feet away from the outlined face of the driver. The head, angled slightly away from her, showed the profile of the man she had seen in the painting at the club.

Her hand was on the butt of the gun in her waistband. But the flare of hatred and perhaps the shock of opportunity paralysed her momentarily. In the instant it took to propel her legs forward, the Mercedes swept passed her into the road and pulled smoothly away in the direction of Meyerick.

Turning, she ran back to her car, her heels clattering on the metalled road. The tension was released now. She threw open the door and slipped behind the wheel. Ahead she could just see the receding glow of the Mercedes' tail lights.

As Cy Stevenson drove the three mile stretch of road between Piebald and Meyerick City, he was experiencing the sort of buzz he used to feel when he still had a cocaine habit. A sharpness, a perception edged by panic, but sweetened by excitement.

A new life. Why not? Perhaps he had been digging in too deep in Meyerick County anyway. Perhaps he had stopped seeing life here as the massive, violent joke it really was, and begun to take their summer fairs and garden parties seriously. Take himself seriously. No, that was no way to survive. He would miss Sunny a little. Probably. Her money certainly. But there was no reason that couldn't be made up by Mary. So a new name. A new life. New women. Perhaps, even, in England or Australia, a new wife. Time to begin anew.

Yet something was troubling him. It took another glance into the rear view mirror to be sure. He had seen the car behind just after he had turned out of his drive. Now as he increased his speed the car behind was doing the same.

The coke-edge left him. Without knowing clearly why, he was invaded by the certainty that it was the girl. Nan Luc. The girl who had tracked him from Saigon to Meyerick City. The girl who was responsible for him losing everything he had built up in the last ten years.

His jaw tightened as the fury flooded him. He was no longer intrigued by thoughts of a change, a new life-style. He was the child again, the ten-year-old boy, ready to scream out of control if his wishes were denied.

He swung the car sharp left, away from the river, away from the direct road into Meyerick. Only the gravel trucks used this road and on a weekend evening they had long stopped. If the lights were still with him he could be sure he was being followed.

He drove on slowly, dropping to thirty to give her a chance to back up and follow if she had missed the turning. But within moments the headlights were there, reaching out towards him across the snowy darkness.

He put his foot down and the car bucked forward. He was not yet certain what he would do. The gravel pits were less than a mile ahead, at this time of night a deserted, waterlogged scar on the hillside. He glanced again into the mirror. The car was still there, keeping a hundred yard distance, cruising along at the same easy speed.

She had a gun, suddenly it occurred to him. She was ready for him to stop. He felt his hands grow clammy at the thought of how close he had been. How certain he had been that in the deserted area of the gravel pits it was she who would be in danger.

'Christ . . .' he spoke out loud, his confidence spiralling down. Like a suicidal fool he had led her there. To the only spot within miles of Meyerick where she could kill him unseen, unheard.

His eyes flicked towards the mirror. With a sudden spurt of speed she had closed on him. The interior of the Mercedes was lit by her headlights. In the rear mirror he could see the outline of her head and shoulders.

He accelerated. The tyres spun and gripped. In seconds the Mercedes was in full flight along the edge of the strange moon-scape of the quarries.

He knew now exactly what he intended, carefully gauging his speed, calculating the moment when the track would come closest to the edge of the quarry.

Ahead a black on yellow plywood sign the size of the side of a truck read: The Meyerick Sand and Gravel Company. As the girl's car came up, filling the rear mirror, he braced himself hard against the headrest and slammed on the brakes.

Instinctively Nan Luc dragged at the wheel. The Mercedes' brakelights reared up at her. When metal struck metal Nan's car was skidding broadside, the impact just barely diminished in ferocity, her head wrenched sideways to crash against the quarterlight. For a moment she sat, her head in her hands, her vision a green anaesthetic haze. When she raised her head and focused her eyes, the Mercedes had gone.

Beyond the car the blackness was pierced by the single beam of her undamaged headlight. She wheeled down the window and gulped air. Slowly the ringing in her ears faded.

She was alerted by the sudden spurt and crackle of gravel in the darkness to her right. Turning her head she saw the dark shape of the Mercedes, then the headlights flicked on and the Chevrolet was filled with white light. Blinded, she jerked her head away. Her hand found the door handle. Outside, the long shadow of the Chevrolet sped out to the edge of the gravel pit.

The impact was terrific. Like a two-ton battering ram moving at ten miles an hour, the Mercedes hit the side of the Chevrolet, sweeping it across the gravel apron, carrying the Sand and Gravel Company sign with it, as it bludgeoned Nan's car over the quarry edge.

The Chevrolet fell ten feet, bounced and rolled across a gravel ledge and dropped again. Hurled across the cramped interior of the car, buffeted like a rag doll, Nan Luc's last sensation was a fierce rush of air in her face. Cy Stevenson, leaning from his halted Mercedes, was too late to see Nan thrown from the driver's door. Craning his neck he saw only the mad patterns of the single Chevrolet headlight beam as the car fell through the darkness into the sump of the gravel pit below.

'Listen,' the voice said in the darkness that seemed to engulf her, 'whatever you do, don't move.'

Under her hands she could feel a sandpaper roughness. If she pressed with one hand then the other, the world seemed to rock gently. If she pressed with both hands at the same time her body seemed to move forward in space. Only the insistent voice of the man in the darkness above her kept her from experiment. 'Just lie still,' he said; 'if you're conscious, if you can hear me, just lie still. I'm coming down to get you.'

A light shone on her. Consciousness came with a rush of fear. The yellow and black plywood board beneath her teetered on the gravel ledge.

Spreadeagled on the board, she dare not risk turning her head to look up towards the voice. She lay, frozen immobile, as every faint gust of wind tugged at the board, rocking her bodyweight gently backward and forward.

A woman spoke above her and the light shifted position. A moment later a rush of sand and small stones scattered across the board. The man was on the gravel ledge now, a yard or two from her. 'Take the end of this rope,' he said calmly, 'and whatever happens, hang on in there.'

Sitting in the pick-up between the driver and the girl, Nan Luc tried her best to answer their questions.

'Until the road petered out into a gravel track,' Nan said, 'I thought I was still on the main road into Meyerick. Then the car ahead of me braked. You saw the rest.'

'And you've no ideas who it could be?' the girl said.

'I only came into the area today.'

'Some crazy kid in a stolen car, I guess,' the driver, Sam Forester, said. 'I've heard of this game ramming patrol cars in New York, but I never expected to see it in Meyerick.' He grinned. 'You're lucky Diane's room-mate needed the place to herself for the evening. We were just killing time up there.'

'I'm lucky,' Nan Luc said.

Ahead the lights of old clapboard houses glittered through the snowfall. On whitened lawns dark cedars and pines extended arms draped with snow. They passed a few stores and diners and saw there were more people on the street now, more cars, a brightly lit yellow bus.

'You'll find the police just to the left of Dampner's the department store,' Sam said. 'Be sure you report it right away, OK?'

Nan thanked them both again and climbed down from the pick-up. Standing on the sidewalk she waved as Sam pulled out into traffic.

Before her, a blaze of coloured lights shaped like a Christmas tree rose forty or fifty feet from the centre of a small square, and across a public building an illuminated banner spelt out the glittering message: A Merry Christmas from Meyerick City.

She was aware of music now as she walked on past Dampner's, melodies in the last few days she had begun to associate with Christmas: 'Jingle Bells' and 'Silent Night'.

She thought of Max and her stomach lurched unhappily. She could feel tears start in her eyes as the clear voice of a child carried 'Silent Night' across the square. Along the sidewalk families were shopping, snow was drifting through lamp-light, a red-robed Father Christmas gave children gifts from a sack. Store windows glittered with goods; on a street corner people rattled boxes for a Christmas charity.

She was walking down to the old river front now. At the end of the steep slope she stopped at the stone embankment. High brick warehouses rose steeply on her left. From each one a timber framework projected above her head, the housing for the pulley which lifted the bales and sacks from the wharf. A more widely travelled visitor than Nan Luc might have been reminded of Amsterdam or the canalside warehouses of small English manufacturing towns. But to her nothing was familiar, neither the narrow dark-eyed buildings, the iron-bracket street lamps nor the incredible, ubiquitous snow.

Further along the riverside a canal ran across her front and joined the river. She stopped before the humped wooden bridge, standing in close to the line of buildings. From where she stood she could see that the warehouse in front of her formed the corner of the canal and the continuation of the wharf. Two or three lights shone on one of the upper floors.

She walked on across the canal bridge. The snow settled on her shoulders and in her hair. Distantly, from the main square, she could hear the strains of Christmas carols. She was no longer close to crying.

On the far side of the bridge she stopped. To her left the side of the warehouse rose steeply from the canal, the black water washing at the lower courses of sodden brickwork. In front of her a dark blue Mercedes was parked on the timber wharf between the warehouse and the river. Front and rear of the car were dented and scarred.

A few steps forward. She could see now that this was the last of the renovated warehouses. Beyond it there were vacant lots and the lights of an elevated roadway crossing the river. On a new glass portico she read a list of companies using the building: a firm of attorneys, realtors, a software house, two or three designers. On the fourth-floor plaque she read: Meyerick Fund, President Cyrus M. Stevenson. Treasurer Oliver J. Digweed.

The door was huge, a carriage entrance designed for horse-drawn waggons. Set into it was a smaller opening, a few inches ajar. She pushed it and entered, stepping over the wooden sill. She was now standing in a cobbled loading bay, dimly lit by a single Victorian bracket lamp above her head. Timber beams braced the white-painted bare brick walls; carved timber struts held the wooden staircase; planking, sanded deep yellow in colour and smelling sweetly of wax, formed the floors.

Moving to the staircase she started upwards.

42

From the safe he took the thirty-five hundred dollars' cash always held for a donation emergency. With his private key he opened the rear section of the metal barrel. Taking out the pictures of Mary and the gun he had kept there since the first day he had taken over the fund, he glanced at the security monitor. In a grey halation, like a ghost, Nan Luc was ascending the main stairway.

The blood pounded in Nan Luc's head. The pains in every muscle of her arms and legs barely registered. Adrenalin surged through her as raw energy. Vividly, it seemed to her, she could sense his presence in the building.

Reaching the top floor she walked quietly along the gallery to the lighted offices at the end. She could hear no movement inside but the outer door was open. In a wide main office black Italian desks carried hooded computers; a small bronze sculpture hung between two sloping loft windows; a runner carpet led towards the far door standing part ajar.

Beyond the inner door she heard a sound, a footstep perhaps. She paused. On the other side of that door stood the man whose name was on her birth certificate.

She had covered the twenty or so steps towards the inner door. She stopped, her hand flat on the brass fingerplate. Very gently she pushed. As she did so her free hand reached into the waistband of her skirt.

She stepped forward and at that same moment her wrist was struck with something of metallic hardness. Her reactions were automatic, instilled in her by service training classes. She dropped her hand under the force of the blow and struck out instinctively with her left. Cy Stevenson felt the taut flat of her hand hit his upper lip. In shock, the fingers holding the gun relaxed. From his hand the gun jumped and skidded, spinning across the polished wood floor.

When she turned she saw a face different from anything she had expected, drawn with a savage intensity, a thick smudge of blood across the upper lip, a face very different from the relaxed portrait in the club. It was a moment she had always known was bound to come. A moment when she would be forced to decide. Was this man with his crude, heavy features, his blue eyes made mean with fear, the man her mother had chosen to father her child?

She stood inside the door to his office, all her questions about this man refined into a numbness in the mind, and a chill that flickered like electricity up her spine.

He was backing across the room. Away from the gun she still held. 'So full of hate,' he said, 'say something, for God's sake.' She watched him, without speaking. 'Jesus, say something, will you?' She moved towards him, the gun held forward. 'You crazy woman,' he exploded, his face flushing, then draining quickly to its uncertain pallor. 'You've pursued someone halfway round the world for ritual vengeance and you've got the wrong man. I'm not your father.'

'You still have to pay.'

'You know how my name got on that birth certificate.'

'I'm talking about Louise,' she said. He sucked air through his clenched teeth. 'And I'm talking about my mother.'

'I hardly even knew your mother, for Christ's sake. She was in the bamboo. As far as I know she was still there when I got out of Saigon.'

'She came back the night the US embassy was evacuated. The night you left.' Nan walked into the middle of the room, kicking the door closed behind her. 'My mother came back to the Eros to a note from Louise, saying I was safely on my way to America. With you. She also came back to a bar room full of North Vietnam soldiers treating themselves to a film show. Using all your old equipment and all the old movies you had left behind. Including the last film you made at the request of Monsieur Quatch.' He was breathing heavily, watching the gun. 'My mother never knew the orphanage had taken me. She believed she had delivered her daughter into the hands of a child pornographer. That same night she killed herself.'

Suddenly his face seemed to regain a flood of colour. Something close to a smile shaped his lips. 'You came to New York to kill a father. But you've been cheated out of that. You know I'm just a guy who was there when somebody was handing out five thousand dollars. You could have had any name on that birth certificate. You know I'm not your father.'

'But you know who is.'

'Yes,' he said, 'I know who is. I'm the only man alive who does know.' She watched him, waiting. He took a handful of Kleenex from his desk and wiped the blood from his face. 'The way I see it that piece of information could be worth a lot.'

'Tell me,' she said.

Tentatively he pressed the flesh of his upper lip. 'I'll tell you so far, no further. Then we'll talk about that gun in your hand.'

'Just tell me.' He leaned back against the desk. 'You were to take me back to America.'

'To Los Angeles.'

'And then what?'

'We were to be met at Los Angeles International.'

'By my father?'

He nodded. 'That was the deal.'

'I want his name.'

'Not yet. There's a trade to be made here. Just got to work out terms.'

'When you arrived at Los Angeles, what happened?'

'No problem,' he said. 'Your Daddy couldn't make it.'

'He wasn't there?'

'Couldn't make it. On account of the fact he was dead.'

She swayed unsteadily. 'He's dead?'

'That much was free. The rest you pay for.'

'Where did he die?'

'I've got to move along. Put up that gun.'

'In Paris. Did my father die in Paris?'

'First put up the gun.'

Nan Luc's face was set. 'Yesterday all I wanted was to see you dead. Today you've got a chance to face a court. But first I have to have that name. Understand me, Mr Stevenson. You have two minutes. Without that name you will not walk out of here alive.'

'That's no deal,' he said uncertainly.

'It's all you're going to get,' she said. 'Two minutes.'

'You wouldn't do it.' He reached over to pick up the duffel bag on the desk. His arm outstretched, he stopped, his head cocked, looking half behind him, his eyes opening in a sudden access of fear.

'You crazy woman,' he said. 'What the hell have you done?' He turned to a door at the back of the office and wrenched it open. Smoke plumed into the room. 'You've set the goddam place on fire!' he screamed. 'Jesus Christ, you're going to kill us both.' Fear galvanised him. He swung the duffel bag through the air and swept the gun from her hand. As blue smoke crept and eddied along the polished plank floor they faced each other.

He was fit, and stronger. He charged forward in confidence.

He never saw the blow that exploded on the side of his head. Something inside his skull, his eardrum perhaps, seemed to whine at high pitch like a maddened police siren. He reeled back, dropping the bag.

He had been a streetfighter in his youth. He knew how to swing and butt and bring up his knee and kick and elbow and gouge and he found now every move was necessary. He found now as blows rained across his head, as his nose poured blood, that he needed every ounce of strength, every barely remembered skill.

He threw himself at her, bawling as loud as he could force his voice. He knew that skill could be combated with sheer aggression. As the blows from the flat of her hands rained on him he seized her round the waist, butting and kneeing her, hearing her gasp and cry out until he threw her against the wall.

He was much more formidable than she had imagined, much quicker, with a readier cunning than she had thought possible. But there was some satisfaction in that for her too. At long last all the adrenalin of hate which had infected her since the day she had watched the film could be burnt off in the fury with which she faced him now.

Sweat poured down his face, soaking his shirt. He was breathing heavily now, coughing, gasping in hot drafts of smoke-laden air. 'For God's sake,' he croaked, 'I can't breathe. Let me past.'

She stood in the doorway, her breathing fast and shallow, but still regular. 'Unless you want to die in here,' she said, 'give me my father's name.'

He knew he was on the edge of defeat. Then as he took the next step back, away from her, his shoe struck the gun. In a second his hand covered it. He raised it and fired twice. The sheer volume of sound shocked him. He sucked in air, the smoke made sharper by the sting of cordite. A short cough barked from his throat. Then another. Through streaming eyes he looked towards Nan Luc. She was moving across the space towards him. A drowning panic seized him. Each breath choked down quantities of smoke. He fired again, but wildly, stumbling backwards. The gun fell as he struck about him like a madman, trying to keep the smoke from his lungs.

In that moment, as he fell across the desk, Nan Luc had time to register what her senses had been keeping at bay. A fantail of flame was pouring under the door. Beyond the office she could hear a dull roar like a crowd's long acclamation. The panels of the door were cracking now and smoke plunged through in an unrelenting stream, isolating each wall light and desk lamp as a point of brightness in a dense grey fog. At her feet Cy Stevenson rolled in pain, retching himself into stillness. Then he lifted his head. In a final effort he pushed himself up to his knees and began to gasp and choke in the thickness of the smoke. 'Please,' he croaked. 'Get me out of here.'

She reached down and gripped his chin, wrenching his head so that he stared up at her. 'I want to know,' she said, 'who gave my mother the five thousand dollars. I want the name of the man you were to meet at Los Angeles.' His eyes closed. The choking died away to a thin gurgle in his throat.

She straightened up. She knew she could leave him and he would be dead within minutes. But with him would go the answer to the one question that meant everything to her now.

Turning towards the window she pulled it open. The cold air struck her face, and the mass of street lamps and store lights seemed like distant salvation. Below her she could see a man running across the canal bridge and others further down the wharf. Standing on the narrow iron-railed balcony she looked straight down to the canal sixty feet below, its surface flat and still.

The man on the bridge was waving his arms. 'Jump,' his voice carried in the cold air. 'Jump!'

She turned back into the room. The lights still burnt whitely through the dense smoke. Other light, flame, blackish-red as blood, sprang from around the doorway. Cy Stevenson lay face down on the floor. She bent over him, the smoke in her lungs tasting black as soot. Taking his jacket collar she hauled him across to the window. Heaving and pushing she brought his body up on to the sill. In the sudden rush of cold air he seemed to be suffering some sort of a seizure, his face twisting into tortured shapes, his tongue lolling.

She lifted his legs. Below, several men had reached the bridge. With one final heave she lifted him clear of the balcony rail, watched him fall silently, arms and legs spread wide, and hit the surface with a gigantic eruption of white water.

With the heat of the fire on her, she stepped back a pace. At that moment flames, rising from the floor below, threw up an impenetrable wall between Nan Luc and the window over the canal.

43

An orange glow had settled in the sky over Meyerick, a dome of light through which snow fell steadily upon the town. By now large crowds were pressing into the waterfront area and fire tenders, klaxons braying, lights flashing, were obliged to force their way through corridors in the crowds opened up by the police.

At the far end of the waterfront the fire blazed uncontrollably. Wooden flooring and old timber staircases fuelled flames which had already collapsed the roof. Sparks and snowflakes swirled upwards and a strange, leaden light was reflected from the surface of the water.

'There were two people, a man and a woman,' the wharf-patrolman said. 'I could see them in the top window.'

'You say they were fighting, you could see that?' Jason Rose said.

'It's not far, Jason.' Ruth turned him slightly to face the burning building. 'From here up to the main office window is no more than thirty, forty yards.'

Jason nodded, turning back to the patrolman. 'Did you see the fire start?'

'No, sir. Perhaps it was smouldering away somewhere downstairs. But when it went up it was like a box of firecrackers. One moment there was no fire. Next moment the whole building had burst into flames. What I don't understand is why the sprinkler system couldn't slow it down.'

'Is it right that the alarm system failed too?' Ruth asked.

'Seems like it,' the patrolman said. 'I sure as hell didn't get no warning.'

'OK, so then what happened?'

'There were lights up on the top floor, the Meyerick Fund offices. That balcony window up there's a long one, Mr Rose.

Goes right down through the length of the room. So as I ran forward I could see clear enough there were two people up there, struggling it seemed as the room filled with smoke.'

'Two people,' Ruth said. 'A man and a woman.'

'That's the way it looked. I'd even be pretty sure the man was Mr Stevenson.'

'Then what?' Jason said.

'I ran back to the canal bridge to sound the manual alarm. I guess I was shouting to them to jump, I don't know. When I looked again the woman had the window open. She was dragging something heavy from inside. She got it up on the ledge and toppled it over.'

'The man she was fighting with? She toppled him out into the canal?'

'He must have been pretty nearly dead then. His clothes were smouldering as he fell. Maybe he was dead already.'

'And she jumped right after him?'

'No. She seemed to disappear in a rush of flame. The next thing I saw was someone at the loading bay there.' He pointed.

'One floor down from the fund office,' Ruth said to Jason. 'Directly above the canal.'

'The doors slid open,' the security man said, 'and the woman stood there for a moment, looking down at the water. Smoke was pouring out past her. Maybe she was scared to jump. I don't know. But then the flames roared out of the loading door and she was blasted clear into the water.'

'Did she come up?'

'I don't know, sir. She was below my line of sight. By this time the police were arriving and that many people running to see the fire, it was chaos. Maybe she swam clear, I don't know. All I know is she went in just down there beside the canal bridge in the same spot the man dropped. If they're down there, they're down there together.'

With shocking suddenness, the warehouse buckled. A crack opened up in the brickwork the length of the building and flames and smoke, like a dragon's breath, roared out across the wharf. From the fire hoses, glittering spouts of water arced through powerful lights. As the front wall crashed on to the waterfront a deep baying sound rose from the crowd cordoned off beyond the canal.

On the canal bridge a powerful searchlight had been set up, its beam pointing down into the water where the figures of two frogmen moved slowly like undersea monsters. Hector Hand bustled through the police line and rejoined Jason and Ruth where they were standing in the lights of a half circle of police cars.

'Appalling, appalling,' Hand said. 'The fire chief says it was almost certainly started deliberately.'

'Arson?'

'Or murder,' Hand said. 'Both the sprinkler and alarm systems had been turned off. Do we know for sure the Vietnamese woman was here?'

'We don't know anything for sure, Hector,' Ruth said.

At two in the morning, with the fire at last showing signs of burning itself out, the first body was brought up from the canal.

Water poured from the black bundle of clothing as the two frogmen manhandled it on to the canal path. Leaving Jason and Hector, Ruth ran quickly up on to the bridge. The body was face down, six feet below her. As one of the frogmen turned it over she saw, with horror, Cy Stevenson's face green in the searchlight glare, water pouring from the side of his mouth. Returning to Jason's side, she slipped her arm back in his.

'I heard someone say it's a man,' Jason said. 'Is it Cy?'

'It's Cy,' Ruth said. 'On the bridge they're saying there's a woman down there too. The frogmen are trying to release the body from all the junk lying on the bottom.' She paused. 'It could be some time yet. Why not come home?'

'I want to wait, Ruth.'

'You can't blame yourself for what's happened.'

'I'm not so sure,' he said. 'I already had a feeling she might be planning to go it alone. Something in her voice. A lot of resolution. A hell of a lot of pain.'

It was an hour later before a woman's body was disentangled from the hundred years of iron junk which lay along the bottom of the canal. Jason and Ruth had already moved on to the bridge. The crowd, hearing the winch begin to whirr, pressed forward. The silvery chains glittered in the searchlights, rippling the flat blackness of the canal as they drew a weight from the depths. The crowd fell silent as a woman's body broke the surface, the whiteness of her dangling legs caught in the light beam.

'They're swinging the body on to the canal bank,' Ruth whispered.

Jason tightened his grip on Ruth's hand. 'Is it her?' His voice was flat.

Ruth was craning forward. 'No,' she said suddenly; 'whoever it is, it's not Nan Luc.'

The body swung slowly past and was brought to rest below them on the canal bank. Looking down from the bridge Ruth thought the face of Mary Page Butler could have been sculpted in pale Italian marble.

44

She awoke to daylight bright enough to hurt the eyes. Ruth Caswell was standing beside the bed, a cup of coffee in one hand and clothes draped on her arm. 'There's a visitor downstairs for you,' she said, putting down the coffee and laying the clothes on the bed. 'There, jeans, sweater, trainers. We're about the same size I guess.'

'This visitor, he's from the police?'

Ruth shook her head. 'Get dressed and come downstairs. Doctor Harkness said it was OK for you to get up as soon as you'd slept it out.'

Nan Luc struggled up in bed. 'Not the police?'

'No. They'll want to speak to you later. Jason's just back from Meyerick. They've established a fingerprint connection with a murder in a motel in the Bronx. A lot of dirt's hit the fan. But Jason says there'll be no charges against you.' She watched Nan Luc tense. 'Now don't tighten up,' Ruth said. 'Whatever you intended last night, you never carried it out. The night patrolman at the wharf was witness to the fact you tried to save Stevenson. No,' she shook her head, 'it was the fire that killed Cy Stevenson. And the police seem to be in no doubt it was started by Mary Butler.'

'The woman who was trapped in the fire?'

Ruth nodded. 'Jason talked to Cy Stevenson's wife on the phone a couple of hours ago. She says her husband and her sister Mary were having an affair. Seems he needed Mary Butler's vote on the board of trustees.'

'Why would she want to kill him?'

Ruth helped Nan Luc to sit up in bed. 'Drink your coffee. Why did she want to kill him? I don't know. I guess a lot will come out in the enquiry into the running of the fund.' She paused. 'A piece of advice, Nan Luc. No need to be too forthcoming about your intentions last night.'

'What do you know about my intentions, Ruth?'

Ruth smiled. 'Only what your visitor tells me. Max Benning's been here since before dawn.'

Max was standing on the long gallery looking up at the Rose family portraits as Nan Luc came out of the room. She ran forward into his arms. For a moment they stood together, arms round each other.

'He's dead, Max,' she said.

'I know. Thank God it wasn't you that killed him.'

They came slightly apart. 'I knew by then he wasn't my father. Perhaps I'd known for some time.'

He released her and they began to walk along the gallery. 'What finally persuaded you that Stevenson wasn't your father? Not what Louise told you. Or what I said.'

Nan shook her head. 'No. It was standing opposite him for the first time. I thought of all I knew about my mother. And I suddenly realised there was no greater insult to *her* memory than to believe she had chosen this man.'

He stopped her and turned her lightly towards him. 'Are you OK now?'

'I think so.'

'My God,' he said quietly. 'I arrived just as the body of the woman was taken out of the canal. I was convinced it had to be you. At that time nobody was thinking of the fire stairs.'

She slipped her arm round his waist. 'I didn't even know they were there. I just ran through the smoke and came out on to them.'

They had turned and walked slowly down the gallery. 'How did you know to come to Meyerick?' she asked him.

'Hal Bolson got himself clearance to tell me a story.'

'Hal Bolson. One of the journalists at Cahn Roc?'

'Lives in New York now.'

They walked down the stairs and along the corridor to where Ruth was standing at Jason's door. 'I don't understand,' Nan said. 'What did Hal Bolson know about all this? Who did he have to get clearance from?'

They were passing a window overlooking the snow-covered garden. Max pointed. 'He had to get clearance from that lady there.'

Nan looked out across the garden. Mrs Rose, bareheaded, but in a coat and thick gloves, was pacing the snow-covered drive. 'Mrs Rose? I don't understand.'

Ruth opened the door and Jason stood up behind his desk. 'Hear this from Jason, Nan.' Max propelled her gently forward.

'How's she looking, Ruth?' Jason asked as they all sat in the deep chintz covered sofas round the fire.

'Everything considered, she's looking marvellous,' Ruth said. 'Just a little bewildered.' She took a briefcase from the desktop and handed it to Jason.

He arranged it before him and sprang the locks. 'I never knew this briefcase existed until a retired journalist named Hal Bolson phoned my mother this morning. Immediately she put the phone down she went up to her room. When she came down she was carrying this case. I could see she was pretty upset, but she didn't want to talk. She handed the case to me and told me to do whatever I had to do with what it contains.' Jason opened the case. 'There are a lot of documents here,' he said. 'But this picture tells the essential story.'

Nan took a yellowing photograph from him. In her hands, as she looked down, she saw she held a copy of the same picture of her mother Bernadette had given her. A long silence fell in the room.

'My father was in Saigon many times from the mid-sixties to his death,' Jason said, taking a pack of letters from the case. 'Max and Ruth have read these letters out to me. They're letters to my mother. The first ones told her, very candidly, about his meeting and falling in love with a Vietnamese nurse, Pham. It's clear from later letters that my mother refused a divorce. Even after a child was born. You.'

Nan Luc sat back, swamped with feelings impossible to absorb. She looked past Jason at the photograph of the man on the table under the window. A face quite different from the severity of the portrait on the gallery, an open face that seemed to merge with flickering, elusive memories. Did she see again that figure, Philip Rose now, on the lawn in front of the white villa? Did she hear her own childhood voice as she skipped and danced across the grass? Even as she sat there, breathless, she knew she was doing what all human beings desperately need to do. She was creating a past.

'My father,' Jason said, 'your father too, as we now know, died in 1975 of a massive heart attack on his way to Los Angeles. He had already founded the Meyerick Fund, the fund Cy Stevenson eventually took over when he arrived in Meyerick on the lookout for new opportunities. I'm afraid the information he held over my mother is what made her originally vote him on to the fund. I genuinely believe that she thought she was protecting her husband's memory.'

Nan Luc glanced again at the photograph on the side table. Feelings of indescribable warmth passed through her. If only she could dredge from the past just one certain memory when she and her father had been together.

Max had reached out a hand to touch hers. 'And Peter Benning.' She turned to Max. 'He and . . . my father knew each other?'

'They worked together in Saigon,' Max said. 'Philip Rose's professorship was in Oriental Studies. He and my father worked on recovery projects together.'

Nan Luc stood up and crossed to where Jason stood. Leaning forward she kissed his cheek. He put his arm round her and hugged her close. 'Jason, I'd like to talk to Max for a few moments,' she said. 'But first, if you don't mind, I'd like to call Edward, my husband, in San Diego.'

45

They lay in a tangle of sheets, charged with elation, still in each other's arms. As the shafts of morning sunlight moved from the glistening whiteness of the snow on the window sill into the Greenwich Village apartment, she eased him out of her and rolled on to her back, breathing slow, deep draughts of air, her eyes half closed.

Max raised himself on one elbow, like her, steeped in a heavy drowsiness. His fingers touched her lips, stroking her until her eyes opened fully. She raised her head and kissed him. Then let her head fall back on the pillow.

They both knew that, if they were to talk, this was the time to talk. But they lay together, beside each other, in silence. Outside they could hear the sounds of New Yorkers beginning another day, the slow swish of trucks across the melting slush, two men's voices raised, the rattle of a skateboard, the sound of someone shovelling snow. At one point he reached out, found her hand and held it tight. She turned towards him, making circles with the flat of her hand on his bare chest, but still the silence persisted between them. Moments passed. Perhaps no more than a minute. Nan Luc got out of bed and put on her yellow robe. From where she stood she could see down into the street.

'Nobody told me that snow in the city didn't stay crisp and white,' she said.

He could feel the turmoil in her. He reached up and took her hand. 'At Jason's house,' Max said, 'when you went to call Edward. What did you say?'

She looked out at the bruised lumps of snow heaped by the kerbside. 'I said I'd take a plane this morning.' she said. She turned to look up at him, her eyes glistening. 'I said for him to meet the flight at San Diego.' She turned her back to the window. 'Whatever happens now has to be Edward's decision, not mine.'

'Even though a lot of things have changed?'

'Nothing's changed, Max. I knew I loved you when I married Edward.'

'He knows about me?'

'A little, not all.'

'If ever you're free,' he said, 'will you marry me?'

'She looked at him. 'If ever . . .' she said.

In the crowded airport Christmas carols intermingled with passenger announcements.

From where he stood at the phone point Max was unable to see her any more. But he kept his eyes on the departure gate as the phone rang.

'Ruth Caswell,' the crisp voice on the phone said.

'Ruth. This is Max Benning. I'm glad I caught you.'

'Where are you, Max?'

'I'm at Kennedy. I just saw Nan Luc off to San Diego. I have a couple of hours or so before my London flight. Is there any chance we could meet for a drink?'

'Nan Luc's gone back west?'

'She just left.'

'My office is in Queens,' Ruth said. 'Jason's with me. We can make lunch.'

'Even better.'

'Let's make it lunch then,' Ruth said. She paused. 'Max, Edward Brompton has been trying to contact Nan Luc at the house all morning. He spent a long time talking to Jason.'

'What did he say?'

'Jason'll fill you in over lunch.' She paused. 'He talked about Nan Luc. About Nan Luc and you.'

From the phone booth Max suddenly made out Nan Luc's pale leather jacket as she passed into the departure lounge. For a moment at the gate she hesitated, as if somehow she too had heard what Ruth was saying. Half turning, she looked past the red-robed Father Christmas and the children surrounding him, towards the spot were Max had been standing.

'If ever . . .' she had said.

'If ever . . .' The words echoed in his head as he strained to catch a last glimpse of her among the flickering shapes of the San Diego passengers passing behind the patterned glass screens.